ASHBURN

ASHBURN

Book 2 of the Storyteller Trilogy

---

pHil Rittenhouse

Written Books

*

Book Cover design by the Author

First edition 2026

ISBN: 978-1-970322-05-7

*

Written Books

www.writtenbooks.com

To Leonard, whom I never met but knew me so well.
You penned my story in so many songs.

PREFACE

HERE WE GO again.

With a character like Ashe, who is quite literally timeless, it seems inevitable to me that he'd get pulled into stories even bigger than himself. This is one of them. Or several, depending on how you look at it.

I'd long been fascinated with the idea of weaving parallel story structures into a cohesive narrative. Ashe's longevity and objectives seemed to be well-suited for such a treatment, and doing so provided me with a way to pull in some more interesting characters and explore the concept of aging and remaining competent not just from the perspective of a nigh-immortal, but from regular people who would be pulled along in his wake.

This one was really a lot of fun to write. I hope it's as much fun to read.

And if you make it through this one, hold on for the end of the Storyteller trilogy, and beyond—we're headed somewhere.

This page intentionally left blank.

Chapter 1 : RESIGNATION

1988

THE SUITCASE WAS tired and worn. Simple black threads, frayed from years of faithful use, parted to expose the scuffed, dead-gray plastic structure underneath, not unlike the exposed bones of a murder victim. How many times had she packed that suitcase? This time felt different. Her routine had always been to pack the suitcase on their—her—bed. Her routine had always been to tell herself it would just be a few days before she would be back again in her—their—bed. This time was different.

Dani Linder stared at the suitcase on the marble kitchen counter, as cold and hard as that little spot she'd learned to push to the back corner of her heart. The counter knew she wasn't returning. It didn't care. Dani accepted it herself now but struggled to define her feelings about it. She glanced toward the dark bedroom and realized the bed had given up some time ago. Dani sighed and laid her holstered service weapon next to the limp, resigned lid of the open suitcase. She had just finished packing the travel bag for what she couldn't imagine as anything but a one-way trip. Finding the strength to close it was another thing entirely.

Dani's reverie was interrupted by a faint but sadly familiar scratching of metal on metal. Her service automatic reappeared unbidden in her hand and she laid the holster quietly back on the counter. Dani slipped down the short entry hallway toward her apartment door on stocking feet. Stopping in the blind side of the door, she silently slid back the Sig's side to ensure a round was properly chambered. The faint click of her gun's slide coincided perfectly with the soft metallic sound of the lockpick dropping the last tumbler into place.

The door opened quietly on oiled hinges, and Dani gripped the automatic firmly in both hands. Her arms extended in one fluid motion as a man's head slid stealthily into the darkened hallway. Dani pressed her pistol's muzzle gently against the intruder's right temple. The man froze instantly. In all likelihood, she was overreacting, but there was always the slim chance that some other idiot had chosen tonight to break into her apartment.

"Hey!" The man said with a smile, not daring to turn his head from its position. "There she is! What's up, Doc?"

Nope. Just the same old idiot. Dani lowered her weapon and stomped away from the man, back down the hallway toward the brightly-lit kitchen.

"Next time, use your key," Dani growled over her shoulder. "I could have blown your brains across half of Alexandria."

"Well, sure, but technically, we'd have to be in the middle of Alexandria for that to be true, right? Not the outskirts." The man closed the door behind him.

Back in the kitchen, Dani secured her Sig in its holster and replaced it by the road-weary suitcase. She turned and leaned back against the marble counter, arms already crossed by the time the man's cap-toe oxfords burst into the bright light spilling across the off-white tiles.

Wolfe Linder had a knack for making the world revolve around him. The trait was always the most pronounced when it was the least appropriate. Linder (everyone referred to him as just "Linder," even Dani) was always the lead actor on stage, whether anyone wanted to watch the play or not. The first thing Dani noticed was the ever-present crooked grin; she'd never seen it fade even in the most serious circumstance.

That look danced across Linder's face: the look that had first drawn her to him at the Academy and had drawn her back a dozen times over the past six years. Sharp, alert, and annoyingly pleased with himself, like he was already several steps ahead in a game only he was playing. Named after Nero Wolfe by his parents, Linder had always exhibited that character's confidence despite an express lack of commensurate competence.

The overhead lights gleamed off his dark hair, tousled as if he'd been up all night running a hand through it while sifting through endless stacks of half-legible notes. His suit. God, did he ever wear anything that wasn't black or dark gray? (She'd bought him a couple suits over the years: dark blue, khaki. Beige for the summer. He never wore them.) His suit fit him well enough, snug in all the right places to highlight his runner's frame. Despite this, as usual, his tie was carelessly loose, the top button of his shirt undone as if he just couldn't be bothered to be any more formal.

"Linder," she said by way of grudging welcome. She kept her voice even, but the way he glanced at her with that infuriating twinkle in his eyes told her he wasn't fooled. He gave her a slow once-over, like she was just another piece he had to fit into whatever bizarre puzzle he was mentally assembling.

"Evening, Doctor Draw," he said, voice smooth, a touch of teasing in it. Dani rolled her eyes. He had to say it, didn't he? She'd long suspected that Linder had been the origin of the nickname back at Quantico, but she'd never proven it. Neither had she gotten him to confess to the act, despite five years of marriage. Like many nicknames, hers was due to the ironic contrast with her previous career: as good as she'd ever been at taking bullets out of people as a trauma surgeon, she turned out to be far better at putting them into bad guys in the field.

Linder stepped further into the kitchen with that lazy stride of his, one hand casually in his pocket, the other holding the latest in his seemingly never-ending cavalcade of manila folders. Like many before it, this one was rumpled like it had recently been driven over by a truck. Sight unseen, she already knew the folder was stuffed with newspaper clippings, scribbled notes, and whatever other dubious wonders he'd dredged from some dark corner of the archives or wheedled from some shady source.

"What is it this time, Linder?" Dani closed her eyes for a moment to summon from some inner well of strength, knowing all the while the well was dry. "What do you want?"

"I need you on this one, Dani. One more case."

Dani's eyes opened wearily. "You don't need me, Linder. You've never *needed* me. What you *do* need is a good psychiatrist."

A contained energy crackled in Linder, evidenced by a slight tension in his shoulders and a spring in his step as he edged slightly closer. Dani could swear his eyes shifted a deeper shade of blue. He broadcast the demeanor of someone who had spent years wading into the depths of the unknown and had grown more comfortable there than he'd ever been in the daylight world. As transformations went, it was hypnotic.

Or at least it had once been, before she'd come to realize how full of crap he was.

"No, seriously! I need you on this one. Come on, partner; I need the Doctor."

"You wouldn't need 'the Doctor' if you'd just learned to shoot on your own. God, Linder! How long has it been since you even qualified?"

"Four years. No. Five. Not since Quantico." Linder's eyes fell on Dani's new service weapon holstered on the counter. "Say! Is that the new P226? Nice! I'd have thought you'd go for the S&W 1076, though. Serious stopping power."

Wolfe Linder pulled the satin-black handgun from its holster. He held it in a just barely competent grip and aimed it at the living room couch.

Dani took two strides and snatched the gun from his hands. "Give me that before you hurt yourself, Linder." Replacing it in its holster, Dani tossed it into the open suitcase, which her husband now seemed to notice for the first time.

"Whoa! Where are you going? You're not leaving, are you? I need my partner!"

Dani was infuriated by Linder's ability to go from childish excitement to deep concern in an instant. Feigned deep concern, of course. The only thing the man cared about was himself and the inane fantasies he called casework.

"Forget it, Linder; I resigned. You know that. Resigned. I'm out."

Linder waved the folder as if to dismiss her claim. "What, that? No, no. I talked to AD Mulgrove. He knows you didn't actually mean 'resign'. We cleared that up."

Dani's blood pressure spiked by twenty points. "You did what?" she hissed.

A broad smile flashed across Linder's face. "Look!" He thrust a hand into his pocket and pulled out a prize, laying it on the counter as if he were a cat presenting a limp mouse to its owner. "AD Mulgrove gave me your badge for you. You're back in business."

Dani was speechless. Her heart thumped in her chest.

Linder seized on the moment and took advantage of her being off-balance. He opened the folder on the counter and started to pull several papers and clippings from it. "This one's right up your alley, check it out. There's a vigilante working his way across America, taking out one drug ring after another. Started out here in Arlington about twenty years ago but working consistently west and south. The guy has racked up over fifty bodies that we can confirm, with an amazing range of technique. That's just the ones we can confirm. The guy's an artist."

"Linder..."

"No, wait a second, Dani. I know what you're thinking; this is something for DEA or even Violent Crimes. But look at this." Linder was pulling papers from the folder and grouping them according to some mystical pattern he alone understood. Dani realized that there were news articles from the 1930s, redacted letters written in German bearing the seal of the Nazi High command in World War II, and sheaves of medical findings from the period. Another pile of documents from Australia were dated 1917 through 1919 and were, strangely, still heavily redacted even eighty years later. Despite herself, Dani found herself drawn to more recent documents on assorted letterheads from the FBI and CIA as well as dozens of local police departments in numerous states. These uniformly described perplexing blood work from several crime scenes and were accompanied by a letter of declaration from the Bureau's newly formed Working Group on DNA Analysis Methods.

Scanning over several of these reports, Dani started to tune out Linder's excited voice. It was the only way she could ever deal with these manic briefings of his: focus on the facts. She realized a common theme starting to form a hypothesis regarding a serial murderer, linked across several decades by the simple fact that his or her blood type could not be identified. Almost as if you could only start to see a picture by realizing what wasn't there...

Dani shook her head, returning to the present. She dropped the papers back onto the counter. "Forget it, Linder. I resigned."

"You turned in your letter, sure, but it's still in administrative review. I told you AD Mulgrove cleared that up. C'mon, one more case," he whined.

Dani marveled again at the whirlwind that was Wolfe Linder. AD Mulgrove was his latest conquest, just as she had been a few short years ago. Swept along by the inexorable current of the Linder vortex. God should never allow introverts to have the kind of inherent charisma that Linder possessed; the man was just plain dangerous.

"Maybe it's still in review, but I'm effectively out of the bureau. I'm done," Dani reiterated.

"You're not *really* out yet, though, right? Come on, what do you say? One more case. I need you on this one! Please? Non-typeable blood? Impossible crimes? A vigilante rising from the dead? It'll be just like old times. You always loved this stuff!"

"I always hated that stuff! And even if I didn't, it's too little, too late."

Linder's eyes widened. "What do you mean?" he asked. The man might as well have been a nine-year old, aghast at the news that Santa wasn't real.

"You're always chasing what doesn't exist: inexplicable mysteries, impossible possibilities, things that are never there..."

Linder looked genuinely hurt. She might have fallen for it if they hadn't already had this exact conversation a dozen times. "Are you talking about the case, or our relationship? My inexplicable allure? What's missing in our relationship?"

"I'll tell you what was missing in our relationship: you!" Dani shouted. "You're what's missing, Linder. You only ever need me for work, or for this, or that, or for..." She paused, working to regain control. "It's always about Wolfe Linder, whatever Linder wants or needs at that exact moment in time. You never address what I need. You never see me. Not unless you need me."

"Come on; we both knew what the job would mean for our relationship. This wouldn't have worked without the job, and you know it. And the job wouldn't work without us! This is what excites you about it all. The job is where we came together, right? And it's what makes us who we are. This is the way you want it, because it can't be any other way."

And there it was: the "Linder Effect." A particularly astute instructor at the Academy had coined the term, using it to illustrate a nuanced form of gaslighting inherent in the mind of a serial killer, of all things. Linder had a way of pulling those close to him into an inexorable vortex within which reality was warped ever so slightly to fit his peculiar perspective and outlook. The instructor had gone on to pass Linder at the top of their class, and Linder had gone on to pull everyone he encountered into that vortex.

"Earth to McKendree... come in, McKendree." Linder's use of Dani's maiden name snapped her out of her brief moment of reverie. It was a tactic he often used when he wanted to demonstrate that she was straying from the path he was trying to lead her down. Linder snatched papers from several stacks on the counter, sorting them into some semblance of order. "Check this out, Mrs. Linder." Referring to her in the matrimonial was the flip side of his tactic, conveying his desire for her to follow along more closely.

"The links are here as far back as World War One, but they're loose. It's the same guy; it has to be, but the picture doesn't really start to pull together until World War Two. He was apparently involved in some Nazi experiments focused on a Super-Soldier serum of some sort."

Dani rolled her eyes. "Super-soldiers," she muttered.

"Yes!" Linder was delighted to have his captive audience back and continued. "There are still a bunch of documents I'm waiting on from MI5 and MI6 in England. Supposedly, there's a lot more to the story with Hitler; this is just part of it. He shuffled the German letters aside to highlight more recent Bureau documents.

"That same blood started showing up in the early seventies in Virginia and Maryland, then moved around a bit. But everywhere it turned up, there were piles of dead bodies. Drug dealers. Gang members. All manner of destruction, but always bad guys. The worst."

Dani, despite all common sense, found herself being swept along with the tide. Maybe Linder actually had something this time. There was too much real, physical evidence for this to be nothing, wasn't there? There was only one thing that wasn't adding up.

"Linder, there are just too many events here for it to be one man. Sure, it follows a pattern, but still... the scope of this could never point to one man, especially if we factor in the unconfirmed reports."

"Exactly!" Linder was nearly bursting with excitement now.

She had to close her eyes to concentrate. "Wait a minute, though. Particularly because it can't be one man, it doesn't follow. With the degree of carnage and violence at a lot of these scenes, there would have to be casualties on the other side."

"Other side? You mean the good guy side?"

Dani fixed him with a scowl. "I mean the vigilante side. What you're talking about is an organized group of vigilantes. Or possibly an elite group of in-the-black operatives with a secret mandate to eliminate the drug cartels. Operatives who never leave a man behind."

"Yes!" Linder exclaimed, clapping both hands together in victory.

Dani rubbed at that space between her eyes. *Here it comes.* "Yes, what, Linder?"

"Yes, you see what I see! You see what's going on."

"I truly don't, Linder."

"Nancy Reagan is using a secret cadre of super-soldiers, using technology developed by the Nazi SS, to wage her War on Drugs!"

And there it was. "Nancy Reagan is part of a vast government conspiracy."

"The head of it!" exclaimed Linder.

"Nancy Reagan is the head of a vast government conspiracy. Linder, I think you're the one on drugs."

Linder looked hurt. "What do you mean? You saw it too! You said you saw it."

Dani started again, speaking slowly to ensure clarity. It was like trying to help a three-year old comprehend heavier-than-air flight. "You work for the government. You know how it all works. Or rather, how it barely works! Large bodies of government as a rule are not capable of a conspiracy like this."

"The fact that I've found what I've found shows the imperfection of their cover up and proves your rule by being the exception!"

Dani groaned, "That's not how rules work, Linder. Your results are just a chain of failed blood tests that each failed in the same way over several years. Occam's razor."

Linder, refusing to give up so easily, rustled through the papers, finally finding what he was looking for.

"Alright, what about this?!" He slapped the papers down in front of Dani. The displaced air blew a few other documents around, and off of the counter. He ignored them.

Dani looked at Linder's "evidence." She didn't read German aside from the few words she had gleaned in her undergraduate studies, and that purely by second-hand exposure. Fortunately, the document was accompanied by a full (but redacted) translation. The topic was Hitler's obsession with certain occult practices he supposedly was undertaking to achieve immortality. The paper went into intricate, but completely unscientific, detail about regular blood transfusions given to Hitler himself as well as his inner circle.

"That proves it," stated Linder smugly.

"Proves what?" Dani was exasperated. "Linder, I have a plane to catch."

"No, you don't. Look at it! Look at the date! The SIS sent commandoes in and stopped Hitler, but they brought back the serum. They must have! The Allies got hold of the serum and got it to work." The look on Linder's face showed he considered the evidence conclusive.

Dani had reached the boiling point.

"Linder!" she shouted. "The world is not a comic book!"

"But—"

"But nothing! This is just another of your stupid theories. Just one more ridiculous case!"

"Ridiculous cases?" Linder took a step back, almost as if he feared her break from sanity might be contagious. "When have we been on a ridiculous case?"

"When have we not been on a ridiculous case?!" Dani's eyes were wide circles of incredulity. "Mutant mole people from Mexico? Polygamist Aliens and their UFOs in Utah? Rodents of unusual size in New York?"

Linder's lower lip protruded like a kindergartener who'd just been told he couldn't have another cookie. "That's not fair. Those were really big rats."

"It was New York! *All* the rats are really big! One case after another of that silliness, for five years! All because you've got AD Mulgrove wrapped around your finger."

"AD Mulgrove is a believer."

"Omigod! There it is! The believer thing! You know what, Linder? I'm a believer! I believe in science. I believe in logic. I believe in empirical evidence and good old-fashioned investigative work."

Linder looked at her like a whipped puppy, but she was in no mood to let off the pressure. "You can't change the rules of nature just by aggregating a bunch of disconnected weird facts and claiming some insane conclusion is real."

Linder shook his head. "That's not what I'm doing."

"That's exactly what you're doing! That's what you've been doing for years. It's what you've done for our entire marriage! And I'm done getting sucked into the vortex!"

Dani flipped the lid of her suitcase shut with enough force to slide the entire case several inches. Thrusting a hand into the worn outer pocket, she retrieved a manila folder of her own. She reached into this and pulled out several official-looking papers, which she slammed onto the counter in front of her husband.

"You want papers? I've got papers. These are for you."

Linder looked at the document, recognizing it at once. "You're filing for divorce?"

"Yes! Finally! You should start getting used to the name Dani McKendree again. I'd file for a restraining order too, if I didn't have to go all the way to Chicago to find a judge who hasn't been infected with the paranormal 'Linder' virus!"

"Don't bring your father into this." Her barb about the Chicago judge had sunk deep. "This is between us."

Dani pressed the advantage. "You finally acknowledge an actual truth, Linder. This is between us. This is all there's *ever* been between us."

Dani zipped up her road-weary suitcase and stormed out of the apartment once and for all.

Chapter 2 : THE STANDISH TRIALS

PRESENT DAY

"I DON'T LIKE the idea of the FBI getting involved in my life again," said Ashe.

It was four in the morning. In the weeks since Task's death, things had slowly fallen back into some semblance of their former life. Amber had returned to work, worried that the time she had been gone might have caused the place to fall to ruin, or that Keith would be mad enough at her for disappearing to fire her. She was wrong on the second count; her manager was ecstatic to have her back.

She wasn't far from wrong on her first concern though; the place had certainly suffered.

That was fine, though. Amber was grateful to have daily (or nightly, as it were) tasks to focus on as she restored the place to its former glory. Before long, it was elevated once more under her attentive care to its position of only the third most shabby and substandard diner on this side of the city center. The mundane and routine work of serving her regulars and cleaning up around the diner somehow helped her deal with the extraordinary strangeness of the recent traumatic events.

And having a night-shift waitress again who cared about her work delighted her manager, Keith. So much so that he never once questioned the presence of Amber's new, near-constant, companion. Nor did he ever complain, not even once, about the amount of food the busted-up old homeless guy ate on a nightly basis. Amber was relieved that Keith didn't mind feeding Ashe (for free, no less), but ever the more grateful that he refrained from asking questions about him.

Amber set down a plate heaping with eggs and sausage in front of Ashe, taking away the smeared plate of biscuits and gravy he had just emptied.

She looked at Ashe. In the weeks since the events in Task's office, Ashe had seemingly become younger, at least in appearance. He was still healing from some of the worst trauma suffered in his fall—or technically, re-healing, in at least one case—but instead of being some apparent indeterminate age between sixty and eighty,

Amber would have to say that scale had shifted maybe five years younger, despite having to hobble around on those mismatched crutches of his. Ashe had no ready explanation for it, and the topic seemed far less fascinating to him than it was to her. Fry was still too ashamed of her part in recent events to bring it up, but Amber knew she had to be curious as well. The one time Amber had broached the question, asking Ashe if maybe the radiation from his cave didn't agree with him, all she got was a grunt and a, "Yeah. Maybe."

"Again? What do you mean, again?" Amber asked.

Suddenly, Ashe did that feral animal thing he did. His face went slack as all his mental abilities turned inward to look for an escape. Amber had started calling it his "resting cornered face." He finally settled on the best solution to his dilemma and spoke.

"Nothing. Nevermind."

Amber placed both hands on hips and smiled at him. "Really? That's the best you got?"

"If I wanted to talk about something, I'd talk about it. What were you saying about the guy?"

Amber decided to let her friend off the hook and return to the original topic. "Fry said he showed up out of nowhere. Creepy guy, bad enough she was calling security when he finally flashed his badge. Went at her and the story for over an hour. Had all the forensic stuff with him and did his best to pick her apart."

Amber paused a moment to stretch her back. Looking around the otherwise empty restaurant, she finally decided to sit down for a break. "Hang on, lemme get a cup of coffee. Want some more water?"

"Yeah. Bring the pitcher."

At the coffee station, Amber poured a large mug two-thirds full with black brew. She cast her eyes around for a full sugar dispenser and found none. Her eyes went next to the beakers of sticky maple syrup, but she wasn't feeling that tonight. Finally, she cast a furtive glance into the kitchen to see Keith involved in a game of solitaire on his phone with his back to her. Amber then dissected a large slice of cake; the top and inner layers of icing went into her cup, while the cake itself was unceremoniously dumped into the trash. She topped off her mug with a generous dollop of whipped cream and grabbed a pitcher of water. She turned.

Before she could start back, the door to the diner opened.

The door squealed in faint protest, and a chilling draft swept through the diner. A man in an austere black suit entered. His presence seemed to warp time and space around him as he approached the table next to Ashe. Tall and severe, the man's silhouette loomed over the entrance, casting a disproportionally long shadow across the cracked floor tiles.

His dark, high-collared overcoat enveloped him like a shroud, giving him a spectral quality as he advanced with a purposeful stride. Cold light glinted off piercing gray eyes, rendering them an eerie shade that seemed to bore into Amber's soul.

The man's face was gaunt, and his sharp features etched it with lines that reminded Amber of a hawk she'd once seen at the zoo as it watched a mouse skitter along the bottom of its cage. His countenance held no warmth, and its coldness was reminiscent of some inquisitor from a bygone era.

Amber shook her head to clear her thoughts. She tended to chase these poetically descriptive rabbits when she was nervous. This man emptied the warren and sent bunnies hopping frantically off in all directions.

The air grew tense as the man took a seat at the corner table next to Ashe. It was a strategic vantage point from which he could survey the entire diner from a distance yet have its only two inhabitants up close. The air between Amber and the man seemed to shudder with waves like the heated air over a desert mirage.

Amber sensed a calculated menace in the man's demeanor. It was clear to Amber that he considered himself on a mission to serve some righteous purpose. No, not righteous. Self-righteous. Something about the man blurred the line between hero and villain. Or maybe she just needed some sleep. Either way, his eyes landed on her from across the room and slid from the red hair under her scarf to her bright yellow sneakers, pausing only briefly to drip judgement upon the grease-stained polyester blend of her uniform.

The man sat and turned his gaze on the only other occupied table in the place. Still as a sphinx, he stared at Ashe.

Chewing a mouthful of eggs, Ashe stared back.

When the man finally spoke to Ashe at the next table, each word was delivered with the disdainful syntax of a judge. His voice carried through the restaurant on a practiced undercurrent of menace. The practice had paid off, Amber thought.

"I am Special Agent Standish of the Federal Bureau of Investigation. And you are...?"

"Eating."

"Clever. Unfortunately, I do not care overmuch for cleverness. I asked you a question."

"Yeah. Unfortunately, I don't care overmuch for questions," replied Ashe. "Get lost, Ichabod."

Agent Standish's face darkened considerably. "The name is Lamentation. Lamentation Standish."

Ashe thrust his fork, dripping with yolk, toward the man. "See? I totally pegged you for a witch hunter."

The two men regarded each other in silence for a moment. The only sound was Ashe's renewed chewing.

It was Ashe that next broke the silence. "No kidding, though? Lamentation?"

"My family has always believed in the importance of preserving our Puritan heritage."

Ashe shoveled another forkful of charred sausage and drippy eggs into his mouth. "Well, my shiny buckled hat's off to your parents. They did a bang-up job," he mumbled through his food. A thin line of greasy egg yolk dribbled down his grizzled chin.

Standish growled, "I should arrest you just for the way you eat. You are disgusting."

Ashe slammed his utensil down on the laminate table, causing the dishes on it to jump. "Look, buddy, if we got a problem, we can solve it right now if you wanna go."

Agent Standish slowly pulled back one side of his overcoat, revealing a wicked-looking handgun in a shoulder holster. The weapon had not been evident until now, such was the way the man's clothes hung loosely on his wiry frame. "Facilis descenus Averno," said the agent with his first smile of the encounter.

Ashe rose halfway out of his seat. "Yeah. Virgil. I read, too. 'Smooth is the descent into Hell.' You have no idea, buddy."

Without rising himself, Standish replied, "Oh, I do, Ashe O'Reilly. I do."

"I don't recall telling you my name," snarled Ashe.

"Nor do I recall asking it."

Amber hustled across the diner in an attempt to avoid bloodshed. Arriving between the two tables, she set down her coffee and refilled Ashe's glass from a pitcher of water.

"Hey, there! Ashe, be polite to the nice man!" She turned to Standish. "Would you like a cup of coffee, sir? You look like a man who appreciates a good cuppa joe. And let me tell you, mine's the best from here to—"

Without breaking eye contact with Ashe, the man said flatly, "I do not partake of caffeine."

"Oh! I'm so sorry. I've got some decaf; it's fresh—"

"No."

"Some pie?" She said cheerfully. "Surely you like pie. The cherry pie here is to die for."

Standish finally shifted his attention from Ashe to Amber, piercing her with his gaze. "Is it now? 'To die for?' You appear to me as someone who should be more careful with her words, Ms. Olsen."

﷼ • ﷼

AN UNEASY CEASE-fire between the tables seemed to take hold. Not a peace or a truce, maybe, but at least a cessation of hostilities. Amber looked at Ashe's face, once he relaxed enough to sit back down. No, he still looked pretty hostile.

At least Ashe had calmed enough to refocus on continuing his breakfast and drinking three more glasses of water as Special Agent Standish questioned Amber on her version of the events at Task Tower several weeks ago. She gave her variant of the story they had all practiced, naturally avoiding any mention of Ashe having been on the scene.

Standish took her through the story five more times, each pass taking a different angle, entry point, or approach. For the last version, he had her tell the entire sequence of events in reverse, starting with Cameron Task lying in a puddle of blood on the pavement and working backwards in a chain of effects before causes. Despite the rigor, Amber was relieved that in focusing his attention on her, Standish was at least not further antagonizing Ashe.

At last, the lawman seemed satisfied and leaned back in his seat. "Yes, that is very close to the story I got from Frymet Cieślak. And an almost word-for-word match with what I got from Owen Spirit when I questioned him. You are evidently far better with words than I gave you credit for."

He ended his declaration with a thin smile. It did little to settle Amber's uneasiness about the man.

"Tell me," he continued. "What was Task working on? In that medical lab of his?"

Amber looked at Standish blankly, her mind racing. Her version of the story was crafted to deliberately omit any mention of the lab; she had not officially seen it. Owen Spirit had removed her ruined laptop, and she had touched nothing in the room save for Ashe's rubber IV tubing and the floor. Spirit assured her that neither would bear her fingerprints, so trampled was the scene. Furthermore, the authorities had failed to get a subpoena for that level of investigation due to Task Industries' standing in the community, the proprietary nature of the company's research, and the widely-held belief that Task had been the sole perpetrator in shooting two of his employees before killing himself.

All of this rattled through Amber's head like a pachinko game that seemed to last an eternity. Suddenly she understood that cornered animal look that Ashe often got.

Sensing a chink in the armor, Standish pressed his point. "His lab. The medical bed set up with a drum of horse tranquilizer running through an IV. The lab that looked like a cyclone had ripped through it on its way out the door. You know the one. What was Task working on?"

"I have no idea," she muttered. *Yep, definitely understand the cornered animal thing.*

Standish smiled again. The expression gave Amber a chill. "Strange. That is exactly what Frymet Cieślak and Owen Spirit said as well: 'you have no idea.'" He looked directly at Ashe. "I have ideas though."

Leaning forward, Standish continued, asking, "Do you know what I think?"

"I haven't yet convinced myself *that* you think," growled Ashe.

Standish ignored the barb. "I think Cameron Task was not the only person who fell from the window that night."

"You don't say. Seems like whoever fell with him would've had a pretty bad day, don't you imagine?"

"I do not waste time imagining things. But yes, it was without doubt a bad day. Not as bad a day as the one wherein I catch him, though."

"Catch him?" asked Amber.

Standish's eyes never left Ashe's. "Catch him. Arrest him."

"For?" demanded Ashe.

"For murder, of course."

"What?" Amber was fighting to not break into a cold sweat. "You think that someone fell all that way, and they're still alive?"

Standish leaned back again. "That would be remarkable, indeed." He nodded as if to acknowledge

Amber's logic. His next question did anything but. "Tell me, Mr. Ashe O'Reilly, you might not have broken your leg falling out of a window, perchance?"

"I've broken my leg falling from lots of windows, actually. Not this time, though."

"Oh? How did you break it this time, pray tell?"

"Dropped a pickup truck on it."

Standish looked skeptical. "Ah. A repair accident."

"Nah. It was on purpose." Ashe stuffed another bite of greasy sausage into his mouth.

Amber reflected. Ashe was the only person she'd ever known who could tell the honest truth and make it sound like a total sarcastic fabrication. She suspected it was because the things he did and experienced were so far-fetched that they were impossible to believe in the first place. Ashe had been forced to re-break his leg because it had not been healing correctly. He had set up an abandoned pickup, missing its tires, on a cast steel jack and carefully positioned his leg. He'd wanted Amber to trip a lever on the jack to cause a controlled drop on his thigh, leading to a clean break from the exposed rim of the wheel. She would then, he said, simply re-engage the jack and lift the truck off of him.

She hadn't been able to do it. She couldn't bring herself to drop a truck on her friend. Frustrated, Ashe had kicked the jack out from under the vehicle and ended up crushing his femur completely. Further, he'd had to manually push the vehicle off of his own leg before dragging himself out from underneath it. That was four weeks ago. No matter how fast Ashe healed, this one was taking some time. At least the leg was now straight, so that was good.

Amber refocused on the conversation. Standish was continuing, "So you see, I have questions."

"Ideas and questions," Ashe snarled back. "Sounds to me like you're all set."

"Not at all. Do you know what else I have?"

In reply to this question, Standish received only stares, nervous in Amber's case, baleful, in Ashe's.

"I have blood," the FBI Agent stated simply.

"I have Task's blood on glass in the office, as well as all over the pavement. Not much left in his body, of course, but enough to identify him. I have Frymet Cieślak's blood from the office floor. I have Owen Spirit's blood from the office doorway. But there is more blood in the office and on limbs torn from high in the oak tree in the courtyard."

Silence filled the diner. Amber thought she could hear the cobwebs growing in the far corner.

"Interestingly, that mystery blood from the office, from the window, from the tree... It is a perfect match for blood in that makeshift hospital lab room I mentioned."

Standish looked at the two of them. "That is a lot of blood with which I have no body to go. Blood I cannot identify, and I like to tie up loose ends like that. Did you know that the mystery blood cannot be typed?"

Amber felt her skin flush. "Typed?"

Standish turned to stare again at Ashe. "It has no blood type."

More silence. The cobwebs advanced their territory by another two percent.

Standish shrugged, then continued, "I asked my lab what would have blood like that. They had no idea. I pressed them for a theory. Any theory at all, I said. They told me, if there was any way to make any sense of it whatsoever, it was that the blood was alien. If not alien, then something terrestrial, but not human. He paused. Alien, or inhuman. Those were the only choices they offered. Alien, or evil."

Silence.

"And I do not believe in aliens," explained Standish.

Amber spoke up, "Maybe the sample was corrupted or something?"

"Funny," the agent's lack of a smile made it clear he thought it anything but. "That is the word that my lab finally used in writing their report. Corrupted." Standish stared at Ashe. "And is not 'corrupted' just another word for 'evil?'"

Standish turned back to Amber, his head moving on a steady swivel like Arnold Schwarzenegger in that robot movie Fry liked. "You are a wonder with words after all, Ms. Olsen."

Standish rose from his bench and dropped his card on the table between Ashe and Amber. "Please call me if any of those words of yours decide to tell me what really happened. Before it is too late to do so. I am going to Ashburn with a few warrants, but I will be back, and I will want to talk to you again after that. At some length, I am certain."

The agent turned to leave as Ashe glared at him. Standish tipped an imaginary hat in the old man's direction. "Ashe," he stated in closing. The word dripped with malice.

Chapter 3 : MONK'S PET PIG

PRESENT DAY

THE PLACE HAD been thoroughly cleaned. That was the first thing Amber noticed. The sterile tang of disinfectant hung thick in the air, a pungent scent that clung to every surface and permeated the atmosphere. She paused at the threshold of the room. Her breath caught in her throat as if to resist ingesting the acrid smell and with it, the unwelcome memories. The last time she'd seen this room, the air had been heavy instead with the metallic tang of blood and a burnt ozone smell left behind by Task's bone drill. Now, the room was sanitized, clinically spotless, every surface wiped to a sterile sheen. The machines stood silent, their blinking displays now cold and unfeeling, like eyes that no longer cared to watch.

The bed, still by the far wall, was empty. Its chrome rails were freshly polished, its mattress bare save for a folded white sheet. It was just a piece of furniture now, devoid of the horror it had contained. But Amber couldn't stop seeing Ashe there, wired into that horrific web of tubes and needles, his body a battlefield of wounds, old and new.

Her fingers brushed the doorframe as she stepped in, her stomach twisting. It was strange. Fry and Ashe seemed perfectly at ease as they shuffled into the room, moving like war-weary soldiers returning to familiar ground. Fry's walking cast clicked softly against the floor with each step, her cane swinging rhythmically in her left hand. She wore a wistful detachment with her typical white lab coat. Looking around at the scattered equipment, she dared the room to haunt her.

Ashe made a circuit of the room, his mismatched crutches scraping faintly against the tile. He moved slowly. Each step was deliberate, every calculated motion a testament to the weeks spent in recovery. Amber envied the old man's calm, his quiet resolve. He spared only the briefest glance at the empty bed; it was no longer worthy of his attention.

Amber, on the other hand, couldn't shake the sense that the room was still alive. Not alive in any warm, welcoming way, but alive like a predator watching from the shadows. Waiting.

"This place looks different," Fry said, her voice breaking the silence as she propped her cane against the wall. "Cleaner than I expected."

"Cleaner than it was," Ashe replied, his tone dry. He moved to the rolling cart near the bed, studying it with an expression Amber couldn't quite read. Amber recalled only too well the drum of animal sedative Cameron Task had piped into Ashe's body. It was gone now. "Guess Spirit wanted to erase the evidence. Can't say I blame him."

Amber shifted uncomfortably. "Evidence doesn't just disappear," she muttered, more to herself than to Ashe. Her eyes traced the faint scratches on the floor where the rolling drum had been, and the ghostly outline of what she imagined to have been dried blood near the base of the bed. How well could it have been scrubbed away if she could still see it there?

Fry looked back at her, one eyebrow raised. "You okay?"

Amber forced a smile she didn't feel. "Fine," she lied. "Just... didn't think I'd see this place again."

Fry didn't press. Instead, she turned to Ashe, who was now testing the balance of his crutches by leaning experimentally to one side. "So," Fry said, looking at the old man, "what now?"

"We're going to burn it all."

Frymet looked at Ashe like he wasn't human. It wasn't much of a stretch for her, having seen what she had seen.

"Burn it? Burn what?"

"Task's research. Your notes. Looks like they've eradicated all the blood, the physical evidence, but—"

"But the police stopped their investigation, right?" Fry asked. Amber watched her lift a notebook and open it. "They weren't even allowed in here."

Ashe glared at her. "Yet, enough evidence got out to get somebody hungry for more. That Standish character is gonna come back, believe me, and there's going to be nothing here when he does. It all goes."

Ashe gestured to the lab equipment by the bed. "Standish was able to reconstruct too good a picture from what he got hold of from the local P.D., despite Spirit shutting them down at the gate. If the FBI comes back around with an actual warrant, I'm probably looking at life behind bars. I have very little desire to spend the rest of my life in a prison that might actually be able to hold me."

Amber, standing just inside the doorway, came to Ashe's assistance. "You talked to that Agent Standish, Fry. He is not going to give up until he gets what he wants. And I think Ashe is right; if the FBI wants to see the test results, they will find a way to get them from us."

Frymet looked sadly around the room. She set down the notebook and ran a finger slowly along its spine before looking up at Ashe.

"Shouldn't we wait until Mr. Spirit gets here and see what he thinks?" she asked.

Ashe had worked his way through the room towards the light panel on the far wall. Next to it was a stack of x-ray films. He flipped on the light panel and steadied himself on his crutches so that he could shuffle through the big, floppy sheets. He extracted one and slid its top into the clip along the top edge of the panel.

"Spirit's gonna agree with me. The last thing he wants is the company getting that kind of attention right before the board votes on whether they're going to make his successorship a long-term thing. Once the lab records don't exist, there's nothing more to discuss." Ashe paused a moment to switch films before continuing. "And right now, we are in a good spot because Task Industries has not yet been officially ordered to preserve any evidence. All you're doing is cleaning up, with a good friend to help you and a random homeless guy you hired to get him off the street."

Fry looked at Ashe quizzically. "Hired? You want to get paid for this?"

"You're too literal. But yeah, I want to get paid." Ashe stabbed a finger at a distinctly-shaped dark spot on the second film he had pulled out. "I want that."

Fry hobbled across the room as Amber watched the scene, desperate to remain a bystander. Frymet stood next to Ashe, apparently having either forgiven him or acknowledged the inevitability of his plan. Maybe both.

"Thirty-seven A?" said Fry. She turned to a locked rolling cabinet and inserted a key into the lock cylinder. "All the extracted material is in here."

Extracted material. Such an innocuous term, but Amber's stomach lurched at the thought of the collection of bullets and shrapnel Task had removed from Ashe's body to satisfy his "scientific" curiosity.

Fry opened the cabinet and Ashe started shuffling through the tagged packets on the stainless steel shelves within.

"Doesn't it bother you to look at those?" Amber demanded. "Doesn't it bother you just to be back here?"

Ashe looked up from his explorations. "Bother me? Why would it bother me?"

"You were hurt here!"

Ashe frowned at Amber, failing to understand her concern. "Been hurt a lot of places. Lot of them, more than once. If I avoided every place I'd ever been hurt, I'd never go anywhere, would I?"

"Says the hermit who lived in a radioactive cave for thirty years," rebutted Amber.

"Shut up," Ashe grumbled and returned to rustling through sample pouches.

Frymet had returned to the lightbox. "Task called 37A the 'heartstopper,'" she mused.

Ashe lifted one particular pouch and slid the tray back into the cabinet. He regarded his find and then opened the pouch, pulling out a bullet. The slug was easily recognizable, despite a slight deformation at its tip.

"Sounds about right," he stated simply.

Ashe gripped the handles of his crutches and slid around Fry toward an equipment tray in the corner. Fry was continuing her recollection of the x-ray film.

"Yes, Task was intrigued by that one. Nine-millimeter, mid-to late Eighties. The bullet passed through either the second or third intercostal space, perforated the ascending aorta, and lodged on the inner surface of the left scapula for about four decades."

Ashe held the bullet up to the light with his left hand and Amber saw it shine in the light. The bullet seemed a small thing, dented along the front end only slightly, but it had a beauty to it. The copper-colored jacket enclosing the bullet was itself about three-quarters plated with a brilliant splash of silver.

"What's that coating on it?" Amber had to ask.

Fry turned to her. "It's silver. From what we could tell, the bullet hit something made of silver (pure silver, not sterling) before entering Ashe's chest. X-rays also indicated the presence of small shards of metal, likely more silver, in the ribs around where the bullet passed. Task never finished looking into it; it would have required cutting sections of Ashe's ribs out, and he just hadn't gotten around to it—"

Fry looked up and realized Ashe and Amber were both simply staring at her. She blushed and apologized. "Sorry... At any rate, it was a well-placed shot. Guaranteed fatal."

Ashe steadied himself on his crutches. Still holding the slug with his left hand, he lifted the drill with his right. He had replaced the bone-sampling bit with a much smaller standard bit.

"Yep," he said with an air of satisfaction. "Hurt like a—
"

Stopping himself short, Ashe looked over his shoulder at the two girls. "Hurt like something that hurt a lot. We'll go with 'heartstopper.'"

The room filled with the high-pitched whine of the drill for a moment. Ashe placed the drill back on the tray and turned toward an unopened box on the counter. Tearing the box at the perforated lid, he ripped open a fresh package marked, "Chromic Gut Surgical Suture" and threaded one end of the brown string through the small hole he had just drilled in the bullet. Tying a quick knot, Ashe slipped the loop over his head and dropped the bullet inside his rumpled shirt, probably right next to its old entry wound.

Amber watched this operation with no small amount of curiosity. "What's so special about that one, Ashe?"

Not only did Ashe not explain, he acted like he didn't hear her at all. It was a habit of his that Amber had started to notice. When Ashe didn't want to talk about something too close or too sensitive to him, he simply went blank. Of all his irritating habits, this one irked her the most.

Ashe swung past Amber on his crutches into the hallway. Grabbing a wire document cart, he spun and struggled to push it ahead of him back into the room. Amber finally came out of her fugue and grabbed the cart's handle. "Where do we start?" she asked.

Ashe favored her with a rare grin. "Good girl," he said. "Start with these," Ashe said, his voice low but steady. He pulled a handful of x-ray films from the table. A faint plastic crackle cut through the room's uneasy silence.

Amber nodded and helped empty the tray, grabbing the films several at a time. The cool slickness of the plastic under her fingers made her stomach churn. She tried not to look too closely at the pale, skeletal imprints depicted by each one, with countless fragments of bullets or other metal bits lodged in and around bone.

"Amber, focus," Fry said, her tone even but pointed. She didn't glance up, busy flipping through a spiral-bound lab notebook on the counter. Her fingers traced the scrawled notes that were her own attempts to capture Task's disturbing experimentation in sterile medical jargon.

Across the room, Ashe opened a drawer and pulled out a thick stack of papers, stapled reports, and printouts. He rifled through them with mechanical precision, pausing only in an attempt to separate what needed burning from what could be ignored. The crutches under his arms creaked faintly with every shift of his weight. Shrugging, he gave up the effort and dumped all the documents into the wheeled cart.

When they were finished loading all the films, photos, and notebooks, Fry capped off the cart with a foot-long plastic bin filled with everything else: samples, vials, syringes, and sharps that hadn't already been disposed of. They headed for the elevator and Fry slapped her badge against the glass panel next to the shiny steel doors.

THE BASEMENT HALLWAY was cold. Fluorescent lights buzzed overhead, and the faint echo of their footsteps followed them as they descended a shallow decline. The air grew stale and heavy as they neared the incinerator, a massive metal beast tucked into a corner of the building's lowest level.

Fry dropped the plastic bin in first, the contents spilling into the incinerator's yawning metal mouth. Amber added a bag of films. The plastic crinkled in the latent heat as it landed. Ashe emptied the remaining stacks of notebooks in an unceremonious heap.

For a moment, no one moved. Amber's hand hovered near the ignition switch, her pulse pounding in her ears.

"You want me to do it?" Ashe asked. "We gotta go."

Amber shook her head. "No. I want to."

She flipped the switch and the furnace roared to life. The incinerator's flames flared blue then shifted bright orange. Shadows danced across their faces. Papers curled and blackened; the X-ray films melted into formless blobs before disintegrating entirely. A plume of smoke twisted up through the vent above, carrying with it the last hints of the horrors they'd endured at the hands of Cameron Task.

"What are you clowns doing down here?"

Amber started perceptibly at the unexpected voice. She had not quite realized how lost she had gotten in reflection. Spinning around, Amber watched the silhouette of a man emerge from the dim light of the hallway. Even before she could make out the details, she easily identified the newcomer by his ego. The room seemed smaller with his arrival.

Owen Spirit strode—hobbled, rather—into view, his tailored navy suit immaculate despite the crutches pressed into his armpits. A crisp white shirt beneath the jacket was accented by his silk tie, hung with intentional precision. His polished Oxford shoes reflected the flickering orange light of the incinerator.

"Hope I'm not crashing the party," Spirit said, his voice smooth and rich, cutting through the tension like a finely honed blade. "Nah, just kidding. I hope I am." He paused near the group, adjusting his crutches with a practiced ease that somehow made Ashe's and Fry's attempts at restricted locomotion look comical.

Amber considered the incongruity of the lawyer's elegance in the grungy, soot-streaked basement. "You're a little late if you're here for the bonfire," she said, crossing her arms.

Spirit's mouth curled into a practiced half-smile. "The bonfire, no. But I figured I'd better show up for the grand finale. Someone has to make sure none of you morons accidentally implicate yourselves while you're tying up loose ends."

Fry turned a half circle on her cane. Her lips curled up in dislike. "Says the lawyer who waltzes in after we've burned all the evidence."

Owen raised a brow, his grin sharp as a scalpel. "What? You didn't save the big smoking gun for me?"

Ashe leaned heavily on his crutches. He stepped forward. "About time you showed your sorry face, Spirit," he said, his tone low but, for some reason, not unfriendly.

Owen Spirit tilted his head, his smile softening slightly. "I've always had a profound appreciation for cleaning up messes. Particularly when it's in my best interest."

Amber glanced down at Owen's crutches. Spirit saw the glance and responded with a wry chuckle.

Amber looked away, embarrassed to have been caught.

"Don't worry, Ms. Olsen," he said smoothly, "I'm not looking for sympathy like this bozo." He gestured in Ashe's direction. "Cameron Task had a habit of shooting the messenger when he didn't like the message. My passion for delivering uncomfortable truths finally caught up with me."

Spirit turned toward Ashe, ready with some quip, but the words caught in his throat. His brow furrowed as his gaze swept over Ashe from head to toe, eyes narrowing in suspicion.

"What the heck—" He blinked, his usual smooth delivery faltering for a beat. "You look... different." His sharp eyes flicked to Amber, then back to Ashe. "When I saw you last, you looked like you belonged in a retirement home. One of those dead-end ones. And now, what? You just decided to shave off thirty years?"

"Been eating my vegetables."

Spirit scoffed. "Yeah? Well, let me know where you're shopping, because last I checked, broccoli doesn't fix that kind of mileage." His eyes lingered on Ashe's face, his mind working through the implications. "This some party trick, or should I be concerned?"

"Take your pick," Ashe said, shifting his weight on the crutches. "Just be sure and lose lots of sleep over it."

Spirit exhaled, shaking his head. "Lose sleep over it? You should be losing sleep over it. The FDA should be losing sleep over it. The Broccoli Growers of America should be losing sleep over it. At the rate you're de-aging, that Standish clown is gonna have to try you in juvenile court." He smoothed his neatly combed hair and muttered, "I hate dealing with stuff that doesn't make sense."

"You're a lawyer," Amber said. "You should be used to it by now."

Spirit shot her an unimpressed look before returning his attention to Ashe. "I'm filing this under 'stuff to revisit when I've had a drink.'" His grin returned, though his eyes still carried a flicker of unease.

Ashe shrugged. "You do that."

Spirit studied him for another second, then shook his head. "Alright. Freakish immortality aside, let's move on."

He looked at the others. "Let's go to my office. We need to talk about Standish."

"Your office?" Frymet looked confused.

"Sure," Spirit said through a beaming smile. "The office formerly known as Task's."

ॐ • ॐ

POWERED BY AN automated switch, the lights came up gently as the group entered. Spirit stood for a moment, making the others fan out around his still form. Amber thought the man looked like a statue erected by himself to celebrate his own greatness.

"I guess it's my spleen's office, if you want to get technical. It paid the price to get here." Spirit's self-satisfied smile made the words dance with misplaced levity. Having made his entrance in style, Spirit moved on his crutches toward the desk in the center of his former employer's office, his feet swinging in precise arcs. "But at least it lets me have the nice chair."

Amber's eyes repeated their prior circuit of the office. Comparing what she saw to her previous visit, Amber was stricken by the transformation. The cool air still carried the faint scent of leather and polished wood, but the smoky aroma of exotic coffee had been replaced by the light herbal earthiness of tea. Not a fan of that change, Amber took a step inside. Her worn sneakers tapped softly against the hardwood floor.

The immense plate glass windows, the same ones through which Ashe had dived with Task in a moment of furious violence, had been restored. New, pristine sheets of glass flooded the room with rich golden afternoon sunlight. The skyline beyond remained unchanged, but the atmosphere inside was lighter.

The walls, no longer adorned with Task's curated art collection, now featured a striking collection of edgier, more modern works. Each piece was provocative and raw in a unique way; the artist's primary tools seemed to be spray paint, stencils, and rebellion. A girl released a heart-shaped balloon. A masked protester hurled flowers. A child in a sweat shop sewed propaganda flags. Others were iconic images by famous artists intentionally remixed with vandalism. The new collection sought to replace Task's traditional refinement with rebellious creativity, but Amber felt Spirit was trying too hard.

The furniture retained its defining dark wood and clean lines, but subtle changes reflected Owen Spirit's personality. Chairs, once pristine and rigid, now bore slight creases in the leather, signs of actual use. A soft wool throw in a muted gray herringbone pattern was draped over the back of one chair, adding a warmth that the lawyer would deny if confronted about. The glass and steel conference table had been cleared of the mountain of cash Task had placed there to tempt her. Amber turned away.

The espresso machine was gone from its central position, shoved slightly back and to one side. The place of prominence now held a wooden box containing an assortment of tea bags and jars of loose-leaf blends: Dragon Oolong, Mint, Jasmine Bud, Cardamon. Amber frowned in confusion, her eyes moving to a plain but elegant ceramic teapot that stood beside the box. Amber ran a finger along the edge of the credenza, passing the teapot and stopping in reverence before the stainless beauty of the abandoned coffee machine. It had been shoved back a few inches to the wall and a soft cloth now draped over it. This, Amber brushed gently aside, revealing more dials, levers, meters, and stainless steel tubes than she thought she'd ever know what to do with. But it was glorious.

"You're listening, right?"

Amber spun around, startled back to the present by Spirit's sharp call. Owen Spirit, Fry, and Ashe were all looking straight at her in expectation. Spirit was slumped against the broad expanse of desk, looking like he belonged in a men's fashion magazine, and Fry had lowered herself into an armchair. Ashe stood propped up and slightly tilted to the left. Amber wasn't sure if it was because of the uneven crutches or the still-healing leg that necessitated them.

"Of course I am," she lied.

Spirit resumed speaking, evidently picking where he had left off during Amber's coffee-inspired fantasy. "If we all stick to the story—or at least each of us stick to our own version—then we're in the clear. Once this Agent Standish realizes there's nothing to find, it'll all die back down."

Amber realized that she hadn't missed much; she rejoined the conversation. "He seemed pretty sure of himself. Do you think he has something?" she asked.

Spirit looked at her with a look like a dead fish. He blinked three times. "That's what I was just saying. He obviously has nothing at this point. What can he have?"

"I don't know," Amber shrugged. "He was talking about murder!"

"They always talk about murder. It's required in the FBI handbook."

Ashe spoke up, looking at Spirit. "You told me Task had isolated and destroyed all the external evidence of my blood. He wanted to keep all the info for himself, right? That's what bad guys do. There should be nothing out and about for Standish to find."

Spirit nodded, "Yep. And he kept everything on an air-gapped network in the lab, which has all been wiped."

Frymet leaned forward in her chair, trying to interject, "Task kept everything on the air-gapped network—"

"That's what I just said. Keep up," chided Spirit. "Plus, I've had a hand-picked team of morally questionables from IT scouring everything inside our firewall and eradicating any mention of Ashe or anything related. If those guys can't find something, it's because it isn't there. Since you guys just atomized all the actual physical records, we're solid."

Fry tried again, "But that's just—"

Spirit waved her off. "That's just the end of it. We stick to the story."

Amber's eyebrows wrestled with each other. "Why are you doing this?" she demanded of Spirit.

"Doing what?"

"You really don't seem like the type to help someone else out of the goodness of your heart."

"Goodness? What goodness? Look, I know Ashe's secret, but it's in my own best interests not to reveal anything, or to do anything at all other than stick with the story that Task killed himself and Ashe was never here. So, sure. I become *de facto* complicit in everything you morons do to cover it all up, legal or otherwise. It's a major gray area. But that's okay. I look amazing in gray."

Fry had not yet given up. "But—"

"But don't you think the FBI will see through all of it?" asked Amber.

"No. How many times do I have to say it?" Spirit was animated now, driven to prove the simple point to the simpler minds. "The FBI has nothing unless we hand it to them. Task gathered every shred of physical evidence and every digital record in the world regarding Ashe across history to keep them for himself. And a mountain of physical records from the time before everything was digital."

Warming to his subject, Owen Spirit gestured off-handedly. "Yes, as hard as it is for you children to grasp, there was a time when physical records were all there was. But Task got hold of it all. Police records, FBI records, everything. It wasn't legal, but it was thorough, and transparent. Task was a genius when it came to that kind of stuff. There's no way Standish has anything actionable, or Ashe would be arrested already. And we all would too, as accessories."

"Mr. Spirit..." Fry sounded more exasperated with each passing moment.

"So where did Standish go after he left the diner?" Spirit asked Amber. Ashe swung over to the plate glass window, looking out at the courtyard of the building.

"No idea," was her reply. "He said something about making a trip to burn Ashe with some warrants, and that he'd be back to talk again.

"Warrants? For what? To 'burn Ashe?' That's a weird way for an FBI agent to speak."

"Well, he did talk weird."

"Are you sure that's what he said?"

Amber thought for a moment. "Well, he said it funny-like. Like I said, the guy talked weird. Kinda like English was his second language, right after Evil."

"Think hard," Spirit directed. "What were his exact words?"

"He said he would be 'going to Ashe burn with some warrants' but he'd be back and would want to talk again."

"Ashburn?! He specifically said Ashburn?" Spirit's eyes were suddenly very wide. His head whipped around to face in Frymet's direction. "Why is he going to Ashburn with a warrant?"

Fry grumbled at the lawyer. "That's what I've been trying to tell you. Your IT goons can't get to everything. Mr. Task mentioned a completely isolated server that he alone had access to. Where he kept everything. In Ashburn."

"What's Ashburn?" Asked Amber.

"Ashburn, Virginia," replied Frymet. "The data center capital of the world. A bunch of factors in the nineties led to everybody setting up their data centers there. And that led to Task setting up his first and biggest data center there to prove it could be done sustainably."

"And he…" Spirit's voice trailed off.

Fry nodded, relieved Spirit was finally listening. "And he made weekly trips there, the whole time I was working with him. Alone. Presumably to upload each week's research and data to his private server."

Spirit's face blanched white as his namesake. "People," he said, "We may have a serious problem."

ॐ • ॐ

OWEN SPIRIT SET the phone on the cradle, eyes closed. "Ashburn, Virginia," he said to the others. The words were no surprise. He opened his eyes to watch dusk start to creep over the cityscape below. Spirit looked decidedly sheepish, like he'd missed something obvious. It was not a good look for the man.

"What is it?" Ashe growled.

"Me and my big mouth. 'If those guys can't find something, it's because it isn't there,' right?" Spirit closed his eyes.

Ashe snarled at him, growing impatient. "You've got about ten seconds to tell me what you're whinging about."

Owen Spirit sighed deeply. "So, my brilliant IT team had found an area of the network they couldn't *actually* find. As if that makes any sense. They said it resembled nothing so much as a black hole. They only noticed it by the shadow it cast. Idiots weren't even able to isolate which data center it was in. Or wasn't in. Or, whatever. They'd chalked it up to some error or gremlin. That has to be what Standish is after. No idea how he knows, but he knows."

Ashe growled.

Deflecting, Spirit fixed Fry with a cold glare. "Woulda been nice to hear about that server of Task's a little earlier."

"Woulda been nice to be listened to a little earlier."

"Okay, fine," interjected Ashe. "What do we do about it?"

Spirit shook his head. "That's going to be a problem. With Task dead, we don't have a good way to quickly locate the servers, let alone wipe them. And now with Standish in the picture, I can't suddenly devote any more resources to it without drawing attention, since it's already on the FBI's radar. Once they get to the server, the FBI will be able to devote nearly infinite time and effort to get to the data."

"So we gotta go find it the old-fashioned way," said Ashe.

It looked like it pained him, but Spirit agreed with him. "Yeah. We're going to need to go there. There's no way I can block an FBI warrant, especially from here, but I might be able to delay it a bit if I'm there. As for getting into the server, that'll be your department, I guess. Anything I do going forward, there's going to be a record of it, as an officer of the company."

"It's a computer, right?" Ashe scratched one of his more recent scars. "Just go out there, go in, and pull out the hard drive. Stuff it in your pocket and walk out, right?"

Fry answered him, "It's not as easy as that. These are undoubtedly rack mounted servers, probably with separate storage arrays on much bigger rack units. Not something you can fit in a pocket."

"So, we're going to have to get creative," Ashe said, looking at her. "Okay, then."

Ashe looked around the room. "I'm the strongest one of us. I'm also the one this matters to the most. I'll be the one to go in and grab the drive and smash it to pieces."

Spirit raised his eyebrows. "Um, that's destructive. Kinda the exact opposite of creative, don't you think?"

Ashe waved it off. "Fine, I'll come up with something, but you'll have to point me to the right place."

"A server rack is a pretty big thing," said Owen Spirit, his voice dripping skepticism.

"Okay, so if I can't carry it, I'll bash it to pieces. Problem solved."

Spirit said nothing for a moment, but looked at Ashe without any expression Amber could easily discern.

"What?" demanded Ashe. "Give me two reasons that plan won't work."

"One, you're a Neanderthal. It's all about brute force with you. And two, you're still on crutches, you moron!"

Ashe scowled back. "Two? I'll be off these crutches by the time we get there, which is more than I can say for you, gimp. And one? I'm not a Neanderthal, I'm an engineer. It's all about the tactical *application* of brute force. There's a difference."

Spirit looked at Ashe again for another long minute. They may as well have been the only two people in the room.

Suddenly, Spirit grabbed the phone from its cradle. "Fine. We'll work it out when we get there. I'll call and get us four tickets to Dulles."

Ashe shook his head. "Uh, no, that's not gonna work."

Spirit looked up from the phone. "What are you talking about? Of course it'll work. I know Reagan has a lot more non-stops, but it's farther away. We'll go through Dulles."

"That's not what I mean."

Amber looked up and joined the conversation. "Right. Um, Ashe doesn't have any ID."

"No ID?" Spirit looked confused.

"Yeah. Can't fly without an ID, right?"

Spirit growled at Amber and placed the phone back in its cradle. "Okay, so no commercial flights. That does wrinkle things a bit. Fine; Task never bothered with a corporate jet, but we can charter a Gulfstream."

Again, Ashe shook his head. "Not for me."

"What? Fear of flying?" Strain was starting to show in Owen Spirit's voice; he was growing tired of the topic.

"No. I just need to go by ground so I can pick up some supplies along the way."

"Supplies? What supplies? We'll get whatever you need when we get there. It's not like we have a lot of time for you to take a road trip."

"Too bad." Ashe's face was set like stone. "We'll have to make the time. It'll take too long to get what I need once we get there. Stuff I already have. Tools. Stored up."

Spirit thought for a minute. "Okay. I'll fly there and get to work on that warrant. Ms. Cieślak will accompany me; we can get into the server facility and try to at least locate the server under the radar."

"Sounds good. How do we get there?"

"Well, you're gonna have to drive..." Spirit's voice faded as he regarded Ashe's crutches. He gestured toward Amber. "Strike that; I guess she'll need to drive. Last time you got hold of a motor vehicle, you dropped it on your leg."

Ashe looked down at his leg and shrugged. "Bone healed up wrong. Had to fix it.

"Right. Tactical application of brute force."

Ashe grinned at the lawyer. "Exactly. Anyway, I'll be fine by the time we get there. You get out there and stop that warrant. Get me the schematics of the building while you're at it."

Spirit's eyes narrowed. Amber thought she could hear the clanking of gears as he considered all the possibilities before having to come back around to where he'd started. "Alright, we're doing this. I'll see what I can do on the plans."

"We're gonna need a car with some range," said Ashe. "I don't wanna have to stop every hundred miles for gas."

"I have just the thing," smiled Spirit. "Go home and get ready. Get back here ASAP. Pack light, and pack fast."

Spirit regarded Ashe's crutches. "Well, as fast as you can, *gimp*."

Chapter 4 : CODE BLACK

1988

THE SCENT WAS the same. It never changed, really. It always lingered in hospitals, no matter how modern the lobbies got or how much peaceful artwork they slapped on the walls. But, Dani preferred that smell to the more cloying variant familiar from the morgues she had frequented all too often in her time with the Bureau.

Dani stopped in front of a door marked *Lena Rosenbaum, Head of Medicine*. There was something distinctly Lena in the air that took Dani back to another time: an undercurrent of coffee, faint but unmistakable, but strong and black. Memories flashed of countless late nights at the free clinic in East Ashburn, of Lena perched on a stool with a chipped purple mug and a tired look. That mug and Dani were Lena's constant companions as they saved the world one patient at a time in an area of 1970s Chicago torn with racial strife and bigotry.

Dani knocked lightly on the frosted glass and opened the door when bidden.

The office was bigger than Dani had pictured it would be, though it bristled with the same energy that had always defined Lena. Shelves overflowed with medical tomes and novels along one wall, spilling onto a cluttered desk to blend with stacks of folders, then papers. The blend, which Lena called her "Chaos Gradient," was organized in some indecipherable pattern that she described as a wave of knowledge off the shores of unknowing that she alone could surf.

A new addition was the gleaming white cast encasing Lena's right arm; it in turn was swaddled in a bright yellow, utilitarian sling that clashed with the tailored cut of her lavender blazer. Her old mentor was seated and scanning a report, but the moment Dani entered, Lena burst from her chair in recognition. Dani smiled at the familiar face that was a welcome mix of surprise and delight.

"Danielle McKendree!" Lena exclaimed, her throaty voice every bit as warm and full as Dani remembered. "Or is it still Agent Linder these days?"

Dani smiled. "Still just Dani, as far as I'm concerned."

"Good. You were never much of an 'Agent Anything' to me," Lena said with a grin. She gestured toward the chairs near her desk with her good hand. "Come in, sit. Let me look at you."

As Dani stepped further into the room, she felt Lena's gaze sweep over her. Despite the trappings of office, it wasn't a doctor examining a patient but a friend evaluating the years that had passed. "You haven't changed a bit," Lena concluded, though her eyes lingered just long enough to catch the subtle lines of fatigue etched into Dani's face. "Except for that. Do they teach you how to frown that way, or is it just a hazard of the job?"

Dani laughed, her tension easing slightly. "It's a perk."

Lena's grin widened as she lowered herself into her chair, cradling her injured arm. "And here I am, arm broken in an attempt to regain my youth on a beginner slope. Clearly, we both have it all figured out."

Dani dropped into the chair across from her. "It's good to see you, Lena." Her purse slid to the floor.

"It's good to be seen," Lena replied and leaned back with a warmth that filled the room. She shoved files and papers aside as if to declare her full attentiveness to her old friend. "But you didn't come here just to check in after ten years. I remember that look. What are you wrestling with?"

Dani's eyes narrowed. Lena had always been able to cut through any of her defenses, even back when Dani had thought she could out-stubborn the older woman. "I need to make a change," she admitted. "I'm leaving the Bureau."

"Good. It's about time."

Dani paused, then continued more quietly. "And I'm getting divorced."

"Whoa!" Lena sat forward, reaching for her coffee. Dani noted that she still had the purple mug. It had remained Lena's faithful companion, though Dani had not; it was still her refuge in which to think. She regarded Dani in silence as she sipped from the chipped rim.

That silence hung in the air longer than Dani liked. Lena never reacted immediately when caught by surprise. That steadiness had once been an inspiration for Dani. Now, it seemed like a spotlight was on her. "And you want to come back to medicine?" Lena asked finally.

Dani nodded, grateful for Lena's other notable abilities. She never accused, and she always cut to the heart of the matter. "I don't know if it's the right move, but... I miss it. I miss the clinic, helping people. Fixing them. I'm not cut out for the Bureau. It's been... draining."

"And so has your marriage."

Dani regarded Lena with a sheepish look. Lena had never married, being fully committed to her vocation, and she had spent hours in that old clinic office trying to help Dani realize that her desire to move into law enforcement was a distraction. Later, over the phone, she had tried to convince Dani that her entanglement with Wolfe Linder was a similar complication to be avoided. Lena had enjoyed success with neither point.

"Hey!" Lena exclaimed with a renewed smile. "No judgments here." Her good hand slapped the desk lightly. "And no 'I told you so's'. Although I did. Of course you should come back to medicine! You were brilliant then, and I suspect your hands are steadier now than they were then." She gestured around the room. "And this place could use you. Lord knows we've been stretched thin. You'd fit right in; just like old times."

Dani blinked, caught off guard by the immediate enthusiasm. "You're serious? Just like that?"

Lena leaned forward, the cast sliding against the oak desk. "Why not? You've kept up with your licensure, I presume?"

"Yes, of course."

"I knew it. Dani, you were a force of nature in that clinic. I'd take you back in a heartbeat. You're still a healer. The Bureau might have given you some new tools, but it hasn't taken the old ones away."

"Sometimes I wonder."

Before Lena could respond to Dani's self-targeted jibe, a nurse exploded through the office door without ceremony. She was out of breath.

"Doctor Rosenbaum! Some sort of drug war on the South Side. Major casualties, various ages. Every ambulance in the city is on the road. Illinois Central and U of C are full up, and since Englewood's closed now, we're getting more than our share of the overflow. We have maybe ten minutes before the ER turns into a meat grinder."

In an instant, the nurse vanished back out the door, her message delivered.

Lena stood up at once, her speed and grace belying both her age and injured arm.

"Trial by fire?" the older woman asked Dani with a wry grin.

"Is there any other kind?" replied Dani.

ֆ • ֆ

THE DOUBLE DOORS of the emergency room swung open with a sharp report, and the wave of sound following behind slammed into Dani like a physical force. Sirens wailed from just outside the main entrance, whipped together with shouted orders and the groans of the injured into a froth of chaos. The odors of blood, burnt flesh, and gallons of antiseptic laid heavy in the room, a pervasive smell that no amount of ventilation would chase away any time soon.

Dani followed close behind Lena, who managed to remain calm despite the sudden carnage. The ER was bursting at the seams. Patients on stretchers lined the hallways, spilled into corners converted to impromptu triage stations. Standard hospital admission procedures were meaningless, a thing of the past. A nurse collided with Dani, her arms full of gauze and IV bags. Dani extricated herself from the jumble of limbs and supplies to see a young boy, no older than ten, clinging to his mother's leg in the middle of the hallway. His wide eyes were fixed on the blood pooling near his mother's feet.

"Jesus," Dani muttered to no one. Her gaze swept over the scene. "This is a war zone."

Lena didn't respond, but her quick, purposeful stride slowed for just a moment, her expression darkening. "South Chicago on a Tuesday," she said dryly, her good hand gesturing toward the overflowing triage area. "Grab a pair of gloves and get busy. I'll be back."

Before Dani could ask where she was going, a man in a rumpled suit appeared at Lena's side, gesturing with an air of urgency toward the far side of the broad room. Lena gave Dani a quick, reassuring nod before following him, her broken arm flopping up and down with every rushed step.

And then Dani was alone in a sea of frantic motion and panic. She pulled on a pair of gloves and headed for the nearest cluster of stretchers, scanning faces and wounds, making snap judgments, surprised at how quickly old habits could return despite a decade of neglect. A middle-aged man with a gunshot wound to the shoulder and burns along his neck. Stable enough to wait. A young woman clutching her side, blood seeping through her shirt, her breathing shallow. Priority. Dani flagged a nurse, pointing the woman toward a room that wasn't ready but would have to get that way real quick.

Sweat began to gather at her temples as she moved to the next patient. A teenage boy, maybe seventeen, his face pale and slack. His shirt was ripped open, revealing multiple gunshot wounds to his chest. Gang tattoos beneath the gore stood out like banners, but they meant nothing to Dani. He was a kid. Whatever he'd done to end up here didn't matter now.

"Oxygen, and prep him for surgery," she told the nearest orderly. The man nodded and rushed the boy's stretcher toward a bay, though Dani had little confidence there would be either surgeon or operating theater available anytime soon.

She continued around the periphery of the room. A man in his thirties, unconscious but still breathing. An elderly woman with a leg injury. Not life-threatening, despite her agonized grip on the stretcher rail. A child cradled in the arms of a shell-shocked paramedic. Too small a child.

"Doctor!" someone called, pulling her from her reverie. Dani turned to see a uniformed police officer standing near the entrance, his face lined with exhaustion and other emotions she didn't have time to decipher. She strode over to the man, wiping her bloodied gloves on a towel slung over her shoulder.

"What happened out there?" Dani barked, stepping closer so he could hear her over the din. Her voice was sharper than she intended, more FBI than field medic.

The officer exhaled, shaking his head as he spoke. "Drug war. Two major factions involved; some kind of peace talk, from what we're hearing. Working out a truce or something. But then it all went sideways. They think a third group showed up and—" He made a sharp gesture with both hands, like an explosion. "Boom. Everything went to pieces. Literally."

Dani frowned, her mind racing. "A third group? Any idea who?"

"Yeah," the officer said, answering her first question, not the second. He scratched at the back of his neck. "Third party. No one knows who, but things went south fast. Explosions, gunfire, lots of both. Whatever the deal was, it tore the place apart. What you got here are the lucky ones."

His radio crackled, and the officer grimaced. "I've got to get back out there," he said. "Good luck in here, Doc." The man left without ever revealing why he had called out to her.

Dani watched him go, her mind churning not as a doctor for the moment, but a law enforcement officer herself. A third party. An intentional escalation? She didn't know what that meant. Did someone want the war to keep going? Someone who didn't care about collateral damage?

She shoved the thought aside and turned back to the fray. People were dying, and she had no time to figure out why.

&ev; • &ev;

THE KILLERS WERE right above her again. They were right above her again and the Good Samaritan was gone. He promised he'd be back, and she believed him. After all, he was a good Good Samaritan, wasn't he? He'd be back, but for now he was gone. The Good Samaritan was gone, and the killers walked over her head.

Dust fell from a creaking floor joist and danced in the beam of light produced by the bullet hole in the floor above. Dani didn't like the smell down here. It was dank and reeked of age, though it wasn't damp like she thought a crawl space should be. It was dry; it was dusty and smelled just like slow-roasted wood.

The Good Samaritan was gone. He said he'd be going on ahead and that he would call her when he had everything prepared. He would signal her that it was time to go. But she didn't know what the signal would be. She didn't know what the signal would be, and she realized now that she couldn't hear.

A spider slunk across its web on eight silent feet, crossing the beam of light. It had been alerted by vibrations in its web as dust fell from the killers above. But it made no noise. Not that she had ever heard a spider walking on a web. That was ridiculous. But she could hear nothing at all now, and that concerned her. The Good Samaritan would make the call and she would never hear it. With the killers right over her head.

All she had now was the light. The single bright shaft of light erupted from a nine-millimeter hole drilled through the linoleum and subfloor and ceramic and subfloor and oak planks and pine planks and dust. She had never known that the floor beneath her feet had been made of so many layers. Not until those layers were now above her head. Layers of age, all pierced in an instant by a bullet. All to bring her the bright, shining light.

The light went out.

A killer walked over her head and stepped over the hole and there was no more light. The Good Samaritan was gone now and now there was no light. The spider bellowed its rage against the dying of the light but she heard not its scream in the dark.

And the killer's hand was on her now. The killer had reached his hand right through the floor despite the floor's age, despite its rock-hard stability, despite her need for its protection.

The hand squeezed.

Dani's eyes burst open. Her right hand flew to her hip, instincts developed over the past decade driving it there in a single fluid motion, faster than her tired brain could follow. Reaching her hip, the hand found nothing but cloth, crusty with dried blood.

"Whoa up there, cowgirl!" Lena jerked her good hand back from Dani's shoulder and raised it in a motion of surrender. The older woman stood in front of her, looking down. "It's just me. I'm sorry to wake you."

Dani stood up from her chair and slid the curtain aside. It made a harsh metallic scraping sound on its track above her head. "I'm sorry, Lena. I must have fallen asleep."

"Don't apologize; you earned a few minutes. Fourteen hours on your feet will wear you out a bit, won't it?"

Dani looked at Lena. It had been a couple hours since she had seen the older woman. They'd crossed paths several times in the carnage and chaos, and the progress of Lena's appearance had been a mirror of her own. Her pastel suit marked with the first few patches of bright crimson from the earliest patients, then the red areas spreading far and wide, the oldest patches fading to a reddish brown as the crimson continued its inexorable conquest of new territory. Lena had abandoned the sling at some point out of need for even a semi-functional right hand as she worked in the trenches alongside her staff to triage and treat the wounded.

Dani's mentor and new boss smiled at her. "Well, kid, I have to say: as far as first days on the job go, you sure can pick 'em. I'm sorry it's not over yet."

Dani cast her eyes around the war zone that had begun yesterday morning as a simple emergency room. Although beds and bays were filled and gurneys strove to contain the overflow across the room, there seemed to be a relative lull in the action they had endured over the past several hours.

"Are there more coming?" Dani asked.

"No," replied Lena. "We've got all we're likely to get. But we did just get what may be the last survivor from this whole mess. Paramedics said they found him buried under rubble alongside a bunch of the dead." Lena's complexion blanched. "Dead women and children, they said. Noncombatants, but it was some of the worst carnage on the scene."

Dani didn't want to think about that until it was all over. It was a tactic she had developed in the Bureau after planting its seeds during her earlier trauma residency. Push down the feelings about the job until the job is done. The feelings never failed to come back later. In force.

"Okay, what do we have, then?" she asked Lena, looking around. "I don't see any new patients in triage."

"He's already waiting for you in the operating room." Lena had anticipated the effect those words would have on Dani's composure. She fixed Dani with a steady, calming gaze, full of confidence that she sought to instill in Dani by osmosis. "You can do this. I need another neurosurgeon."

"I'm not a neuro!" exclaimed Dani. Her hands grew clammy as she felt their heat rush away and into her neck and cheeks and ears. "You're the neuro!"

"I am." Lena's voice remained steady and calm. She lifted her broken arm. The cast, now covered with bloody marks and prints, flapped like an impotent chicken wing. "But I'm in no shape to operate at the moment. I have two neuros on staff, and they are both elbows-deep already. As are all my generals. Even my OB/GYNs are doing trauma."

Lena locked eyes with Dani and her voice picked up an edge that took Dani back a dozen years. "You are what I have. And I will be the angel on your shoulder. I will walk you through every step of it."

As she had done so many times over the years, Dani closed her eyes and took a deep, composing breath. A need was a need.

She opened her eyes. "I'm good. What do we have?" she repeated.

Lena gave the tiniest of nods. That was something Dani had always loved about her mentor: the more intense Lena's emotion or approval, the less demonstrative she was about it. "Male Caucasian, forty-five years old," she said in a matter-of-fact voice. Her surgeon voice. "Double shotgun blast, buckshot, at close range to the upper back. Severe trauma at C3 through C5, inclusive, and throughout."

Dani's eyes closed as she digested this information. "Lord. Complete or incomplete?" She asked, referring to the degree of spinal compromise.

"Looks complete, but we can't fully tell yet. There's too much blood, and the patient is non-responsive. Second- and third-degree burns over much of the back, possibly fourth-degree in spots. The collar placed by the EMTs blocked an earlier full analysis. You'll have to assess live in theater."

"That's quite a list," Dani stated. "Are you sure about this? I haven't been in an operating room in years, and you're the neuro, not me. I am under-qualified for this."

"Yeah, well, you're all there is. You said you'd maintained licensure, right?"

"Sure, but I—"

"Then you're qualified. And you're not just some locum tenens off the street. I don't care if you weren't a neuro; I've never seen anyone with hands as steady as yours. Steady hands are what I need right now. I just hope you haven't lost it all. You're the only hope this man's got."

Dani fell silent. She'd run out of words.

Lena Rosenbaum waved down an orderly and pulled Dani by the elbow in his direction. "This is Doctor McKendree," she said to the harried-looking young man.

Dani didn't bother to correct her. "Please get her scrubbed and prepped at OR Seven. I'll be right behind you both."

Turning to Dani, she noted her wide eyes. "You've got this, Danielle. I'm going to get scrubbed, and I'll be right there. I'll be over your shoulder for the whole procedure. It'll be just like old times."

"Sure," Dani muttered. "Just like old times."

               ∻   •   ∻

OPERATING ROOM SEVEN was not large, even when empty. Holding six medical professionals and a patient prone on the bed, the room shrank fast. The walls closed in, the space constricted by the weight of too many surgeries and too little time. Lights overhead bathed the space in a harsh white which reflected off stainless steel trays crowded with hastily arranged instruments.

The patient lay face-down on the table. His head and face had been shaved in preparation by someone on staff in the expectation of a surgeon to continue the work. The man's back was a horrid tapestry of charred skin, puncture wounds, and deep gashes exposing bone. One look told Dani that the man's neck might as well be gone for all the good it would do him for the rest of his life. However long that might be. She had to look hard to find a square inch of skin and muscle intact between the man's shoulders and the base of his skull. Blood oozed from his other wounds to saturate the temporary dressings. His neck was swollen, the edges of shredded muscle visible beneath the trauma. Dani's gaze rested there a moment. Her hands flexed involuntarily, subconsciously rehearsing movements she hadn't made in years.

Lena entered quietly, the cast on her arm tucked against her side like a shield. "You've got this, Dani," she said. Her voice was steady but low. The words were no longer an encouragement; they were an order.

Two nurses, a young man whose eyes were somehow still sharp and a woman whose fatigue broadcast itself from her slumped shoulders, worked to prepare Dani's theater. Across the operating table, the anesthesiologist adjusted several monitors while her assistant quietly called out vitals. Blood pressure was going to be a concern; the pulse was steady but weak.

For a moment, the soft beeping of the machines was the only sound in the room, a rhythmic pulse that sought to express a man's life in numbers. Dani took a slow breath, her fingers brushing the handle of a scalpel. She no longer had the luxury of doubt. "Let's get started," she said, her voice firmer than she expected.

"He's lost a lot of blood," commented Nurse 1, his eyes locked on a monitor.

"Prep another unit of blood; he'll need it for the operation," Dani told the man.

"I got it," Nurse 2 called out from her position at the far wall. "What's his type?"

Several seconds passed.

"I said, what's his type?" repeated Nurse 2, an irritated frown evident above her surgical mask.

"Um..." Hesitation poured off the male nurse.

Dani's instincts kicked in hard, and she suddenly became the undisputed boss of the room. "Nurse!" she snapped at the man. "Time is the most valuable thing in the world to this patient right now. Blood is a close second. Please focus. What is the patient's blood type?"

The nurse's face reddened above his mask. He looked directly at Dani, eyes wide. "I... He... He doesn't have a blood type."

"That is patently impossible, nurse. Type it again."

"I've done it twice." The young man turned to Lena for support. "Dr. Rosenbaum. The patient does not conform to any of the known blood types."

"I am not the surgeon in charge, Nurse Higgins," Lena chided her employee, compounding his humiliation. "I am here in an advisory capacity. You will address your comments to Doctor McKendree, not me."

Dani's expectant gaze drilled into the young nurse, and he immediately busied himself running the test a third time. Watching him, Dani could tell he had skill and confidence. It was strange that he would have had so much difficulty with such a basic process. She was starting to grow agitated by the time the nurse finished the test. Dani took a breath and chalked it up to the long hours of work. She shook her head to clear it. Fatigue was a luxury no one could afford right now.

"Um, Doctor..."

"McKendree," Lena reminded the nurse.

"Doctor McKendree, the results are consistent. The patient does not conform to any of the four blood types."

Dani's eyes drilled into the man. Her teeth ground one against another. She was going to have to do the test herself.

Seeing the imminent storm, the nurse continued. "A and B antigens are both simultaneously present and absent. It's like he's Type A, B, AB, and O, and also none of them. All at the same time. And the Rh protein is both there and not there. The test doesn't know what to do with this guy."

Dani stared at the nurse. He stared back, nervous but unflinching. Good; she could respect that. Before Dani could formulate a response, she was startled to hear a faint groan from the operating table.

The room fell silent.

Dani turned at once to the anesthesiologist. "Doctor! The patient is still responsive. I need him anesthetized, stat! Do I need to remind you of the risk of adverse outcome to this patient with insufficient anesthesia?"

The assistant took a tiny step to the left, as if to distance herself from her targeted superior. The anesthesiologist registered shock. "You certainly do not, doctor," she fired back at Dani. "I've already given him the maximum prescribed dosage. He should be out like a light."

Dani glanced at the patient's vitals again. "His temperature and heart rate are spiking! Are you pushing Enflurane? He's going into malignant hyperthermia. How much did you push? Did you even check his history for epilepsy?"

"He's a John Doe! How *could* I check his history? And, no, I am *not* using Enflurane. Do you take me for a first-year? I'm pushing Isoflurane."

Dani wasn't backing down. It was her room, and this patient would die if they did not get the show on the road. "Regardless, we have to address the hyperthermia. Hit him with Dantrolene, now," she directed the anesthesiologist.

The woman complied at once, casting Dani a baleful eye.

Dani turned back to the patient after confirming the downward trend in his monitor. She noted the shreds of a silver chain buried in the flesh of the patient's neck. Something familiar clicked in the back of her mind.

Focus! she told herself.

"Those bits of silver will all have to be removed from his neck. That's likely to be more work than the buckshot," Dani said aloud, more as a roadmap for herself than instruction for the room.

Nurse 2 stepped back toward the table. "The man was brought in barely alive, but the EMT mentioned his hand was clutching some kind of locket," she offered.

Dani looked down at the patient's right hand, still balled into a tight fist. Something to worry about later; right now, this man had far more urgent issues, and lots of them. She looked back to his upper back and pulled the small tray-table holding her surgical tools into a more accessible position. She returned her attention to the patient's upper back and continued the mental cartography that would guide her through the next several hours.

The anesthesiologist spoke up again. She had composed herself; professionalism was evident again in her tone. "The drugs aren't knocking him out, it's already taken a lot more than it should. I don't think I can give him any more."

"You don't think you can, or you can't?" Dani asked the woman. Clarity mattered.

"I can't."

Dani paused, her mind racing. It didn't take her long to consider alternatives; there were none.

"We will have to operate anyway, even without full anesthesia." Dani looked to Lena, as per procedure drilled into her by her mentor a decade before. "Doctor Rosenbaum, do you concur?"

"I concur. Proceed, doctor."

Dani took a deep, cleansing breath and lifted a shining scalpel in her right hand. The familiar heft of the instrument felt to her hand far more natural than the thin layer of sterile latex separating its cold surface from her skin.

Lena stated for the recording, "Note administrative concurrence. Doctor Danielle McKendree attending. Procedure begins." In a less professional tone, she added, "I feel bad for the poor slob. He's gonna feel every bit of this. Let's pray he can handle pain."

Dani's eyes ticked rapidly upward and to the left. Something continued to nag her. Her mind struggled to connect the man's silver chain and her mentor's statement about handling pain. Dani suddenly recalled Lena using that phrase about someone long ago...

Hooking a toe into the foot stirrup of a floor reflector, she slid the angled mirror over to get an unobstructed view of the patient's face, hanging towards the floor. The man had been intubated and tape covered much of his face, but he was familiar nonetheless.

"Omigod. Ashe?" Dani whispered, almost inaudibly.

Nurse 1, noting Dani's sudden pallor, asked, "Are you alright, Doctor? You look like you've seen a ghost."

Dani blinked. "Yes, yes. I'm fine," she lied.

She steadied the scalpel in her hand for the first cut.

Chapter 5 : BURN NOTICE

PRESENT DAY

"WHO WANTS A coffee?"

Amber pulled the espresso machine forward on the polished surface of the credenza. The chrome-plated marvel slid gracefully forward, pulled back into its rightful place by several thin hoses clad in fine steel mesh that led under the top of the sideboard into a cabinet below. It stopped with a faint squeak from its rubber feet and awaited Amber's instruction.

Two LED displays lit up at Amber's command, one over each of the black-handled filter heads. Amber thought the displays looked like two cute little eyes, wide and bright, watching her in ready eagerness so they wouldn't miss whatever she did next. Not that she was all too sure what to do next. She'd watched the process countless times at the coffee shop, though. Surely she could figure it out.

The grind was first, right? Amber rummaged around in the cupboard doors and found everything she was looking for. Two large bags of coffee beans labeled with words she didn't dare try to pronounce came first. One was sealed and still held its vacuum, but the other had been opened and was about two-thirds full. She undid the wire clip that held the folded bag top and nearly swooned with pleasure at the rich, velvet aroma that filled the air with its soft caress.

Where the beans had been delicate and delightful, Amber found the grinder a rough beast. Not that it was ugly, far from it. But it was big and heavy and commanding, handsome in its own brutal way. Every bit of its appearance spoke of power and authority.

Amber set the grinder on the credenza surface and scooped in some beans, enjoying the happy tinkle they made against the powdery metal. She was again nearly overcome by the aroma. Not knowing anything about how to customize the machine, Amber opted to just leave Task's dial settings and reached out a finger to push the device's single button.

A horrendous screaming metallic whine pierced the room at once. Sounding like a drilling competition at a convention for dentists, the noise continued for several seconds, and Amber found herself having to cover her ears against the din. She felt rather than heard the soft conversation between the two men behind her grind to an instant halt and turned around just as the device finished its violent task.

Ashe and Spirit stood by the large desk, backlit by the earliest pink hints of approaching sunrise starting to slip through the city skyline. The two men stared in her direction, a disapproving look plain on each face. Whatever quiet conversation they'd been having as they awaited Fry's arrival had come to a screeching halt.

Amber pulled her palms from her ears. "What?" she said, hoping her petulant scowl made her look serious. "It's like five in the morning! I haven't had any coffee. Who wants an espresso?"

Owen Spirit shook his head and looked at Ashe. Waving a hand at Amber in dismissal, Spirit dropped into his chair and responded to the question Ashe had just asked with one of his own. "Didn't you hear her? It's like five in the morning. No, I don't have the schematics yet. We just hatched this idiot plan late last night, right? I'll text the schematics to you once I get to Ashburn and you can study them as you drive."

Ashe looked confused. "You'll *what* them to me?" he asked.

"I'll text them to you. On your phone."

"I don't have a phone."

"That, I did take care of." Spirit handed Ashe a pair of boxes with apple-shaped logos on them, one larger than the other. "Have your ginger Gen-Z whippersnapper set this stuff up for you."

Amber looked at Spirit's reflection in the polished chrome of the espresso machine. "I heard that."

Both men ignored her. Ashe set the boxes down on the desk. "How important is this, really?"

"The phone? Very. We're not going to do this without communication. Stay in touch, grandpa."

"Not what I mean, mouthpiece," Ashe growled. "I mean, how critical is us getting to this fabled computer? The company is practically yours now, right? If you're having so much trouble getting to this 'mysterious maybe' data, what makes you think the FBI can get to it?"

"Infinite resources, for starters. Legal ability to lock us out with a warrant. The list goes on. And it's not 'maybe' data," Spirit rebutted. "I should have pieced it together earlier. I knew Task intimately. The man was a weasel on a cataclysmic scale, but he was thorough. He wiped your existence from the world's eye, but the data *has* to still exist somewhere. The FBI will eventually find it and figure you out. And we're all screwed, once they do. We're all accessories after the fact, at the very least. And you're in for life because of Task. Too high profile a death; they're not going to let it go."

Ashe grunted noncommittally.

There was a brief pause as Fry entered the office. She placed her small suitcase on the floor between Spirit's designer hardshell rollaboard and Amber's ratty backpack. Amber looked up from the espresso machine and waved to her friend.

Spirit went on. "And it'll get far worse if your history is as bad as Task indicated."

Fry took up residence in the same chair she had been sitting in during the previous night's discussion. "What exactly are we talking about, anyway?" she asked.

Spirit, unwilling to go back and catch Fry up on the conversation, continued his discourse. "There is no statute of limitations for federal crimes punishable by death, nor for certain federal crimes of terrorism, nor for certain federal sex offenses."

Spirit stopped and cast a snarky look that bounced between Ashe and Amber. "Wait a second. We're not talking about...?"

"You so much as even finish thinking that thought and I'll kill you here and now," Ashe snarled at Owen Spirit. The old man leaned forward menacingly on his crutches.

"Okay!" A broad grin split the lawyer's face and raised both hands in a placating gesture. Having goaded Ashe to the precipice of violence, he decided to back off. "Just murder, then. I totally get it."

$$\approx \quad \bullet \quad \backsim$$

"OH, MY GOD! You're Pusher's End!"

"I'm what?" Ashe asked, a confused look on his face.

Ashe had been describing some of the events that had eventually led to his decision to isolate in the radioactive wasteland cave, away from the rest of humanity. It had been a heavily redacted version of those events, of course; there were young ladies present. But the story had featured enough details about Ashe's interactions with certain less desirable groups of humanity to excite Owen Spirit.

"The Pusher's End killer," Spirit explained. "The mysterious serial killer targeting drug rings in the eighties?"

"Pusher's End. That's the best the newsies could come up with?"

"What are you talking about? That's an amazing name!"

Amber turned away from the coffee machine. This was getting interesting. "You mean, the news and everybody actually knew about Ashe?" she asked.

"Yes and no," replied Spirit. Ashe just leaned on his crutches, looking uncomfortable. "They called him a number of things in different cities, at first: 'The Overkiller' in Virginia due to the extremity of rage evident in the earliest cases, 'The Withdrawal Killer' in Philadelphia. He was 'Judgment Day' in Pittsburgh. You see the pattern. Other names ranged, but they all followed a similar motif.

"Once somebody in the FBI pieced together that it appeared to be the work of a single man with an identifiable objective, the name 'Pusher's End' took hold. The media loved it at the time, early CNN days and all, they loved a catchphrase. The name had a dual meaning, referring not only to the focused objective of the killer but also the nickname of the neighborhood in Alexandria where the killings started."

Ashe scowled at the lawyer. "You sure know a lot about me, shyster."

"Ashe, buddy!" Spirit smiled widely. "Of course I do, now that I know it's you! You're famous. I wrote a paper on you at Harvard."

Ashe rolled his eyes as Spirit continued, "We studied you in my Criminal Law and Procedure classes, regarding proportionality and the defense of necessity. Wow. Ashe is Pusher's End."

"It's still a stupid name," muttered Ashe.

"It's a great name," insisted Spirit. "It makes sense, you know, with the timing and all that Task was able to find. You were Nancy Reagan's right-hand man! 'Just Say No, or Else,' am I right? Then you just vanished. They said you died, and the FBI closed the case, because there was no real proof of anything. No real connections between the cases, no meaningful evidence, and when it all stopped, the news moved on to something else. When they didn't care, neither did the FBI. I mean, so what? You killed a bunch of drug peddlers and smugglers."

Ashe's face clouded over.

Amber asked, "So, he's off the hook, since the case was closed?"

Spirit shook his head. "No, not remotely. I mean, if they ever tie things together, it'll all come rushing back. And if they get Task's treasure trove of hidden data, tying it together will be so easy they'll be done by breakfast."

Amber continued, momentarily distracted from her coffee-making ventures. "What about that 'necessary defense' thing you mentioned?"

"No, he's totally screwed. That was just a crazy theory in a law school classroom. It ceases to be a rational and proportional response when it turns out to be a premeditated, calculated effort spanning several states over two decades."

"But I thought you said the FBI closed the case?" Fry asked, curious as well.

"They did, but there were all kinds of conspiracies about it. The FBI was accused for years of hushing the case up, just letting it drop. People claimed it was because the FBI itself was operating outside the law, or that CIA agents were operating on American soil to cover up their prior involvement in drug trafficking. You name it, some crackpot had a theory about 'The Pharmacist.' That one was from Cleveland." Spirit winked at Ashe, whose stare just became more baleful. "I guess nobody was imaginative enough to figure it was just some grumpy old immortal with a vendetta."

Amber was still confused. "So what, though?"

"So what," Spirit explained in a deliberate voice, "is that if this thing surfaces and the FBI somehow gets proof that Pusher's End is still around, they'll fall over themselves trying to get hold of someone to parade on the media and prove that the conspiracies were off-base, and that they can still get their man. Plus, someone with that kind of rep killing Cameron Task? That's the biggest media circus of modern times, looking for a field to pitch its tent."

Amber looked at Ashe. "So he's screwed."

Owen Spirit gave her a nod. "Yeah. 'Several lifetimes in prison' kinda screwed." Spirit turned back to Ashe. "Which for you, means something. At least as a vigilante, you'd be in there with your uh... 'target' demographic."

Ashe turned away. "They got nothing, or Standish would already have made a move."

Spirit asked, "Are you sure? I did some checking into this Standish guy. He's known in the Bureau as a bulldog. No imagination. Not a great profiler, due to his biases, but once he gets scent of something, he's never failed to chase it down. Not once. Legend is the guy can find a grain of salt in the Mojave Desert."

"There's lots of salt in the Mojave Desert," said Ashe.

"You're missing the point. An FBI agent wants to link you to Task and call it murder due to the DNA evidence. Once that evidence links out to the Pusher's End killer, I repeat: it's going to be the biggest carnival since Manson. They will literally taste blood in the water, and it's gonna be yours."

Spirit had warmed to his subject, and continued, "Once they have that link, this Standish guy's gonna make his career on officially re-opening every single one of those cold cases. Declaring Task's death as murder, not suicide, will get him all the attention he needs to get that ball rolling. And it won't stop once it starts." The lawyer took a deep breath.

"And we're all accessories."

Ashe turned back to the seated man. "Okay. So, we're back full circle. Task had a server in Ashburn. All the proof in the world about me is probably on that server. So... we get to the server first."

Owen Spirit nodded, pushing his chair back. "For once we agree. I've already got tickets for Frymet and myself; we leave around eleven this morning from LAX."

Amber, still fiddling with the espresso machine, flipped a lever. A loud hiss was followed by a sharp report as the filter cup burst loose, covering the wall, credenza, and Amber in an explosion of steam, brown water, and hot espresso grounds.

Spirit turned to Ashe. "I am glad I'm flying. Owen Spirit doesn't spend 50 hours in a car for anybody. Let alone a car with *her*."

"I heard that!" said Amber, mopping furiously at the wall with a cloth.

Spirit swung atop his gleaming crutches toward the door. "That's because I said it out loud," he told her. Grabbing a couple stacks of cash from a cabinet, he handed the money to Ashe, who looked at him blankly.

"For expenses. Come on, let's go get you a car," he stated, and headed for the door of the office.

"Hey! What about my cup of coffee?" asked Amber as Spirit passed her.

A bewildered look overtook the lawyer's face. "Look," he said softly, as if speaking to a child, "Let's get this job done, and once none of us is any longer faced with, I dunno, life in prison, you can have the stupid espresso machine. All yours."

"No way! Seriously? The grinder too?"

"All of it. Yours. I'll even have a tech flown in from Italy to teach you how to use it the thing."

Amber smiled widely. She finished mopping her jeans with the towel and dropped the soiled cloth atop his teapot. "Well, why didn't you lead with that? Let's go!"

Spinning toward the door to follow the others, Amber snatched the large bag of beans that probably cost more than two months' rent at her apartment. She popped a couple beans in her mouth and munched them, crunching loudly.

"Oh, man! These are amazing just like this!"

"I WANT THIS one."

Amber stood before the little convertible and admired the vast expanse of spotless cherry red paint. She walked around the front, gently caressing the hood and stopping just at the rectangular yellow badge with its black rampant stallion. A perfect match for the larger horse on its grille.

"Nope, not that one," said Owen Spirit. He swung past her on his crutches and led the group farther into the building's enormous garage. The place might as well have been a museum; it was filled with a mouth-watering collection of sports cars and other vehicles, each a part of the late Cameron Task's personal collection, and each a unique piece of automotive history in its own right.

Amber looked around the room and saw many such vehicles. But this was the one that had caught her eye. She stood her ground.

"Why can't we take this one? It looks fast."

"A girl with priorities so far out of whack doesn't deserve such a fine automobile," Spirit called back over his shoulder.

"Priorities?" Amber asked. She hustled to catch up with the rest of the small group, weaving through the cars. Each one was pristine. She resisted the urge to touch them all, figuring Spirit would just make her wipe them all down if she did. "What priorities of mine are out of whack?"

Spirit just gave her an enigmatic grin. "The very fact that you are asking that question proves you don't deserve that car."

Amber looked at Ashe, who was also grinning. He was actually *grinning*! It was clear that he and Spirit were sharing some inside joke at her expense. She decided to ignore it.

"Back me up! Let's take the red one," she pleaded with the old man.

"Absolutely not. I'm not crossing the country in something with the gas tank the size of a teacup that gets three miles to the gallon. We'll save Ferris in something else."

"Come on, Ashe! How often do you get to drive across the country on someone else's money?"

"Based on recent experience? At least once too often." Ashe turned to the lawyer. "You said you had something that was good on gas?"

Owen Spirit smiled. "I've got just the thing. You'll even be doing me a favor getting it to DC."

In the center of the back wall sat a smallish vehicle draped under a heavy tarp, its shape unmistakably classic despite the covering. Spirit hobbled forward on his crutches.

"Here she is," Spirit said with some gravity, stopping next to the shrouded car. "You get to drive a piece of history." He handed one crutch to Fry, who steadied him while he grabbed the edge of the tarp with his free hand. With a theatrical flourish, he yanked it back, revealing the car. Its checkerboard paint, flat black alternating with semi-reflective gray, seemed to shimmer under the overhead lights. The effect felt more organic than mechanical.

"Task's very own 1963 Split-Window Corvette," announced Spirit. He looked around for a reaction. Of his audience, only Fry seemed to recognize the significance of the vehicle.

Amber tilted her head, her brow furrowing. "Huh. It's... kind of weird-looking. What's with the paint? Did Task lose a bet?" she said, stepping closer. The checkerboard covered the car's entire surface. The pattern was mapped out with mechanical precision, somehow maintaining its integrity across and over the many curves of the vehicle.

Upon closer inspection, Amber saw that the black areas were the car's original paint whereas the thick, goopy silver-gray paint appeared to be full of tiny silver prisms and had been applied as a heavy slop. The corners of each grayish square were connected to the corners of its neighbors by a hair-thin copper wire integrated into the paint. Despite looking like a kindergartener's art project, the car did have a certain beauty to it. The strange squares of paint were black when looked at directly, but shifted to a dull, leaden shimmer when viewed at an angle.

Fry, leaning lightly on her cane, handed Spirit his crutch. "No," she told Amber. "That's a photoconvertive coating. It's functional. This was Task's first hybrid solar prototype."

Amber blinked, her fingers trailing over the strange finish. "Wait, this thing's a solar car?"

Spirit smirked. He settled onto his second crutch as he gestured toward the car. "Not just a solar car. *The* solar car. Task converted it himself. This beauty is the first hybrid solar vehicle ever made. It's an engineering milestone." He tapped his crutch lightly against a rear tire for emphasis. "And you guys are taking it to the Smithsonian for me."

"Solar," Ashe mused. "Good on gas."

"Well, hybrid. Not pure solar," Spirit explained, "but definitely good on gas. Each wheel has a solar motor that's used in concert with an LS1 V-8 crammed into the engine bay. The solar/electric motors run at the same time as the gas-driven wheels, so the car sips gas like it's idling when you're cruising at eighty. It was Task's special take on a hybrid; you'll still have to fill it up, but you might get almost a thousand miles on a tank of gas if you're careful."

Ashe did some fast calculations in his head. "So, you're telling me we'll get to the DC area with just one extra stop? Nice."

Spirit looked at Ashe, then over to Amber.

Amber had been still admiring the red Ferrari from across the cavernous garage but snapped to attention and looked at Ashe before pivoting to regard Owen Spirit.

Spirit broke the awkward silence. "Extra stop?"

Ashe nodded. "Supply run. We can fill up where I gotta stop, and then once more in the Appalachians somewhere."

"Oh yeah," Spirit stated. "I'd forgotten about the supply stop. What are you picking up?"

Before Ashe could reply, Amber interrupted. "Wait a minute. We're still making pit stops and eating, right?"

Ashe's face took on a look indicating it might have been the first time he'd considered that. He looked at Amber, then the Corvette, then his leg, still in a splint.

"Oh no! You are *not* peeing in a bottle all the way to Virginia. Not in this thing!" Spirit's loud voice echoed in the garage. "Look. The Smithsonian. Big museum. They want the 'Vette as a loan for a permanent exhibit. So, if you take this thing, you will not pee in a bottle. You will not eat in it. You will not sneeze in it. You need to ensure it's driven carefully."

"I thought the goal was to drive fast," Ashe said to the lawyer.

"Carefully and fast. I'm serious, Ashe."

"What? I'm not serious? Do I look like I'm joking?"

"You have to promise it will be driven very carefully. Maybe this is a mistake. This thing is a piece of history."

Ashe waved a hand at the car. "You think I'm doing this for fun? This thing barely has enough room in it for my crutches!"

"You're so confident you won't need crutches once you get to Ashburn, why don't you just leave them here?" asked Spirit.

"Me? Why don't you leave yours here? Oh, yeah - because you need them to hold up that colossal head of yours."

Amber had had enough of the bickering. "Boys! We can stand here all day while you two argue about which one of you has the biggest crutch, or we can load up and get going."

Spirit leaned forward, pinning Ashe with a menacing look. "You have to promise it will be driven very carefully."

"I promise it'll be driven very carefully," Ashe replied.

Chapter 6 : THE SAMARITAN

1976

THE AIR REEKED of diesel exhaust and summer heat. Dani walked briskly along the cracked sidewalk, headed northbound on South Oakley. Ashburn was quieter than many Chicago neighborhoods, but there was no missing the ever-present tension. Recent changes to the demographics in the neighborhoods to the east of South Western Avenue were severely unwelcome to many of the area's residents west of that dividing line on Chicago's map. It was exactly those changes that made her work with Lena Rosenbaum at the Ashburn Free Clinic mean something, but the tension here could still be palpable.

A group of small children bustled past her near the corner. They weren't doing anything, not really, but their presence and appearance was an irritant to many nearby throughout Ashburn and Marquette Park to the north who didn't want the average skin color of the neighborhood to darken.

Ahead, the clinic came into view, its squat brick exterior defiant against its backdrop of decay. The building itself had seen more years than Dani knew, and many of them showed. But it was still a good place, where they were trying to do some good. Not that it could keep up the fight much longer, she imagined. To her knowledge, this was the last of the free clinics in the Chicago metropolitan area, and there was constant pressure to make it fade into memory like the others. One could argue that the demise of free centers like hers was an indication of a broader trend in national health policy whereby the system sought to diminish the health care options of poor Americans in large cities. In fact, she had argued that exact point with her father, many times. But even though he largely agreed with her logic, even a senior US District Judge's hands were tied against matters such as progress. Progress was unstoppable, whether it was progress or not.

Approaching the clinic, Dani's eyes landed on Doctor Lena Rosenbaum standing outside the building. Lena's current efforts served to illustrate that not all of the bigotry tearing the city apart was based on skin color. Dani's friend and mentor stood proudly at the street-side wall of the clinic with a bucket of soapy water and a stiff-bristled brush. She worked methodically, scrubbing at the large swastika that stretched across the wall in black spray paint. She braced her wiry frame and leaned into the task of scrubbing the brick and mortar.

Dani sighed, picking up her pace. It wasn't the first time Lena had been forced to scrub off the vile symbol and it probably wouldn't be the last. The building's red brick, painted white, bore the faint ghosts of previous graffiti; no amount of scrubbing or repainting had been able to fully erase the marks. The clinic's location in mostly-white Ashburn, and its mission of freely serving humanity regardless of race, color, or creed, made it a prime and frequent target. Add the fact that the clinic was operated by Dr. Lena Rosenbaum, a Jew and survivor of the Holocaust, and it was a perfect storm.

"Need a hand?" Dani called as she approached.

Lena straightened, pausing mid-scrub. Her face lit up despite the streaks of sweat on her brow. "Danielle! You're early." Her voice carried its ever-present warmth, despite her current activities.

Dani stopped next to her mentor and crossed her arms, looking at the half-cleaned wall. "Again?"

Lena shrugged. She dipped the brush into the soapy bucket and resumed scrubbing. "Another gift from our friends up the street." She motioned vaguely toward Marquette Park. "They're branching out."

Dani regarded the older doctor. For the past two years, Lena Rosenbaum had been her mentor. Not quite two decades her senior, Lena had experienced more in her lifetime than Dani expected she ever would. Born in 1933, Lena had told her about the years spent in Buchenwald and the struggles she and her mother had faced ever since their rescue at the end of the war. Lena had had it better than many in the camps and had weathered it as well as anyone could hope for.

Lena's mother had not fared so well from the experience. Lena's father had died during the liberation, and her mother had recovered physically from the trauma there, but the psychic scars were deep and lasting. In the thirty years since the war, Lena had cared for her mother more than the other way around and done it with aplomb and a compassion Dani had never seen in anyone else. Moving first to Montreal, Lena raised herself and cared for her mother with the help of her new community and the synagogue there. Medical school in New York followed her undergrad at McGill in Montreal, and she eventually found her way to Chicago's South side. Here she started the clinic, building it as a beacon for the poor out of the crumbling pre-war structure it had been when she found it.

Dani had been with her at the clinic for two years, deciding to take the slow path through her residency to learn as much as she could from Rosenbaum. Lena herself had specialized in neurology and was bright enough to tenure at Hopkins or anywhere else she chose. Instead, she elected to be here, where she felt she could do the most good. Someday, of course, she would be forced to move on to something bigger, but for now, her heart was in this little clinic nestled in the northeast corner of Ashburn.

Because of that, Dani knew it must have been difficult to relocate her residence northward to Skokie, but Lena had finally moved there to better provide for her mother as she advanced in years. Dani imagined it wasn't Montreal, but Lena was able to find in Skokie a greater community of people with shared experience. It was important enough to Lena that her mother have a sense of home that she continued to make the southward drive every day from Skokie to the clinic in Ashburn. Only in the past two years, with Dani's arrival, had Lena relented from making that trek twice every day of the week.

It tore Dani's heart out that the prejudice that had shaped Lena's life had followed her to Skokie in the past couple of years. Prejudice of more than one form was percolating throughout the city. It enraged her to see that prejudice and ignorance splashed in black paint across the clinic that had become her labor of love as well as Lena's.

Lena was not only her role model as a doctor, she was also the main inspiration for Dani's upcoming career change, despite it meaning a divergence in their paths. It was going to pain her to leave Lena and the clinic, but they both knew it was inevitable.

"I got in," Dani told Lena.

The older woman looked up, dropping the brush into the bucket. She or Dani would return to finish the job later. "You were accepted," she said.

"Well, no, not yet. But they completed my application, and I got the invitation. I'm scheduled for my Phase I test in two weeks. I... I really appreciate your recommendation."

They started toward the clinic doors. Dani reached past the nearest of the glass double doors to open the second. She noticed the tape holding up the "Please use other door" sign on the door with the bad hinge was giving way again.

"Thank yourself," Lena responded as she stepped through the open door. "Although, I never should have agreed to do it. I wouldn't have if I thought you'd actually join the FBI and leave me."

"Lena..."

"I mean, really! How can you leave this paradise?" The older woman smiled as she reached over to push the sign's tape against the door from the inside. The sun-bleached and stiffened paper of the sign pulled the yellowed tape back off the glass before her hand had even returned to her side.

"I want to join the FBI and make a difference," Dani said, repeating that point for the umpteenth time.

"You know you're making a difference here." Lena stepped to a hand-wash station and scrubbed at her hands. "You are a brilliant surgeon."

Dani started to demur, but Lena persisted. "Look at how you handled Mr. White's surgery after he was attacked by those dealers. I'd say you made a difference in his life. You have a gift, and I don't want to see you waste it."

"But what if I can do something about dealers attacking homeless people before they do it? What if I can be part of legal action to stop hateful idiots from painting swastikas on your clinic before they do it? Won't that make a bigger difference?"

"Legal action? Is that the Honorable Justin McKendree talking?" she said with a grin.

"No, my dad isn't in favor of the move either. He wanted me to be a lawyer like him. It was bad enough I disappointed him and went into medicine, now he's pitching regular fits that I'm going to be 'enacting frontier justice with a gun' at the FBI."

"Guess he shouldn't have taught you to shoot so well, then, huh?" Lena referred to competitive shooting, the hobby Dani shared with her father. That was one area where she had not only followed in her father's footsteps, but marched right past them. Although Judge McKendree had recently won the National Pistol Championships twice by age fifty-four, Dani had just won the top medal a third time as a young woman half that age.

A twinkle entered Lena's eyes. "At least you won't have any problem with the handgun qualifications."

"I guess not," Dani laughed.

❧ • ☙

"HOW MUCH LONGER, do you think?" Dani asked Lena.

Lena frowned at the younger doctor. The two of them were conducting their morning rounds and had just stepped out of Mrs. Hurston's room. The woman's condition conformed to Dani's "three Bs": bad, bedridden, but breathing. She wondered aloud how long the woman might have, and Lena took her to task for it.

"First, that doesn't matter. She will have the best care here that we can give her, whether it's for a day, a week, or a year. Second..." Lena deflated a bit. "Not long," she admitted. "I wish we could do more. But we will give her the best care possible as long as necessary, because we are all she can afford."

"Of course, Lena. Sorry."

A few steps later, the pair arrived at the clinic's only other overnight room and stepped through the door.

"Good morning, Mr. Jackson!" Lena said in a cheerful voice.

Lena and Dani smiled at their patient. Though the old man's dark skin was pulled tightly enough across his frame to catch the light in blue-brown highlights, its texture was still elastic, and he appeared to be in far better health than he had just last night. Of the clinic's two overnight rooms, they had given Mr. Jackson the largest, and the one with an integral bathroom and shower. Unlike so many of the other homeless patients that made up a large part of their clientele, Eddie Jackson had immediately set out trying to avail himself of the shower. Dani had been forced to change his dressings three times last night because the man repeatedly wanted to luxuriate in the clean hot water.

Making a notation on the man's chart, Dani asked, "How are you feeling this morning, Mr. Jackson?"

"Well, I'd be better if you could get me somethin' to drink," was the reply.

Dani poured him a glass of water from a plastic jug on the table by his bed.

"Aw, honey, you know that's not what I'm talking about."

Dani smiled. "I know full well, Mr. Jackson. But I also know that your liver function isn't all that great, and the beating you took didn't do any good for your liver, or your kidneys. You don't need alcohol making your problems worse."

The old man's face turned serious, and he looked at Dani with thanks in his eyes.

"Dr. Lena tells me you was the one what fixed me up last night. She says you did a real good job, and I feel pretty good about it too. Still hurts like the ol' devil hisself, but I gots you to thank I can feel it at all, Dr. Dani."

"You need to thank the Samaritan, Mr. Jackson."

The old man looked down and away, wringing his hands. "The who? I don't knows no Samaritan."

"Come on Mr. Jackson," said Dani, "you know we're all friends here. No police, and nobody's going to bring it up again. You'll tell me who he is, won't you?"

"No, ma'am, I's tellin' ya. I don't know nobody what goes by that name. I came in myself last night. Walked right down here from up Marquette Park way."

Dani could tell that the old black man was growing increasingly agitated.

Lena patted the man's shoulder. "That's all right, Eddie. You just get some rest. We'll be in to check on you later."

Exiting the room, the two doctors turned right to head up the short hallway to the storage closet they had repurposed as an office space.

Once in the cramped office, Lena poured several ounces of coffee into the chipped purple mug that she favored.

"They all want to protect him. The Samaritan," she said, blowing air on the hot liquid.

Dani ran a glass of water from the tap. "How much did he leave this time? For Mr. Jackson?"

"Close to three thousand dollars." Lena took a tentative sip from the mug. "More than enough."

"Ever seen him?"

"The Samaritan? No, not up close. The man's brought us over two dozen homeless patients just this year, though. All victims of drug peddlers or racial violence. Left us enough money earmarked for their care to finance the clinic flat out. And I have not once seen him."

"Or her," Dani pointed out.

"No, he's a guy, for sure. Not too tall, but very strong. He's physically carried in several of the patients he brings. Mid-forties, dark hair, grizzly beard."

"Mid-forties, dark hair, grizzly beard? Pretty descriptive for someone who's never seen the guy."

"Well, I've seen him from a distance on a couple occasions," replied Lena. "Pretty torn up one time, covered in blood and limping. Still managed to carry in someone worse off than he was and then split before I could get close. Whoever the guy is, he can sure handle pain. Anyway, a few of the patients have described him to me. Some of them I'm pretty sure even know him, but not one of them ever offers up any real information."

"They protect who they respect," mused Dani.

"Who they love," Lena corrected.

Dani shot back: "Oh! So you think he might be lovable, then?"

"Most everybody's lovable," Lena smiled, "Not all, but most. Just depends how hard you want to work at it."

∂ • ∽

THE SUN DIPPED behind the nearby buildings, casting long shadows across the cracked sidewalks of Ashburn. Scents of fried food and exhaust wafted in, carried by a light breeze to mix with the sharp tang of fresh paint.

Dani stood outside by the clinic wall, her arm moving rhythmically as she rolled a fresh coat of white paint over the remains of the jagged swastika that had marred the bricks that morning. Lena and Dani had decided that all the washing they could do would not be enough to erase the graffiti, so Dani had slipped out to buy more paint in the early afternoon, leaving Lena to close up shop. By the time Dani returned from the Ace Hardware down the street, Lena had gone home and left a note. The note informed her that the afternoon's delivery truck had dropped off several gas canisters and a few large boxes of other supplies, a fact that Dani could see for herself. Dani decided that moving the heavy canisters and restocking supply cabinets could wait until morning. After a quick round of the clinic's two overnight guests, Dani had decided to enjoy the cooling of the day while repainting the outside wall.

Her old lab coat hung loosely, the fabric thin and frayed at the cuffs, but it served its purpose. It was now splattered with streaks of paint, but at least her jeans and top were safe. She figured that the paint, once dried, would just blend into the tired whiteness. She watched the last rays of full sunshine fade, grateful to watch the day shift into a less frantic routine. With most of the lights off inside and the streets emptying, the world felt smaller. Almost peaceful.

The graffiti on the wall disappeared inch by inch beneath the roller. It was satisfying in a way Dani couldn't quite explain, watching the hateful marks vanish under clean, bright paint. She paused to dip the roller into the tray at her feet, the faint clink of metal on brick the only sound.

A dog barked somewhere nearby, a sharp, solitary sound that faded quickly enough. A sound like several car doors slamming sounded in the distance, and a group of teenagers laughed as they passed on the opposite sidewalk. The clinic's neon sign buzzed faintly above her, its red letters casting a faint glow onto the wall behind it.

It was the tiniest of beacons, surely insignificant against the backdrop of the city, but Dani still hoped it meant something to the people who came here.

Dani's arms ached from the repetitive motion, but it was a good ache. It furnished proof of effort, of her impact on the neighborhood. She wiped her forehead with the sleeve of her lab coat, leaving a streak of white paint she didn't notice.

The wall was almost restored now, the new paint stark against the patches of older coats that layered the bricks like a timeline. It wasn't perfect; nothing ever was here. But it was enough. For tonight, it would be enough.

The quiet was strange. Dani glanced down the street, watching as the lampposts flickered to life one by one, their light pooling in uneven circles along the cracked pavement. The neighborhood wasn't asleep yet, but it was headed in that direction, anticipating its rest between one day and the next.

She lifted the roller and continued her work, the motion steady and deliberate. There was still a little more hatred to cover, and dusk had given her just enough time to finish before the night fell in earnest.

Before she could finish, an approaching commotion caught her attention. Around the corner came a hurried group of people; it was immediately clear that the clinic was their destination. Leading the procession was a stocky white man, possibly a bit less than average height. He was rough around the edges and Dani would have presumed him to be homeless passing him on the street, but his shoes were in good condition; strong and sturdy yet silent enough to indicate they probably were not cast-offs, but carefully chosen and fitted for purposes of stability and stealth. The man carried in his arms an unconscious teenage black boy without discernible effort. Close on the man's heels followed a middle-aged black woman with three young girls in tow. The group passed Dani without seeming to notice her and burst through the doors to the clinic after only a minor altercation with the dysfunctional left door. Realizing her momentary distraction, Dani dropped the paint roller and sprinted to catch up with her new visitors.

"Folks!" Dani called out upon re-entry to the clinic. She was slightly out of breath. "I'm Doctor McKendree. What happened?"

Her question seemed to burst open a dam. Words poured from the distraught mother as the man laid the boy gently on the sole gurney in the waiting area.

"What happened? I don't *know* what happened! What was he even doin' there? He wasn't supposed to be there! We was just comin' back from the store. Just finna get a soda, that's all! Then they started shootin', and—" Her voice broke, her words stumbling in the turbulent flood. "Marcus ain't mixed up in that stuff! He a good kid! I told him to stay away from that corner, told him stay close. Why didn't he listen? Why didn't I just go myself and leave him home with his sisters? All we wanted was a soda!"

She looked around the room like a cornered animal, eyes settling on the three little girls clinging to her legs. Their wide, tear-streaked eyes were fixed in turn on her.

She wrapped her arms around them, pulling them close as if they might disappear, too. Her voice cracked, quieter now, as her gaze returned to the doctor. "Please. Please don't let him die. They need they brother. I need my Marcus. He all we got."

The boy was bleeding on the gurney. Dani's focus snapped to the spreading stain on the rough bandage someone had tied around his abdomen. The man who had carried him in stayed close, his hands still on the gurney's rails. Even shorter than she'd first registered, he was solidly built. He was also filthy. His clothes were stained and rumpled, his dark hair matted against his forehead, and his heavy beard formed peculiar clumps on his cheeks and jaw. Dani thought again that the man resembled a homeless beggar, but there was a deliberate nature to the way he moved. The sharpness in his eyes as they darted between her and the boy also supported her growing suspicion that his appearance was a ruse, a costume.

"Hold this," Dani barked, tossing a fresh stack of gauze into his hands as she cut away the boy's blood-soaked shirt. "Press here. Hard. You're keeping pressure on that wound until I tell you otherwise. Got it?"

The man nodded, stepping into the role without hesitation. His hands pressed down firmly, and Dani noted with mild surprise how steady they were. He'd done this before and done it often enough to get good at it. She scanned the boy's injuries: one bullet wound just below his ribs, another near the right clavicle. Exit wounds on both, but she was concerned about tearing in the shoulder. Blood was pooling fast under the lower wound. Her hands worked automatically, prepping a seal pad to stem the bleeding from the abdominal wound. "Blood loss isn't great, but he's stable. Shoulder wound is non-critical, no open pneumothorax," she muttered, more to herself than to him.

"What happened?" she demanded sharply, glancing up at the man. Her voice softened just enough to coax a response. "When did he get hit, and where?"

"Ten minutes ago," the man said evenly, though his voice carried a gravelly edge, like it hadn't been used in a while. "Two blocks over. Caught in crossfire. He wasn't part of it."

"Crossfire? With who?" Dani asked the man.

"Bad people," he replied.

"They just came outta nowhere!" the mother sobbed. She stood clutching her daughters as she tried to steady her shaking voice. "We were just... just comin' back from the store. Just a soda and stuff. Just normal stuff! And then... then these two men, they ran out from the alley, right in front of us! Oh, God. I saw 'em before. I know I seen 'em, hanging around the corner sometimes. Pushers. Those pushers!"

Her words tumbled out between gasps of air, her chest heaving as tears streamed down her cheeks. "They were bleedin', both of 'em, bleedin' bad! One of 'em walking like his leg broke or somethin'. And they—oh, God—they shootin' back! Just shootin' back behind them like the devil hisself was on they tail!" Her voice cracked. "Only it wasn't—oh, my baby—it wasn't them that got hit. It was my boy. It was my boy!"

Dani nodded briskly, filing the information as her hands moved to start an IV line. "Saline. I need saline," she muttered, scanning the tray for the bag and catching the man's eye again. He passed her the fluid-filled bag. "Okay, listen. I'm going to stop the bleeding here first, then stabilize him. You keep holding that pressure and don't let up. Understand?"

He didn't hesitate. "Got it."

She caught something in the man's expression. Concern, guilt, resolve? The look unsettled her, but she pushed it aside. The boy wheezed faintly as she worked, but his pulse was strong under her fingers. She barked another set of instructions, explaining what she was doing in plain terms. "I'm going to close this wound enough to stop the bleeding, but he's got another injury near his shoulder. I need to be sure there are no fragments. He's got to be stable before I move him for imaging. You're doing good; keep the pressure steady."

He nodded again, silent and focused, and Dani realized that this man was almost certainly Lena's Samaritan. But there was no time to unpack that mystery. Getting the teenager's wounds handled was all that mattered at the moment.

A few minutes passed while Dani worked. The man proved a capable field nurse and had even managed to don a pair of gloves without releasing pressure on the compress, which impressed Dani.

"Friend of the family?" Dani asked the man.

"No. Just helping out. Wrong place, wrong time."

"Lot of that going around tonight," Dani realized her tone was harsh, and she softened it a bit. "Well, you were in the right place at the right time for this kid. What's your name?"

"Ashe."

Dani looked over at the mother, who had moved near the wall with her young girls. "Ma'am, I need to take your son back for some x-rays and get him stitched up a bit. I promise you he's going to be fine. Would you mind having a seat out here for a bit? You can take the girls to that vending machine there…"

The woman looked up. Her eyes were sunken and hollow. "Thank you miss, but I don't got no change…"

Dani put on the biggest smile she had and directed it at the three girls. "Well, lucky for you girls, that vending machine is a little defective. All you have to do is thump the one on the right real hard on the side, and it'll dispense anything you want. But don't tell anybody I told you." She winked at the little girls, who rushed off in delight and started pounding on the vending machine. Raptured squeals announced the arrival of the first treats. The girls would no doubt have tummy aches before the night was through, but they'd also still have their brother.

Dani pushed a small amount of a painkiller into the port on the boy's IV and unlocked the casters on the gurney. Grabbing the IV bag off the stationary hook, she thrust it at Ashe. "Here, carry this. Make sure you keep it at least as high as your chest."

The man looked horrified. He'd clearly intended to help out and vanish as soon as possible. "Wait a minute," he said, "I can't... I mean, I'm not a nurse—"

"You are now. And if I hear the words, 'I can't' come out of your mouth again before this kid is on his feet, you'll wish to God you'd stayed in bed this morning. Now come on; we're moving."

ॐ • ॐ

"THAT SHOULD DO it," Dani told the man. She arched her back, relishing the popping sounds from her too-long hunched back. The x-rays of the teenage boy's shoulder and abdomen had shown no bullet fragments had been left behind; she was relieved that both were simple through-and-throughs. The lower wound had even been at oblique enough an angle to miss everything important. She had just completed a thorough cleaning and suture of each wound, and the boy should come through fine. He'd wake up with nothing too much worse than scars, bragging rights, and a hyper-protective mother.

She ensured the boy's fresh bag of fluids was flowing sufficiently and turned toward her on-demand nurse. She looked at the man.

The man looked back.

"Ashe, right?" Dani asked. "You did good, Ashe. Got a last name?"

"No. Not for a long time. It's just Ashe."

"Huh. Okay, just Ashe." Dani's eyes narrowed. Since the boy was now stable, she was able to allow her mind to wander down other paths for the first time since the group's arrival. "Haven't shaved for a while, huh, just Ashe?"

Ashe shrugged.

Dani thinks back to Lena's description of the Samaritan. "So... How old are you?"

Ashe looked back at her, his eyes registering surprise.

"I'm just curious, just Ashe. You look to be in your mid-forties..."

The man scowled. "I've been mid-forties a long time. Long as I can remember. Longer than you've been around, for sure," he said enigmatically.

Dani looked at him slyly. "How do you know how long I've lived here in Ashburn?"

"I meant longer than you've been alive."

Dani chuckled, but stopped when she realized the man didn't appear to be kidding.

Ashe pulled off his bloodied latex gloves and brushed talcum powder off on the thighs of his dirty blue jeans. "Look, I gotta get going. We done here?"

"Well, Marcus here will be fine. He's going to need rest, and I'll move him to our last overnight room in a bit. But I'd like to ask you—"

Before she could finish her question, Dani was interrupted by the sound of gunfire and screams ringing from the front lobby area. Ashe turned quickly and slipped out the door without a sound.

Rushing around the boy's gurney, Dani pushed through the still-swinging door. Even though she had been right behind Ashe, the man was simply... gone.

ॐ • ॐ

DANI BARELY HAD time to wonder how Ashe had vanished so quickly before three thugs came running around the hallway corner. The three men pointed guns at her and checked the small operating room. Judging the unconscious teenager on the gurney to be no threat, they yanked Dani with them back to the lobby area.

Despite her whirlwind descent into peril, Dani breathed a deep sigh of relief to see that her new patient's mother remained unharmed, and that the three girls were clustered tightly around her, also unhurt.

The small waiting area was now tightly packed due to the presence of eight gang members, a few of whom wore bandanas or ski masks. Dani took this to mean that these were probably local kids or new additions, uneasy about being identified by people they might know.

Scanning faces, Dani quickly identified the group's leader. The thugs had fanned out, but he stood at the center of the group, more commanding than the others in presence despite his slight frame. His white felt hat, worn over a red paisley bandana, seemed almost comical. Calling it a cowboy hat would be as inaccurate as it was generous. It seemed like a hat better suited for a ten-year-old's birthday party rather than gangland violence. The hat's front was pinned up flat in a silly manner, but the set of the young man's jaw and the sharpness of his gaze wiped away any desire to laugh. His denim jacket, frayed at the shoulders and adorned with mismatched patches, hung open over his shirtless torso.

An edge was prominent in his dark eyes, a spark. This wasn't a man who fought; this was someone who led, who had others fight. A faded flag patch on his jacket hinted at an older allegiance, though whether to heritage or ideology, Dani couldn't tell. There was nothing casual about the way he stood: feet apart, arms loose but ready. The others circled around him, their eyes flicking to his as if awaiting a signal.

A slight trail of smoke wafted from the muzzle of his gun as he lowered his arm. The pistol was an ugly thing despite its satin nickel plating, a hulking piece of steel that seemed too large to be practical. The gun's vented rib barrel gave it an aggressive, predatory look. Dani couldn't help but notice the way the thug's fingers lovingly held and caressed the pistol, as if he drew confidence from its weight.

A brittle old drop-ceiling tile in the far corner of the room had cracked in half, nearly destroyed by his bullet. Rather than being aimed at anyone in particular, the gunshot had been a warning or announcement.

Dani looked around the room, curious about Ashe, but not seeing him. She didn't have much time to wonder because the gang leader backhanded her new patient's mother and yelled at her to pipe down. The woman cowered back, and he shoved her brutally with his free hand. She slipped backward into a hard plastic chair, the girls close around her.

"Thank you," he said sardonically. He turned to Dani. "You the doctor?"

Dani pulled at the grip of the thug holding her arm. "Who wants to know?"

The gang leader waved his gun casually in her direction, its muzzle pointing lazily downward. "I do, chica," he answered. "Di'n't you hear me ask?"

Dani glowered at the man. "I'm the doctor. What do you want? We don't have any money here. And the drugs are all locked up; I don't have the key."

The thug laughed. "You hear that, boys? The lily-white doc just automatically assumes we came for her drugs!"

One of the other thugs laughed loudly. "Hey, I'll take her drugs!"

The leader's smile was an evil crack across his face that failed to involve his eyes. Dead eyes. "Oh, for sure, we'll get the drugs too. But that ain't why we came."

Dani jerked roughly against her captor. This time, the large man released her arm, confident she couldn't cause any trouble they couldn't handle. "Then why are you here? What do you want?" she demanded.

"Ain't a 'what,' I want, it's a 'who,' chica. Where's the *gringo cabron* that brought the kid in here? The kid who got shot?"

Dani looked over at the mother, who was sobbing quietly and trying to comfort her wide-eyed girls. Dani turned back to the leader.

"I don't know who you mean."

The leader's pistol, which had formerly been waved around loosely in a casual grip, was suddenly held level and rock steady two feet from Dani's face. She could see the square notches of the rifling in the shiny round circle of the barrel. "Don't you try to be cute here, chica! I ain't got a lot of time here tonight, and my boss, he wants to see that old man. He really wants to see him."

Dani weighed her available options and decided the truth offered her the best chance of surviving the next few minutes. "I don't know where he is. He was with me in the operating room back there, then he just disappeared."

The leader frowned in irritation. "Disappeared, huh? What do you mean, disappeared? Like he vanished? Like a ghost?"

"No, I mean he stepped through the door, and by the time I came out, he was gone."

"This place got a back door?" The leader leaned to one side to look around Dain and down the hall. The man's automatic pistol had not wavered.

Dani shook her head. "No, just the front door and the side windows. And they're all barred. CFD wants us out of the building, because there's no alternate exits, but we're just going to have a rear door added next Spring."

The leader looked more annoyed by the second. "Do I look like I care about next Spring, here, chica? Where's he at now?"

"That's what I'm telling you. I don't know."

The leader dropped his gun hand to his side in a resigned gesture. "Well, he didn't come by us. He's still in this place somewhere." He looked to his gang. "You guys fan out. Go through every one of those rooms back there and bring him back here."

"Wait a minute!" Dani cried out. "I have patients back there!"

The evil smile spread farther across the leader's face. "So much the better!" He pointed at three of the men in particular. "You three make a lap and bring everybody you find back there to the party. The more the merrier."

He saw Dani's discomfiture about her patients and pointed the gun at her again. "And you can just be happy about it, chica."

Chapter 7 : CRUNCH AND REPEAT

PRESENT DAY

THE DESERT STRETCHED to the horizon ahead, flat and unforgiving under the glare of the morning sky. The Corvette's cramped cabin was stifling despite the air conditioner cranked to full blast. That was the bad part. On the good side, the engine rumbled pleasantly at idle despite its wheels eating up the highway at posted speeds. The low purr provided a bass score for the papery rustle of the bag of coffee beans Amber was picking through. She grabbed a small handful of beans and popped a couple into her mouth, crunching noisily. Amber's fingers tapped some imagined tune on the steering wheel, and her eyes flicked from the road ahead to Ashe as she chewed her morning cup. Crunch. Tap. From Ashe to the road. Crunch. Tap, tap. Back to Ashe. Crunch.

Ashe's jaw tightened with every bite. He sat slumped in the passenger seat, arms crossed, his expression darkened with all the clouds that were absent from the clear morning sky. They had been on the road for just under two hours.

"Seriously," Amber said, her tone far too perky for the situation. "What difference does it make? That's all I'm asking."

Ashe leaned his head back against the seat, his crutches digging uncomfortably into his ribs where they were wedged beside him. He wished his leg would hurry up and heal so that he could drive and maybe she could sleep. For that matter, he wished he needed more sleep than he did. Grabbing a fresh water bottle from behind his seat, he drained it in one long swallow. Along with his accelerated healing came an almost perpetual wakefulness which gave him fitful respite only when he was the most severely injured. Being awake for two thousand years seemed hardly as bad as being awake for two hours in a car with Amber's constant chatter. He exhaled slowly through his nose. "You're a writer. You figure it out."

"Oh, I *am* a writer," Amber shot back, waving a coffee bean at him for emphasis. "Don't you mock me."

"Then you should be able to see the difference," Ashe replied, staring straight ahead, his eyes fixed on the endless desert road.

"Okay, Mr. Smarty Pants," she said, tossing the bean into her mouth. "I'm just saying, okay, I get 'along the way.' But why is 'in the way' any different from 'on the way?' It's dumb."

Ashe let his head roll to the side, leveling a flat look at her. "Because this conversation we're having *on* the way is getting *in* the way of me having a minute to think."

Amber squinted at the road ahead, chewing loudly. She considered his statement for what she judged to be a suitable amount of time, then shook her head. "Nope. I still don't get it."

"Yeah, well, that's on you," Ashe grumbled, squirming in his seat, as though that would magically make the cramped space less miserable.

Amber pursed her lips, thought for a moment, then grinned. "Okay, what on earth?!" She exclaimed.

Ashe turned his head sharply, his eyes narrowing as he scanned the horizon and leaned forward to check the passenger side mirror. "What on earth what?"

"That's another one!" Amber said, pointing at him with an air of triumph. "The earth is the world. Our world is the earth. If you say, 'what *on* earth,' why can't I say, 'what *in* earth,' or even, 'what *on*—'"

"Amber," Ashe cut in, his voice a growling rumble in tune with the car's motor. "Enough. Just... enough. Do you know what I want?" he asked.

For a moment, blessed silence filled the car. Ashe briefly thought Amber knew what he wanted and was finally giving it to him. Then she tossed another coffee bean into her mouth and proved otherwise. She munched with extraordinary finesse, drawing out the process of chewing and making it as loud as possible for as long as possible. Ashe closed his eyes and pressed his fingers to his right temple, praying she might at least refrain from talking for longer than thirty seconds.

She didn't.

"You know," she started again, her tone breezy, "you ever think about what the world wants? Maybe it wants something and gets disappointed when it doesn't get it."

Ashe didn't open his eyes. "Yeah, well," he said, his voice flat, "that's on the world."

Amber's head snapped toward him, her green eyes sparkling. "Nice! I see what you did there," she smiled.

"Of course you do," Ashe said dryly. "You're a writer."

Amber giggled, unfazed, and grabbed another bean. "Fine, fine. Just making conversation. It's not like we've got a crazy long way to go or anything."

Her eyes widened in feigned surprise.

"Oh, wait, we do!"

"NEEDLES."

The vast expanse of sand and scrub had changed little in the past hours; the ribbon of Highway 40 had just shifted slightly southward, shimmering in the midday heat. The road sliced through the landscape like a scar. Amber seemed immune to the monotony of the scenery, her voice rising and falling with unflagging energy, punctuated by the crunch of coffee beans she pulled from the bag in her lap.

Every few minutes, a fresh crunch punctuated her words as she rattled through a stream of disconnected thoughts. Ashe's responses to Amber's stream of consciousness had dwindled to occasional grunts or one-word replies, but it didn't seem to faze her. If anything, his silence only seemed to provide more space for her to fill. She'd already covered a dizzying range of topics: conspiracy theories about highway naming conventions, an in-depth analysis of the role of trash diners in the American experience, her latest theory about why the desert smelled like "toasted earth." No topic was off-limits. No topic was particularly meaningful, but none was off-limits.

"What?" asked Ashe.

Amber gestured at the road sign. "Needles. Do you think they call it that because they make needles there? Or...?"

Ashe looked at her blankly. Needles. This had to be the twentieth meaningless landmark Amber had commented on in the past three and a half hours.

Ashe fixed his focus on the wavering horizon. He leaned back in his seat, his injured leg stretched awkwardly, crutches crammed uncomfortably behind his shoulder.

"Maybe it's some geographical feature," mused Amber.

Ashe closed his eyes. He opened them and looked back at her. "Are you going to point out every piddly little road sign we pass? All the way to Virginia?"

Amber popped another couple of the roasted beans into her mouth and munched on them loudly, filling the cramped cabin of the Corvette with the rich, earthy aroma of Sumatran coffee.

"Probably, yeah."

She took a swig from her water bottle, swishing the liquid around in her mouth to create a makeshift cold brew. For his part, Ashe opened and emptied his fifth bottle of the trip in one long drag. He crumpled the bottle to save space and tossed it into the tight space behind the passenger seat.

"The desert's so weird, isn't it?" Amber said, her voice cutting through the silence. "It's like, dead, but not really. You'd think nothing could survive out here, but then there's all these tiny plants. Like, how do they even do that? They're just... out here. In the middle of nowhere."

Ashe didn't look at her. "Yeah. Just like us."

Amber snorted, "I know, right? Except we've got AC and snacks." She popped another bean into her mouth, crunching loudly. Ashe winced at the sound, pressing two fingers to his temple.

"I'm bored," said Amber.

"I'm aware," replied Ashe.

"Remember the old days, when you used to tell me stories?"

"Old days? I've only known you for just over two months."

"I know! Remember the good old days, though?"

Amber set her bottle between her legs and grabbed the steering wheel at ten and two. "Look, this is mind-numbing." She drove for a few moments like a zombie, still as a statue, staring at the road ahead. Exchanging her deadpan for a smile, she looked back over at Ashe with tilted head. "You could always tell me a story."

"Hey, I've got a great idea. You want to be a writer. Why don't you quietly think about your next book? How's that for a fun plan?"

Amber thought for a moment, then spoke, having found the trap. "Nah, I'd have to have a first book before I could have a next book."

"Okay, so write your first book."

"I can't write a book. I need a life. Nothing ever happens to me."

Taken aback, Ashe stared at his traveling companion in disbelief.

"You've faced down an egomaniacal multi-billionaire and were a part of the end of his evil empire," Ashe reminded her.

"Yeah, but that was then. And I was kind of just a bystander."

"You're driving across the entire country in a one-of-a-kind piece of automotive history and headed off to destroy evidence before the FBI can get their hands on it."

"Yeah, but that hasn't *happened*. All we're doing so far is driving. And it's boring," she complained. "Tell me a story."

Ashe folded his arms.

"I know! You could tell me about that bullet you've got around your neck. The one you saved from Task's lab."

Ashe stared out the passenger window, ignoring her.

"Come on, Ashe. Please?" she wheedled.

"Not gonna happen."

"Please?" repeated Amber.

"I said, 'no.' I'm not gonna talk about that."

Amber harrumphed, annoyed. "Fine. Don't talk about it. Tell me how you came to be living in a cave in a radioactive wasteland."

"I'm not gonna talk about that, cause then I'd have to tell you about the bullet."

Amber's eyes grew wide. "Ooh! Sounds meaty!" She got no reaction from Ashe.

She looked at the road ahead of them.

She looked back at Ashe.

"No," Ashe repeated.

"Okay, fine. Some other story, then... Oh! I know! When we were in the coffee shop and talked about the Spear of Destiny... Something about that triggered the snot out of you and you went off on Task, comparing him to Hitler."

"Yeah," muttered Ashe. "And?"

"And? Tell me the story! What was it that set you off?"

Ashe inhaled a bushel of cold air and heaved a deep sigh.

"Okay, fine. How much do you know about Hitler?"

"I dunno, the basics, I guess. He was a bad guy. Worst mass murderer in history. Stuff like that."

"So… you know nothing, then. Fine, we'll start before the first time I met him."

"Wait - what? Wait a second. You met Hitler?"

"I think that's what I just said."

"Okay, then. The obvious question: why didn't you kill the guy? You would've survived, right?"

Ashe rolled his eyes. "That old chestnut. 'Why didn't you kill Hitler?' Do you know what you should do right this second based on what might happen in the future?"

Amber glanced at an approaching road sign and turned on her blinker.

"Sure! Right now, I should pull off because in the future, I'll wet my pants if I don't."

Chapter 8 : NO EXIT

1976

THE WAITING ROOM was oppressive, the air thick with fear and an acrid blend of sweat, cheap cologne, and smoke-saturated clothing. The gang's leader paced near the front desk, his heavy boots thudding against the linoleum floor. His fingers drummed on the butt of the pistol he'd tucked back into his waistband, a nervous rhythm that elicited anxious glances from some of his men. The mother sat frozen in the corner, clutching her three daughters close. The youngest of the girls whimpered softly, her wide eyes darting between the gang members and Dani, who sat stiffly on a worn chair, her lab coat smeared with the boy's blood. Dani didn't look at the mother, afraid that even a glance might provoke the woman to break down.

The leader snapped something in Spanish, his voice sharp and commanding. Dani didn't catch much of it, but the meaning was clear enough. Three of the gang members nodded and moved toward the hallway leading deeper into the clinic. The leader gestured impatiently. "Check everywhere," he called after them in English. "Bring back anyone you find."

Dani's pulse quickened as the three disappeared into the dim corridor. Her mind raced. They were looking for someone. Ashe. She was certain of it. Her chest tightened, but she kept her expression neutral, her gaze fixed on the cracked tiles beneath her feet. If they found him, things could go from bad to worse. Much worse. She'd only just met the man, but Ashe did not strike her as the type to come along meekly.

Minutes ticked by, the silence punctuated by the sounds of the leader's boots and an occasional sniffle from the girls in the corner. The man's agitation became palpable, his contained pacing becoming erratic as he muttered under his breath. His frustration boiled over into an angry stream of Spanish invective, directed at the remaining thugs in the room. Dani caught enough to piece it together: he was angry about how long things were taking. His men weren't moving fast enough, weren't finding what they were looking for. And he wasn't going to pay the price alone if they went back to his boss empty-handed. His tone sharpened, shouting out demands for answers from people who weren't there to give them.

The tension snapped when the sound of shuffling feet and squeaking wheels came from the hallway. Dani's stomach dropped as two of the three thugs reappeared, the first pushing a wheelchair in which a resolute-looking Mr. Jackson sat, stiff as a board. Dani figured the man had not put up a fight, but she could tell from the set of his jaw that he'd been no help, either.

Close behind, a second thug pushed Mrs. Hurston's heavy wheeled hospital bed, gasping for breath. Dani was gratified to see that the punk had shown at least enough compassion to bring along her oxygen tank. The poor woman looked terrified, her gaze darting between her captors and Dani as though her doctor might have the answers.

The leader exploded in a rapid-fire tirade of Spanish, jabbing his finger at the patients. His men shot back heated responses, their voices rising as they gestured toward the empty hallway. Dani couldn't follow all of it, but the leader's tone was unmistakable; he was furious. The patients weren't who they were looking for. They were wasting time.

And worse, Ashe was still missing.

The leader paused his abuse of his men for a moment, realizing that three men had gone out but only two had returned.

Dani kept her eyes down, her mind a whirlwind. The waiting room felt like a tinderbox, ready to ignite at the slightest spark. She needed to stay calm, be invisible, and hope that wherever Ashe was, he hadn't deserted them. Even better, that he had a plan.

The gun in her face brought Dani's attention back to the gang leader.

"How many more patients you got back there, chica?" demanded the thug.

"Just the one," she answered, "the boy who was just brought in with the gunshot wound. He's still on the gurney in the OR"

The leader pointed to another of his group. "You go get Alejandro and bring him and the kid from the OR here. I want everybody together." He pointed to the original pair of lackeys. "You two go out and find the gringo. Remember, El Jefe wants him alive. Move!"

A brief lull ensued, in which wheels spun furiously in Dani's head. A picture was becoming clear in her mind's eye. Ashe was the Samaritan that Lena spoke of, that Mr. Jackson and others refused to talk about. The Samaritan, who frequently dropped off sick and injured homeless people who would almost certainly die on the streets otherwise. The Samaritan, who had a penchant for leaving wads of cash behind as donations to the clinic to help with the care of those homeless people. The Samaritan, who, by all current indications, had gotten himself hip-deep on the bad side of local drug dealers and gangs. It didn't take much of a mental leap from there to figure where the wads of cash came from.

The Samaritan was Ashe. Ashe, who treated wounds like a battlefield medic. Ashe, who moved with purpose and grace. Ashe, who had somehow vanished right in front of her eyes.

The thug that the leader had just sent after Dani's newest patient returned, pushing the boy's wheeled gurney. The teenager was still unconscious, a result of the pain medications Dani had given him. His mother leapt up and tried to get to her son but was shoved roughly back into her seat by a thug nearby. The leader pointed his gun at her. "Just sit down, lady. Your boy's fine; I'm sure Doc Chica here did some good work stitching him up."

He looked around the room, then back to the man who'd brought the gurney. "Where's Alejandro?" the leader demanded.

"He's not back there. I checked the whole place."

The gang leader addressed the room. "We're just here looking for the gringo been messing with us, hitting our dealers and stealing our cash. That's all. We get him, and we go. And you all be fine." He turned to look at Dani. "And we won't even raid your drugs, chica."

One of the other thugs smiled at this and commented, "Yeah, we got our own!" A chorus of laughter among the other gang members seemed to lighten the tension slightly.

The merriment was not long-lasting. "Where are those three?" Grumbled the leader. He yelled down the hallway after his two missing men. "Oso! Carter! Where you at?"

No answer. Silence.

"Don't you tell me you two need help with one old man!" More quietly, he turned to speak to two others as he waved his gun toward the hallway. "Jiminez—you and Paco go check on them."

A few moments passed and the two men, Jimenez and Paco, came back to the waiting area. They reported having been unable to find any of their three missing comrades or "the gringo."

Furious, the leader spun to Dani. He pointed his pistol at the head of the boy unconscious on the gurney. "Yo! Doctor Chica! Why didn't you tell me there was a back door to this place?"

The boy's mother screamed and the thug guarding her slapped her in the face. The three little sisters sobbed quietly, nestled closely against their mother.

Dani was mystified. "There's not! I swear it. High windows, but not something a person could get through. Leave these people alone."

"Leave them alone? Oh, okay. I'll leave them alone. But you, chica? You're coming with me," the man snarled. He seized her arm roughly with his free hand and yanked her to her feet. He waved his gun at his gang, indicating the two that had just returned and the man nearest them. "You two, and you—on me. You other two, stay here and make sure the gringo doesn't come past here. He shows his face, you shoot him in it."

One of the thugs tasked with guarding the lobby worked up the nerve to question his boss. "But what about Ming, ese? The man wants the little gringo alive, you said."

The leader scowled. "Yeah, Martin, only I'm starting to not care as much as I should, maybe. Just shut up and keep everyone quiet in here. We'll be back." He addresses Dani, "You're gonna take me on the guided tour of this 'ain't no back door' clinic of yours."

⤐ • ⤏

"IT'S LIKE I told you, boss," Paco told the gang leader. "Ain't nobody back here."

Dani had led the group at gunpoint through every room in the small clinic. As Dani had previously told the leader, there was no rear exit to the building. She pointed out the two small windows she had mentioned before. Both of these were in the long, narrow break room along the back wall of the building. They were high in the wall and only about ten inches tall by twenty wide.

"That gringo isn't real big," commented Jimenez. "He might fit through one of those windows."

"Yeah, maybe, but they're both locked from the inside," said the leader. "And they both got bars on the outside."

"And what about our missing guys?" Asked Paco. "Where'd they go?"

"Carter's not too big. He might fit through there," replied Jimenez, clinging tenaciously to his logic.

The leader slapped Jimenez across the head for this. "Yeah, but what did he do? Squeeze through the bars? And do you think Oso would fit? He's as big as a house."

No one commented. All four of Dani's captors looked around aimlessly.

An idea then seemed to click in the leader's mind. He snapped his fingers and ordered one of the crew out to take a lap around the outside of the clinic.

"Looking for what?" Paco asked.

"Look for any doors out there that might be hidden in here behind a cabinet or something. Look for open windows. Look for footprints. Use your head, you idiot!"

Paco departed. While he was gone, the leader, Jimenez, and the other young man, a quiet boy whose name Dani had not picked up, continued their search inside the clinic. The leader had taken to dragging Dani along roughly by the arm in his agitation. The thugs made a royal mess of every room, shoving stacks of supply boxes over, tipping over cabinets, ripping informative medical posters from the walls.

Paco returned from his scouting trip. He reported finding no additional windows, and that the ones they'd seen were secured by solid bars. There was no secret door to be found. The only thing of note had been some vents along the ground outside, a few inches above the sidewalk, but they were barely big enough for a cat to fit through.

Standing in the hallway between the patient rooms, the leader rattled a doorknob, surprised to find it locked.

He turned to Paco and Jimenez, who had searched earlier. "What's in here?"

The two men looked at each other and back at the leader. "We don't know... it was locked," replied Paco.

The leader released his grip on Dani's arm and used his free hand to slap Paco across the head. "*¿Son burros o qué? ¡No ven nada!*'" he yelled at his men. "I said check the place out, you idiots!" he hissed, backing away from the door. The group spread out a bit.

The leader gestured at the unnamed boy, clearly the junior member of the current group. The boy wore a ski mask rolled into a beanie atop his head and was the only one without a pistol. He grabbed Dani when instructed by his boss.

The gang leader pointed his gun at Dani's head and started groping at her, checking pockets. Finding the lab coat's breast pocket empty, he thrust a hand into each blood-stained hip pocket. Empty as well. The man ripped open the lab coat; Dani squirmed. The leader shoved a hand deep into her first jeans pocket, yanking it inside out. The second pocket finally yielded a set of keys and a small tube of lip gloss.

"Always the last place you look," the leader snarled. "Which one is it?" he demanded, tossing the lip gloss aside. Dani noted that he was speaking in a hushed voice, convinced that Ashe had taken refuge behind the door.

Dani indicated one of the keys. "It's just a little supply room. Not even big enough for—"

The leader cut her off. "You'll excuse me if I don't trust you, chica. I think we'll find out for ourselves."

The leader gave hand signals to his men, who responded in silence. For the first time, Dani started to get the idea that this group was working a little above the capability level she'd expect from common street thugs. Paco and Jimenez fanned out and stacked on either side of the locked door. The one holding Dani backed up, keeping her as a shield in front of him as he backed into an open doorway across the hall.

The leader, struck with an inspiration, picked up the tube of lip gloss and slathered the waxy substance on the key. The key then slid silently into the keyhole. He held up three fingers, counting his team down. On "zero," the leader's hand closed to a fist and he moved quickly. In a single smooth motion, he flipped the key, turned the knob, and yanked the door open before reaching back to his waistband for his gun.

His two men slipped into formation, instantly moving to clear the room. As Dani had stated, the small closet was quite small, and the two men collided into each other in their zeal. The closet was empty except for a few cleaning supplies.

The leader and the two front men looked into the closet, stunned. It was clear that they had all expected something more.

A muted thump suddenly drew their focus, above them and just down the hall they had come from.

The leader identified the source of the sound above them and pointed to a spot in the drop ceiling. He pointed his gun upward and opened fire; big booming coughs deafened everyone in the hallway. The two front men joined in and the group riddled the ceiling with nearly a dozen bullets. Dani's ears rang as the sudden noise abated and the smoke-filled corridor fell silent save for the tinkling of brass casings chattering along the linoleum floor.

Blood started dripping from the bullet holes and the leader made an excited outburst. He grabbed a broom from the closet and shoved it hard upward against a reddening ceiling tile. The tile broke and a body fell through, almost hitting the leader. He jumped back out of the way.

        ❮   •   ❯

TWO ADDITIONAL CEILING tiles next to that first one gave way in a cloud of dust and a much larger body fell through, crashing on top of the leader. The two of them crumpled to the floor in a jumble of arms and legs atop the first body.

The leader scrambled up, his face white.

Dani observed that the two bodies which had just fallen from the ceiling were the two missing thugs that had been sent out in the first foray to look for Ashe.

The leader and the two front men spun around in shocked circles. They pointed their guns all over, focused on trying to locate and identify the new sudden threat.

The young man holding Dani took a few additional steps back. He was the only one of the group without a firearm, a fact he seemed suddenly very self-conscious about. Dani struggled against him, but he was too strong, his wiry muscles fueled by adrenaline. He pulled her back into the room behind them.

Without warning, Dani felt a rough jolt and the man's grip on her vanished.

Unbalanced by her sudden freedom, Dani lurched against the wall and spun to see Ashe manhandling the thug like a puppet. The older man held the punk in a stranglehold and was clearly about to extinguish the younger man's life. His and Dani's eyes met.

Ashe appeared to note Dani's horrified expression. He scowled, relenting his hold a few seconds after consciousness faded from the young man's eyes but before his life could follow suit. Amid the continued loud shouts and occasional gunshots from the hallway, Dani heard no sound as Ashe slid the thug to the floor.

Dani was forming a question when Ashe slapped a hand over her mouth and "shushed" her, gesturing with the universal sign for silence: one stiff finger held upright to his pursed lips.

Ashe released Dani, who was shocked at the old man's strength and speed. He grabbed some surgical tubing and tied up the thug with an economy of effort, leading Dani to surmise that assisting in field surgery wasn't the man's only skill. Ashe wadded the unconscious man's mouth full of gauze and shoved him into a blind corner of the room.

"What is going on? Who are you?" Dani demanded in a hushed voice.

"Told you; I'm Ashe."

"No, not 'what's your name.' Who *are* you? Are you a cop?"

"No," was Ashe's reply. He risked a glance out the doorway.

"Then who are you?"

"I'm the hero," answered Ashe. "Come on, we gotta go."

Ashe gestured for Dani to follow. He bent down and grabbed the edge of a floor tile. Dani reflected that she had caught her shoe on that very tile more than once.

Ashe lifted the tile. With it came up what Dani suddenly realized must be a trap door that had been covered over by several decades of floor refreshes under cheap linoleum. Ashe gestured for her to drop through the opening and waggled his bushy eyebrows to indicate urgency.

Dani followed his suggestion, deciding it would be best to not be found when the thugs inevitably came looking for their latest fallen comrade.

❧ • ❦

IT WAS CRAMPED and dark beneath the floor and smelt of age and dirt. Startled by their intrusion, something furry skittered over Dani's exposed ankle between her jeans and track shoes. The rafters of the floor above creaked slightly and she heard muffled voices above.

The voices rose to shouts, although Dani could not make out any words. Wet-sounding thumps were heard followed by more yelling.

Eventually a shot rang out, muffled by the floor above. A single hole appeared in the floor a few feet to Dani's left. She instantly feared an oncoming hail of bullets, thinking the gang had deduced their location. Dani felt Ashe's hand clamp once again tightly over her mouth, preventing an outcry.

Instead of the rain of lead she anticipated, there was just another wet thump, then the voices and footsteps receded. Ashe's hand pulled slowly away from Dani's face.

"What..." Dani whispered, confused.

Deciding it was safe enough to speak quietly, Ashe whispered back, "The one who was holding you? Julio shot him. This crew doesn't take well to failure."

"Oh, my God," was all Dani could say.

"God's got no part of this," said Ashe. "It's alright, though. Idiot wants to shoot all his men, that's okay with me. He's down four now. How many did he come in with?"

"Eight, plus himself; nine total. Six of the eight armed with various small-caliber handguns, plus the leader..."

"Julio," supplied Ashe.

"Julio, with one of those new Auto Mags."

Ashe grunted. "You know your guns." His voice carried a tone of approval. For some reason Dani did not understand, she felt her cheeks flush. She was relieved to be in the dark.

"Yeah, Julio likes making big holes," continued Ashe. "Thing won't hit much outside of thirty yards, though. What else of note?"

"The one up here," she pointed up, then shook her head when she realized Ashe couldn't see her. "He and the other guy without a gun had folding knives. In all, six Hispanics, two Caucasians, one black. All late teens to mid-twenties except Julio, who I put maybe around thirty. All moderately fit except the large one that..." Dani fell silent, interrupted by the sound of several sets of footsteps overhead.

Yelling.

Fast footsteps.

Shelves falling over.

More yelling.

Receding footsteps.

Ashe's voice came again. "Okay. We gotta go. Julio's not super bright, but he is thorough. He'll eventually come back and find that trapdoor. Come on."

Dani paused, still trying to process everything.

"Did you hear me?" Ashe growled at her. "We gotta go. Kinda limited options down here, and it's just gonna get worse."

Dani snapped her mouth shut on the next question. He was right; they had a definite need to be somewhere else. "Okay, hero," she said. "Lead the way."

Dani felt rather than saw Ashe crawl past her.

Ashe heaved at the trapdoor above them. The wood groaned but refused to budge. Ashe shifted slightly, planting his feet for better leverage, and pushed again. This time, the trapdoor cracked open an inch, spilling a thin ray of silver light into the darkness. The beam cut across Ashe's face, highlighting heavy lines etched into his skin and streaks of gray threading through his hair and beard. Once again, Dani observed how carefully unruly his appearance was: his ragged clothes, the smudges of dirt on his face. It was all too intentional to be real.

Her breath caught. She should have been alarmed by how easily this man, who looked like someone you'd ignore on the street, had handled the gang and led them on a wild goose chase. Instead of alarm in his presence, she felt something else, something she wasn't ready to name or even admit. The sharp angles beneath the fur of Ashe's grizzled jaw and the calm intensity in his eyes absorbed her entire focus.

"This figures," Ashe muttered, his voice low and gravelly. He gave the trapdoor another shove, but it resisted completely, stuck against something above. The faint light framing his face cast shadows across his features. He seemed both rugged and untouchable. Dani shook her head slightly, trying to clear the fog that had settled into her thoughts.

"Are you all right?" he asked, his eyes meeting hers in the dim light.

She nodded a little too quickly, grateful for the semi-darkness that hid the warmth creeping back into her cheeks. "I'm fine. Just wondering what I've walked into."

"A mess," Ashe replied, his lips twitching in what might have been the ghost of a smile. He turned back to the trapdoor, his focus sharp and unwavering. Dani continued staring at him a moment longer than she should have. Now wasn't the time to figure him out.

"Okay," he said. "There's another exit from this crawlspace, but it's not in a good place."

"How did you even know about this crawlspace? I've worked here for six months, and I never knew it was here. Lena never mentioned it either; she's been here for years."

In the scarce light, Ashe looked at her. He seemed a little put off. "Where did you think your heat came from?"

"What do you mean?"

"You've got radiant heat. Post-war construction. Same principal as a Roman hypocaust, but more efficient."

Dani was confused, and said so.

Ashe grunted. "Steam heat. Low maintenance, but stuff still breaks. How are you gonna work on it? You can't just tear up your floor all the time."

"Okay, I guess that makes sense. But how would I know that? I'm not a builder."

"Yeah, neither is Julio. But he's gonna eventually figure it out. Come on. We gotta move."

Ashe shut the trapdoor and they started their slow, dark journey across the width of the building, feeling ahead of them as they crawled.

❧ • ❦

DANI AND ASHE wormed their way in the dark for a few moments in silence. Dani finally broke the silence. "Ashe, right?" she whispered.

"Yeah."

"These guys friends of yours? You called their leader Julio."

"I know of them. They know of me. I'm familiar with Julio. Hardly friends. Mostly, I know Julio's boss."

"The guy that wants to speak with you?"

Ashe was quiet for a moment. "Julio said that?"

"Yes," Dani replied. "Said the boss, el jefe, wants to take you alive so he can talk to you."

"Talk to me? That what he said?" Dani couldn't see Ashe's face in the darkness, but she thought she could hear a smile on his rugged face.

"I think so. Maybe not. I don't remember. One of the gang called his name Ming, I think."

"Yeah, Ming wants me, I'm sure, but not for talking," said Ashe. "We go back a ways."

"So, you're old friends with a drug lord, then?"

"We served together. Until he decided he was better off serving himself. Crossed some lines. Big lines."

By this time, Dani estimated that they had crossed under the building to a spot near the front lobby. She heard voices above, sharp outbursts blended with a faint murmur of fear.

Another tiny sliver of light appeared ahead of her as Ashe carefully pushed up another trap door. With a gesture, Ashe cautioned her to silence.

A shot rang out above, startling Dani.

Ashe didn't flinch.

Fearing for her patients, Dani surged forward toward the trapdoor. Ashe placed a firm hand on her shoulder, easily restricting her ability to move any further. He let go and wedged a tiny pebble into the opening, maintaining the small amount of light.

Glancing up through the small crack, Ashe reported back to Dani that the gunshot had been Julio firing into the ceiling in an attempt to get the patients to settle down. Discussing their situation, Ashe stated his concern that Julio was starting to boil over.

"Someone nearby is likely to report the gunshots," Ashe said matter-of-factly. "That puts Julio on a ticking clock, which puts us on one."

Looking Dani in the eye, he asked Dani if there were any guns or weapons in the clinic.

"Of course not!" she exclaimed, still whispering. "It's a clinic."

"You know guns pretty well. I just figured you might have something here for self-defense."

"Never been an issue."

"Until now."

Dani couldn't argue with that. "Until now. Plus, I'm morally a pacifist."

"Seriously?" Ashe asked her. "I don't see how the world can afford pacifism. Killers like those scum upstairs love pacifists. Pacifism isn't an appropriate response to the world. That's why legal responses to stuff like this fall apart."

Dani bridled at this. For some reason Ashe's disapproval sliced through the situation and turned her into a defensive little girl. She suddenly felt she was having yet another "philosopholegal" discussion with her father.

"I said I was a pacifist. Doesn't mean I'm weak. Doesn't mean I can't shoot. And legal solutions?" Dani paused, cringing inside at the realization that she was about to quote something she'd heard on many occasions from her father, current chief judge in the United States District Court for the Northern District of Illinois. Cringing or not, she'd come this far with her argument. Might as well finish it. She layered as much conviction into her voice as she could muster, hiding out from the drug gang that had invaded her clinic and taken her patients hostage. "That attitude is why legal responses fail."

"Says the pacifist doctor." Ashe worked to squirm around to re-orient himself back in the direction they'd come.

Dani, desperate in this situation to have the last word, shot back, "Says the just-vetted FBI rookie agent!"

Ashe paused. He looked at her in the low light for a long moment.

"FBI agent?" he asked, "So you don't mind killing bad guys?"

"I don't mind *shooting* bad guys. You don't have to kill someone to put them out of service."

Ashe looked pleased. "Okay, I'll take it. Beggars can't be choosers."

He pulled a handgun from his waistband. "Here. I took this off that big guy back there."

Ashe reached into a pocket and came out with a metal tube which he then screwed onto the muzzle of the pistol.

Dani was skeptical. "You're telling me the big dumb guy—what was his name? Oso? Oso had a Walther with a silencer?"

Ashe regarded her with a blank look, much like a kid caught with his hand in the candy jar. He followed her eyes to the gun, which looked exactly like something that would simply be swallowed up in Oso's ham-sized hands.

"Um... yeah," Ashe said after a pause. He handed her the gun.

Dani checked the clip and jacked the slide to confirm there was a round chambered. "Whatever. What's the plan?"

"I'm going to go back to the other trap door and get back upstairs. It's bound to make some noise, so it should draw them my way."

A creaking floorboard just over Ashe's head caused him to pause in his instructions. The patrolling thug moved on after a moment and Ashe continued. "They'll probably clear out, looking for me. Especially since I've been thinning them out; they're not going to want to come in small numbers. Soon as you can, get up through that trapdoor and get your patients out. Fast. Don't look back. Get them out of the area and call the police."

"The gun's for any of them they leave behind to guard the patients?"

"Exactly. Although, with the reward their boss has on offer for me, it may not be too likely anybody's gonna stay back."

"What about the leader?" Dani asked, knowing the leader's .44 outgunned her little Walther by a country mile.

"Julio? You can bet he's gonna be first through that door after me. He's aggressive as a pit bull, and he's got a personal stake in this. You just worry about the stragglers."

"How do I know when it's time?"

"You'll know. Just wait for the signal."

Ashe moved off and Dani moved into place beneath the trapdoor.

Chapter 9 : THE SAMARITAN'S DEBT

1988

IT WAS MID-MORNING when he stirred. The surgery had lasted long into the night, with Dani and the entire OR staff working tirelessly to save his life. Lena had wondered aloud throughout the procedure how a man could have that much metal invade his body, have it taken out, and live to tell the tale. Exhausted, Dani had simply stretched out in a chair in Ashe's room once he was stabilized. Presuming her patient hadn't woken while she slept, he'd been out for nearly twelve hours, and so had she. How Ashe was not in a full coma, she had no idea. She could say the same thing about herself—twelve hours in a hospital room chair constituted rest, but only in name.

Ashe finally opened his eyes and looked at Dani for a long moment.

Dani looked back at the man lying in the hospital bed before her. The room was dim, lit only by a faint blue-gray light filtering through the blinds. Ashe lay motionless in the bed, his body a patchwork of gauze and sutures. The sight of him caused Dani's chest to tighten, both with professional pride and personal anguish. His head and half his face had been shaved for the surgery. *Why hadn't they just shaved it all?* she wondered. A raw, pink line of sutures stood out against his white scalp, trailing down into the immobilization collar bracing his neck. A rigid back brace, wired to traction rods that were in turn affixed to the bed, held his body still. It was an intricate prison of metal and wire and fabric designed to keep him alive.

Dani moved closer, her footsteps tapping on the tile floor. Her eyes traced the contours of his face—leaner than she remembered, but unmistakably the same man. The Samaritan. Ashe. The shaved area of his beard revealed deep lines around his mouth and eyes, but the characteristic streaks of gray remained on the other side of his grizzled jaw. But even as she stood over him, haunted by the memory of the man he had been, she was startled by the clear recognition in his eyes as they opened and found hers.

"Long time, no see," he rasped. The words were barely audible, but they hit her like a slap. Dani's throat tightened, and she looked away for a moment, pretending to adjust an IV line as her hands shook. She'd spent hours in surgery fighting to save this man, to piece him back together, but now she was the one feeling fractured.

She was surprised that he recognized her, and flat out astounded that a quip about their reunion would be the first thing out of the injured man's mouth. It had only been twelve years, but she knew she had changed quite a bit from the young doctor he'd known only briefly. Beyond that, she figured he'd made far more of an impression on her than the other way around—especially considering the circumstances of that first encounter.

She looked back at him, unsure what to say. "They... They could never identify any of the bodies. In the clinic back then, I mean. Well, except for that big guy from the ceiling. He was pretty easy." She paused. "I thought you were dead, Ashe."

"Yeah, that's a pretty common misconception. Where are we?"

"You're at Sacred Cross. Ashe, you were injured. Guess you were in the wrong place at the wrong time again." Dani fought to restrain tears.

Ashe looked around. Sensing his range of motion restrained, he tried to turn his head. Dani could tell immediately that he regretted the attempt, despite having moved only a couple millimeters. Dani was shocked he could move his head at all.

"Easy there, hero! You just had major surgery! You can hurt yourself even worse."

Resisting the urge to try and move his head again, Ashe sent his eyes around the room on a reconnaissance mission.

"I'm not sure it could hurt worse," he muttered. "Although that surgery sucked eggs pretty bad."

"You remember the surgery?"

"Yeah, at least the rougher bits. About nine or ten hours, right?"

Dani was horrified. "Eleven," she whispered.

Misinterpreting the tremble in her voice, Ashe tried to reassure her. "Hey! You did good work. Good hands."

Dani didn't acknowledge the compliment. "They told me the anesthesia wasn't working... You felt the work on your head, then?"

Ashe smiled at her, despite the obvious pain it caused him. "I felt the work on all of it, darlin'. I think you missed a pellet in my butt. Drugs don't do me a lot of good."

Dani was saddened. Jumbled memories were common in severe spinal trauma cases like this, as was a patient's initial belief that he or she could still feel. The mind expected pain and was quite skilled in creating the illusion of it at such times.

Ashe's eyes had finished their trip around the room. "Okay, I'm caught up now," he said. His expression became earnest as he looked up at her. "Listen, Dani. I can't be here."

"What do you mean?"

"The hospital. I can't be here." His voice was plain, authoritative, matter-of-fact. "I need to get out of the hospital."

Dani had to try and be encouraging for him. She knew how big a part mental attitude played in the healing process. Ashe would never walk again, but he could still have a life if he stayed positive.

"Ashe, I'm so sorry, but I remember you as a pretty straightforward person. There's no easy way to tell you this. You've suffered a terrible injury. I was able to re-attach the spinal cord, but..."

"Yeah, I remember. Thanks for that. Seriously. That will speed things up, I'm sure. But I need to go." Ashe saw the sadness in her eyes and surprised her with a fresh attempt to comfort her. "I'm gonna be fine," he grinned.

"That's the spirit," Dani said, mustering a weak smile.

Ashe was strangely adamant. "No, look. I'm going to get better, but I can't do it here in your hospital."

"It's not my hospital; it's actually my friend, Lena's. You might remember her, too, from the clinic. I kinda got, well, conscripted."

"Not your hospital? You are still a doctor, right? You just said you reconnected my spine."

"Well, technically, yes, I'm still a doctor. I've kept my license up and stayed current as much as I could. But I've been an FBI agent for about nine years."

Ashe smiled. "You? An FBI agent? So you made it then. Good for you."

"You remember that?" Dani asked.

"Yeah, I've got a decent memory of most the conversations I've had with pretty girls in crawlspaces."

Despite herself, Dani felt a blush rise to her cheeks. *Stop acting like a giddy schoolgirl,* she chided herself. Changing the subject, Dani took a few moments to explain to Ashe his integral part in her decision to ultimately join the Bureau.

"Great!" Ashe exclaimed. "Then you owe me one. Get me out of here."

Dani chuckled. "Anyway, I'm quitting. I feel like I'm a bit too widely known in the Bureau for putting bullets in people. I'd rather go back to taking them out."

"Awesome! So you owe me one twice." Ashe's expression was becoming more and more intense. "I'm serious, I need to not be here. And I need to not be here pretty soon."

"You can't go. It's just not possible; I'm sorry, Ashe." Dani watched her patient's battered face. Ashe was clearly experiencing severe discomfort. That was to be expected, but it was getting worse. Dani felt for the man, knowing that no painkillers would address his phantom pain, with or without the resistance to drugs he claimed to have.

Ashe raised his voice a notch and spoke through gritted teeth. "Listen to me! I have got to get out of here. If I stay here, my life is essentially over! You're still in the

FBI, right? Go get my records and tell the hospital I'm a suspect. Or a witness or something. Tell them that you have to take me to another facility. If I stay here for too much longer, I'll be in a lab till the end of time!" Ashe's voice had grown deep and husky in anguish, either physical or mental. Possibly both.

Dani shook her head, tears welling in her eyes.

Ashe's voice rasped, "You said the other doctor from back then, Lena. You said this was her hospital now. Go tell her that her Samaritan is here, and he needs paid back."

What happened next burned itself into Dani's memory so vividly that she knew she would never forget it. Against everything Dani knew to be possible in the world of medical science, Ashe moved his arm. The motion was faltering and weak, his muscles trembled with the strain of the effort, but he moved his arm. Establishing a feeble grip on the mattress, he sought to pull himself toward the edge of the bed. Of course, he made no headway. He had too much stacked against him: the scaffolding of traction rods, the tightly-wound bandages. And, of course, the fact that he was destined to be a quadriplegic for the rest of his life.

Ashe's hand slipped on the sheet and broke loose, causing his body to lurch back. He had moved less than an inch, but the sudden undoing of even that small amount of progress caused him a prodigious amount of pain, and he groaned loudly. The spell broken, Dani burst forward to stop him. She wasn't sure how he was able to move at all—she had no illusions about her surgical skills being that good—but she couldn't let her patient mess up whatever was going on and ruin his chances at a partial recovery out of haste.

Dani laid both hands on him. Ashe was as weak as a kitten, of course, so she had no trouble stopping him from moving. However, she noticed immediately upon touching him that he was burning up; Dani had never felt a fever so high. Grabbing for a thermometer, she thrust it into his armpit and grabbed his wrist. Pulse was racing at over 150 beats per minute. She pulled the thermometer and looked from her watch to the glass tube; Ashe's temperature was nearing a hundred and five.

Dani was halfway around the bed to grab for the emergency button before Ashe could stop her or get her attention.

"No!" Ashe's pained cry was loud enough to cut through her thoughts and catch her up short.

From her new vantage point, Dani noticed with confusion that the large IV bag that had recently been started was already drained. She looked from it to Ashe's face. He looked back at her, pain etched in every line in his face, the weak muscles in his neck trembling with effort. Dani stood for the briefest moment holding the emergency call button, unable to figure out how the man could still be coherent.

"Look, I don't have time right now to argue. I'm going to be fine, but you have got to get me to my house. It's across town. And you have to get every copy of my records from the hospital, especially my blood work. I can try to explain later, but I *can not* be here through this."

"You can't be anywhere else!" Dani exclaimed.

"I have to be!"

Something in his voice, a desperation such as she had never seen in anyone before, convinced her to act against any and all logic. She set the emergency call button gingerly on the mattress and hastened to the door. "Hang on—I'll go get Lena."

THE HALLWAY BLURRED past Dani as she sprinted back to Ashe's room, Lena just behind her. Neither doctor thought the frantic pace was unjustified: heart rate 150, temp 105... Dani's mind raced as she considered the implications. A temperature that high could be catastrophic—organ failure, brain damage—and with his injuries, Ashe shouldn't have been conscious, let alone moving. So why had she decided to delay and to get Lena? Lena had asked that question herself and Dani had tried to describe Ashe's conviction as they started racing back to his room. The more she tried to explain, the more foolish it sounded, and by the time they rounded the last corner, she was berating herself for the delay. She had just saved Ashe's life only to let him talk her into killing him.

The two women burst into the room, the door slamming against the wall. Ashe was still there on the bed, his skin pale and glistening with sweat, his muscles trembling from effort. Despite the immobilization of his neck and the frame securing his shattered spine, he had somehow managed to push himself to the edge of the mattress. His feet dangled precariously, and his arms, useless and limp, hung like dead weight at his sides.

"Ashe!" Dani rushed forward, her heart pounding. "What do you think you're doing? You're going to kill yourself!"

His head tilted slightly, and his eyes locked onto hers. They were glassy with fever but still sharp, still focused in a way that she couldn't fathom. "I can't stay here," he repeated, his voice cracked and raw. "You're not listening. I have to leave."

"You're not going anywhere!" Lena snapped, moving to the other side of the bed. She grabbed a cold pack from the nearby tray, pressing it against an unbandaged area of his neck. The older woman somehow fought down the urge to shove the man back onto his bed. "You've got an impossibly high fever. You'll seize if this keeps up."

"I can't stay," he insisted, his words slurring a bit. His desperation was palpable. "I'm not safe here. None of you are." He tried to shift again, the motion sending a jolt through his tortured frame.

A small group of nurses and staff had begun to gather in the doorway. There had been no alarm, but they could plainly see their head of medicine and the new doctor frantically trying to deal with a difficult patient. His neck restrained by the collar, Ashe saw them out of the corner of his eye. "Get out!" he yelled at them.

"Ashe, stop it!" Dani barked, one hand on his shoulder to steady him. "Your spine is stitched together with duct tape! Do you even realize what you're doing to yourself? You'll ruin what's left of your spine!"

Her words seemed to hit him, and for a moment he froze. Then, in one sudden motion, his body tipped forward. Dani lunged, but it was too late. Ashe's dead weight pulled him over the edge, and he crashed to the floor with a sickening thud and a clatter of metal.

"Oh my God!" Dani dropped to her knees beside him, her hands trembling as she checked for new injuries. Lena crouched on his other side. She barked at the nurses and orderlies at the door to assist them.

Ashe's head lolled against the immobilization collar, his breath ragged but steady. His eyes fluttered open, his gaze locking onto Dani's again. "I mean it," he whispered, his voice weaker now but no less urgent. "You have to get me out of here. You don't understand."

Dani's chest clenched inside as she looked at him. He was broken and burning with fever, yet still fighting with every ounce of his reserve of strength. Strength he shouldn't even have. Whatever danger he believed was coming, the fear of it was enough to drive him past the bounds of reason.

Within moments, they got Ashe back into his bed with the assistance of the onlookers. Lena gestured at one of the nurses and the woman handed her a thermometer. At Ashe's weak insistence, Lena told the nurses and staff to vacate momentarily as she checked his vitals.

Lena struggled to believe her eyes. "107 degrees. This isn't possible."

Ashe's voice was as dry as a rustling newspaper. "You know, I kinda feel like it is. Am I anywhere near a record?"

Lena looked at him, bewildered. "Considering the record is room temperature, no. But you're headed that way."

"Look, Lena. Dr. Rosenbaum. I can't be here right now. Those questions you got? They're just the tip of the iceberg if you keep me here. And you won't be the one asking." He turned his head nearly two inches to look at Dani. "Please," he implored her again, "Get me out of here. No records. I saved your life; you owe me."

His eyes shot back to Lena. "I saved a lot of lives. You two both owe me."

Lena stepped around the side of the bed. Turning Ashe's head, she peeled back the edge of the heavy wound dressing. Wide-eyed, she looked at Dani. "The wound is closing," she muttered.

Dani nodded. "Well, yes, I stitched him up. You watched me."

"No," stated Lena. "Three days' worth of healing, at least. In less than twelve hours."

 ∾ • ∾

LENA LOOKED SHAKEN.

They had started a fresh IV bag and placed every cold compress on the floor strategically around Ashe's body.

These efforts had stabilized him but had done little to slow or reverse the direction of his fever.

Lena commented to Dani that she had barely recognized her Samaritan without his unruly mop of hair and his scruffy beard. "Where have you been?" Lena asked their patient. "We thought you'd died in that drug war ten years ago."

"I'm real sorry about your clinic that day, doc," Ashe rasped through obvious pain. At Lena's insistence, Dani had injected enough pain meds and antipyretics to treat an entire ward, but as Ashe had repeatedly assured them would be the case, the drugs had no real impact. Despite this, he continued to find the strength to talk, albeit with increasing effort. "I know how much you cared for your work there. But you have to let me out of here, or you know that drug war you're talking about? It's going to land all over your doorstep, and I promise you it'll make that mess at your free clinic look like a playground."

Lena was torn. Dani knew Lena felt she owed Ashe for his endeavors long ago as her Samaritan, but the path was clear for a case like his. And that path did not lead away from a hospital.

Heaving a sigh, Lena sat by his bed. Dani watched her mentor's face as the woman observed Ashe's face from an angle such as that from which a child might regard a taller man.

Lena's face went suddenly white.

An uneasy moment passed before Lena spoke. In a hushed voice, she asked, "Ashe, did your... father... serve in the War? The Big One?"

Gritting his teeth, Ashe replied that his father had served in a war, and he guessed it was big enough.

Lena placed a palm gently on Ashe's fiery chest and stood up. She walked to the door.

Ashe groaned in frustration, agony, or both. Dani rushed out to meet Lena in the hallway.

"Lena, what is going on? What's the matter?"

"Seeing him there, with his head shaven, lying down like that... it reminded me of my father. In Buchenwald."

"Ashe reminded you of your father?"

"No. Well, yes. Only peripherally. He reminded me of another man: the soldier who carried my father out of the camp after the liberation. He looked exactly like Ashe. Exactly. I never saw it before, through the moppy hair and the beard. And I never saw him up close, at the clinic."

Lena slumped heavily against the wall outside Ashe's room, her arms folded tight across her chest like a scared little girl. Dani stood nearby, her expression soft as she watched her mentor stare back into Ashe's room. The hallway was quiet now. The nurses and orderlies had returned to their normal routines but cast furtive glances at their boss as she considered Ashe's fragile condition.

"I was a child," Lena began, her voice barely above a whisper, as though speaking the words aloud might break something inside her. "Twelve years old. The Americans came to liberate Buchenwald, but it was chaos after eight years of death and suffering. My father was frail. Too far gone to stand, let alone walk. I clutched his arm, crying and begging him to get up, but he couldn't move. And then... this soldier came."

Dani stayed silent, letting the story unfold, despite knowing how little time they had to decide Ashe's condition. The weight of Lena's tone anchored her to the moment.

"He was strong, fierce," Lena continued, her eyes seeing another time. "He scooped my father up like he weighed nothing. His face was set like stone. I clung to his web belt, terrified of being left behind. My father... he didn't make it to the truck. He died in that soldier's arms. But the way the man laid him down on the truck bed... so gentle, so reverent. He treated my father like he was still alive, still someone worth protecting."

Lena's voice caught, but she pushed on. "And the way that soldier spoke, Dani. He looked at the others, the ones loading the bodies, and he told them what would happen to them if they didn't show respect for this man. His voice was like the thundering voice of God himself; I'll never forget it. I remember thinking, 'I want to be like that. Fierce. Unyielding.'" She smiled at Dani, but the expression failed to reach her eyes.

"But it wasn't just that. It was the way he looked down at me after it was all over. His face softened, despite the sorrow in it. It was like... like he'd broken a promise he'd made to someone, and it crushed him."

Her gaze returned to Ashe. "And now, looking at him... it's the same face, Dani. The same pain, sorrow. The same unfulfilled promise." She paused, her voice barely audible.

"I don't know how it's possible. But it's him in there. It's him."

Dani stared at Lena. "Lena, that's…"

"I know how it sounds," Lena said, waving a hand to cut her off. "But I can't unsee it. It's weird, though. I thought he was older back in the seventies, but I guess I never really saw him close up."

Dani saw Lena's expression transform in an instant from remembered pain and bewilderment to a mask of determination. "He wants to go home? He goes home," she declared. "Go get him ready. I will obfuscate or destroy every record I can, and I have a couple orderlies who can be discreet. They'll help you transport Ashe wherever he needs to go."

She gestured to a nurse and gave the young woman a pair of names and terse instruction before continuing. "You're on sabbatical, effective immediately, Dani. Your only concern is his care. You'll have whatever equipment and supplies you need until he's either finished healing or done living."

Lena's eyes locked on Dani's. "I don't think he's long for this world," the older woman finished sadly. "And if he is, he'll never walk again. But it won't be because we didn't do our part."

Chapter 10 : SIGNAL FIRE

1976

DANI'S HEART THUDDED loudly, like a drum in her ears. The crawlspace felt tight and thick with dust and was heavy with the sharp smell of old wood. Every noise was amplified, the creaking floorboards above and the low murmur of voices she couldn't quite understand.

She held her breath, straining to listen. The jumbled words were incomprehensible, like she was trying to read a book with missing pages. Her hands trembled as she peered through the small crack provided by the rock Ashe had placed in the trapdoor. She caught glimpses of the room above.

Julio paced, his movements jerky, and she saw the frequent glint of his gun reflecting the lobby's dim light. Beyond him, her patients sat huddled, with the mother clutching the three little girls close near her son's gurney. Dani's breath caught, but she exhaled slowly, fighting to stay calm. For now, they were safe.

She leaned back against a rough wooden support, trying to slow her racing heart. Ashe had told her, "Wait for the signal," in a calm voice, as if this were just a scene in a movie. But this wasn't a movie; it was chaos. Ashe, with his calm voice and cryptic instructions, had disappeared, leaving her with little but a promise and the small bit of trust she had begun to have in him. Well, that and a silenced pistol. Maybe it was a movie after all.

Her fingers clenched around the small handgun's grip. What signal? What was he waiting for? Each second felt endless. Above, Julio's voice grew louder, sharp and angry, then faded again. Dani's stomach churned; her mind raced through possibilities. When it all came down to it, she was a surgeon, not a soldier; this wasn't her kind of battlefield. But that didn't matter now. What mattered was holding out long enough for the signal Ashe had promised, whatever it was.

Despite her predicament, she found her thoughts returning to this man that Lena called her "Samaritan." Who was this guy? Moreover, who did he *think* he was? Calling shots like some action hero and yanking the damsel around like she couldn't defend herself. Then, leaving her to do just that! So what if she was a pacifist? Yes, there were certainly occasions where violent action was necessary, but it should only and ever be as a last resort. Every possible legal and diplomatic action had to be exhausted before violence became a legitimate answer.

Ashe was a veteran, so she understood his perspective a bit, even if she didn't fully agree with it. She'd been in college at the University of Chicago in 1968. She'd been at Grant Park for the protests and was nearly yanked out of school by her father as a result.

Like her father, Dani was an awkward mix: a non-liberal pacifist. She looked at the gun in her hand, shiny in the small sliver of light from above. She wasn't in favor of violence but wouldn't shy away from it when it was needed.

Wait for the signal, he'd said. Like she even knew what the signal was going to be. Wait for the signal. Like he was Dirty Harry or something.

Dani smiled, despite her situation. Ashe was hardly Clint Eastwood. He was far too short to be some leading man in a Hollywood blockbuster. She shook her head. She needed to focus. Think about her next actions. She glanced through the floor, reassessing the room once again.

Think about her patients.

Don't think about Ashe.

Wait for the signal.

෬ • ෬

THE SIGNAL CAME with a loud and resounding crash. Dani glanced back along the way they'd come to see a flare of light as Ashe burst upward in the back of the building. He apparently shut the trapdoor immediately after emerging, since the light vanished as quickly as it had appeared.

Smart, she reflected. Preserving the secret of where he had come from, protecting her position.

Dani turned an eye to her own cracked trapdoor, although she barely needed visual confirmation for the sudden jumble of frenetic activity above her. Julio sent the majority of his remaining gang charging down the hallway after Ashe, who'd given away his location.

Watching this, Dani realized at once that Ashe's plan had been only partly successful. It missed being correct in one important point: Julio had sent his men after Ashe, rather than charging off himself. Although this tactic left just Julio himself and one other thug in the lobby, it also left Julio's hand cannon, a fact which did not fill her with enthusiasm.

Ashe had promised her Julio would lead the charge, being the most aggressive of the crew. Instead, the man had stayed back.

Whatever her next thought was on the topic was violently interrupted by gunshots and mayhem erupting from the back of the building.

Dani wrestled with her limbs to reposition herself in the small crawlspace as the battle raged closer. A glance showed Julio becoming increasingly agitated and waving his huge gun at the hostages. Dani began to fear for her patients as the situation deteriorated, and she scrambled to develop a plan of action.

Julio had his back turned. Dani placed a hand against the trapdoor but faltered. What would her father say about his daughter shooting a man from behind? What would she think of herself, shooting a man at all?

Her self-examination was interrupted as two of the men burst back into the room. They tried to stammer some sort of explanation in fast-paced Spanish, but Julio stopped the man by pistol-whipping him across the face and shoving him back to the doorway after Ashe. Dani noted that Julio was positioning the two men as a shield in front of him as the three of them stepped cautiously through the door into the clinic.

Dani decided there was no better time to make her move and pushed the trapdoor open as quietly as she could manage. She was halfway through to the lobby when a nail caught the leg of her jeans and she fell, alerting the remaining thug.

The punk spun toward her, wide-eyed, but his fear dissipated in a heartbeat as soon as he saw it was just Dani. He lifted his gun to point at her. Dani and the young gang member both froze, each locked in the other's sights. She mentally willed him to back down, but Dani knew she was at a disadvantage, lying on the floor as she was.

The thug's finger twitched on the trigger; Dani could see his knuckle whiten, seemingly in slow motion. Dani's mind raced for options she knew she didn't have. The moment stretched unbearably, her heartbeat hammering in her ears.

Then came the sound of a sickening thud and the thug's eyes flew wide. His smirk collapsed as his face went slack and he crumpled to the floor. Dani's eyes followed his gun clattering across the scuffed linoleum. Looking up from the pistol, Dani regarded her unexpected savior. Standing behind the thug on swaying, unsteady feet, was the teenage boy she had just stitched up. His face had a greenish hue and was shiny with sweat, but his grip was firm on Mrs. Hurston's green oxygen bottle, now dented deeply at the base.

For a moment, the room was utterly still, the only sound the labored breathing of the boy as he tried to stay upright. Then his mother rushed forward, her arms wrapping around him to steady his trembling frame. Mr. Jackson followed close behind her, his movements shaky. He reached past the cluster of little girls now swarming their older brother and grabbed the oxygen bottle from the boy's hands. Together, the boy's mother and tall, lanky old man eased the boy back onto his gurney. "Way to go, son," Jackson said with a wide smile. "You lie back down and let us handle it from here." The boy nodded weakly, his head falling against his mother's shoulder as she whispered frantic reassurances, her trembling hands wiping sweat from his brow.

Dani scrambled to her feet, her hands trembling as she grabbed the edge of the gurney to steady herself. Her gaze darted to the lobby door, beyond which Julio and his goons were searching for Ashe, and she bolted toward it. Gripping the handle, she slammed the door shut and leaned her weight against it, her breath coming in short, panicked bursts.

"Help me block this!" she barked, her voice sharp with urgency. Mr. Jackson and the boy's mother sprang into action, each grabbing a side of the heavy desk against the wall. Together, they heaved it toward the door, its legs screeching against the linoleum. The desk wasn't much, but it was the best choice they had.

A heavy metallic clang behind her made Dani flinch. She spun to see one of the tall metal oxygen tanks that had been delivered earlier rolling lazily across the room, the sound reverberating through the clinic like a gunshot. Her stomach sank. Julio would have heard that. *No time now; just move.*

"Everybody out!" she commanded, her voice tight as she shoved the boy's gurney into motion. The mother was already back at her son's side, one hand gripping the rail. He stirred, trying to sit up, but Dani pressed him back down. "Stay down! You're faster like this."

The glass double doors were just ahead. The boy's mother yanked the working door wide, but her two youngest daughters threw their weight against the other, their small hands slapping the unmoving glass.

"No, sweeties, that door's broke!" Dani shouted, breathless as she reached the entry. "It won't open! You just get outside."

The girls hesitated for only a moment before darting out into the night. Dani thrust the back of the gurney into Mr. Jackson's hands. "Take him!" she ordered, already spinning around toward her remaining patient.

Mrs. Hurston was still in her wheeled bed, her thin frame frail against the stark white sheets. Dani cursed under her breath, realizing the problem. The left-side door was completely jammed: rusted hinges frozen in place. Mrs. Hurston's bed was too wide to fit through the single working door, and there was no way she could walk, not in her condition.

Dani pushed against the bed, trying to angle it through the opening. The wheels caught, refusing to budge, and she felt her frustration boil over. In her frantic effort, her foot snagged another oxygen canister, sending it clattering to the floor. She stumbled, catching herself on the edge of the bed, and shoved again.

The bed slammed into the doorframe with a dull thud and lodged there just as a pounding sound erupted from the back of the lobby. Her stomach flipped. The noise grew louder, the slamming rhythmic and violent. Julio had heard her; he'd realized what was happening.

Dani froze, hearing the sound of fists on the door echoing through the clinic. Then she shook herself, her hands gripping the edge of Mrs. Hurston's bed. She had seconds. Maybe less.

"Come on," she whispered to herself, digging deep for strength she hoped she had somewhere. The pounding continued, relentless. She wasn't giving up. Not now.

ॐ • ॐ

"COME ON, DR. McKendree! That door ain't gonna hold 'em for long!" Mr. Jackson's voice boomed through the chaos. His lanky frame stretched across the doorway as he tried to maneuver Mrs. Hurston's bed through the jammed glass doors but his efforts were in vain; the bed was stuck fast. His face glistened with sweat and his arms trembled under the strain but he refused to stop. "We gotta move!"

The bed was wedged at an impossible angle between the warped doorframe and the narrow entryway. Dani looked between the bed and the doorway to the inner clinic, blocked by the desk they had pushed against it. The thud of boots and distant shouts echoed through the clinic, alerting her to how little time she had to get her patients to safety. Dani pushed herself off the floor, her vision swimming as she reached for Mr. Jackson's outstretched hand. Her fingers brushed his, but her heel slipped on the dented oxygen canister rolling beneath her. She stumbled hard, crashing to the floor.

Dani's eyes darted to the floor, catching a glint of metal. Her Walther. It lay just out of reach, the small, silenced pistol that looked woefully inadequate now. She hesitated, torn between helping with the bed and retrieving the gun, when the inner clinic door was hit hard from the other side and the desk groaned ominously against the scratched floor. The desk shifted slightly, and Dani's stomach clenched.

The door opened a foot, then stopped. Through the gap, Julio's arm thrust forward, the hand cannon in his grip looking grotesquely oversized in the confined space. He fired wildly into the room, each blast deafening in the narrow lobby. Wood splintered, and glass shattered as bullets tore through the walls and fixtures. Dani hit the floor again, her chest pressing into the cold linoleum tiles as adrenaline surged through her body. Ashe's assurances about Julio's inaccuracy with the Auto Mag suddenly meant less than nothing.

She crawled toward the Walther, her hands trembling as she grabbed it and rolled to her side. The silenced shots were soft and sharp in contrast to Julio's booming weapon, barely audible over the chaos. She squeezed the trigger three times, planting bullets into the wall near Julio's arm. The slide on the Walther locked back; it was empty. Her heart sank, but her return fire had done the trick, at least for now. Julio cursed loudly in Spanish, recoiling and yanking his arm back through the door.

Dani abandoned the Walther and scrabbled toward the outer doors. Mr. Jackson and the teen's mother were still working to free Mrs. Hurston, struggling with the bulky hospital bed. Dani climbed atop it next to her gasping patient, reaching back to free the latches holding the mattress to the frame.

"Go, go, go!" she barked, sliding out through the blocked door to help Mr. Jackson and the boy's mother. Together, they pulled against the mattress, trying to dislodge it from the doorframe. Mrs. Hurston, pale and frail, lay motionless atop it, her small oxygen tank rattling against the rails. "We've gotta get her out!" Dani shouted.

The mother shook her head, panic flashing in her eyes. "It's stuck!"

Bodies slammed against the inner door, making Dani's pulse quicken further. They didn't have time. "Forget the bed!" she snapped. "Get her on something smaller!"

"I'm trying!" Mr. Jackson growled, his wiry frame straining as he wrestled with the bulky mattress. It wouldn't budge, despite his efforts to fold Mrs. Hurston up in it like a taco.

"Here!" The teenage boy's voice cut through the noise, and Dani turned to see him wheeling his gurney toward the door. His face was pale, his movements shaky, but he pushed with determination. The gurney rattled to a stop, and the group scrambled to transfer Mrs. Hurston onto it. Her body was light but awkward, and her oxygen tank made the struggle no easier. Finally, the group got her through the door and secured. The gurney's small wheels creaked as Dani and the boy's mother pushed the bed-bound Mrs. Hurston toward the street.

"Get out of here!" Dani shouted, glancing over her shoulder. The feel of the night air finally penetrated Dani's awareness, hitting her face like a splash of cold water. Her heart pounded as she turned back toward the clinic, pausing just long enough to make sure the group was moving. Mr. Jackson stepped up, working with the mother to push Mrs. Hurston's gurney down the cracked sidewalk. The old woman was pale and unresponsive but safely out of harm's way. The teenage boy limped along behind them, one hand clutching his side as his sisters tugged at his sleeve, urging him forward.

The inner door was wide open now, the desk cast aside by the remaining gang members' combined effort. Julio stood framed in the doorway, his gun raised, his face twisted with rage. Dani's breath caught as he saw her and swung the big handgun toward her.

Then Ashe burst into the room.

He hit Julio with the force of a wrecking ball and the two men crashed to the floor in a violent tangle of limbs. Julio's gun roared, the deafening report filling the night. One of Julio's men, stepping through the door behind him, crumpled with a strangled cry, clutching his chest where his leader's stray bullet had struck.

From Dani's vantage point on the sidewalk, the fight was a brutal, chaotic blur. Ashe moved like nothing she'd ever seen, his body a blur of raw power and controlled chaos. Every motion was deliberate, brutal, efficient: a mix of techniques she couldn't name, blended with animal ferocity. Julio fought back with increasing desperation, his strikes wild and unfocused, but Ashe's intensity gave her a clear indication where the fight was headed.

Dani flinched as Julio managed to land a blow, the butt of his huge pistol connecting with Ashe's jaw in a sickening crack she could hear even outside. Ashe barely reacted, twisting Julio's arm in a motion so fluid it looked rehearsed. The handgun clattered to the floor, but Julio wasn't done. He lashed out with his other hand, clawing at Ashe's face before grabbing unsuccessfully to retrieve his gun.

Julio's desperation was palpable, his wild punches and kicks landing with diminishing effectiveness as Ashe bore down on him. Ashe's strikes were precise, each one targeting a weak point with surgical intent. Dani had never seen anything like it—like every fighting style she'd ever encountered had been fused into one seamless, savage technique. There was no hesitation, no wasted motion. Just pure, irresistible force, like a tornado.

But Julio refused to give up. With a growl of frustration, he twisted free long enough to grab his weapon. He fired wildly, the deafening reports echoing through the clinic. Dani gasped as two bullets tore into Ashe's body, sprays of blood spouting from his back, darkening his tattered shirt. Ashe staggered but didn't fall. With a bellow, his hands slammed into Julio with a force that made Dani wince.

The fight devolved into a frenzied tangle of limbs, the two men grappling across the floor slick with fresh blood. Julio's face twisted into a grimace of panic as he realized the end was near. With trembling hands, he raised the gun again and fired indiscriminately. The thug's last shots ricocheted wildly, shattering glass and striking the clustered oxygen and nitrous oxide canisters which had rolled and been kicked in the fracas to the wall near the clinic's ancient propane heater.

Dani's stomach dropped. She saw the flash before she heard it: a brilliant burst of light that illuminated the clinic's interior for a split second. Then came the explosion.

The fireball erupted with a thunderous roar, blasting out what remained of the shattered doors and windows. The wave of heat rolled over Dani like an inferno, searing her skin even from the relative safety of the sidewalk. She threw herself to the ground, shielding her head as debris rained down around her. The group she'd ushered out screamed in unison from a half block away, the teenage boy pulling his sisters close while Mr. Jackson shielded Mrs. Hurston with his body.

Everything fell silent except for the roar of the flames. Dani pushed herself up on shaky arms, her ears ringing and her chest tight with the acrid smoke filling the air. She stared at the clinic, her eyes brimming with tears.

The lobby was gone, replaced with a roaring furnace.

And Ashe was gone with it.

Chapter 11 : BAD COFFEE, WORSE COMPANY

PRESENT DAY

AMBER SHUT THE car door and looked at the old man in the passenger seat. Ashe fixed her rigidly with a steely glare.

"What?" She started the car, hearing its electric servos spool up a second before the rumble of the big gas engine.

"That was our third rest stop since we left the city."

"'The city?' Why don't you ever call it Los Angeles like the rest of us?" asked Amber.

"Because there ain't no angels in it. Don't change the subject. We're never going to get to Virginia if you have to stop every hundred miles. That's why we needed to drive this cramped museum piece in the first place."

"Well, when you gotta go, you gotta go, right?"

"You'd have to go a lot less often if you hadn't washed down a half bag of coffee beans with a gallon of water."

"It was two water bottles!" Amber exclaimed as she merged into the sparse late morning eastbound traffic along Interstate 40.

Suddenly, Amber turned to look at him. "Wait a minute! You drank half a dozen bottles! How is it *your* eyeballs aren't floating?"

"My metabolism must work better than yours," deadpanned Ashe.

"Okay, that's ridiculous. That's not how it works." She frowned. She glanced at him. "Wait... is it? No. No, it isn't. It can't be. Can it? No. No way." Amber's gaze flipped back and forth between the road and her traveling companion as quickly as her rapid-fire questions, fueled by her cumulative intake of caffeine over the past several hours.

The car's tires ate their next mile of pavement in relative silence.

"Is your bladder just really big, or what?"

Ashe groaned audibly. "Okay, shut up about my bladder already. Just drive."

Amber expressed her opinion wordlessly.

"And I'll rip that tongue out if you stick it out again," Ashe assured her. "Kill two birds with one stone."

Amber's tongue vanished. She frowned at him before asking, "Why don't you get back to that Spear of Destiny story you promised me?"

"Sure, why not?" Ashe paused. "That research you were doing on the so-called Spear of Destiny. Did you read about Hitler's first encounter with the Spear?"

"No, I don't think so."

"Alright, it'll come into play later on, so we'll start there. Hitler started out as kind of a loser who didn't have anything much going for him. He was beaten a lot as a child, had a crappy relationship with his father, but his mother babied him something fierce. He was a poor student across the board; never did well in school. Did even worse after his father died. When he turned eighteen, his mom died and he moved to Vienna. Applied to Vienna's Academy of Fine Arts and failed the entrance exam miserably; the Academy didn't want anything to do with him."

Amber took a sip from her water bottle. Ashe frowned but continued, "Hitler's devastated. Massages his bruised ego with the idea of German superiority while he struggles to survive as an artist in Vienna. Lives in a lice-infested dump of a boarding house. Escapes from the cold by constantly moping around the Hofburg Museum or the library, reading every musty old book he can get hold of. Mostly occult stuff and bogus paranormal crap throughout history. Junk filled his head with all manner of nonsense.

"One day, the museum opens an exhibit. It's the Holy Lance, a prized part of the Habsburg imperial treasure.

Hitler meets a guy at the exhibit. Named Stein, I think. Guy's some kind of expert on the Holy Grail. Well, Hitler catches Stein's ear and goes on and on, obsessed with his destiny to one day wield great power. Hitler told Stein that he saw the Holy Lance as the key to unlocking that future."

"Did it work?" Amber asked.

"No, of course not! Hitler was just getting an early start as history's most dangerous crackpot. Do you know anything at all about how the Nazis came into power?"

Amber didn't bother dissembling on the topic; she just shook her head, looking forward along the highway. She had learned by now that Ashe could be harsh and abrasive when he thought she should know something, but he was always willing to fill in the gaps in her knowledge.

"Alright, well, we're gonna get to that," said Ashe. "First though, Hitler gets exposed to all kinds of racist propaganda and super-national rhetoric in Vienna. He eventually goes to Munich and is conscripted into the army."

"So that's where he got started? He's in the army now?"

"Not yet. He was conscripted but determined to be unfit for service. A few months later, World War I breaks out, and he tries to enlist in the Bavarian army anyway. There's a clerical error somewhere, since he should have been returned to Austria as an Austrian citizen, and now, he's finally in the army, even if it's technically the wrong one. This is 1914. Couple years later, he's at the Battle of Fromelles."

Ashe was interrupted by a piercing ring from the phone that Amber had set up for him. He juggled the small device for a moment before Amber reached over and showed him how to answer a call.

"Anyway, Fromelles. That's where he killed me the first time." Ashe finished his thought before shifting his attention to the person on the other end of the call.

Ashe lifted the phone toward his ear and then commenced a strange dance, placing the phone to his ear, pulling it away to look at it, placing it back. Frustrated, Amber reached over and stabbed a finger at the screen. He batted her away and their slapping hands fought for dominance. "Just put it on speaker!" she commanded.

Ashe's face demonstrated that he had no idea what she meant. Amber finally managed to poke the speaker button on the screen and Owen Spirit's voice came from the device. "Ashe? Are you there? What are you talking about? Who killed you?"

"Nevermind. Different conversation." Ashe glowered at Amber. Shifting his attention to the call, he asked, "What do you want?"

"We're at LAX, getting on the plane," said Spirit. "Where are you guys?"

"Just crossed over into Arizona," Ashe told him.

Amber looked at Ashe. "How did you know that? The map's on my phone!"

"There was a sign. You know, the one sign you didn't jabber about," Ashe snarked.

"Look, you two argue on your own time; we're boarding," admonished the lawyer's voice. "I just sent you a PDF of the schematics for Task's Ashburn data center. I need—"

"Sent me a what?" Asked Ashe.

"A PDF. A file. Geez, Ashe, catch up! Amber will help out. I need you to get after reviewing those plans and figuring out a few possible solutions if we can't get into the servers in a more normal way."

"Cool!" Amber smiled. "This is gonna be just like a heist movie!"

 howmuchwood • howmuchwood

AMBER WAS PRACTICALLY dancing in her seat in need of a restroom by the time they passed Albuquerque. She'd done her best to not stop more than absolutely necessary as Ashe studied building schematics on the screen of his phone. He'd been so absorbed in his studies that he hardly grunted during the one stop she'd had to make five hours ago.

She tapped the brakes, hitting her indicator to finally exit the roadway.

Ashe looked up at last, pulled from his screen by the slowing car. He looked around. "We're east of Albuquerque."

Amber marveled again at his ability to know where he was. She was sure that Ashe had not looked up at any of the signs for hours, not even the one she had seen alerting her to the presence of a roadside truck stop.

"Yeah, by about an hour. I made it as far as I could; we're in the middle of nowhere. We may as well fill up with gas, too."

"Good. How are you for sleep?" Ashe asked her.

Amber pulled into the truck stop and they rolled up to the gas pumps. "I'm good," she told him. "Those coffee beans of Task's are a-ma-zing. I'm pretty rumbly, though. I could use some food that doesn't come in a wrapper."

Ashe looked at the clock on the dashboard, and over at the empty truck stop building. It boasted a restaurant. "Yeah, me too. We can eat."

Amber stepped out of the car and stood with some effort. Sitting in a sports car for over twelve hours had taken a toll. Standing by Ashe as he grabbed the lever for the gas pump, she noticed that he was only using a single crutch now, rather than the pair. She explained her need for a restroom and rushed off, taking cash to pay for the gas inside.

Several minutes later, she walked slowly back to the car. Bracing her hands on her hips, Amber arched backwards to stretch her back. She folded her arms over the top of the car and looked at Ashe.

He looked back. "What?"

"You were telling me about the first time Hitler killed you?" she reminded him. "You kinda left me hanging to look at those schematics."

"Yeah, okay then." Ashe grabbed the nozzle of the gas pump and put it into the car with a click. "You remember that song about losing my legs in Suvla?"

Amber frowned, remembering. "Sure. That was World War I?"

"It was," he replied, relieved she'd learned something. "You were in the Australian army, right?"

"At the time. So, after Suvla, I was sent back to Australia and spent six, seven months healing up. I reenlisted and sailed out again, part of the new Fifth Division forming up in Egypt. We shipped out through Marseilles to Fromelles and joined the two other divisions already there.

"The Battle of the Somme was already underway, and the British were taking it pretty hard on the chin. The higher-ups shuffled all of us all over the place, and we ended up finishing our training at Blaringhem."

A half-smile teased from the corners of Amber's mouth. "You were still in training?"

"Well, not me," he said. Ashe looked indignant. "I knew what I was doing, of course. But overall? Yeah, we were the greenest of the green. The most inexperienced of the Australian divisions in France, and of course, we were the first to see major action. Been there a week, and the Germans had had plenty of time to dig in. They cut us to pieces. Five thousand Aussies lost in twenty-four hours.

"I saved most of my unit, but eventually I was pinned by two German machine gun squads at once. They dropped me there on the field in no-man's land and I started the long, slow crawl back to my boys."

"And Hitler was on one of those machine gun squads?"

"No, Hitler was a message runner. Bavarian Reserve. During a lull, he's sent to deliver an update to his superiors or something. Dang fool runs out in the open, and trips over me. He *trips* over me. I couldn't believe it. So he scrambles backward, looking completely spooked. I didn't have a lot to go on at the moment, even if I had a weapon within reach, which I didn't. Adolf's eyes are big as saucers, and that stupid spiky helmet is all crooked on his head, and all I can do is look at him. A minute or two of that, and he catches up to the situation: I'm basically helpless. So what's he do? He pulls his pistol and puts nine millimeters of lead through my neck."

The gas gauge stopped pumping with a loud "clunk." The car's tank was full.

"He shot you? In the neck?" Amber grimaced.

"Yeah, I think he was aiming for my head. Point-blank range and he missed. But it did give him the chance to crawl over and enjoy watching me as I bled out."

Like so many times before, Amber had no idea how to respond. She just watched him replace the gun-shaped handle in the pump with a clatter.

"Hungry? I need food," Ashe stated bluntly and got back into the car.

The Corvette rumbled quietly to life as Amber started it and they rolled across the lot, avoiding potholes that yawned like craters in the dim light. The place was nearly deserted, save for a couple of big rigs parked along the edge of the property, their cabs dark. Amber pulled the car into a far corner, where the pool of overhead light barely reached. The fluorescents above buzzed faintly, their glow flickering like a dying pulse.

Stretching as she stepped out of the cramped car again, Amber rolled her shoulders. "Wow. Twelve hours. My spine is, like, permanently shaped like a bucket seat now." She ran a hand through her unruly red hair and grabbed a pair of coffee beans from the crumpled bag on the dash, popping them into her mouth. Crunch.

The truck stop's flickering neon sign barely illuminated the cracked asphalt outside the building. The building itself was a squat, tired structure, its facade a patchwork of yellowed stucco and sun-bleached advertisements. For some reason, Amber's attention was drawn to a can of Spam in the store window. Its label had faded in the sun, bleaching all the red dye from the label and making the meat concoction even less appealing than it typically was. The diner lights glowed a sickly blue-white that cast elongated shadows over the dusty pavement. Inside, a few rows of metal shelves held cheap plastic trinkets: dreamcatchers made in China, faded postcards of Route 66 which ran along their path down Route 40, and racks of off-brand sunglasses with chalky lenses. The whole place smelled like old fryer grease and stale cigarette smoke, even from outside.

Two men emerged from the diner as Ashe exited the car. They were the only other customers, judging by the empty lot, and they moved with the slow, unbothered gait of long-haul truckers who had seen too many late nights fueled with too many bad cups of coffee. The first one was quite thick around the middle, his gut stretching a faded T-shirt graced with a pin-up girl on a Harley. He squinted at the Corvette as they walked past, then stopped short.

"Well, ain't that a shame," he drawled, shaking his head. "Some moron took a '63 split-window and slapped a bad eighties paint job on her." His voice carried the tone of a man who took personal offense at such things, as though he'd just stumbled upon a desecrated grave. "Look at this thing, Homer. Dang thing looks like my kid's skate shoes."

Ashe ignored the man, shutting his car door with a dull thunk. He turned toward the diner, seemingly intent on finding something resembling food before they got back on the road. Amber, however, lingered, casually leaning against the car as she smirked. "Bad eighties paint job?" she echoed. "Oh, you mean the checkerboard? It's kind of growing on me."

The first trucker scoffed. "Growin' on ya like a fungus, maybe. It's a tragedy." His voice was laden with judgment, but he seemed content to grumble about his opinion rather than escalate further.

The second man, Homer, taller and thinner with a grease-streaked baseball cap pulled low over his forehead, stopped beside his friend and let out a short, derisive laugh. "Aw, you idiot," he muttered, shaking his head. "Those ain't paint squares. They're solar panels or somethin'. I seen stuff like that before."

Amber tilted her head, gesturing at the tall trucker with a pointed finger and a sarcastic wink. "Ding ding ding! We have a winner."

The round trucker made a disgusted noise and spit a gob of brown tobacco juice onto the pavement. "That's even worse," he sneered. "Ruinin' a classic 'Merican automobile to push your little tree-huggin' agenda. Bet it don't even sound right anymore."

Amber grinned and leaned toward Ashe. "I think we just got called 'greenies.'" She turned to the man, "Oh, it sounds right." Then back to Ashe, "Should we start it back up and pop their eardrums?"

Ashe ignored her. He stepped past the men toward the diner entrance, and Amber reluctantly followed, gloating with a casual wave over her shoulder. "Enjoy your drive, boys."

The first trucker just shook his head, muttering about the decline of civilization as Amber and Ashe walked away. The second trucker glared after them as well, but neither made a move to follow.

Amber nudged Ashe with her elbow as they stepped inside. "I think we really won them over."

Ashe exhaled through his nose. "Let's just eat." Navigating the racks of stale candies and useless merchandise, Ashe made a beeline for the diner area of the building.

Amber grinned. "You really don't like people, huh?"

"I like people fine," Ashe muttered. "Just not sure I like people here."

Amber chuckled, aimlessly spinning a rack of dusty keychains as she passed it. "Well, lucky for you, this place looks full of empty."

ᕯ • ᕯ

THE TRUCK STOP diner was silent except for the faint hum of the old ceiling fan struggling against the stagnant night air. A single fly buzzed lazily between the neon "OPEN 24 HOURS" sign in the window and the dented "PLEASE SEAT YOURSELF" sign near the counter. Amber drummed her fingers on the sticky tabletop, casting a glance toward the counter, where two coffee pots sat untouched. They had been waiting for nearly fifteen minutes, but no waitress had appeared.

"Maybe they don't know we're here," she muttered, stretching her arms over her head before slumping forward dramatically.

"Okay, even that dump you work in isn't this bad," grumped Ashe.

"You better say that!" she said, but then softened. "I guess they're short-handed. While we're waiting, tell me more of the story. Did you get back to the war after that? After Hitler shot you?"

"Not that war, no. I migrated back to England in the twenties. An old comrade from Fromelles, British guy, he looks me up and convinces me to join Military Intelligence. Says they need somebody with experience like I had."

"Somebody with experience? If only he knew the whole story, right?" Amber smiled.

Ashe grunted, then continued. "I suppose. He knew a bit, though. Some of us were closer than brothers. Happens under those circumstances. Anyway, I find myself part of Admiral Sinclair's Section D in MI6."

"What? MI6? You were a spy? Did you know Ian Fleming?"

"Ian Fleming? Why?" Ashe asked her. "Big fan, are you? Have you read any of his books?"

"Well, no, of course not." Amber scowled. She knew what was coming next.

"Then shut up. Anyway, Section D work was a lot of fun, but let's skip ahead. In 1931 I got sent to Berlin. Officially, I was there as a low-level liaison, working with Frank Foley to exchange information about Communism with officials in the Gestapo. Behind the scenes, I—"

"Wait a second!" Amber interrupted. "You worked with the Gestapo? What was that about?"

"If anything, it was about diplomacy, and that's not my strong suit. But you have to keep in mind that history can look completely different before it becomes history. It was a weird time, for sure."

"What were you really there to do?"

"If you can cool it with the questions, I'll tell you," growled Ashe.

Amber held up a palm. "Tell me in a minute. Here comes the manager."

A wiry blonde man in a grease-stained apron hurried toward them, a coffee pot in one hand. "Sorry, folks. Sorry, sorry," he said breathlessly, quickly filling their mugs. "My waitress went home sick, and I'm all that's left. Makes me cook, waiter, dishwasher, and manager, and I got wrapped up trying to fix a clog in the sink. I guess I'm the handyman too."

Amber perked up, scooting forward. "You mean you're running this place solo?"

Jim—his name was stitched on his apron—nodded. "Trying to, anyway. Just for a few hours, till the night girl can get here. If she even shows."

Amber glanced around the empty diner. It wasn't exactly Grand Central Station, but a place like this would still have occasional customers. Late-night truckers, weary travelers, and any other night owls who preferred bad coffee and greasy eggs to sleep.

"Well, tonight's your lucky night," Amber said, stretching her arms forward and bridging her knuckles palm outward to crack audibly. "I work at a place just like this. I'll help out."

Jim's eyebrows flew upward. "You serious?"

"As a heart attack," Amber replied. "I can pour coffee, sling hash, and pretend to like people with the best of them."

Jim hesitated for half a second before nodding. "You do that, your ticket's on the house."

Ashe was glaring directly at Amber. He tapped his left wrist with the first two fingers of his right hand.

She ignored him. "You might wanna reconsider," she told Jim. "This guy—" she jerked a thumb at Ashe, "—eats like a black hole."

Jim scoffed. "Young lady, I'll take that chance if it gets me a waitress." Before Amber could respond, the diner door swung open, and a pair of men walked in, their presence shifting the atmosphere immediately.

They were rough-looking: denim jackets that had seen better days, boots heavy against the floor, the kind of men who looked like they lived on the road and didn't particularly like company. One had a thick beard and tired eyes; the other, younger and wiry, scanned the room like he was casing the place.

Jim took their order and muttered something about getting the grill hot. He disappeared into the kitchen. Amber, however, was eyeing the coffee pot as Jim replaced it on the warmer. "No offense," she said to Ashe, picking up her mug and taking a sip before making a face, "but this is... undrinkable."

"So what? The place serves bad coffee," Ashe muttered.

"Not anymore! This calls for emergency intervention." Rushing out to the car, Amber hustled back in with her bag of top-shelf beans from Task's office.

She took it behind the counter, Ashe shook his head as she ground the beans with an industrial hum. The smell of fresh coffee soon flooded the stale air, causing Jim to pause from the grill and raise an approving eyebrow.

The two new arrivals had settled into a booth, and Amber approached her first customers, pot in hand. "Coffee?"

The bearded man nodded, but the younger one grinned at her, leaning an elbow on the table. "Well, you're a sight for sore eyes."

Amber smiled, unbothered. "If your eyes are sore, you could try sleeping instead of hanging out in sketchy diners at one in the morning."

The older man chuckled, but the younger one's grin faded a bit. "Sassy, huh?"

"You have no idea," Amber said smoothly, topping off their mugs before walking away. Jim rang a bell from the kitchen, indicating Ashe's order was up.

Passing Ashe's table, she glanced at him. He had watched the exchange with an unreadable expression. She could sense the quiet storm gathering behind his scowl.

"You good?" she asked as she returned to the table and slid into the booth across from him. She placed his plate in front of him and grabbed a slice of bacon from it.

"Fine," Ashe muttered, picking up his fork. "You don't need to take tables. Let Jim handle them."

Amber waved her purloined bacon in dismissal, munching. "Relax. I can handle a couple of truckers."

Ashe grunted but said nothing, instead focusing on the food. Amber watched, fascinated, as the contents of the plate vanished with inhuman efficiency. After a few minutes, he pushed back the plate. "More?" she asked.

Ashe nodded, draining his glass of water.

"I know I keep saying this, but you eat a lot."

Ashe wiped his mouth with a napkin. "Healing takes fuel."

Amber shook her head, muttering something about the failure of medical science before getting up to check on Jim. The pair of customers was served and left after a while, and a second pair entered. Nothing remarkable, but Ashe watched them nonetheless. He barely said anything when they left after a light meal, but an hour later, when a third pair arrived, his focus sharpened.

In between helping customers and feeding Ashe, she had hung out at the table with him. Amber noticed him now, squinting in thought. "What's up?" she asked.

"One of them was here before," Ashe said, his voice low.

Amber glanced over. It was true: one of the new arrivals was the bearded man from the first pair. But now, he was wearing a different jacket.

"So? Maybe he's still hungry, like you," Amber said, unconcerned. Ashe had just finished his third plate of food.

"New jacket," Ashe mumbled.

"Yeah. Maybe he got something on the other one."

Ashe didn't look away. "Or maybe he wanted to change how he looked."

Amber rolled her eyes. "Not everything is a conspiracy, old man."

Ashe said nothing, but his attention remained on the men until they eventually got a phone call. The bearded man dropped a twenty on the table to cover their coffee and toast, and they left.

An hour and a half and two more plates of food later, Amber's replacement finally arrived, thankfully before Ashe could drain the diner's supplies. The girl, maybe a year or two younger than Amber, already looked haggard and exhausted. Her blonde hair was wadded into a messy bun, and dark circles lined her eyes. As she tied her apron, she gave Amber a grateful look. "Jim told me you filled in for me. You have no idea how much I appreciate this. I couldn't get hold of my sister right away, and she had to finish up her factory shift before she could watch my baby. He's just now sleeping through the night."

Amber's heart went out to the girl. "You're raising a newborn and working night shifts? That's rough."

"Gotta do what you gotta do," the waitress smiled weakly and went back to clock in.

Ashe stood up without a word, reaching into his jacket. Amber watched as he pulled out the thick stack of bills Spirit had supplied them. Without hesitation, he counted out ten hundred-dollar bills and placed them under his empty coffee cup.

Amber stared. "That's a thousand-dollar tip."

Ashe met her eyes. "I know."

"Where's my tip?" she asked with a grin.

"Here's a tip: it's time to go."

Amber waved at Jim, who waved to thank her, and followed Ashe out of the diner. As they headed toward the convenience store area, they passed three men walking back toward the diner area. Ashe's eyes flicked toward them.

"They're back," he said quietly.

Amber shrugged. "Hungry again?"

At the counter, a scrawny, pimple-faced cashier was talking to the other two familiar customers. Ashe observed them for a second before exiting the building, "That worker looks shifty."

"Everybody looks shifty to you," Amber snorted, following him out into the early morning air. "You're paranoid, Ashe."

"Maybe."

❧ • ❧

AMBER TUGGED THE Corvette's door handle, then froze. "Wait a second," she said. "I forgot my coffee beans."

Ashe, already settling into the cramped passenger seat with a sigh, turned his head toward her, his expression a mask of irritation. "It's three in the morning, Amber."

"I know, I know," she said quickly, already stepping back from the car. "But I just made one pot in there. The rest of the beans are still in there, and I'm not leaving them behind. I'll be quick, promise."

Ashe frowned and slumped against his seat, clearly resigned. "Fine. Hurry it up."

Amber jogged toward the door, yawning as she pushed into the convenience store. The fluorescent lights buzzed overhead. The cashier was gone; probably on a smoke break. She barely noticed as she weaved between shelves, heading toward the diner entrance.

The moment she stepped inside, she froze.

Jim and the night waitress sat on the stools at the bar, rigid and wide-eyed. The waitress clutched a coffee pot with both hands, knuckles white, as if she were considering using it as a weapon. Jim looked like he wanted to sink into the floor.

Amber's stomach twisted and she looked around the small diner.

Three of the men from earlier were back, their postures casual and relaxed in a way that worried Amber. One leaned against the counter, fiddling with a toothpick between his fingers. The second sat on the far end of the bar, legs stretched out like he owned the place. The third, the one with the beard who had changed his jacket earlier, turned slightly at the sound of her entry.

"Well, well," he murmured. His eyes flicked over Amber. "If it isn't the pinch hitter with the Corvette."

The second man snorted, his lip curling. "That thing ain't a Corvette no more. That paint job is a crime." He tilted his head, giving Amber an up-and-down look that made her skin crawl. "But I'd take the little red one for a spin."

Amber's feet shifted backward toward the door.

That was a mistake.

A claw-like hand clamped down on her upper arm, jerking her back. The shifty store clerk, the one Ashe had seen earlier, materialized behind her with an ugly grin.

"Not so fast, sweetheart," he said, pulling her into the diner.

Her breath caught as she felt something hard press against her ribs: his other hand, tucked inside his jacket. A gun, she presumed.

Jim swallowed hard, shifting slightly on his stool, but new jacket guy—Amber was starting to figure he was the leader—shot him a warning glance. "Stay put, old man," he said.

Amber's brain reeled. She'd walked straight into some kind of a mess. Typical. A robbery? Extortion? It didn't matter. Before she could say a word, the front door jingled again.

Ashe.

He stepped inside, his crutch tapping lightly against the floor as he took in the scene. His face remained inscrutable, but Amber could see the shift in his posture: the barely perceptible tension in his shoulders, the way his fingers flexed against the crutch handle. She knew from experience what would come next.

"Let her go," Ashe said evenly.

The leader smirked. "Well now, you don't look like you're in much of a position to make demands, geezer." His tone was dismissive. "You should've stayed in your car."

Amber felt the grip on her tighten as the store clerk started to pull her toward the bar. Ashe moved to intercept—

And crumpled to the floor in a heap. Echoes of a sickening metallic crack rang through the empty diner as Ashe's crutch skidded across the linoleum.

Behind Ashe stood another man Amber hadn't seen before, holding an aluminum baseball bat. He exhaled, rolling his shoulder. "Well, that was easy."

Chapter 12 : GHOST HOUSE

1988

"THANK YOU FOR getting me away from the hospital," whispered Ashe.

His voice was barely audible, a rattle shaped into words, but Dani had learned by now to recognize the difference between lucidity and delirium. He was lucid, for the moment. That wouldn't last long. His fever had peaked at 108 and keeping him conscious was a delicate balancing act. She had discovered that opening the V-track controller on his IV all the way brought him back from the edge, but if she restricted the flow even slightly, he tanked.

She frowned, glancing at the clear saline dripping steadily through the tube. At this rate, she was going to need to rig a catheter. The thought made her grimace. She should have asked one of the male orderlies to handle that before they left for Sacred Cross to retrieve more supplies. *You've been away from medicine too long if you're having girlishly embarrassed thoughts like that.*

"You're welcome," she murmured, checking the IV site at his arm. "Just don't make me regret it. Or Lena. The amount of juggling she had to do to keep you anonymous and get you out of there is nothing compared to what we'll both have to do if you die."

Ashe didn't respond. His head tilted slightly against the pillow. His shaved scalp was still mottled with bruising from the injury, but the skin pale beneath showed the faint shadows of regrowth.

Dani sighed and stepped back, finally taking her first real look around the room.

The row house felt... wrong. Not in the immediate sense: no threats, no lurking danger. But something about it unsettled her.

The room itself had good bones, the kind of structure that suggested thoughtful design beneath layers of neglect. The walls, unadorned, stretched clean and unbroken except for where the sofa had been positioned as a makeshift hospital bed. It was a large sectional, repurposed out of necessity. Beside it, an IV rack stood like a sentry, the fluid bags swaying slightly from her examination of the IV lines. That was all that had been touched; the main room of the first floor. The rest of the place sat like a piece of history.

Dani turned slightly, taking in the armchairs covered with drop cloths, their draped forms squatting like forgotten ghosts. In the dim lighting, she could make out a faint sheen of dust collecting along the fabric's folds. The boxes stacked haphazardly nearby were a sharp contrast: new, cluttered with medical supplies Lena had insisted on sending. They were the only things in the room that betrayed any evidence of recent habitation.

Beyond the sofa, a partial wall divided the space. It extended across two-thirds the width of the room, unmarked by art or photographs. No shelves, no decoration, no indication that anyone cared it was there. It was a divide, not a display.

Through the opening, her gaze fell on the dining table. It was also draped in cloth, but the cloth there had been disturbed, pushed back enough to accommodate a single chair, the others stacked upside down like abandoned chess pieces. Someone—Ashe, she figured—had carved out just enough space to sit, to eat, to exist in solitude. Dani's throat tightened.

The air felt thick, like a house that had fallen into neglect waiting for its owner to come home. She'd been in plenty of houses, apartments, even sterile safehouses during her time with the Bureau, but something about this space felt different. It was a space carved out for someone who expected to be alone. *This isn't a home*, she thought. *It's a bunker. A waiting room. A place to hide, not to live.*

She turned back to Ashe, watching his chest rise and fall in slow, even intervals. Even now, battered and unconscious, he seemed out of place here. Or maybe it was the other way around. Maybe this house was out of place around him.

"Will you be back tomorrow?" Ashe asked.

Pulled from her reverie, Dani smiled. She hadn't noticed him waking. "Back tomorrow? How do you figure you'll do without me here? No way, buster, you signed up for the full package. I'm staying here until you're stabilized and we can figure out how to have you cared for."

"You mean until I'm back up on my feet." Ashe's optimism tore at her heart, but his stubbornness was growing increasingly frustrating. Again, now wasn't the time for that discussion.

Dani checked Ashe's forehead. It was still so hot she could barely touch it.

"Good thing you're not tall," she said with a smile. "Leaves this half of the sofa for me." Dani was referring to the unused half of the sectional that had been pushed aside to make room for supplies.

"No," Ashe demanded, eyes closing. "Danged if you're sleeping on the couch. Take a bedroom upstairs. There's three."

Dani could sense that Ashe was nearing the end of this lucid period. Best to placate him and then decide what to do. "Which one should I take?" she asked.

"Any of 'em. All of 'em. Take turns like Goldilocks if you want to. I don't really use 'em when I can climb the stairs, let alone right now."

Ashe's voice trailed off, and his labored breathing became more regular. Dani let out a slow breath in time with his, watching the IV drip before stepping away. There was nothing more she could do for the moment.

Looking at Ashe, she considered the extent of his injuries. Her mind always came back to that: how he had been injured so badly, and yet remained optimistic about his chances. How she at times, almost believed him.

She ran her practiced fingers around the edges of a bandage, ensuring it was placed well. In doing so, she encountered an unexpected lump and peeled back the gauze to examine it.

Ashe's silver locket. The one he had so tightly gripped in the operating room. Somehow, not having use of his hands—of anything, really—he had managed to place that locket against his chest, inside the gauze of his bandages. She was unsure how he'd gotten it squirreled away in the bandages, but when a person is determined enough to do something, they'll find a way.

Dani slid the locket gently out and opened it.

A woman grinned shyly at her in faded sepia tones. The photograph was undoubtedly very old, its crackled surface and yellowed edges seeming to date back to sometime in the last century. Ashe's grandmother? Whatever the case, it was very important to the man. She slid it back into place and patted the gauze down.

Dani took a slow circuit through the row house. Her steps were measured, careful not to let the old floorboards creak too loudly. The house felt solid beneath her feet. Aged, but enduring. She ran a hand along the banister as she climbed, feeling the worn smoothness of the wood. This place had been built to last, probably sometime in the early 1900s. The neighborhood, however, had changed around it.

She had noted that much as they arrived. Ashe's home was one of four row houses, second from the left in a block that had seen better days, and seen them long ago. The other three: first, third, and fourth, were unmistakably abandoned, their windows boarded up, their doors sealed against intrusion. Condemned, left to rot. And yet Ashe remained, a lone holdout in a place most had long since fled.

Her father had mentioned the Auburn Gresham neighborhood on occasion; he'd watched its transformation in real time. Once a solidly white, middle-class community, it had flipped demographically in a short period. Despite the speed of that shift, the area hadn't suffered quite as much from overt racial tension as some of its neighboring communities. The decline of the buildings around Ashe's house was impossible to miss, however: worn-out businesses, patched graffiti. But Ashe's house, despite its location, made sense for him. It was a place on the fringe, still standing where others had crumbled, a fortress in the middle of nowhere.

She walked through the upper floors, noting how much the row house matched his personality: spartan, functional, deliberately impersonal. Two bedrooms on the third floor, another on the fourth. A single couch sat in the fourth-floor hallway, along with a desk and chair in the adjoining bedroom. No warmth, no sign that anyone lived here. Just space, occupied and used, but unloved.

Downstairs, she found a storage area tucked away at the back of the lowest floor. Stacks of boxes teetered in uneven piles, their labels faded with time. A few 55-gallon drums sat against the wall, covered in tarps. She hesitated, looking over the clutter. There was something about it that struck her as less like storage and more like... stuff left behind. Whatever was in those boxes had been placed there long ago and forgotten.

Returning to the main floor, she paused near the dining room, where a wide bookcase stood against the wall. She ran her fingers over the dust-free spines, surprised by what she found. Bibles in multiple languages, some so old they looked like they belonged in a museum. Engineering books, poetry, philosophy, all in a variety of tongues and spanning centuries. But no fiction, which, upon reflection, didn't surprise her. What did surprise her was the lack of general history books. Given the other content, she would have expected them. Their absence seemed deliberate.

Her fingers traced the rich leather binding of an old volume before stepping away, making her way back to the living room where Ashe lay. His face was damp with sweat, his chest rising and falling in a steady but labored rhythm. The fever still raged in him, hotter than any body should be able to endure.

She couldn't explain it.

She wasn't sure she wanted to try.

But despite everything—his impossible condition, the madness of sneaking him out of a hospital, the way his body was tearing itself apart and healing at the same time—she was starting to believe him. Maybe it was the conviction in his voice when he was lucid. Maybe it was his sheer stubborn refusal to die.

All she could do now was watch and wait. Care for his needs. Keep a phone nearby, of course.

For now, she had a job to do.

Whatever ghosts lingered in Ashe's house, they would wait.

                                      ✥ • ✥

THE SUN HUNG low in the sky, stretching the shadows of the row houses long across the cracked pavement. The heat of the day had withered into a stagnant warmth, and the air smelled faintly of hot brick, dry weeds, and distant cooking grease.

Dani had taken advantage of Ashe's relative stability to slip out and retrieve her belongings from the hotel she had initially checked into. Two days. Just two days ago had she arrived back in Chicago. Seemed like a lifetime already. Regardless, it looked like she had accommodations for the duration of Ashe's recovery, whatever form that would take.

Dani stepped out of the taxi, her suitcase bumping against her leg as she shut the door and took in the street again.

The block looked as lifeless as it had that morning. Worse, now, in the approaching twilight. The row houses stood shoulder to shoulder, ramshackle and abandoned, their windows boarded like patched eye sockets. Paint peeled in long, jagged strips. A broken downspout hung from the third house, swaying slightly in the evening breeze, knocking rhythmically against the weathered brick. The block was the kind of place that had stopped hoping a long time ago.

Except for Ashe's house.

Not that looked much better than the others: just as weathered, just as empty from the outside. But at its base, along the narrow, chipped concrete steps, clusters of white lilies stood like quiet sentries. Their stark petals glowed faintly in the dim light, an unexpected softness against the backdrop of urban decay. They'd been planted there with intent, tended with care. It wasn't much, but it was something.

Dani hoisted her bag onto her shoulder and started for the stairs.

A small figure stood at the foot of them, looking up at Ashe's door.

The boy was young, his frame thin but sturdy in a pair of too-short jeans and a faded T-shirt that had once been bright yellow. His sneakers were scuffed, the rubber-capped toes dirty. He had his hands in his pockets, standing with the sort of self-contained stillness that children sometimes have when they're thinking very hard about something.

Dani paused a step away and, careful not to loom over him, sat down on the lowermost stair.

"Hello," she said.

The boy turned his head just slightly. "Hello."

"What's your name?"

"I'm Jaxi."

"Well! Hello, Jaxi! My name's Dani." She smiled. "Our names rhyme a bit, don't they?"

Jaxi squinted at her like she'd just said something deeply incorrect. "Nah, not really. To rhyme, the vowel sounds and the cons'nant sounds gotta be the same. X and N ain't the same."

Dani blinked, momentarily caught off guard. "Is that so?"

"Yeah. Mr. Ashe, he been teachin' me about poetry."

Dani raised an eyebrow. "He has, has he?"

Jaxi nodded, looking proud. "Uh-huh."

"How old are you, Jaxi?"

"I'm six." He straightened a little, as if that indicated he'd passed a very important milestone.

Dani studied him, impressed. "That's a sharp mind you've got there."

Jaxi's face scrunched up for a moment in thought, then he tilted his head. "You gonna be Mr. Ashe's new girlfriend?"

The question took Dani so completely by surprise that she nearly laughed. Instead, she managed to compose herself. "Does Mr. Ashe already have a girlfriend?"

"Nah." Jaxi kicked a loose pebble, sending it skittering down the sidewalk. "Mr. Ashe ain't never had a girlfriend. He's always alone."

Dani felt a tightening in her chest.

Jaxi continued, as if this was all very matter-of-fact. "I asked him about it once, but he said he can't help us little kids if he had some lady tellin' him what to do like my mom does me."

For the first time since they'd started talking, Jaxi's expression changed. His eyes narrowed slightly, a flicker of suspicion crossing his small face. Dani got the distinct impression that she owed him an answer.

"No, no," she said, shaking her head. "I'm not Mr. Ashe's girlfriend. I'm... well, I'm kind of his doctor."

Jaxi looked skeptical. "Mr. Ashe don't like doctors."

"He's going to have to deal with this one," Dani said dryly. "Jaxi, Mr. Ashe will need to stay inside for a while. Maybe a long time."

Jaxi's brow furrowed. "Why?"

Dani hesitated, then said gently, "Jaxi, Mr. Ashe got hurt."

The boy didn't look particularly surprised.

"Yeah, Mr. Ashe, he gets hurt a lot."

It was Dani's brow that furrowed now. "Oh?"

"Yeah, he gets hurt a lot," Jaxi repeated. "But he always gets better, so he says it's alright. Mr. Ashe says he's different a little bit. Sometimes he does things to help folks and gets hurt, but he always says he'll get better real quick, and he does."

Dani's pulse ticked up slightly. "What kind of work does Mr. Ashe do?"

Jaxi tilted his head.

Dani rephrased. "You know, what does he do for money? Does he build houses? Or fix cars?"

Jaxi's face brightened. "Sure! He do both of those! One time he helped Mr. Ambrose fix up a hole in his roof. Another time he put a new thing in Mrs. Taylor's car to make it run again. Mr. Ashe told me it was a thing what made sparks so the gas would 'splode. I was real worried about that, but Mr. Ashe told me it just 'splodes real small, so she won't get hurt."

Dani smiled slightly. "So Mr. Ashe does these things, and he gets hurt then?"

"Nah," Jaxi said, shaking his head. "Mr. Ashe never gets hurt that way. He's real good at fixing stuff."

"Then when does Mr. Ashe get himself hurt?" Dani pressed. "Have you ever seen him get hurt?"

Jaxi thought hard about that. "No, I guess I never seen him get hurt," he admitted. "I think he always gets hurt at night. Lot of times, he'll be okay one day and got bandages or something the next day, like in the morning."

A woman's voice rang out from across the street. "Jaxi!"

Jaxi turned, his mother standing in the doorway of a weathered row house, arms crossed, her stance weary but expectant.

"I gotta go now," Jaxi said, hopping off the step. "Bye, doctor lady!"

He took off toward the house, his sneakers slapping against the dusty pavement. As he ran, he called out, "Mommy! Mr. Ashe got himself a new doctor!"

His mother glanced in Dani's direction, hesitated, then lifted a tentative hand in a wave. Dani returned it, watching as the boy disappeared into the house.

She exhaled, turning back toward Ashe's steps.

The lilies stood watch in quiet rows, catching the last glow of the sun as it dipped below the skyline. Dani reached down and gently plucked a small cluster from the edge of the box; maybe Ashe would like them inside.

She mounted the steps to the door, glancing one last time down the quiet street, then let herself into the house.

ᔧ • ᔦ

IT HAD BEEN a long three days.

Dani had spent most of that time bouncing between exhausted vigilance and mindless monotony as she tended to Ashe's extensive wounds. He had remained unconscious for nearly all of it, his complexion shifting between the gray pallor of death and the flushed crimson of fever. The redness of fever had worried her, but the moments where he drifted toward that lifeless ashen shade had been agonizing.

She had worked through it the way any good doctor—former doctor?—would. Keep the emotions in check.

Change dressings. Check vitals. Keep the saline flowing. Watching the IV drip at a steady rhythm had given her something solid to cling to, something measurable to pass the time.

So, when she came downstairs that morning, still groggy from a fitful sleep, she had no reason to expect anything different.

She stepped into the living room and froze.

Ashe was sitting up on the sofa.

Not fully upright, of course. He looked like a rag doll that had been unceremoniously propped against the couch. But still, he was up. His arms lay dormant at his sides, his posture sagged, but his head was tipped forward slightly, his eyes open. Awake. Present.

Dani's pulse quickened. "How did you—" She rushed forward, staring at him like he might disappear. "How did you get up?"

Ashe let out a rattling breath, sounding almost amused. "Took a while. Better part of an hour. Surprised you didn't hear me, all the grunting I was doing."

Dani's jaw tightened, torn between relief and frustration. She stepped closer, looking him over with a clinical eye. He still looked like death—pale and fevered, his shaved scalp swollen and bruised, skin slick with sweat—but she saw a sharpness in his gaze that hadn't been there before.

"I don't remotely understand how any of this is possible," Dani repeated yet again. She shook her head, unable to contain her frustration. "How on earth are you even moving?"

Ashe made a slow, deliberate effort to glance down at his body, but even that small motion took a visible toll. His shoulders tensed; his breathing quickened. His head barely dipped before he had to stop. "Not too well, from the look of things," he admitted, his voice rough.

Dani sat gingerly beside him on the couch. The heat radiating from his body was still shocking, unnatural. Without thinking, she pressed the back of her hand lightly against his forehead, then shoved a thermometer between his lips before he could argue.

His pulse came next. She caught his wrist, pressing two fingers into the space between tendons. One eye on her watch, she counted. His temperature was still inhumanly high, but lower than before. A small victory.

She should have felt relieved. Instead, her throat tightened with the same anxiety that had gnawed at her since she'd first seen him in that hospital bed. His body was giving all the wrong signals, defying everything she knew about medicine.

She removed the thermometer and read the number. Still fatal.

She swallowed. "Ashe," she started carefully. "I need you to understand—"

"No." His voice was resolute.

Her brow wrinkled. "No?"

"I already know what you're gonna say." His gaze locked on hers, eyes fever-bright but unyielding. "I don't want to hear it. Keep your negativity to yourself."

"I'm not being negative. I'm just stating the reality of—"

"Well, keep your reality to yourself. I've got my own."

Dani opened her mouth to argue, but Ashe cut her off before she could form a rebuttal.

"When can I start working on physical therapy or something?"

She blinked at him. "Are you serious?"

"Dead serious," he grinned.

Dani nearly laughed at the absurdity of it all. The man sat there, barely able to move, held together by sheer stubbornness and whatever strange quirk of biology that kept him from just... dying—and he was talking about physical therapy.

She didn't know how to respond.

Maybe he sensed it, because his voice softened. "Thank you," he said quietly. "For everything. I know I don't seem like it, but I appreciate all that you're doing." His lips twitched, almost a self-deprecating smirk. "I'm just not used to needing help."

There was something about hearing vulnerability in his words that caught her off guard.

Ashe murmured, almost absently, "Your skin is soft."

Dani's breath hitched. She looked down and realized she was holding his hand.

How had he felt that?

Ashe's fingers twitched almost imperceptibly in hers.

She jerked her hand back, trying to compose herself. "I'm serious, though," Ashe continued, his voice still soft but determined. "When do we start getting me back on my feet?"

Dani hesitated, her breath quivering. "Alright, Ashe," she relented. "If you insist. We'll get started tomorrow. I'll need to go to the hospital and get a few things. But we start small."

Ashe's head tipped slightly in something resembling a nod. "Small sounds good to me," he murmured. "I'm exhausted."

Dani rose from the couch, running a hand through her hair. "And hungry?"

"Starving," Ashe admitted, shifting just slightly against the cushions. "What's for breakfast?"

Chapter 13 : FREEZER BURN

PRESENT DAY

"HE'S DEAD!"

The leader of the gang straightened up after checking Ashe's neck for a pulse. He rubbed a hand over his bearded jaw as he turned to face the others. His lips curled in impotent anger.

Silence gripped the diner, thick and suffocating. The bent aluminum baseball bat wobbled on the floor where its wielder had let it drop. Unable to roll on account of the dent it had earned from the force of impact against Ashe's skull, the ruined bat made a weak creaking sound as it worked out the last of its energy against the floor.

"You idiot!" The leader's voice was low and furious. His gun snapped up, leveled at the bat-swinger's face. "This was simple! What did you have to do that for?"

Bat-boy took half a step backward, hands up, his confidence fading. "He... he was about to get the drop on you!"

"Get the drop on me?" The leader's jaw clenched, but he lowered the gun. He ran a frustrated hand through his thick hair. "He was a cripple, stupid! What was he gonna do? Hook me with his crutch?"

Across the diner, the young waitress sobbed quietly into her hands. Jim, the diner manager, still sat on the stool next to her. He lifted his head to meet Amber's eyes. "I'm so sorry," he mouthed.

The inside man, the greasy-looking store clerk holding Amber's arm, vibrated with nervous energy and too much caffeine or whatever else he had taken to get himself ready for the job. His eyes darted to the front windows. "Come on, man! The Brinks guys are gonna be here at four, and we gotta get gone way before then!"

The leader exhaled sharply, dragging a hand down his face. "Fine." His glare shot back to the bat-swinger. "You. You're staying behind to guard the hostages."

The thug stiffened. "What?!"

"Lock them in the freezer." The leader jerked his head toward the back. "But cut the power first. We don't need any more dead people in this mess. Can you handle that, stupid?"

"Yeah... yeah," the thug muttered, but his gaze kept darting back to Ashe. Blood had begun to seep from the wound on his head and drip onto the floor. A thin red line crept in a slow, lazy arc across the linoleum floor.

The leader followed his stare and snarled. "Hey! Snap out of it! We're gonna be across the border before they even get after us. But only if you pull it together!"

The leader and three other robbers peeled away, following the jittery inside man, who was fumbling with a set of keys as he led them toward the back of the store.

The bat-swinger turned, waving his pistol at the hostages. "Up! Move!"

Amber rose slowly, her hands balled into tight fists at her sides. Her heart thundered in her chest. The manager helped the waitress to her feet, guiding her toward the back with a gentle hand on her shoulder. The three of them—Amber, the manager, and the waitress—were herded through the swinging door into the back of the diner.

"Where's the power?"

Bat-boy's voice boomed in the small space. He seemed to regain some of his cockiness in the absence of the group's leader.

The manager hesitated, but eventually nodded toward a rusted electrical panel bolted to the wall near the industrial sink. The thug stomped over, scanning the labels with squinted eyes before yanking down a switch.

He jerked the freezer door open, sending a rush of cold air tumbling across the greasy floor in a thick, white fog.

"Inside." He waved his gun at them impatiently.

Amber stepped in first, suppressing a shiver as the freezing air lapped at her. Metal racks of boxed meats and bags of frozen fries loomed in the dim glow of the solitary overhead bulb. The others followed, huddling close.

The door swung shut. A pre-determined number of seconds later, the light cut out.

The waitress shrieked involuntarily before regaining her flagging composure. "Now what?" she asked.

"Now we wait," replied Amber. She exhaled, her breath a white cloud made invisible by the pitch dark.

෨ • ෬

THE FREEZER WAS warming. Amber had been telling herself that for the past several minutes, trying to sound convincing. But now, she believed it might actually be getting less cold in their little meat-filled prison. The air had seemed to shift a little bit from biting cold to just super unpleasant. Frost still clung to the metal walls, she knew, its crystalline edges hiding in the darkness. She'd made the regrettable move of touching the wall a few minutes ago and although the icy crystals dissolved a little easier than she might have expected, she'd paid a price: she was positive she could still feel her hand throbbing. The faint scent of packaged meat, maybe thawing, drifted past her nostrils, mingling with the sterile metallic tang of the freezer's surfaces and the stale, nervous breath of trapped bodies.

The walk-in was small, and Amber imagined it wouldn't be long until their combined body heat thawed enough meat and other frozen goods to give Jim a really bad day. Then, she rethought that and realized a bad balance sheet was probably not the worst outcome, under the circumstances.

Okay, maybe it was warming up, but Amber was still shivering. Thinking about the diner's accounting woes could only distract her for so long. She told herself it wasn't the cold. It was the lingering tension coiled in her muscles: tension born from being powerless in a bad situation.

Nah, it was the cold. She hugged her knees tighter, feeling a tremor start in her core and quake outward, fading into her limbs. Shivering meant her body was still regulating itself, right? That didn't make it any easier to be happy about her predicament, but it was something.

No one spoke. The silence was thick, broken only by the occasional sniffle from the young waitress huddled somewhere off to Amber's left. She could hear Jim, the manager, shifting his weight near the door, his breathing shallow and quick, like he was trying to keep from panicking but enjoying only marginal success.

Amber broke the silence with a soft voice, "Hey, we're going to be okay. Ashe is coming."

Amber heard a snort from Jim's direction. "That old guy? He... he was dead. I saw it. We all did. That leader guy said he was dead."

Amber turned her head toward the sound of his voice, though she couldn't see him in the dark. "What, the 'change my jacket so you won't recognize me' guy? Not exactly doctor material, do ya think? He was wrong. Ashe will be here. Trust me. He's coming."

Jim snorted again, this time in apparent derision of Amber's faith in her friend.

The waitress sniffled again, her voice small and tight. "But what if he doesn't? What if we're stuck here? What if...?"

Amber crawled over, guided by sound and instinct, and found the waitress's trembling hand. She wrapped her fingers around it, squeezing gently. "He'll come. I know it. Ashe is... he's stubborn. Stubborn and nasty. Getting knocked down is just a speed bump."

A sound outside the freezer captured Amber's attention, cutting through the darkness and chill. The noise started softly, a soft shuffle outside the heavy door. Then the dull thud of something, or someone, hitting the other side. A muffled grunt, the scuff of shoes against tile. The waitress gasped, her breath hitching. Jim turned sharply, bumping into Amber as he reached out instinctively to shield her from the door, as if expecting it to fly open any moment with death on the other side.

The noise grew louder: more movement, more shuffling. A harsh curse. The unmistakable crack of something solid—bone, maybe—meeting an unforgiving surface. The vibrations of impact shuddered through the metal door.

Amber felt a smile spread across her face. She knew that sound.

∾ • ∾

SOMETHING CRASHED INTO the freezer door loudly enough to make the waitress scream, but Amber just sighed in relief. "There he is," she whispered to herself.

A second crash, louder than the first. Something heavy slammed into the diner wall, followed by the metallic clatter of chairs skidding across linoleum. A body, maybe. Hard to say. The waitress whimpered in the dark, while Amber could feel that Jim's back had gone rigid.

Shots rang out, sharp, deafening in their proximity. Several of them in quick succession. The waitress squealed louder with each burst, her sobs now uncontrollable. The action on the far side of the freezer door faded, and a tense, eerie silence settled over the diner outside.

Then, the scream.

It wasn't panic. It wasn't fear in the voice. It was undiluted agony, raw and desperate, scratching like nails on glass. The sound drilled into Amber's ears, but she found herself strangely calm, her heart anchored by a certainty she didn't dare explain to the others.

Jim mumbled something Amber couldn't catch, his voice shaky. The waitress was still sobbing softly, her breaths hiccupping between tears.

Amber waited.

Click.

The latch released from the outside, and a sliver of dim yellow light cut through the cold darkness of the freezer. The contrast was blinding after the pitch-black, and Amber's eyes pinched shut to squint against it. She raised a hand, peeking through her fingers like shades.

A shadow loomed in the doorway. A broad, hulking shape, blocking most of the light. The silhouette was unmistakable to Amber, even if the others couldn't believe it.

A consistent whimpering drifted from the other side of the door. The voice was pained beyond endurance and suddenly cried out, "I can't feel my legs! I can't feel my legs!"

The shadow slumped and shifted slightly, moving away from the freezer. The door swung closed again, but this time it didn't latch.

A final loud crack sounded: the wet, unmistakable sound of mistreated bone, and Amber recognized Ashe's voice, gruff and annoyed.

"Yeah, and now I can't hear your mouth."

Jim, bathed in the faint light from the cracked door, looked like he was about to pass out.

The freezer door swung open fully, revealing Ashe, backlit by the harsh lights of the kitchen. His face was smeared with blood. Amber guessed that little of it was his own. A cut ran down along his temple, the slow trickle of blood sneaking in an uneven line down his cheek. His shirt was rumpled, half-untucked, the skin of his knuckles scraped and bloodied up to the wrists. His eyes were sharp and dangerous.

He looked like... Ashe.

Ashe's left fist gripped his crutch, now bent into an unusable angle. Amber grinned when she realized he no longer needed it to stand.

Ashe's eyes flicked to Amber, scanning her for injuries. "You okay?" he asked.

"I'm great," she said, rising to her feet.

"Let's go," he said, his voice low, gruff, like he hadn't quite burned through all his irritation yet.

Amber smiled, deciding to poke the bear. "Took you long enough."

"Seven guys. Seven," Ashe grunted.

"Seven?" Amber asked, looking around corners and counting unconscious thugs on her fingers.

"Driver. Out back," Ashe replied.

"Uh-huh."

The waitress, pale and shaking, finally inched her way out of the freezer. "What... what do we do now?"

She was staring at the group's leader curled near the griddle, his breath coming in wet, pained gasps. It looked like Ashe might have done something to the man's spine. Maybe several somethings.

"Whatever you want to do," Ashe said, walking away. "We don't care; we were never here."

Amber looked at Jim. His heart was finally slowing from its steady drumbeat of tension. She reached out, steadying the man with a hand on his shoulder. "See? Told you he'd come."

No response. Jim just stared after Ashe, as if watching a ghost.

Chapter 14 : TRUCE

1988

DANI WOKE TO a faint gray light seeping through the heavy drapes. The quilt covering her was rough, smelling of cedar and time. She'd found it tucked in an ancient trunk at the foot of the bed when she first settled into this room. She had deemed this room the most livable of the three upstairs bedrooms, though "livable" was a generous term. The bed was solid enough, the linens clean if not exactly fresh, but the room conveyed the same hollow feel that permeated the house, like it was waiting for someone to give it purpose.

She'd decided to carve out her little corner here, just one floor above Ashe. That made it easy to check on him, at least. Not that he made it simple; nothing seemed simple with Ashe.

Stretching, Dani crossed to the window and pulled back the drapes. With reluctance, pre-dawn light crept into the room, casting a pale streak across the floorboards and sparkles in the dusty air, highlighted against the darkness. She stared outside for a minute, focusing on little beyond her reflection in the window.

Four days. She was starting to adjust to the strange rhythms of the house. Three of those days she'd watched Ashe drift from fevered unconsciousness to stubborn defiance and back. She found herself wondering—not for the first time—how he'd become who he was. She wondered also—again, not for the first time—why she was doing what she was doing.

Not just taking care of the mortally wounded man confined to the makeshift hospital bed downstairs, stitched together and somehow alive when he shouldn't be. Her reasons for that spoke for themselves, fueled by an oath she took some time ago as a physician. But what was she doing *here* with him?

Dani let her focus drift outward past the ancient glass of the window. The panes of glass each carried the warping signature of time, surfaces subtly rippled like heat rising off asphalt. The street beyond the window was outlined with gentle distortions, its edges wavering slightly as if the world outside couldn't decide on its shape.

That pretty much summed up her feelings about Ashe. The man seemed to be a fixture in this neighborhood, exhibiting a quiet but true gravity among its residents.

She had found the opportunity to speak with several of them over the past three days, taking walks around the neighborhood as Ashe rested in fitful sleep.

This wasn't the kind of place that revealed itself easily to someone like her. Cracked sidewalks framed by tired buildings, windows watching with hooded eyes... These were more than just descriptors of the neighborhood; they were reflections of the wariness of its people. It had taken many of them some effort to overcome their initial skepticism about the white woman—one who dressed like a law officer, no less—in their neighborhood, but they had all visibly relaxed when they learned the reason for her presence. Little Jaxi's vocal endorsements behind the scenes had also helped a great deal, she found.

Her first interview had been with an older man. Mr. Thompson sat on his front stoop like it was a job, his cane resting across his knees, tapping out slow, thoughtful beats. When Dani asked if he knew Ashe, the man chuckled, the sound low and rough, like gravel sliding in a tin can. "Know him? Yeah, I know him. If it wasn't for that man, this block'd be held together with duct tape and spit." He rattled off a long list of repairs Ashe had made for the locals: patched roofs, rewired old lamps, fixed door hinges that creaked like broken bones. "Ain't about money with him, though. Half the time, I think he just likes things to work."

Jaxi's mother had eventually spoken with her as well. The woman juggled two jobs and three kids, trying to keep her exhaustion tucked behind a sharp tongue and sharper eyes. Those eyes had remained suspicious until she accepted Dani wasn't there to sell anything or ask for favors. Once she softened, she spoke of Ashe in short sentences, as if the full weight of her gratitude was too heavy to carry a long distance. "He makes sure my boy's got books," she'd said, glancing back toward her small apartment. "Real books. Reads with him, too. Not 'cause he has to. 'Cause he wants Jaxi to have a life."

Dani's conversation with Señora Ruiz, an old Hispanic woman, had been short on words for another reason. She didn't speak much English, but her gratitude didn't need translation. She'd pressed a hand to her heart, nodded toward Ashe's house, and whispered, "Él es un hombre tan bueno." She indicated her small garden—a patch of stubborn green amidst the faded concrete—and through pantomime finally helped Dani piece together her story of Ashe's assistance: repaired fencing, heavy bags of fresh soil carried in, weeding when the woman's arthritic hands refused to do such work.

Dani considered all these fragments now as she looked out the window on the street, brightening as the dawn broke. Ashe wasn't just a man who lived here; he was a man woven into the fragile existence of this place, a lifeline disguised as a gruff recluse.

She shook her head. Ashe was also something else: a vigilante, by every technical measure. She should've been writing reports, making calls, asking questions. Instead, she was changing his IV, watching his wounds heal. Heal faster than they had any right to.

She wasn't sure which unsettled her more: the impossibility of his body's ability to recover from the absolute brink of death, or the truth that she was just beginning to come to terms with: despite everything, she wanted him to keep living. And maybe even keep doing what he did, serving as... as what? Guardian? Protector? These were simple words, but the picture she was forming of Ashe was anything but simple.

She thought back a dozen years; Ashe had changed little, on reflection. Lena had referred to him as her "Good Samaritan," based on his habit of bringing in the less fortunate and providing for their care. Even Ashe's treatment of her had followed that pattern. He'd protected her, allowing her time to escape and vacate her patients before they could be harmed further by the gang invading the sanctity of the clinic. He'd been her protector as well.

But protectors generally didn't end up half-dead, spines devastated by buckshot. Guardians didn't wear shadows like second skins.

No, she thought, *that's what vigilantes do.*

And Dani Linder was an FBI Special Agent. To her knowledge, nothing had been proven about Ashe's involvement in any crime, recent or historical. But she hadn't spent much effort in looking, either. Dani thought back to the folder Linder had brought her, seeking her involvement in one more case. Like most of Wolfe Linder's wild goose chases, the material in the folder had been a fat lump of trivia, hyperbole, and fantasy loosely connected in a web of conspiracy theories. Linder's cases never turned into anything real.

But maybe one had this time? Linder was convinced there was a super-human vigilante attacking drug dealers. Over years, decades. How had she missed that connection when Linder came to her? The answer to that was simple enough. She hadn't made the connection earlier because she'd long thought Ashe to be dead, killed in the battle at the clinic. She hadn't made the connection recently, because she was so astounded that Ashe was still alive, and had become engrossed in watching his unnatural recovery process in real time. Or was there more? Did she just not want to make the connection, until it finally forced its way into her consciousness? She wasn't supposed to ignore that kind of thing.

But here she was.

She shook off the thought and headed downstairs, her bare feet whispering on the cool wood. Moving from the stairwell near the kitchen through the dining area, she glanced at the supplies stacked neatly near the wall. She'd picked up several items from Sacred Cross last night: stability belt, walker, some physical therapy basics, though she'd known they wouldn't get much use. Ashe had negotiated his way into the promise of physical therapy, but he was simply too stubborn to admit it remained an impossibility.

She stepped into the living room and froze. This was turning into a daily occurrence.

Ashe was prone on the floor. Flat on his face, arms awkwardly sprawled, legs twisted like he'd gone down hard. He wasn't moving. His face was mashed against the floor but tilted up just enough to glare at her with sharp annoyance.

"You gonna help me up or stand there looking at me?"

Dani blinked, then let out a breath somewhere between exasperation and disbelief. "Well, I was going to make some coffee, but I guess you had other plans?"

She crouched beside him, quickly scanning his condition. No fresh blood, thank goodness, but his breathing was labored from exertion. She slid her arms under his shoulders and hauled him up with careful leverage. Despite the awkwardness, she somehow managed to avoid ripping open any stitches.

Once she had him settled back on the makeshift recovery couch, she leaned in to more closely inspect his wounds. The bandages covering his side and back were damp with sweat, clinging slightly as she peeled them back. She expected angry, livid tissue, but what greeted her was… different.

The redness was fading into patches. Tender, thin skin glistening beneath the gauze where raw flesh should have still been exposed. Where the sutures crossed his flesh, the skin was knitting in spots over the threads themselves, starting to enclose them. In other areas, the stitches looked like relics, unnecessary holdovers from much older injuries already past the re-epithelialization phase.

His scalp, once shaved clean for surgery, was now shadowed with dark stubble, like it had decided to reclaim territory without permission. The same faint scruff crept along his jawline, giving him the ghost of a beard.

It was patently impossible, but as was typical with Ashe, Dani was unable to deny what she saw. She refused to react. She'd learned quickly that Ashe thrived on challenging expectations.

"What were you thinking?" she snapped, adjusting his position with the stability belt.

"I was thinking I was thirsty."

Her eyes took in the IV setup beside him. Both bags had been sucked dry and flapped there, shriveled like empty husks. She cursed softly, grabbing fresh saline and re-spiking the line with quick, practiced efficiency. Then she held a glass of water in front of his face.

"If you're so convinced you're going to get better, you need to work with me. Not like this. You pull another stunt like that, and I leave you there like a dead fish next time. I don't care how stubborn you are, I'll walk out that door."

Ashe drained the glass, glaring at her over the rim like she'd personally offended him.

"You're a doctor. You can't do that."

"Oh, I can." She stood and crossed her arms, leveling him with a look. "I'm also a Special Agent with the FBI.

Technically, I can't just ignore the elephant in the room. Maybe I should start asking you about how you got these injuries."

Ashe's jaw clenched. His glare deepened, but he didn't respond.

She didn't need him to.

Silence stretched between them until, finally, he muttered, "Fine."

"Fine, what?" she demanded.

"I'll work with you."

Dani didn't smile, though the small victory warmed her heart to a degree she didn't expect. She was unsure if it was the threat of being left alone or the idea of being interrogated that cracked him, but either way, she'd take it.

"Well," she said, settling onto the armrest beside him, "looks like we've arrived at an uneasy truce."

Ashe snorted, trying to shift slightly and failing visibly. "Uneasy's right."

But beneath the gruffness, there was something else: a flicker of respect, maybe even trust. She couldn't look away.

And Dani knew, in that quiet moment, that whatever rules she had been trained to follow didn't stand a chance against this.

ॐ • ॐ

THE CLATTER OF utensils announced the end of another stubborn battle between Ashe's appetite and his pride.

The Battle of Dinner on the Second Day of Therapy was finally over. Dani set the empty plate aside with a sigh and regarded Ashe for a long moment. Just as the sectional sofa had lost sight of its purpose and surrendered to being used as a makeshift hospital bed, Ashe seemed to be a fish out of water in his role of helpless patient, leaning back on the couch. Only he didn't surrender as easily.

"Well," she muttered, brushing a lock of stray hair from her face, "as far as patients go, you certainly have a healthy appetite." Dani was simultaneously gratified and concerned for the amount of food Ashe was able to put down. On the one hand, he'd need nourishment for the slow process of healing. On the other hand, it was supposed to be a slow process, and with the way he ate, he'd eventually regain his mobility just by learning to roll around like that blueberry kid in *Willie Wonka and the Chocolate Factory.*

"As far as cooks go, you're certainly a good doctor," Ashe shot back, frowning as she wiped his mouth with a napkin like she would a child.

The man was barely able to lift his hand, yet somehow he'd devoured two full portions of their modest dinner like a lumberjack after a twelve-hour shift. She'd cooked a simple meal of roasted chicken, rice, and steamed vegetables, and despite the effort required, Ashe had eaten as if he expected every bite to be his last.

She'd been feeding him, spoon by careful spoon, like he was a toddler learning motor control: small spoonfuls, careful pacing, making sure he didn't choke. Frequently, he'd grunt in frustration and attempt to reach for the fork himself, muscles trembling with the effort, barely able to flex a few fingers with the intensity of someone lifting a boulder. Ashe's nerves cooperated maybe twenty percent of the time. Watching him struggle should've been frustrating, but Dani was fascinated. When the fingers did move, it was fleeting: tiny, jerky movements that left him exhausted. Feeding time was probably the best therapy session in their new regimen.

Medically speaking, she had no idea what she was doing anymore. These waters were completely uncharted. A patient with spinal injuries as severe as Ashe's should have been immobilized for weeks, months. His body should've been fragile, every movement risking more damage. But Ashe wasn't fragile. He was stubborn, infuriatingly so. And he was making progress. He remained largely paralyzed, but he continued to try. And somehow, impossibly, he made progress.

His wounds had progressed beyond what was scientifically possible, the angry red edges now smooth and pink, the skin knitting itself together at a pace faster than absorbable sutures could stay ahead of. Some stitches had been swallowed whole by new tissue, as if his body had decided it could do a better job without Dani's help. That was a problem for another day. Even his shaved scalp had betrayed her expectations, dark stubble creeping in like nothing had happened.

She checked his temperature, frowning at the digital readout. His temperature had fallen into a range that would denote only severe sickness rather than impending death in a normal person.

"Your temperature spikes after you eat," she noted, "but it drops back to your new baseline shortly after."

Ashe's head lolled toward her slightly, his eyes sharp despite the exhaustion. "Really? Well, it's gonna spike again if you don't get me some water."

She blinked. "What do you mean?"

"I mean," he drawled, each word dripping with sarcasm, "I'm thirsty. I would like some water." He over-enunciated each word and accentuated the pauses between.

Rolling her eyes, Dani grabbed the quart-sized hospital pitcher from the side table and shoved the straw toward his mouth. Ashe drained two-thirds of it in one go, his throat working with deep, greedy swallows. When he finally stopped, his head dropped back against the couch, breath heavy, like drinking had been its own form of physical therapy.

Tension between irritation and awe sat like a knot in her chest.

Vigilante. The word echoed in the back of her mind, a label she was finding it harder to ignore. She should've been questioning him, documenting every detail of how he'd ended up with injuries. Probably creating a crime report to file. But instead, she was feeding him, adjusting his IV, rooting for his healing body to do things it had no right to do.

He's not just a case file, she told herself.

And that was the problem.

Chapter 15 : RED MEANS GO

PRESENT DAY

THE MOTEL DIDN'T need a scary name to warn you off; the chipped neon sign did a great job of that, sputtering half-heartedly against the harsh daylight, its letters flickering erratically like a dying heartbeat. The parking lot was more gravel than the asphalt it may have once been, with weeds thriving in every crack. The Corvette sat tucked against the far side of the building, mostly hidden by a dented ice machine that hadn't dispensed anything colder than lukewarm disappointment in years.

Amber shut the door behind her with a hollow thunk, the lock rattling its protest against being called on to do some work. She tossed her bag onto the sagging mattress, sending up a faint puff of dust. The room smelled like it had given up trying to be clean sometime in the late '90s: its aroma was a mixture of stale cigarettes, mildew, and something vaguely metallic she didn't want to identify.

"How are you feeling?" she asked, peeling off her jacket and frowning at the mysterious stain on the armrest of a chair she was definitely not going to sit in.

Ashe sat on the edge of the other bed. His remaining crutch was propped against the nightstand, which wobbled on three fourths of its legs under the weight of a dusty lamp sporting a crooked shade. He rubbed the back of his head, his fingers pressing into the swollen bruise left from the truck stop incident.

"Got a headache the size of Montana," he muttered. "I'll be fine in the morning."

Amber snorted, abandoning common sense and dropping onto her bed with an exaggerated flop that made the springs shriek in protest. She stared at the water-stained ceiling, where the texture looked like it might peel off and land on her face if she breathed too hard.

"You afraid the robbers will talk to the police?" she asked, her voice muffled against the lumpy pillow.

"Afraid? No," Ashe replied without looking at her, his gaze fixed on the battered TV remote like it owed him money.

Amber sat up. "So you don't think they'll talk to the police, then?"

"No," Ashe said flatly. "I *know* they'll talk to the police. You asked me if I was *afraid* of it."

She groaned, dragging her hands down her face. Her freckles stood out against her skin in the sickly light. "Ugh, you're impossible."

Ashe finally glanced at her. "I'm accurate."

Amber pushed herself off the bed, pacing to the window. The curtain was more of a suggestion than a functional barrier, thin enough to let in too much light but just heavy enough to not hang aside when you wanted it to. She peeked through the gap, confirming that yes, the parking lot was still as depressing as it had been when they arrived.

"Where are we, anyway?" she demanded, turning back to Ashe. "This place is horrible."

He shrugged, leaning back slightly. "It's safe."

"Yeah, but it's nasty." Amber walked over to the ancient air conditioning unit under the window and poked at the rusted controls. The knob promptly fell off, clattering to the floor and rolling toward the crack under the door like it had been waiting for an opportunity to escape.

She pointed at it dramatically. "See? Even the furniture wants to leave."

"Don't make a fuss. It can always be worse."

Amber raised an eyebrow. "Worse than a murder-themed air freshener and a bed that's probably seen more crimes than you've committed?"

"Yep," Ashe said, settling back onto his lumpy mattress with a grunt. "Could've been two murder-themed air fresheners."

☙ • ❧

AMBER PERCHED ON the edge of the second bed and tried to ignore the reek of a century's worth of tobacco that had seeped into the walls and was now seeping back out. Her legs dangling off the side, scuffed sneakers tracing lazy arcs on the threadbare carpet. Ashe sat opposite her, the screen of his phone glowing faintly in the dim light as he dialed.

He put the call on speaker as Amber had taught him to do, resting the phone on the nightstand between them. It rang twice before Owen Spirit's voice snapped through the speaker, sharp and impatient.

"Well? Are you clowns alive, or do I need to start drafting obituaries?"

"Miss you, too. Laying low for the day. Something went sideways at a truck stop east of Albuquerque."

A beat of silence. Then, "Sideways? What does that mean—sideways?" Fry's voice chimed in, distant but distinct, layered with concern beneath her faint Polish accent.

"There was an attempted robbery," Ashe said, his tone flat. "It's handled."

"Handled?" Spirit repeated, his voice dripping with sarcasm. "What did you do? You know what's not handled? The fact that you're a walking headline! 'Elderly man dismantles armed robbers with crutch and bad attitude.'"

"Whoa!" Amber exclaimed. "Is that for real? Where did they print that?"

Spirit paused, taken aback. "No, it's not for real. Wait a second - is that what actually happened? What about that low profile we need you to keep?"

Amber snorted, earning a sharp glance from Ashe. She shrugged, unrepentant, and flopped backward onto the bed, staring at the stained ceiling paint.

"It's low enough. We're not moving during daylight, though, just in case," Ashe continued. "Too risky. The car stands out, and we've already drawn too much attention."

Spirit sighed on the other end. Amber thought the lawyer sounded tired. "You're killing me, Ashe. We don't have time for a sightseeing tour of roach motel America. Standish isn't just a bureaucrat pushing papers around; he's a bloodhound. If he serves that warrant before you guys get here to Ashburn, we're done."

"I'll be there," Ashe said simply.

Amber tuned out as the conversation shifted to logistics: timelines, routes, contingency plans. Spirit's voice blurred into the background, all sharp edges and clipped words, while Fry occasionally interjected with technical details about the route. She was evidently serving as Spirit's digital assistant.

Amber's attention drifted around the room as she followed. It was a depressing collection of bad decisions and worse maintenance. She wandered over to the dusty dresser, pulling at a drawer that groaned like it was protesting her existence. Inside, she found nothing but a crumpled receipt from 2017 and what she guessed—hoped—was just a petrified french fry.

In the bathroom, she flipped the light switch. The flickering bulb overhead buzzed angrily, casting the cracked mirror in harsh relief. She leaned in, studying her reflection, wondering where they'd bought a mirror that made you look that tired. Or maybe the lighting was just that bad.

By the time she returned to the bed, the call was wrapping up.

"Fine," Spirit's voice snapped. "Lay low, but get moving as soon as it's dark. Ashburn can't wait."

"Noted. We're headed straight there, fastest route possible," Ashe replied, ending the call with a sharp tap of the screen.

Amber flopped back onto her bed, propping herself up on her elbows. She looked across the gulf between the two ratty beds. "So," she said, stretching the word out like taffy, "now that we're officially checked into the luxury suite and Spirit is okay with the minor delay, you want to pick up where you left off? The story?"

Ashe rubbed the back of his head again. "Not really."

"Too bad. Now talk. Who was this Foley guy you mentioned?"

"Fine," Ashe sighed loudly. "Frank Foley was the Berlin chief of station. Remarkable guy. Mostly what I did was the physical stuff; the stuff that usually led to injury or death, and I was pretty good at it."

Amber grinned broadly. "You don't say."

"I do say. Foley was the one bending the rules and helping the Jews there. However good I was at my job, he was better at his. I managed to keep a low profile for the couple years I was there. All the while, Foley recruited agents and we both dug up every detail we could find on the Germans' infrastructure and their military research and development.

"Late 1932, I had struck up a relationship with this Dutch kid, name of van der Lubbe. Big brute of a kid, and a good fighter, but he always wanted to swing in the big leagues. Communist zealot, the kind that we'd kept our eyes on to see if we could anticipate trouble. He already had a record with the Gestapo, political rabble-rousing, stuff like that. A few arsons. Nothing big, but I'm pretty sure that's what all led to what happened.

"The Nazi Party—well, Hitler, specifically—had been working one angle after another, climbing towards power. He was close, Hitler was. He got himself appointed Chancellor in January 1933, but the president, Hindenburg, still held power above him. It looked like Chancellor was about as high as Hitler could climb.

"Until February, when the Reichstag burnt."

"What's that?" asked Amber.

"The Reichstag was their version of Parliament. Congress, to you, I guess. The building caught fire, and they somehow arrested van der Lubbe for arson while the building was still barely heating up. It always struck me as too clean a catch, and van der Lubbe never struck me as capable enough for something of that scale.

"I was called to the scene, since I knew van der Lubbe, and that's where it all starts to go south for me. Turns out, the Chancellor is there himself, taking a tour of the smoking ruins of the building by the time I arrive. I'm introduced to him, and I can see the recognition in his eyes immediately. I guess maybe you don't forget the face of the first defenseless man you kill in cold blood, even if you're somebody like Adolf Hitler."

Amber sat on the edge of the bed, her hands resting on her knees, her body leaning forward to betray how completely she was absorbed in Ashe's storytelling. The usual flicker of restless energy was gone. Her green eyes locked onto Ashe's, wide and unblinking, as if his words themselves might disappear if she dared to look away. She didn't fidget, didn't interrupt. Rare for her. It wasn't just the story, though. It was him: the way his voice carried the weight of the events. He wasn't just recounting history but pulling it, piece by piece, from somewhere deep inside.

The room felt smaller in the hush between his sentences, the hum of the air conditioner a dull, distant thing. Amber barely blinked. Her breathing grew shallow as she tracked every shift in his expression, every subtle pause. Ashe showed no need for embellishment, no dramatic flair. Just the quiet, brutal simplicity of someone who had been there. The idea still hadn't fully settled in her head, that she was sitting here, in a dive motel off some nowhere highway, listening to a firsthand account of Hitler's rise to power. And yet, she didn't question it. Couldn't.

"So, the building was practically destroyed, and there's no missing that on the news cycle, even back then," Ashe continued, his voice rough under the weight of memory. "Adolf jumps all over the opportunity, claiming that communist agitators were plotting against the government, and he got Hindenburg to—"

"Hindenburg, the president," Amber murmured, her voice thick with exhaustion but still following.

"What other Hindenburg was there?" demanded Ashe.

Amber frowned. "That balloon, right?" She stifled a yawn.

Ashe shook his head.

"Yeah; Hindenburg the president," he said. "Hitler got Hindenburg to essentially declare martial law. Under that umbrella, Adolf cleans house. The Nazis pass legislation to give Hitler full legal power without Hindenburg's approval. President Hindenburg croaks in 1934, and Hitler declares himself president as well. Adolf Hitler is now in control of everything."

Amber's head dipped, her shoulders sagging. Ashe kept going, his voice softer now.

"And he knows who I am."

He glanced over, only to find Amber slumped against a pillow, eyes closed, her breathing slow and even. A soft, barely audible snore escaped her lips. Reaching over, he pulled the thin motel blanket up over her shoulders before settling back against his pillow, staring at the water-stained ceiling.

        ∽   •   ≍

AMBER WOKE TO the harsh sting of sunlight cutting back into the room, searing directly into her face. She squinted, groaning as she instinctively reached for her phone on the rickety nightstand. Three hours, the time on the screen told her. She'd slept for three hours. The clock on her phone glared like it was personally offended she hadn't slept longer. She could relate.

She sat up, disoriented, her stiff neck protesting from the awkward angle she'd crashed in. Ashe stood near the window, curtains thrown wide, letting the unfiltered daylight spill into the room like an unwanted guest. The air felt thicker, heavier for having been confined while she slept.

"What was that for?" she grumbled, rubbing her eyes. "Feels like waking up inside a microwave."

Ashe didn't bother looking at her. "Time to move."

Amber swung her legs over the edge of the bed, glaring at him. "I thought we were laying low until dark. 'It's too dangerous to travel in the daylight,' remember? Your words."

"There's more than one solution for most problems," Ashe replied, his voice flat. He was being cryptic, as usual. He grabbed his crutch and made his way without using it toward the door with that same stubborn efficiency he applied to everything. Patience was a resource he'd long since burned through.

"So why is violence always top of your list?" Amber asked, stretching.

"It's efficient," he replied. "Come on, get up."

Amber groaned again, forcing herself to stand. She shuffled toward the bathroom, turning the tap for some water to splash on her face. A rusty trickle sputtered out, the color somewhere between weak tea and regret. She stared at it, disgusted.

"Oh, great. Perfect. I was hoping to wash my face with liquid tetanus." She glared at the faucet like it had personally wronged her. "This place is a biohazard. Pretty sure the CDC would just burn it down and call it even."

"Don't make a fuss," Ashe said again, glancing over his shoulder. "It can always be worse."

Amber mumbled something unladylike under her breath, grabbed her bag, and followed him outside.

The parking lot hadn't improved during her nap. In fact, it had probably gotten worse, but she didn't want to waste energy cataloging how. Same cracked pavement, same stubborn weeds. But one thing had changed. She stopped short, blinking hard.

Where the silvery-gray and black checkerboard-coated Corvette had been, there now sat a candy-apple red version of the same car, gleaming under the mid-day sun. Ashe was at work peeling masking tape from the windows and chrome trim. Crumpled strips of painter's paper littered the pavement at his feet.

Amber's jaw dropped. "You painted the car? Spirit's going to explode!"

Ashe didn't even pause, methodically yanking a strip of tape from the windshield. "Our goal isn't to impress Spirit. Our goal is to stay under the radar."

Amber stared at the car. "Bright red is 'under the radar?'"

"When it comes to classic Corvettes," Ashe replied, tossing the last wad of tape onto the pile, "a bright red one is invisible. Nobody notices it because it's what they expect. That funky checkerboard stuff stood out like a neon sign saying, 'here's the guy; arrest him.'"

"I can still see the checkerboard pattern!" exclaimed Amber. "It's just red now."

"Yeah, but you're right on top of it. Cops seeing this thing go by at seventy miles an hour won't even bat an eye."

Ashe gave the car a once-over, then turned to her. "We'll take back roads to Abilene. Longer route and we've lost our solar advantage, but we'll make it, and we'll make it faster. That's what matters."

Amber shook her head in disbelief, watching as Ashe tossed their bags into the car. He'd moved well past the need for his crutch. He shoved it into the car along with the paint-covered masking paper, not wanting to leave behind any more evidence than necessary.

"Come on, get in," he barked over his shoulder. "We gotta get going. We're moving too slow."

Chapter 16 : BLOOD TYPE ATYPICAL

1988

"YOU'RE MOVING TOO fast," Dani snapped, her voice sharp in the stillness of the room. The words escaped her lips with more bite than she intended, but frustration had recently started to find ways to slip past her professional veneer.

Ashe grunted in response, bracing his trembling arms against the battered armrest of the sectional. His fingers, gnarled and pale, gripped with white-knuckled determination as he strained to push himself upright. His face was drawn tight with effort, every muscle trembling like a wire pulled too taut. Sweat beaded along his brow, slicking the graying stubble on his temples.

"I've been hurt a lot of times," he rasped through gritted teeth, "and I've never had to recover this way. Shouldn't be taking so long. It's not like I'm missing any parts, right?"

Unsure what that meant, Dani crossed the creaking floor to crouch beside him. The faint medicinal scent of fresh antiseptic mixed with Ashe's sweat: a sharp reminder that new wounds still hid beneath the bandages. New by her standards, anyway.

She adjusted the IV bag hanging from a metal stand that had been Ashe's constant companion for the past two weeks. The saline was nearly drained, the bag crinkling like an empty sack. In reaching for the bag, her fingers brushed against the tape securing the line to his arm. His skin felt like paper: too dry, too warm. Whatever game his body was playing, she feared it may have played too long.

"Look, Ashe, I understand the frustration, I do," she said, her tone softening. "But however fast you think this process should be, the nerve connections have to be reprogrammed. Even after flesh knits together. It all takes time. And—"

She hesitated, studying the dark hollows of his eyes, the bluish tinge around his lips that had deepened recently even when he was properly hydrated.

"—And you're doing great."

The lie tasted bitter on her tongue, but she knew he needed to hear it. He needed to believe it. *And maybe*, she thought, *I need to believe it too*.

It had been two weeks since they'd left the hospital. Half that spent in long, grueling days of fever spikes, restless nights, and futile attempts at movement. His temperature had remained in a zone she considered dangerously high, stubbornly refusing to settle, and his skin had taken on a sickly, blue pallor that triggered alarms in her head. The dark circles beneath his eyes stood out like day-old bruises, shadowing the sharp lines of his cheekbones.

He still seemed to rally after eating or drinking, albeit less and less. It was like food was some kind of temporary fuel keeping him tethered to the world. And he ate. A lot. More than she thought his body could handle in its weakened state. Non-medical wisdom would suggest that an appetite was a good sign, a mark of recovery. But staring at him now, Dani felt the gnawing dread that it was the opposite. He was losing weight.

"I'm not moving fast enough," Ashe muttered, sagging back against the cushions with a wince. "This is taking too long."

Dani stood, pacing to the small medical kit she'd kept within arm's reach since bringing him home. The repetitive motion helped steady her thoughts. *You shouldn't even be moving at all*, she wanted to scream. But Ashe wasn't like any patient she'd ever treated. Or anyone that had ever been discussed in medical literature.

"You've taken two steps, Ashe," she said, glancing over her shoulder. "That's nothing short of miraculous."

Except it wasn't. Those steps had doubtless been more reflex than intent: random neural signals breaking through scar tissue, like faulty wiring occasionally sparking to life. The control just wasn't there. Not yet. Probably not ever.

"I want to check your blood work," she announced, grabbing a syringe from the kit. "I'll clear it with Lena first, but I need to see what's going on beneath the surface."

As she approached, Ashe's body shuddered with a sudden, involuntary tremor that rippled from his shoulders down to his legs. Dani froze mid-step, her medical instincts flaring.

"What was that?" she asked sharply. "Are you in pain?"

Ashe exhaled through his nose, his face impassive. "I'm in extreme pain," he admitted. It was just another fact, as simple as commenting on the weather. "But that's not the problem."

Her brow furrowed. "Not the problem? Ashe, most people would consider 'extreme pain' a pretty big problem."

"Pain is just pain," he replied flatly, his gaze distant, as if the words belonged to someone else. "You wouldn't understand."

Frustration surged again, but Dani tamped it down. She needed answers, not another argument. She sat on the edge of the coffee table, leaning in until their eyes met.

"You're right," she said quietly. "I don't understand. But that's kind of my job—to figure this out. And for what it's worth, feeling pain is a good sign. It means your nerves are reconnecting." She forced a smile. "Even if it sucks."

She studied him for a long moment, then added, "You never ask for painkillers."

"They don't work."

The simplicity of this reminder hit like a slap. She blinked, processing. She'd forgotten that detail, lost it somewhere in the chaos of his impossible recovery. "What do you mean they don't work? None of them?"

Ashe shook his head, jaw clenched. "I'm immune. Painkillers, anesthetics. All of it."

Dani's breath caught in her throat. The surgery. That horrid, eleven hour surgery. She remembered the tension in the operating room, the spike in Ashe's vitals when scalpel touched skin, the subtle signs the staff had ignored, refusing to confront the truth. Unable to do anything about it if they did confront it.

"That explains..." She swallowed hard. "That would mean you really did feel everything during the surgery."

Ashe didn't flinch. "Every second of it."

The words landed like a punch to her gut. She straightened, fighting to remain upright on the coffee table. She was glad she wasn't standing; her legs had gone wobbly.

"But... you never said a word. You didn't even make a sound." She stared at him, disbelief etched into her face. "How? How could you go through that without—" She swallowed, the words lodging in her throat. "Without screaming? Without anything?"

"I kinda felt like whining about it wouldn't help."

༄ • ༄

DANI SAT BESIDE Ashe, sleeves of her top rolled up to the elbows. The shirt was one of her work shirts: the Bureau's idea of tactical fashion, suited for immediate identification of the female wearer as an agent with or without a jacket, with just enough femininity to show how badly the designers had failed at their job. Dani usually referred to the shirts as "Government-issued personality suppressors," although they did make great clothing for hard work, if only because she didn't care what happened to them. Although she often joked that the crisp, white shirts were stiff enough to double as body armor in a paper cut battle, the current instance was crumpled and softened with her sweat equity to the point that it resembled one of Ashe's soiled bandages.

Dani's hands methodically worked through the routine of changing Ashe's gauze cocoon. The bottle of antiseptic nearby wafted a pungent odor throughout Ashe's living room. Unwrapping the gauze from Ashe's abdomen to get a look at the injuries on his back, she noticed a long, jagged scar that traced an angry path from his lower ribcage down to his pelvis. The scar was juxtaposed against the fresh, rapidly healing surgical wounds from the recent chaos, white and lumpy compared to the pink and tight edges of the recent wounds against the ever-deepening blues and purples of his flesh.

She paused, fingertips lightly brushing the thickened line of scar tissue. "This one isn't recent," she murmured, more to herself than to Ashe. Her gaze lifted to meet his, searching. "Vietnam?"

Ashe's face hardened, a subtle but unmistakable shift. His silver-gray eyes darkened, not with anger but with a shadow older than the years etched into his rugged features. "Vietnam," he replied, voice gravelly and low.

The tension thickened between them, heavy with the presence of the unspoken and unexpected land mine Dani's question had just exposed. She continued cleaning his back, her hands moving with practiced precision. "You know, from the way you react to some of these scars, I get the sense that there's a lot more to it than just battlefield wounds. Like you're still fighting something—or someone—from back then."

Ashe's jaw clenched, the muscles twitching under skin that bore a distinct hint of cyanosis. Over the past few days, the bluish tinge that had started in his eyes and face had spread downward to his neck and torso like a slow, relentless tide. Dani noted the discoloration, her clinical mind racing even as she pressed forward.

"Could you ever just... leave it behind? Deal with things as they are now?" Her voice softened, full of both curiosity and concern. She'd seen men haunted by wars past, their battles continuing long after the guns fell silent.

Ashe's voice was a dry, bitter rasp. "Kinda hard to leave it behind."

Dani set down the used gauze, leaning back slightly, her arms crossed. "So many of you brought that place back with them. Men who, like you, couldn't leave it behind. Sometimes it's just a choice you have to make." Dani wanted to wince at the inadvertent quote her father had once used on her, but she fought down the urge and stared at Ashe.

His eyes locked on hers, sharp and unyielding. "Ain't no choice about it. It was all still waiting for me when I got here."

His words hung in the air, heavy with the weight of some hidden truth that she wasn't privy to. Dani didn't press further. She could see the steel wall behind his gaze, the immovable boundary he'd erected against her invasion.

Turning back to her task, she continued her examination. As she peeled back more of the bandages, her breath hitched slightly. The surgical incisions, fresh from the hospital two weeks prior, were nearly gone. Smooth, taut skin had replaced what should have been raw, tender healing tissue.

"This..." she whispered, awe peeking through her clinical detachment. "These should still be in the inflammatory phase. Yet here... epithelialization is finished, and maturation is nearly universal in this area. The dermal layers have closed, and there's minimal granulation tissue."

Her fingers hovered over the blue-tinged skin surrounding the healed wounds. Dani's medical instincts screamed at the evident ischemia, maybe hinting at early gangrene, but the tissue was warm, supple, and surprisingly resilient to touch. No necrosis. No crepitus. No signs of compromised perfusion beyond the discoloration.

She frowned. "The tissue's oxygen-starved, but it's not necrotic. It's like... the healing process is pulling oxygen away from the surrounding skin, diverting resources to regenerate at a rate that shouldn't be possible. But the surrounding tissues aren't suffering significantly for some reason."

And then she saw it: along the nape of his neck, tiny, taut lines where the skin had begun to grow over the sutures themselves. Dani leaned in, incredulous. "The skin's completely enveloping the stitches. This would normally take months, if it happened at all. The remodeling phase hasn't just started, it's nearly done."

She sat back. "Ashe, your healing mechanisms defy everything I've ever studied. Cellular turnover rates, collagen deposition, it's like your body's working on overdrive without any of the expected systemic strain."

Ashe looked at her, his eyes half-lidded with exhaustion. "I don't understand most of what you just said, but I do know it itches back there like crazy. You wouldn't want to take those stitches out for me, would you?"

֍　•　֍

FLUORESCENT LIGHTS BUZZED softly overhead. Glass-fronted cabinets cast wavering reflections onto the linoleum floor of the basement lab at Sacred Cross Hospital. The room was utilitarian, but utility is why Dani was here. Beige tiles lined the walls, their sterile monotony broken only by the occasional safety poster or outdated anatomical chart curling at the corners. Rows of metal cabinets stood like silent sentinels, their contents— glass slides, petri dishes, and neatly labeled specimen jars—twinkling in the dim glow.

A spinning centrifuge hummed in the corner, its rhythmic vibration a lonely heartbeat in the quiet space. Beakers, pipettes, and test tubes were meticulously arranged on stainless steel countertops, interspersed with bulky, analog diagnostic equipment—manual microscopes, spectrophotometers, and hematology analyzers whose readouts flickered with amber light.

Dani Linder—the lab coats Lena had provided her bore the name "McKendree"—sat hunched over a microscope, her eyes reflecting fatigue. She adjusted the fine focus, her face illuminated by the cold, white wash of the microscope's light source. On the slide beneath her lens, Ashe's blood sample refused to reveal its secrets. It had so far been an evening without answers. The cells floated in suspension, deceptively ordinary until observed more closely. Dani leaned back, running a hand through her hair, and reached for her notebook, the pages already filled with hastily scribbled notes and diagrams.

She thought back to the perplexed nurse in the operating room. He'd tried several times to type Ashe's blood, and she was now confirming his results again. No AB antigens. And yet, the samples could act like both antigens and both antibodies were present—on both the red cells and the plasma. But also like neither factor could be found in either component. No Rh protein. Yet evidence of it all over the place. Universal donor... but also universal recipient. As if that wasn't weird enough, there was more.

She'd observed the cells under different conditions: deprived of nutrients, they didn't die as expected. Instead, they entered a dormant state, like hibernating organisms. When reintroduced to nutrients and water, the cells didn't just recover, they repaired themselves. Not through traditional cell division, but actual repair of damaged structures, reversing what should have been irreversible.

Dani spoke softly to herself, her voice the only human sound in the room. "Not apoptosis. Not necrosis. No senescence. It's like... they just wait."

She flipped back to an earlier page in her notes. The rapid healing of Ashe's surgical wounds defied everything she knew about human physiology. Incisions that should have taken weeks to begin proper closure were already nearly gone. The fibrin she expected to be newly formed was instead replaced by neatly woven tissue, seamless and robust.

She scribbled another jumble of notes: *Cellular repair mechanism—exothermic? Matches febrile response observed; check timeline. Oxygen depletion localized to healing areas. Surrounding tissue oxygen-starved, yet healthy.*

Dani pushed back from the desk, her chair scraping softly against the linoleum. She stared at the wall, her mind racing through possibilities. Radiation? No. Genetic anomaly? Too stable, too systemic. Something else: something beyond her training, but not beyond her curiosity.

She needed to talk to Ashe. Needed answers.

Gathering her notes, she muttered, "How long have you been like this, Ashe? What on earth happened to you?" The lab didn't answer, but the questions lingered in the sterile air.

Chapter 17 : A BRIDGE TOO FAR

PRESENT DAY

THE LOW RUMBLE of the big engine and hum of the tires on the cracked asphalt provided a constant drone beneath the occasional whistle of wind rattling through the Corvette's slightly misaligned passenger window. Amber hadn't noticed the window noise earlier, but since Ashe had recovered enough of his legs to drive, she had been relegated to the right-hand seat. They'd been rolling east for some time. The sun was now a muted glow behind them, painting the horizon with strokes of orange and purple. Amber traced a finger along the dashboard's curve, marveling at the cool, smooth feel of the vintage leather, worn thin in places but still holding onto its stubborn charm.

This was her first time in the passenger seat. It smelled faintly of aged leather and engine oil, and Ashe added some undefinable quality to the aroma, like a mix of tobacco and gunpowder, though she knew he didn't smoke. The seat creaked under her weight, the upholstery cracked with age and stitched over in spots where time had won minor battles. She briefly wondered why Task had never fixed up little flaws like that, as wealthy as the man had been. The dash was a sprawl of analog dials and chrome-rimmed gauges, the kind that seemed to tell you everything and nothing all at once. A small crack ran diagonally through the corner of the speedometer, and she found herself idly tracing it with her eyes, as if it mapped a secret path to mysterious faraway lands.

They had just peeled off US 40 for some reason, the familiar highway giving way to a narrower, less-traveled road. The sign for a small town had flashed by in a blink, its bold letters doing little to justify the town's existence. Amber snorted softly.

"Santa Rosa," she muttered, shaking her head. "Sounds like it should be prettier than a gas station and a couple of sad-looking trailers. You think they named it after someone's grandma or a cactus?"

Ashe didn't respond. His eyes remained fixed on the road, hands relaxed on the wheel but with that ever-present tension of his lurking underneath. Amber shifted in her seat, stretching her legs out as far as the cramped space allowed. Her knees bumped against the faded glove compartment that rattled slightly with every pothole.

Moriarty, seemingly comprised of little but empty fireworks stands, had been the last town of any size after Albuquerque, before that truck stop fiasco. The name lingered in her mind like an itch she couldn't scratch. Moriarty... why did that sound so familiar? Probably something from a book she didn't read or a show she never finished.

"I keep thinking about the truck stop," she said after a moment, her voice quieter, laced with something that might have been guilt. "You didn't have to hurt those guys so bad."

Ashe didn't flinch, didn't glance her way. "We didn't have time to play around. They'll live."

Amber chewed on that, having munched on what was probably too many coffee beans for one day. She stared out at the endless stretch of nothingness. An occasional tumbleweed did its best to act out an impression of a cliché desert against a dusty backdrop of dust. "Sure, but don't you think it's gonna draw some attention? Spirit said we needed to lay low, or Standish will figure out we're headed for Ashburn."

"Anything we did about the truck stop mess was going to draw attention," Ashe replied, his tone flat. "This way, it'll teach those morons a lesson, too."

Amber rolled her eyes, slouching deeper into her seat. The seatbelt buckle dug into her hip, but she didn't bother to adjust it. "Jeez, remind me never to enroll in any of your classes."

Ashe grunted, a sound that could have been a laugh but was probably just the engine vibrating through him as he exhaled. "We have to get to Abilene and ditch the car."

Amber shot up straighter, her face contorting in mock horror. "Ditch the Vette?! No way!"

"I thought you didn't like this thing? Didn't you want the Ferrari anyway?"

She folded her arms, defiant. "Well, sure, but this one's way better now that it's red."

Ashe finally glanced at her, the faintest trace of a smirk tugging at the corner of his mouth. "It's not about the color. The robbers, the manager, and the waitress will all describe the car to the cops. As soon as they do, any advantage we had from painting it is gone. Every cop will be on the lookout for a classic Corvette."

Amber huffed, her fingers drumming an annoyed rhythm on the door panel, her thumb catching on a strip of peeling vinyl. "You know, you could just let me enjoy one thing without making it all doom and gloom."

"We'll change things up once we get to Texas," Ashe said, his tone brokering no argument.

Amber perked up slightly. "Okay, so just a little detour, then?"

Ashe scoffed, shaking his head. "A *little* detour? Have you ever been to Texas?"

                            ❧ • ❧

AMBER WOKE SOMETIME later, more than a little disoriented. She wiped wetness from the corner of her mouth with a sidelong glance at Ashe and was relieved that he was occupied and probably had not noticed her drooling in the glow of the dashboard lights. The car still hummed along beneath them, but night had fallen, turning the world outside into an expanse of endless black, broken only by the occasional glint of distant headlights or the pale glow of the moon.

Ashe was on the phone, the device balanced precariously on the dash, set to speaker. That must have been what woke her up. *Maybe I should teach him how to use his headphones,* Amber thought groggily.

"You're headed where?" Owen Spirit's voice crackled through the speakers, sharp and filled with disapproval, the kind you could feel like static against your skin.

"Abilene. Actually, a little north of there," Ashe replied, his tone casual. Maddeningly so to the lawyer. Amber could sense Spirit's incredulous glare even through the phone.

"Wasn't there maybe an... I don't know... *direct* route you could have taken?"

"Not one with Abilene on it. I checked," Ashe shot back, not missing a beat.

"Look, we are on the clock here! We don't exactly have a lot of slack in this schedule for you to jolly across every podunk town you want to tourist-hop through."

"Too bad. Isn't a side trip. It's a necessity." Ashe's voice was firm, but there was an edge of forced calm, like he was trying to pacify a volatile client.

Spirit sighed audibly. "Grrr. Make it quick. Why Abilene?"

"I told you. I need to pick up some stuff. And we need to ditch the Corvette."

There was a pause, the kind that made Amber wince in anticipation. She'd been on the receiving end of enough pauses just like that to know what was coming next.

"Say what?!" Spirit shouted. "Over my dead body! That thing is a museum piece!"

"Maybe so, but it's a little on the notable side."

"I don't care! That 'Vette is priceless! You are not just going to leave it along the road somewhere!"

Ashe exhaled slowly, like he was counting to ten. "Calm down. We can move quicker if they don't have eyes on us. We need alternate long-range transportation. The only way we're gonna make it in time is to stay at the speed limit, under the radar, and cover as much distance between stops as possible."

Spirit's voice dropped to an icy whisper, each word enunciated with the precision of a teacher scolding a difficult student. "Listen, you troglodyte. You will take care of that car and make sure nothing happens to it. Nothing," he stressed the last word, speaking it at half speed.

"Of course," Ashe replied smoothly. "I'll stash it somewhere safe, and you can send for it when this is all over."

The reluctant silence that followed was more victory than Amber expected they'd get.

"You better be sure it's safe," Spirit muttered in defeat.

"Stop worrying. How's things working out on your end?" Ashe asked, steering the conversation away with practiced ease. Amber hadn't seen much of this side of Ashe, but anyone able to talk their way around someone like Owen Spirit deserved her respect.

"Not great. Local judge denied my motion to dismiss the warrant, mostly because he couldn't find it in the system. Spent entirely too much time looking for it and set off all kinds of bells with the FBI. If they weren't interested, they sure are now. The judge must have some kind of a rock in his shoe about Task Industries. He asked the FBI if they want to push for fresh warrants and if they wanted to move up the date."

"Maybe he just saw through your shoddy shyster act and figured he better act quick too."

"Har, har. Look. Bottom line is, we might not have the whole week. You need to get your carcasses up here."

"Working on it," Ashe replied, his voice calm but his knuckles white on the steering wheel.

Amber listened, her mind rattling with questions she knew Ashe wouldn't answer if she asked.

৵ • ৶

THEY VEERED EAST onto an even smaller road after a few hours and drove toward what Amber mentally dubbed as a "little bit of nowhere," about an hour northeast of Abilene. The town didn't even register as a blip on her mental map: a scattering of lights swallowed by the vast Texas darkness, the kind of place that existed to be passed through. Amber did see a sign as they passed declaring that the town had once served as the home of legendary Old West figure, John "Doc" Holliday. So, it had that going for it.

As they rolled into town under the cover of darkness, Amber inquired as to the reason for going out of their way to make such an obvious detour to such an obvious lack of a destination.

Ashe spoke softly, almost as if the place could hear him. "Place is small enough that we can drive in unnoticed. No one's awake to care, and even if they were, they won't remember us come morning."

Amber glanced around at the silent streets. Ashe was right about that, for sure. "So, what's the plan for stashing the car?"

"There's a long bridge across the reservoir," Ashe replied. "It's got a mezzanine-type platform under the west side. We'll park the 'Vette there, under the main bridge, and cover it up."

Amber frowned. "Why not just park it in your storage unit?"

"Like I said, it's a small town. Real small. We can drive through without too much notice, but stopping a car like this at a storage unit after dark would make the front page. Trust me on this one."

They reached the bridge only to find barriers blocking the entrance. A bright orange metal sign warned that the bridge was closed ahead but offered no additional detail. Barricades and barrel-sized cones completed the definitive "go away" vibe. Ashe stopped briefly, assessing.

"This is even better," Ashe muttered, shifting gears. He appeared unfazed by the blockade. "It means it'll be even longer before anyone finds the car."

They maneuvered around the barriers and drove cautiously across the bridge. Amber swore she heard the beams groaning faintly under the car's weight, but Ashe pressed on, guiding them to the far side and the mezzanine platform beneath.

Navigating the tricky descent, they managed to park the Corvette snugly under the bridge. As they climbed back up, Amber couldn't resist. "Are you sure this is a good idea? Those supports look like they haven't had a good day since the '80s. If one more pigeon poops on that thing, it's probably all over."

"I'm an engineer. It'll be fine. Let's go."

As they reached the top, a deep groan echoed beneath them. The metal underpinning of the road surface shuddered, followed by sharp reports, sounding like cannons in the still night air. Huge pieces of the bridge's understructure began splintering off, cascading into the dark water below with thunderous splashes.

Amber's breath hitched and they turned to watch the inevitable. The platform beneath the Corvette sagged, held for a beat by sheer stubbornness before giving way entirely. The car plunged into the reservoir with a resounding roar.

Silence followed, broken only by the soft lapping of water against the remaining bridge supports and nearby shore.

Ashe stared down at the ripples. "Well, crap."

Amber's eyes were circles reflecting the moonlight. "Some days you're the pigeon, and some days you're the bridge, huh?"

Ashe shot her a withering look.

Amber's head tilted at the old man. "I thought you were an engineer?" she said.

Ashe shrugged, already turning to leave. "Don't pin this on me! I didn't build the dang thing. Let's get going."

Chapter 18 : GUNS CHECKED OFF

PRESENT DAY

THE NIGHT WAS cool and indifferent as Ashe and Amber trudged along the dusty roadside. The air had already forgotten the shrieks of collapsing metal and the sad fate of the Corvette. Amber had found a flashlight in the car's glovebox—solar, of course, but with ample charge—and waved it about erratically as they walked. The yellow beam danced over uneven patches of gravel and bursts of scratchy grass, casting long, twitching shadows. They walked in silence for a while, their steps crunching on the dry Texas dirt. The darkness was nearly absolute out here, far from city lights, the sky an endless sprawl of stars stretching from horizon to horizon.

Inevitably, Amber broke the silence.

"So, let's recap. Your master plan was to stash the car, keep it safe and hidden from prying eyes, and instead, you drove it onto a collapsing bridge." She spread her arms wide and waved them around as she spoke in an attempt to recreate the event through hand signals in case anyone should miss out. "The whole thing gave way like a wet paper towel. Splash! Bye-bye Corvette. That about sum it up?"

Ashe focused on walking.

"You know," Amber went on, her voice cutting through the quiet like a persistent mosquito, "the look on Spirit's face when he finds out about the Corvette? That's going to be priceless. I hope you're ready to be his personal handyman for the next decade."

Ashe sighed, rubbing his temples as he kept walking. "Are we still doing this?"

"Oh, we are absolutely still doing this," Amber shot back, grinning broadly and adjusting the straps of her backpack. "This is officially my new favorite thing. Because I know exactly how Spirit is going to react. He's going to combust! He'll turn purple. You think you've heard him yell before? Just wait."

Ashe sighed, thrusting his hands deeper into his pockets and looking like he wanted to crawl in after them. "Yeah? Well, maybe I'll get to charge him for emotional trauma and cut my sentence in half."

Amber chuckled, undeterred. "Oh, sure. Emotional distress. Try that and he'll double your sentence for aggravated insult. You heard the guy talk about that car. He practically considers it family. I mean, you do realize you just drowned his beloved 'priceless museum piece,' right? I give it a week before you're back to fixing leaky faucets and unclogging drains in my apartment building to pay him back."

Ashe kept moving, his pace keeping time like a grandfather clock. A grumpy grandfather clock. "Spirit will get over it," was all he could manage.

"Oh, no. No, no, no." Amber shook her head. Curls bounced in a delighted "let's mock Ashe" dance around her freckled face in the moonlight. "You don't just 'get over' losing a priceless car, Ashe. That thing was a one of a kind! He is going to turn you into his private handyman for the next decade. You will be fixing sinks. Patching drywall. Replacing locks. Painting walls. Whatever weird rich-people things need doing in his fancy penthouse, you are *on* it. That's your to-do list."

"I am not painting Spirit's walls."

"You will, and you'll do it with a smile." Amber's grin was wicked. "Oh, and you better believe I'm going to find a way to watch it happen."

"Look, can we please talk about something else?" Ashe's voice was flat, but there was a profound weariness beneath the gruffness. He made Amber think of someone who'd been trying to swat the same irritating fly for two days. Amber grinned in the darkness, despite knowing she was probably the fly.

Not letting up, she said, "Sure. But I can just imagine him standing there, all smug and lawyerly, arms crossed, tapping his foot. 'Ashe, where's my car?'" She mimicked Spirit's clipped tone and then shifted an octave lower to imitate Ashe. "Oh, I parked it somewhere safe, Owen." She laughed at her own impressions. "You know, the kind of place that no one can even breathe on it...."

"Seriously. Anything else. We can talk about anything else."

Amber let the silence stretch for a beat, trying to assess how much farther she could push the old man. Finally, she relented. "Okay, okay. Tell me more of your story. What happened with Hitler after the fire? What did you do?"

Ashe groaned. "Great. That's better."

Amber smirked, stretching her arms as they walked. "You were telling me about the fire. What happened after that? What did you do?"

Ashe was quiet for a moment, his pause measured against the rhythmic crunch of gravel in an off-beat four-count beneath their feet. When he spoke, his voice was a low rumble blending with the night sounds. "I got out of there. Requested a transfer back to London."

Amber frowned. "Just like that?"

"Not exactly. It took some work. Sinclair wasn't keen on letting me leave, but Churchill pulled some strings."

"Were you scared?"

Ashe was quiet for longer this time. "Not the way you think," he finally said. "I wasn't worried about getting killed. What I didn't want was some kind of public event or spectacle where my... peculiar nature got exposed. If that happened, then things would spiral out of control, and I'd spend the rest of my life in a lab, or worse."

Amber pursed her lips, considering. "But in hindsight?"

Ashe grunted. "I probably should've stayed and gone that route. At least then, maybe..."

"Maybe you could've killed Hitler."

A long exhale. Amber was sure he stretched it out on purpose. "There we go again," he said simply.

Amber shrugged. "I mean, I was going to say, 'maybe you could've stopped the war before it started,' but sure, let's talk about the obvious."

Ashe didn't argue. "Yeah," he admitted. "I guess I can't even disagree with that. Either way, I didn't. I left. And it wasn't long before I was pulled into something else. By 1938, I was back in London."

Amber kicked a stray rock, sending it bouncing off into the darkness. "And?"

"Remember that Stein guy?" Ashe asked. "The one Adolf ran into at the museum in Austria?"

Amber nodded. "Yeah. The one who told baby-Hitler he was special. You saying he moved to London?"

"Yeah. Stein showed up in '33, just after the fire in Berlin. Spent the next few years making a name for himself in certain circles: esoteric types, mystics, academics who entertained the weirder side of history. Eventually, he caught the attention of my immediate boss in SIS."

"And?"

"And by 1936, Sinclair had discovered the Gestapo had penetrated several of our stations. It became a scramble to undo the damage, figure out who we could still trust, and, more importantly, figure out what the Nazis were really up to."

"Sinclair was your boss?" Amber asked, unsure if Ashe had already covered that.

"My boss' boss, at the time," replied Ashe.

Amber frowned. "Wait. Wasn't that around the time they started doing all those crazy artifact hunts?"

Ashe gave her a surprised glance. "What do you know about that?"

Amber lifted her hands. "Pop culture stuff. Links from that research I was doing. You know, crazy Nazi superweapons, 'Raiders of the Lost Ark,' all that jazz. It's all kind of mixed up in conspiracy theories and Hollywood and history now."

"Most of it's nonsense, for sure," Ashe muttered. "But not all of it. You think hard enough, you'll realize that. And in 1938, my boss started taking it very seriously. You see, Stein had been talking about Hitler's fascination with the Spear of Destiny for years."

"The what?" Amber blinked in feigned innocence, just to irritate Ashe.

It worked; Ashe cast her a withering scowl. He went on, "the spear that pierced Christ's side during the Crucifixion. The one in the Habsburg was fake, of course."

"But Hitler believed in it?"

"Oh, he believed in it, all right. At least according to Stein. Adolf thought it would grant him victory, supreme power, all that." Ashe's voice dripped with contempt. "And in a truly ludicrous bit of irony, my boss thought I should be the one to stop him from getting it."

Amber wasn't sure she got the joke, but she wasn't about to let on. "Okay, that's actually funny."

"Yeah. Real laugh riot. I told them it was ridiculous. There's no such thing as a mystical spear that grants ultimate power to its wielder." He shook his head. "Didn't matter. The boss pulled rank, Sinclair nodded along, and suddenly, old Ashe is on the case."

Amber let out a soft laugh. "Of course. Because nothing shouts 'military strategy' like chasing after a magic stick."

Ashe smirked faintly. "Now you're getting it. In October, Hitler orders the lance and all the other Habsburg goodies onto a special train. Once the SS gets it to Nuremberg, they house it in St. Catherine's Church. That's my job. Church robbery."

Ashe paused for effect, or perhaps to underscore some point of irony that Amber felt she was missing. "Church robbery," he repeated, "under the noses of a short company of heavily armed SS guards. No problem."

"And let me guess," Amber said, "you failed spectacularly."

"Spectacularly," Ashe confirmed. "They nabbed me, pretty heavily injured. At least I sent about forty of them along to Lucifer before they got me, so there's that."

Amber gave him a sidelong glance, her smile returning. "You're nothing if not consistent, Ashe."

"I'll choose to take that as a compliment." Ashe shrugged, his silhouette barely distinguishable against the dark landscape. "Consistency counts for something."

They walked on. The rhythm of their steps ate up the distance, blending with the fading echoes of history.

THE STORAGE FACILITY sat like a graveyard for forgotten lives packed away in neat little boxes. Rows of corrugated metal doors stretched into the dark, each one a sealed tomb of someone's past. The overhead lamps lining the lot were mostly burnt out, leaving pools of shadow between islands of flickering, sickly orange light. The few remaining bulbs buzzed faintly, casting a jittery glow that made everything seem slightly unreal, like the edges of the world hadn't rendered properly.

Amber and Ashe crouched in the shadows near the entrance, hidden behind a sagging chain-link fence overgrown with patches of dry, stubborn weeds. The air smelled of rust and asphalt cooling after the heat of the day, tinged with faint bites of oil and dust. In a peculiar twist, the scent of honeysuckle drifted along with the mix from atop the fence.

A lone pickup truck rested near one of the units, its headlights casting skewed shadows across the lumpy gravel. The man loading up his truck looked like he'd been poured directly from an aged vat of "Texas Local." Worn jeans, a trucker cap pulled low, and a stained T-shirt advertising a bar that probably hadn't passed a health inspection since Amber was born. His movements were slow, methodical: shuffling boxes from the unit to the truck bed like each one contained the last vestiges of his will to live.

Amber squinted, watching him. "You know," she whispered, her voice low to avoid detection, "we could just tie him up and steal his truck."

Ashe didn't even look at her. "Shut up."

Amber smirked, leaning back against the cool metal of the fence. "I'm just saying. We'd be doing the guy a favor."

Ashe grunted, which Amber took as tacit acknowledgment that she wasn't entirely wrong.

She nudged his boot with her sneaker. "So... while we're waiting... How about you pick up where you left off? You know, the part where you failed spectacularly and got yourself captured. That's where the story gets good, right?"

Ashe sighed, shifting his weight slightly, the worn leather of his footwear creaking softly. "Fine. But keep your voice down."

Amber mimed zipping her lips and leaned in, eager.

"I was captured," Ashe began, his voice low and even. "Dragged through half of Germany. Patched up just enough to keep me breathing. They took me to Wewelsburg Castle."

Amber raised an eyebrow. "Castle? Sounds like the setting of a bad horror movie."

Ashe snorted softly. "It might as well have been. It was the SS headquarters, a hub for all their occult nonsense.

The place was built like a fortress, perched on a ridge like it was daring the world to try and knock it down. They kept me in the dungeon. No windows, just dripping stone walls and chains bolted into the rock."

Amber shivered slightly, pulling her jacket tighter around herself, though the night wasn't cold.

"Then came Kristallnacht." It was a whisper.

"Crystal knocked? What's that?"

"Kristallnacht," Ashe repeated after a deep breath, correcting Amber's pronunciation. "The Night of Broken Glass. For a lot of people, it was the worst night of their life. Until every night afterwards was worse than the one before. After Kristallnacht, they brought in a group of Jews from a nearby town called Salzkotten. Seventeen of them. They were held in the same dungeon I was before being shipped off to Buchenwald. Some of them..." He paused, his gaze distant, lost in memories that weighed more than the present.

"They were kind to me," Ashe said finally. "Despite everything. Despite what I looked like, what they had themselves just been through. One man in particular, he tended my wounds. Helped me through the worst of it when my body was regenerating slower than usual."

Amber tilted her head slightly. "Why was it slower?"

"Because the Nazi pigs never let me heal," Ashe replied. "They kept reopening wounds, testing my limits. Pushing to see how much I could take."

Amber swallowed, the smirk gone from her face now.

"That man... I met his daughter years later," Ashe added quietly. "I did what I could to return the favor. She ran a clinic in Chicago."

Amber didn't press. Something in his tone made it clear that was all he'd say on the matter.

"Hitler and his goons started experimenting on me in earnest after that," Ashe went on, his voice a little tighter. "Draining my blood, measuring how long it took me to recover. But the worst part wasn't the pain. It was what they did with my blood."

Amber leaned forward slightly, her brow furrowed.

"Hitler," Ashe said flatly. "He demanded my blood be used for transfusions. No explanation to his staff, no scientific reasoning. Just orders. Regular transfusions, my veins to his."

Amber blinked. "Wait. What?"

"Yeah," Ashe said, his face blank. "The first transfusions happened right there in Wewelsburg. And wouldn't you know it? Things started going well for him. Poland fell. Blitzkrieg after blitzkrieg. Unstoppable, like he couldn't lose."

Amber's brain spun, trying to reconcile the surreal details with the history she'd learned in school. "So... are you saying your blood made him—?"

"No," Ashe snapped, sharper than she expected. "It doesn't work that way. My blood doesn't do what it does for anyone but me."

Amber pursed her lips. "But Hitler thought it did, right?"

"Yeah," Ashe admitted, his jaw tight. "He did. What an idiot."

Amber was silent for a long moment as she processed Ashe's story. Portions of it nagged at her, tickled at the back of her mind. Slowly, the pieces came together: Ashe's fury about that magazine article regarding Task's blood research, his getting so angry at the coffee shop about her research... Her research. Her research about Hitler. About the Spear of Destiny.

Amber's eyes flew wide. She covered her mouth with a hand to stifle a gasp.

"Hitler wasn't after the Spear. He was after you. You were the Spear of Destiny that granted him invincibility!"

"Yeah, or so he thought. Like I said: what an idiot. The spear was just bait, and it wasn't even the genuine article. The real spear. I'd have known. But the bait worked."

Amber shook her head, the absurdity of the situation settling over her like a blanket. "So what then? He just kept going?"

"He expanded the program," Ashe said. "Decided if it worked for him, it'd work for his top brass too. Göring, Himmler, all of them. Regular transfusions, all at my expense."

Amber shook her head slowly, trying to wrap her mind around it. "You know this all sounds super pop-cultury, right? Like something out of a conspiracy theory podcast."

Ashe gave her a sideways look. "Every myth has to spring from somewhere. You realize that, don't you?"

Amber opened her mouth to reply, but the rattle of a metal door snapped both their heads toward the storage facility. The man they'd been watching finally finished, slamming the roll-up door shut and locking it with an exaggerated yank. His truck sputtered to life with an ear-splitting roar that echoed through the empty lot, headlights slicing through the dark as he pulled out, the suspension groaning under the weight of whatever bits of life he'd just loaded.

Amber watched the taillights disappear down the otherwise deserted road before turning back to Ashe. "Well," she whispered, "I guess it's showtime."

Ashe pushed himself to his feet with a groan. "Yeah. Let's go."

∽ • ∾

ASHE'S STORAGE UNIT, a double-sized one served by a single overhead-track garage door and a separate entry door, sat tucked away in the farthest corner of the facility, graced by a flickering security light that buzzed like a lazy hornet. The metal roll-up door was caked with decades of dust and grime, its faded blue paint peeling like sunburned skin. Ashe approached it with the same wary precision he gave to everything: hand on the lock panel of the smaller door but eyes scanning the empty lot as if shadows themselves could betray them.

Amber stood beside him, arms crossed, her exhaustion battling curiosity. "So, what's the plan here?

We camping out with your forgotten Beanie Baby collection?"

Ashe didn't bite. He opened the dusty cover to the lock panel with a creak. This revealed a dial-type combination panel within, and Ashe spun the dial of the lock several times fluidly in each direction until a soft click was heard in the lock mechanism. Amber was surprised for a moment at how smoothly the lock operated, given the thick layer of dirt on it. It must have been a very high-quality piece, she decided, possibly installed by Ashe himself before she'd been born. Ashe pulled the door open just enough to slip through. He motioned for Amber to follow, ducking through the half-opened door with practiced ease.

"Keep your hands off my tools," Ashe muttered as they stepped into the darkness.

Amber laughed. "You men and your tools. What harm could I really do? Pick up your hammer and bring down civilization?"

Ashe gave her a sharp look in the dim light as he shut the door behind them. "Just keep your hands to yourself."

Before she could frame a reply, she heard Ashe reach for a dangling cord near the ceiling and give it a firm tug. Click. The single bulb flickered, then hummed to life, casting a harsh, sterile glow across the space.

Amber froze.

She'd been expecting dusty boxes, maybe some old military junk. Lots of water, knowing Ashe, having seen his hermit cave. What she found herself faced with instead was an armory. The walls were lined with racks of weapons: guns of every imaginable type, from sleek sniper rifles to battered shotguns, all meticulously oiled and cared for and arranged with obsessive precision. Boxes of ammunition were stacked like bricks, labeled in Ashe's tight, no-nonsense handwriting. Black tactical bags squatted in neat rows along one wall of the unit, each one zipped shut with military-grade precision. Larger, more heavily-worn green nylon bags sat along the opposite side, pouches stuffed with contents that were no doubt equally deadly.

In the center of the unit loomed a hulking shape, covered by a heavy canvas tarp. The thing dominated the space, its silhouette rugged and angular, like some forgotten relic of war.

Amber's mouth opened, but no words came out. She blinked, half-expecting the room to change if she looked away and back again. Half-hoping.

Finally, she found her voice. "What. In. The actual. Earth... Ashe? What is this place?"

Ashe didn't even flinch. He moved through the space like it was the most natural thing in the world, fully at home in the arsenal surrounding them.

Amber spun to face him. "Where did all this come from? I thought you were homeless."

Ashe shrugged, kneeling to unlatch a crate. "I have a home. I just don't go there often."

"But the money!" she exclaimed, waving her arms at the room. "You've been doing grunt work in my apartment building for promises and pennies! Now you're telling me you didn't need money at all?"

"I got money," Ashe replied, rifling through a box of ammunition. "Just not easy to get to. Most of it's in use anyway."

Amber stared, her mind racing to make sense of his words. "In use? Doing what? What money?"

Ashe sighed, standing up and dusting off his hands. He answered her string of questions in reverse order. "Military pensions from more than one war, a few investments that aged better than I did, and I've 'appropriated' some funds here and there from the bad guys. Most of my free money goes automatically to veterans' causes and the families of men I served with. The rest funds... this. You know. Thirty years of storage payments, here and there around the country."

Amber opened her mouth, then closed it again. There were no words.

"Look," Ashe said, pulling the tarp off the monstrous shape in the center of the unit. "Get some sleep. I wanna get back on the road in about three hours."

Amber's retort died in her throat as the tarp hit the floor with a crumpling thud, revealing an old, black Ford Bronco. It was a beast of a thing, lifted on short stands. Thick, knobby tires were lovingly wrapped in plastic to resist the passage of time and cattle-catcher-like bars framed the front bumper. The paint was chipped in places, but the metal beneath looked unyielding, as if the vehicle could drive through a wall just to prove a point. It practically reeked of "ex-military"—not too heavy on the "ex."

"Get some sleep?" Amber repeated, glancing around at the walls of death and destruction. "Oh, sure. Let me just snuggle up with the nearest grenade."

Ashe kicked over the tarp and tossed her a couple of scratchy green wool blankets. "Be my guest. They're in the far corner."

"Ashe! This is not okay!"

The old man regarded the blankets he had just thrown her way, confused. "Well, it's all I got. Sleep, don't sleep. Whatever; I got work to do. Stay outta my way."

Amber grumbled, working the tarp into a half-hearted nest on the cold concrete floor. "'Don't make a fuss,' he says," she muttered under her breath, mimicking Ashe's gravelly voice. "'There's always worse hotel rooms,' he says."

Ashe was fiddling with something under the Bronco's hood when his phone rang. Without missing a beat, he answered, putting it on speaker.

"Owen," Ashe greeted flatly.

Spirit's voice crackled through the tiny speaker, sharp and agitated. "The FBI succeeded in accelerating the warrant. I got the weird impression they were caught flat-footed by the judge, but they weren't about to admit it and caught up quick. There's no way they're going to miss a chance like this, I guess. We've got until Friday at noon to get what we need from the data center."

Ashe glanced at Amber. "That's right at sixty hours from now."

"Correct," Spirit snapped. "Where are you? Are you going to make it?"

"We're a little outside Abilene, Texas. I'm arranging for alternate transportation."

Amber regarded the massive truck in their midst. "You could say that," she mumbled.

"You've already found a place to stash the Corvette?"

Amber couldn't resist. "You could say that," she said again, much more loudly.

Ashe shot her a glare sharp enough to blister paint.

"What was that?" Spirit barked. "Ashe, tell me the Corvette is safe."

Ashe hesitated, clearly struggling between the urge to lie and the inability to do it convincingly.

Amber saved him the trouble. She sat up slightly and called out, "Safe as bridges."

Ashe's head snapped toward her, his jaw clenched so tightly she feared he might crack a molar. "Houses," he growled.

Amber blinked, feigning confusion. "What?"

"The saying is 'safe as houses,'" Ashe hissed.

"Oh," Amber replied sweetly. "Are you telling me bridges aren't safe, Ashe?"

Ashe's face was a mask of barely-contained rage: a mix of squinting fury and wide-eyed disbelief, like his brain couldn't decide whether to reach out and throttle her from his new position under the bus or lecture her about proper idiomatic expressions.

Spirit groaned. "Can we please drop the semantics lesson and get back to business? Are you going to be able to make it to Ashburn in time?"

Ashe reached into the Bronco, unlatching the convertible top with a few swift motions. "We'll make it. It's only about twenty, twenty-five hours of road time from here."

"What about stopping for gas? Are you building in enough time for that? If you're leaving the Corvette behind, you'll have to account for refueling more often."

Ashe folded back the canvas top to reveal two large aftermarket fuel cells bolted securely into place in the back of the vehicle. "I said we'd make it. Your new-fangled solar cars aren't the only way to eat up the road."

Spirit sighed, acknowledging defeat. "Whatever your plan B was, Ashe, it's starting to look like it's now Plan A. Don't screw it up."

The line went dead.

Ashe turned to Amber, his expression softening slightly. Just enough to not completely resemble someone who wanted to kill her in her sleep. "Get some rest. I'll get the old horse ready. I'll wake you in three hours. We'll fill up just outside town."

Amber flopped back onto her makeshift bed, the tarp doing little to cushion the hard floor. She tugged a scratchy blanket over herself and muttered, "'Don't make a fuss,' he says. 'It can always get worse,' he says. You never told me you could tell the future, too."

And with that, exhaustion pulled her down into restless slumber.

ॐ • ॐ

AMBER WOKE WITH a start, the gritty chill of the concrete floor seeping into her back through the thin layer of tarp she'd wadded into a makeshift mattress. The dim light flickering from the single bulb overhead cast creepy, stretched shadows across the walls of Ashe's armory. She blinked hard, her neck stiff from the awkward angle she'd slept in, her mind sluggish as it tried to acclimate to her surroundings.

Then she saw Ashe.

He stood at the workbench, methodically loading a pair of wicked-looking pistols with the kind of focus most people reserved for defusing bombs. *I'd hate to see what he does with a bomb*, she mused, then banished the thought immediately. She did not want to think something like that into existence. The old man's hands moved with practiced precision, sliding rounds into magazines with mechanical efficiency, the faint metallic clicks punctuating the silence like tiny gunshots themselves. Next to the pistols was a black canvas bag filled with several boxes of ammunition: neat, organized, and entirely too casual for her comfort.

Amber sat up fast, her blanket cocoon unraveling like a startled snake. "Whoa! What do you think you're doing?"

Ashe shrugged. "Getting ready."

"For what? A war?" She scrambled to her feet, her hair a tangled mess, her heart pounding for reasons that had nothing to do with just waking up. "We don't need guns!"

Ashe finally glanced over his shoulder, his expression noncommittal. "We might."

"No. No, no, no." Amber marched over, her finger jabbing the air like an angry exclamation point. "You are not taking guns with us!"

Ashe raised an eyebrow, clearly confused. "Why not?"

"Because—" Amber flailed for words, her brain racing to articulate the gnawing fear gripping her. "Because of Chekhov's rifle! That's why!"

Ashe blinked, his brow furrowing slightly. "Come on, what does a Russian playwright have to do with this?"

Amber groaned, running her hands through her hair in frustration. "It's a literary principle, genius. Chekhov's rifle says that if you introduce a gun in the story, it has to go off before the end. You can't just... have it sitting there. It means something bad is going to happen. It's like a rule of the universe."

"I know about Chekhov's rifle. I'm the one who reads, remember?" Ashe asked her. He stared at her for a beat, then snorted. "You're being superstitious."

"Says the guy with supernatural blood," she fired back, her hands on her hips. "I'm serious! Remember in your cave? I saw your old service weapons, and I said something to myself about Chekhov's gun. And what happened? Task shot you! That's not a coincidence."

"That *is* a coincidence. In fact, if you look up 'coincidence' in the dictionary, it's got a picture of me getting shot by Task. It wasn't because of some stupid 'rule of the universe,'" Ashe stated, turning back to his bag. "It's because Task was a narcissistic maniac with a forty-five."

Amber remained resolute and undeterred. She stepped closer, grabbing one of the pistols from the bench and holding it like it was a venomous snake. "No way. You are not taking any guns. That is only going to go wrong."

Ashe sighed, his jaw clenching. For a long moment, she thought he was going to argue. Maybe even snap at her. But then, with a low, guttural grumble that sounded like it had been dragged out of him against his will, he plucked the pistol from her hands, dropped it back on the bench with a clunk, and did the same with the other one. The magazines followed, sliding into place next to the guns with a reluctant sound of metal scraping on metal.

Amber crossed her arms, glaring at him as if daring him to defy her again.

Instead, Ashe grabbed a heavy-looking ALICE pack from the corner of the bench, slinging it over one shoulder with a grunt. Its battered straps were frayed only slightly from years of use.

"What's in there?" Amber asked, narrowing her eyes.

"Just some other supplies I'm gonna need."

"No guns?"

"No guns," Ashe replied, holding up his free hand like he was swearing an oath. "I promise."

Amber didn't move, her eyes squinting with suspicion. "Like, zero guns?"

Ashe let out an exaggerated sigh. "Zero guns," he repeated loudly.

She huffed, but relented. She stepped back slightly, though her wary gaze lingered on the bag as if she expected a rifle to jump out of it on its own. "Fine. But if you secretly packed a gun, and you get shot because of it, I am never letting you live it down."

Ashe didn't respond. He just shut the Bronco's rear hatch with a decisive thunk, the sound echoing through the storage unit like a period at the end of an argument. It was obvious to Amber that he'd used more force to shut it than necessary.

Amber crossed her arms again, muttering under her breath as Ashe stepped toward the door to the storage unit.

"Chekhov's gun," Ashe muttered, shaking his head. He waved Amber towards the Bronco, indicating it was time to mount up.

"The universe is watching," Amber admonished, heading toward her door on the far side of the vehicle.

Ashe's jaw twitched, but he didn't say another word as he opened the big overhead door.

Chapter 19 : UNSAID UNDONE

1988

THE DINING ROOM was lit by the late afternoon sun filtering in from the front room. Second-hand sunlight cast wavering patterns on the worn wooden floor and faded past the dividing wall where weak artificial lighting tried to pick up the task. The air was thick with effort and fragrance from the candle Dani had burned earlier, an attempt to create some sort of sanctuary in this place of rehabilitation and tension. Ashe's dining room furniture had been pushed aside, replaced with physical therapy equipment provided by Lena: parallel bars, resistance bands, large rubber balls, and an assortment of weights. Amidst it all, two yoga mats lie unfurled, side by side on the floor, the unlikely setting for today's session.

Months had passed, and the shattered shell of a man she had first tended to had become something else entirely: still fragile, still healing, but undeniably stronger. A miracle, if she believed in those. Looking at Ashe, she wasn't sure why she'd ever doubted them.

Dani sat across from Ashe on the floor, their mats aligned side by side. Yoga wasn't his style. He grumbled about it incessantly, muttering about the indignity of it, of how he should be straining his body in ways that felt like work, providing pain and proof of progress. And yet, here he was, a man built from war and stone, breathing in sync with her, his body slowly relearning its capabilities— sometimes even showing patience. She didn't know if he had come to see value in the process or if he was just humoring her, but she had discovered it was best to take small victories where she could find them.

Her heart had surprised her over these months. It had betrayed her with every lingering glance, every moment spent watching him push himself past his limits, every fleeting smile. Smiles at his growing progress. Even some returned smiles, ones that appeared to be just at her, allowed when he thought she wasn't looking. She had spent years wading through the murky detritus of her failing marriage, drowning in Wolfe Linder's obsessions, his constant detachment, and yet, with Ashe—someone so impossibly closed off—she felt something else.

Something raw, something real. Something she had only glimpsed twelve years ago as a much younger woman. And now, sitting across from him, watching the slow, even rise and fall of his chest as they worked through their breathing, the weight of not acknowledging those feelings was unbearable.

Wolfe had never made her feel like this. Their marriage had been more of a partnership of convenience, a merger of minds rather than hearts. Wolfe had always been chasing shadows, hunting ghosts that existed only in his mind, while Dani craved something tangible, something grounded. She remembered countless nights lying awake, wondering why the bed felt colder when Wolfe was in it than when it was empty. But with Ashe, it was different. Here was flesh and here was blood, scarred and battered and real. One moment of his silence spoke more to her than all of Wolfe's endless words ever had.

Dani looked at Ashe, at the hard lines of his face, at the silver-gray eyes that seemed to hold centuries of weariness even though she knew he couldn't be much older than fifty. Fifty at most. There was a moment where time seemed to slow, where the world beyond this room ceased to exist, and then he shifted, just slightly—enough to throw himself off balance. His arm brushed against her, and in the next instant, he tumbled, catching her in the process. They landed in a tangled heap, his weight pressing into her as she caught her breath.

His hands, calloused and warm, pressed against her arms as he moved to push himself up, but he stilled when he saw her face: flushed, eyes searching his. His jaw tightened, the flicker of something unspoken, shy and peeking out from behind his guarded expression. Dani's heart pounded, an erratic drumbeat she was sure he could hear.

"Ashe," she whispered, barely aware that she had spoken at all. The words tumbled out, unbidden. "I have to tell you how I feel about you."

He stiffened, a visible tension locking his muscles.

"No, you don't."

A pause. Dani's breath hitched. "I don't?"

He exhaled slowly, as if trying to keep something tightly contained. "I'm not an idiot. I can see how you feel. And I wish you didn't. I'm sorry you do."

The words cut deep. But she'd heard a hesitation behind them, just the slightest falter, and it sent her mind racing. She saw it in his eyes, the undeniable struggle he fought against himself, as though he were fighting to hold back an inexorable tide.

She sat up, still breathless, and helped him back onto his feet. He grasped for his walker, his movements deliberate, mechanical, a man retreating behind familiar defenses.

Dani took a step closer. "What do you mean?"

"Look," he said, looking away, his voice quieter now, "I'm grateful for your help. I am."

"It's more than that, though, isn't it? Tell me you don't feel the same way."

A silence fell into the space between them, thick with unspoken truths. Ashe didn't move, didn't even breathe for a moment. But he didn't deny the feelings she knew he had to have. His hand gripped the walker tighter, knuckles white, as if it were the only thing anchoring him.

Finally, he muttered, "I'm too old for you."

Dani let out a short, incredulous laugh. "No, you're not! You can't be more than ten years older than me. When we met twelve years ago, it might have been an issue, but not now!"

Ashe shook his head, his expression impossible to read. "You have no idea how old I am."

Something in the way he said it—firm, absolute—made her pause. She could see it now, the weight he carried, not just in his injuries but in his soul. A man haunted by more than just physical scars.

She swallowed. "Well, how old are you? I got your blood tests back. It seems like you have some condition that—"

His head snapped up. His eyes were suddenly aflame. "You what?!"

Dani blinked, startled by the unexpected shift. "I tested your blood. It has regenerative properties that—"

"You said you were going to test it," he snapped, his voice rising. "Not have it sent off!"

"Well, there are some things that I was unable to—"

"I never gave you permission for that," he roared.

Dani stepped back, thrown off balance by the sheer intensity of his anger. "Well, of course, I sent it off. But it was anonymous. John Doe. I had to—"

"Had to what?" Ashe's voice was raw and guttural, his face dark with something close to panic. "Had to what? Had to figure out the freak? Had to see what you could get out of it? Where's the reporters? When's your article going to be published? Huh?"

Dani recoiled from the sting of his words like she would a physical slap. "What? No, I don't— I'm not—"

Ashe pulled himself up onto his walker, his body trembling—not from weakness, but in fury. Dani reached out, pressing a hand against his chest, trying to ground him. "Ashe, what is going on?"

He shoved her hand away. The violent action, fueled by frustration and sheer force, knocked him off balance. His body lurched, and before she could catch him, he crashed back to the floor.

Dani lunged to help, but his voice cut through the air, a raw, thunderous bellow.

"Get out!" he shouted.

She froze.

The rage in his eyes wasn't just anger, it was fear. A deep, animal fear. Behind it, she could see the flicker of something else, something buried beneath layers of self-imposed isolation. Regret? Longing? She couldn't be sure.

Dani stepped back, chest rising and falling with heavy breaths. She wanted to fight, to argue, to reach him, but something told her that this wasn't a battle she could win. Not here, not now.

She turned, fists clenched, and walked stiffly out the door.

Outside the room, Dani leaned against the cool plaster wall, her legs trembling beneath her. Her heart raced, not from the confrontation itself, but from the rawness of what had just unraveled. She could still feel the echo of his anger, the sharp sting of rejection mingling with the wet jumble of her feelings.

Dani was a woman who had navigated complex investigations, handled hardened criminals, and dissected the wreckage of human behavior with clinical precision. But nothing had prepared her for the complexity of Ashe. Not the man. Not the history etched deep into his scars. And certainly not the emotions he dragged out of her like old skeletons pulled from dark closets.

Her hands trembled as she pressed them to her chest, feeling the rapid beat of her heart—a heart that had betrayed her with its reckless vulnerability. Wolfe had never made her feel like this. Not even in their best days, before the distance between them had turned into a chasm. And now, after all these years, after the wreckage of that marriage, here she was again, aching for something she couldn't have.

Dani slid down the wall, knees drawn up to her chest, as tears blurred her vision. Tears not for Ashe. Not even for herself. But for the fragile hope she'd tried to nurture, now shattered under the weight of his rejection.

She knew she couldn't stay here, couldn't just sit in the shattering silence of words left unsaid. But for now, she mourned the loss of something that had not been allowed to begin.

Chapter 20 : RESTITCHED

1988

DANI STOOD BEFORE the door to Ashe's house, her hand hovering inches from the chipped wood. The late afternoon sun cast long shadows across the porch, streaks of gold cutting through the dust that danced lazily in the still air. She'd been standing there for ten minutes, rehearsing words in her mind that never seemed to come together the way she needed them to. Apologies were simple in theory, but the weight of her last conversation with Ashe made this more complicated.

Her heart thudded against her ribs, a mix of fear and anticipation. She had crossed a line with Ashe, violated a fragile trust, and now she wasn't sure if an apology would be enough. After two nights sleeping on Lena's couch, stewing in her guilt and regret, she knew she couldn't leave things the way they were. She needed to see him, needed to bridge the distance she'd created.

As so many times before, Lena had been her anchor during those sleepless nights, offering wisdom wrapped in dry humor and clinical detachment that only someone like Lena could deliver, holding that omnipresent purple mug of hers. They'd talked late into the night, Lena relating stories of her father, of the war, and the mysterious soldier she believed had carried her father out of Buchenwald. The math didn't add up, of course. Lena knew that. The man would have been Ashe's current age back then, in 1945. But the resemblance was uncanny, and Lena couldn't escape it. They'd rationalized that if anything, the man must have been Ashe's father. Maybe. Something about it kept Dani from shaking off the impossible question of Ashe's identity and his meaning to Lena that lingered just beneath the surface.

The topic had strayed on several occasions to the emotional minefield Dani was failing to navigate. Dani was fighting to reconcile complex feelings of guilt, curiosity, attraction, and a growing, undeniable bond. Lena had easily characterized the struggle between Dani's professional instincts and her feelings for the man. There was a vulnerability that came with genuinely caring for someone you couldn't hope to comprehend, Lena had told her. "That's why I'm still single," her mentor had added with a twinkle in her eye.

Lena's next words had stuck with her. "You're not just trying to solve a puzzle this time, Dani. You actually care about him. That's what scares you."

She'd hated how right Lena was.

Before she could summon the courage to knock, the door creaked open. Ashe stood there, leaning heavily on his walker, his frame backlit by the dim glow from inside. His face, etched with lines of pain and resilience, softened slightly when he saw her.

"I'm sorry," they both blurted out in unison.

A brief, awkward silence followed, both of them caught off guard. Dani managed a nervous laugh, tucking a loose strand of hair behind her ear.

"You first," Ashe said, stepping back slightly to give her room.

She hesitated, then stepped inside. The familiar scent of old wood and fading antiseptic greeted her, mingling with the memories of countless hours spent here during his recovery. Suddenly, she realized that Ashe meant she should be first up the stairs. Mounting the small half flight, she stopped on the landing to the living room and turned to watch him.

Ashe began the slow, laborious climb up the narrow staircase to the living room. Each step was deliberate, his hands gripping the walker with white-knuckled determination. Dani's chest tightened, not from pity but from awe. Despite the strain, his breathing remained steady, controlled. Dani wondered if sheer willpower fueled him more than strength.

At the top, Ashe paused, not out of breath but as if waiting for her to clear the way for him. She stepped aside, allowing him to precede her now to the couch. The living room had been stripped weeks ago of many of the trappings of invalid care, and Ashe had somehow returned the living room to its normal state while she was gone. She sat on the sectional opposite him.

"I'm sorry," Ashe said again once they were both seated. His voice low, almost gruff. "I've been used as a guinea pig more times than I care to count. It's made me… sensitive. I shouldn't have lashed out."

Dani's eyes traced the faint lines of exhaustion around his eyes, now softened with something she didn't dare name. "I should've respected your boundaries. I got so caught up in the mystery of it all—your blood, your healing—I forgot you're not a puzzle to solve. You're…"

He raised a hand, stopping her gently. "You can't know what it's like," Ashe murmured, his gaze distant, as if he were looking back through time. "To be stripped down to nothing more than a specimen. They poke, prod, take pieces of you. Because to them, you're not human anymore. Just an anomaly. Something to be dissected, cataloged. It's not the tests themselves. It's the way they look at you, like you're less than human… or worse, like you're more than that. And that you're their property, their pet project."

Dani's throat tightened. She could hear the echoes of memory in his voice, shadows of a past he hadn't shared and wouldn't. The weight of those experiences spread over the moment like a fragile truce.

She swallowed hard. "I'm sorry, Ashe. I shouldn't have treated you like that. Despite everything, you're still—"

She stopped mid-sentence, realizing how much her emotion had crept back into her voice, and with it, Ashe's face had clouded. She forced herself to breathe, to shift gears.

"You're nearly ready to be out and about on your own," she said instead, offering a tentative smile. "I think that calls for a celebration. How about I go out and come back with a bottle of wine?"

Ashe gave a small shrug. "No need to go out. There's a cabinet in the basement. Against the far wall, under some old boxes. You'll find it. Grab whatever you want."

Grateful for the excuse to move, Dani headed downstairs. The basement was dim, lit only by a single bulb hanging from the ceiling. She navigated the clutter until she found what must have been the ornate antique chest Ashe had described. Its dark wood gleamed faintly under the thin layer of dust, intricate carvings hinting at a history she couldn't begin to guess.

Opening the cabinet, she whistled audibly. Inside was a collection of wines and liquors, each bottle a relic in its own right, labels faded but still legible enough for her to recognize names she'd only seen in high-end restaurants or luxury auctions. She picked a middle-of-the-road bottle of red, though even this "average" choice was far pricier than anything her father, despite his distinguished career, had ever been able to afford—connoisseur though he was.

Back upstairs, she set the bottle on the table. "Ashe, do you have any idea what's down there? That's not a liquor cabinet; it's a treasure chest. There's probably half a million dollars in that collection."

Ashe glanced at the bottle, but Dani saw no recognition in his expression. "They were gifts. I don't drink, so stuff just piles up."

"Gifts? From who? Some of those bottles are over a hundred years old! You live in a neighborhood where people leave broken lawn chairs out like decorations."

He shrugged. The motion was casual, dismissive. Dani shook her head, deciding not to press further. Some answers, she realized, would come in their own time, if at all.

"Well, it's your loss," she teased, uncorking the bottle. "I'm making dinner to go with this."

She headed toward the small kitchen, already imagining what she could throw together with the odds and ends in Ashe's pantry.

"I'll help," Ashe said, following her with slow, shuffling steps.

Dani paused at the threshold, turning to look at him. The tension between them had eased. Not vanished, but eased. She was grateful for the small victory. "Sure," she said softly. "I'd like that."

అ • ઈ

DANI AWOKE TO the rustling of thin curtains in a morning breeze. She blinked against the light, her head pounding with the dull ache of too much wine. And rum... And whatever that third bottle had been. She took a breath of cool late October morning, suddenly grateful for whoever had left the window cracked. She sat up slowly, realizing she was still fully dressed, her boots neatly placed beside the bed. Her visual exploration of the room drifted outward in small concentric circles, and she realized she was back in her room on the third floor of Ashe's row house.

She frowned, trying to piece together how she'd gotten there. The last thing she remembered was laughing in the kitchen, her head light from drink and exhaustion. She certainly didn't recall climbing two flights of stairs. That's when it hit her: Ashe must have carried her.

The thought sent a warmth through her, even as she swung her legs over the side of the bed and stood, bracing herself for the wave of dizziness that was sure to follow. It did. Eventually she padded downstairs, each creaky step an added layer to the day's assault on her headache, until she reached the living room. Ashe was there, sitting by the window, his silhouette framed by the soft morning light spilling through the dusty glass. He didn't turn when she entered.

"Hey," Dani said, her voice rough with sleep and the aftermath of drink. "Good morning. I wanted to ask you something last night..."

Ashe shifted slightly, his gaze still fixed outside. "Look, I'm really sorry. After a while, you passed out, so I took you to bed."

He paused, his posture stiffening as if realizing the implications of his words. "I mean—" he stammered, glancing over his shoulder, his face tinged with an uncharacteristic blush, "—I just carried you upstairs. That's it."

Dani arched an eyebrow, fighting a grin at his discomfort. "You carried me upstairs? I said you were fit to go out and about, not to do strenuous things like that."

Ashe shrugged, the faintest smile tugging at the corner of his mouth. "I need to get back in shape."

She stepped closer, folding her arms. "The strong wine. And the rum. And whatever round three was. You're lucky you didn't drop me."

Dani watched him for a moment, until she realized that he had no idea how much he had risked with that stunt. "You should have let me sleep it off on the stupid kitchen floor! Do you realize it's been just over two months, Ashe? Two months!"

The man was still confused, so she continued, "Your spinal cord was severed, Ashe. Severed," she said the word very slowly to ensure he didn't miss the point. "And the shotgun trauma. And the burns. And the surgery to try and put Humpty Dumpty back together? Normal people would just now be getting their stitches out. And expecting to be fed like a baby for the rest of their life. Yet somehow, you've received a second chance. A gift! You shouldn't even be walking. And you risked it all to carry me up two flights of stairs."

"I'm sorry if I overstepped," Ashe said, his tone quieter now. "I wasn't sure how you slept, and I sure didn't want to think—" He trailed off, rubbing the back of his neck, looking everywhere but at her.

Dani took another step forward, her heart beating a little faster. "Maybe it wouldn't be such a bad thing if you thought..."

Their eyes met, and for a moment, the room seemed to shrink around them. She could feel the tension, electric and fragile, as she leaned in slightly. But just as their lips were about to meet, Ashe stepped back, shaking his head.

"No," he said softly, his voice again a rough whisper. "That's really not a good idea."

The moment shattered like glass, leaving Dani standing there, her face flushed with both embarrassment and frustration. She opened her mouth to say something, anything, but then her mind caught on a different thread.

"Wait a minute," she said, narrowing her eyes. "I was completely trashed last night. You were matching me drink for drink. You said you don't drink, so you should have no resistance. You should've been plastered. How were you sober enough to walk, let alone carry me up two flights of stairs?"

Ashe shifted uncomfortably. "Um... alcohol doesn't have any impact on me. I was drinking just to be polite."

Dani stared at him. "You were drinking to be polite?"

"Yeah. I hate the stuff. It doesn't affect me the way it does you, and it tastes like rotten fruit, or worse. Usually worse. Not really my thing."

Her doctor's instincts flared, curiosity purging any remnants of her embarrassment. She dropped onto the couch across from him, her headache momentarily forgotten. "Doesn't affect you? Like your resistance to anesthesia? Why doesn't it affect you?"

"It did at one point," Ashe admitted, his gaze distant again. "But that was a very long time ago. Same thing with any painkiller. With the really strong stuff, there's a little relief, but it fades out in seconds. Way too quick for me to even care."

Dani sat back, processing his words. Every time she thought she was starting to understand this man, he revealed another layer, another impossibility.

"How... how is that even possible?" she whispered.

"It doesn't matter," Ashe said quickly, his voice a little sharper. "Don't worry about it." He stood, shuffling into the small kitchen. She just watched him go. He returned momentarily with a cup of coffee, setting it in front of her. "What were you going to ask me last night?"

The warmth of the mug seeped into her hands, grounding her. The coffee, her lingering headache, and Ashe's skillful deflection were enough to steer her thoughts back to the conversation she'd been meaning to have.

"After I left a couple nights ago, I crashed on Lena's couch," she began, her fingers tracing the rim of the mug. "She couldn't make sense of anything either, but she helped me realize I'd overstepped by treating you like an experiment."

She looked up, meeting Ashe's steady gaze. "She gave me something to help try and mend things a bit, if we were interested. Another gift. Would you want to…"

Her voice trailed off, uncertainty catching the end of her sentence.

Ashe tilted his head slightly. "Want to what?"

Chapter 21 : FRONT TOWARD ENEMY

PRESENT DAY

THE BRONCO'S ENGINE rumbled in contentment to have Ashe back at the wheel, the vibrations coursing through the seats as they rolled eastward, leaving the storage unit behind. Amber had been barely awake when they pulled away. Her head had lolled against the seat, eyes fluttering shut almost as soon as Ashe had locked up the unit and climbed back into the driver's seat.

Ashe stole a glance at her in the pre-dawn light, her fiery red hair spilling like a flame across the worn upholstery. In sleep, her face softened, peaceful and untouched by the jagged edges of the world she came from. It was unsettling, the resemblance: Aurelia's face, Ashe's daughter long dead, was mirrored in the girl beside him. That's all it was, he told himself. Just the resemblance. Nothing more. He was incapable of forming new attachments. Couldn't do it, not after all this time. Protecting her wasn't about anything real; it was just the echo of a father's instinct, long buried and best left that way.

But it wasn't just the resemblance, and Ashe knew it. No matter how often he recited that lie to himself, the truth gnawed at him and broke through. The curse wasn't just that he lived, it was that he felt. Every time he thought the pain had dulled, that his memory had finally faded enough to leave him be, someone like Amber came along and shattered the illusion. Whatever the memory, it was always there. This time, it was Aurelia. Amber's unruly red hair, the sharp defiance in her green eyes, the stubborn tilt of her chin—it was all Aurelia, wrapped in the fragile armor of someone he couldn't afford to care about. Because caring meant loss. Always had. Always would.

Aurelia's death had hollowed him out in ways little else had, either before or since. The image of her at the end, her once-vibrant face ravaged by the sickness that spared only him and not a single person he loved. It haunted him still; it was a specter he'd never outrun. He remembered Aurelia's weight in his arms and the last rattle of her breath. The light fading from her eyes even as they accused him with her silent question. No amount of suffering since had ever been enough to answer.

Turning his gaze back to the road, Ashe calculated the Bronco's range. With only about ten gallons in the tank, they'd just make it to Weatherford before a refill became critical. The town was small enough, sleepy this time of morning, and far from the FBI's prying eyes. Perfect.

The Bronco had roared back to life with surprising vigor after 25 years in storage. At least, that had gone right. He'd done the prep: conditioned the fuel, drained fluids, disconnected the battery, protected the tires. The beast had awakened like it was just another morning, not decades later. A small point of pride in his machine, one of the few things that still prompted any sense of satisfaction in him.

Amber stirred beside him, rubbing her eyes and glancing around groggily. "Wow. This thing rides pretty smooth for a crusty old antique. Who would've thought?" She straightened, stretching her arms overhead. "Do you need me to drive?"

"I got it for a while. You rest," Ashe replied, his eyes fixed on the dark ribbon of highway ahead.

"Nah, there's no way I'll be able to sleep anymore right now." She reached into the floorboard behind her seat, rummaging until she produced her bag of coffee beans and a bottle of water. She handed the water to Ashe, who drained it before she'd even fished out a second one for herself.

Amber's green eyes sparkled despite her lingering drowsiness. "So... you gonna keep going on that story?"

Ashe sighed, his grip tightening on the wheel. He glanced at her, then back to the road. "You really want to keep going? We've covered most the important stuff."

"No way you're quitting on me now," she said, stifling a yawn. "You're still trapped in Hitler's creepy castle with him and all his Nazi vampires. You gotta tell me how you got away."

"Fine," he muttered. "We'll pick up where we left off. May 1940. Belgium and Holland fell to the Blitz. Hitler rolled into France soon after. That's when he moved me to the Felsennest."

Amber perked up. "What's that?"

"The Felsennest. 'Rocky Eyrie.' One of Hitler's command posts. Cramped, just four rooms, near Bad Münstereifel. He liked it because it was close to the action. He was there on May 10, 1940, when the invasion of France kicked off."

Ashe's voice grew quieter, darker. "They kept me there, drained me dry more times than I can count. They actually believed my blood made them stronger, invincible. Hitler, his inner circle? They fed on it like parasites. You were right about the vampire bit."

Amber winced, her curiosity mingling with discomfort.

"June 14," Ashe continued. "The swastika was raised over Paris. All through that time, I was nothing more than a resource to them. Hooked up to machines, bled out like livestock. They thought they were gods, standing on the bones of men better than them."

The Bronco rolled into Weatherford just as dawn threatened the horizon. Ashe pulled into a dimly lit gas station, parking beside a pump. He climbed out, opened the back of the Bronco, and flipped the switches on the auxiliary tanks: two massive, armored 58-gallon cells he'd installed years ago. He left the back door ajar as Amber joined him.

"That's a lot of gas," she remarked.

"Long range," Ashe replied, "the old-fashioned way."

As he began filling the tanks, he resumed his story, assuming Amber was still listening. "Late June, Hitler moved me to the Berghof. His retreat in the Bavarian Alps. He spent more time there than anywhere else. Like it was his throne. They kept draining me, trying to capture whatever it was they thought made me different."

He paused, realizing he'd been speaking to empty air.

"Amber?" he called but received no reply. Frowning, he listened. Footsteps, someone rustling through his gear in the back of the Bronco. Ashe sighed deeply. He did not want Amber rummaging through his ALICE pack back there.

Rounding the vehicle, Ashe encountered not Amber, but a young man: early twenties, scruffy, trying hard to look tough with a straw hat and cheap tactical pants that screamed "wannabe." In between the hat and the pants was a bright yellow t-shirt sporting the Gadsden flag logo, its snake warning anyone who might tread on it, or by extension, the wearer. The boy was rifling through Ashe's gear, a delighted grin plastered across his pimpled face.

"Dude, you a prepper? I'm a prepper too! This go bag is legit, bruh," the kid chirped, just as he accidentally knocked a Claymore mine out of Ashe's backpack. He juggled the green plastic brick clumsily, catching it up just before it hit the ground.

His grin faltered. "Dude, What's this?"

Ashe's expression darkened instantly. He let the gas hose clatter back into its place in the pump and stalked over, snatching the Claymore from the kid's hands. The kid tried to hold on, but Ashe shoved the mine against his gut, walking him backward with irresistible force until he was pinned against the station's concrete wall.

Ashe's fingers curled around the Claymore mine, the green plastic case pressing firmly against the boy's belt buckle. Ashe's gray eyes were devoid of warmth, focused solely on the taller man he had pinned against the concrete wall. The faint scent of gasoline wafted over from the Bronco, borne by a gentle morning breeze.

"This," Ashe began, his tone flat and clinical, "is an M18A1 Claymore mine. They call it a directional anti-personnel device. Know what that means? That's a fancy way of saying it's designed to turn everything on the business side of it into a pulpy red mist. See the words? 'FRONT TOWARD ENEMY?' Oh, right. I guess you can't see 'em right now, because it ain't your eyeballs mashed against the thing at the moment. Anyway, pretty simple instructions. You'd be surprised how many people need that reminder, though."

He leaned in slightly, pressing the raised letters of the warning deeper into the kid's waist. Ashe's voice sounded like he was teaching a class to a group of bored students who'd rather be playing outside. "Inside this innocent-looking plastic shell is a pound and a half of Composition C-4, a plastic explosive. Pretty impersonal stuff; doesn't care about anything but doing its job. Packed in front of the explosive inside the shell are 700 steel ball bearings, each one just over an eighth of an inch in diameter. When the mine is triggered, the balls are blasted out in a sixty-degree arc, traveling at over 3,900 feet per second. That's faster than a rifle round. You realize that? Faster than the human brain can even register what's happening."

The young man whimpered, trying to slide along the wall to freedom, but Ashe stopped that by shoving the mine harder still against him, his expression unchanging.

"The effective kill range is a little over fifty meters," Ashe said and spared a glance around. "But you don't really care about that because it looks like you don't have fifty meters here. You don't have one. At this distance, it wouldn't just kill you, it'd atomize every bit of you north and south of your tighty whities. Muscle, fat, lungs, heart... Bones, even. All gone. Just a wet mist embedded into this brick wall like paint. The backblast would mess me up a bit, sure. Probably break my hand, maybe shatter my arm. But I'd take those odds. I've had worse."

Ashe's voice remained eerily calm, the words precise. "The mechanism's simple. A blasting cap fits into the detonator well here. Oh, look! There it is. One click of a clacker, and boom: fireworks. Except I left the clacker in that ALICE pack over there you liked so much. But that's okay; I can just yank on this tripwire firing pin here."

The kid's eyes went wide, his bravado long since crumbled, right alongside any desire to be in the same county as this crazy old man. Ashe continued, his voice becoming low and menacing.

"Even if you're lucky enough not to be in the direct cone of death, the fragments can still reach out to a hundred meters. But if you're thinking of making a move, keep in mind that this thing is fifty years old, if it's a day. And you know how unstable old stuff can be, right?"

The kid's mouth opened and closed like a fish trapped on the beach. He was apparently beyond the ability to form a coherent response.

"Well, let's just say old stuff like this can be... twitchy," Ashe said.

The kid whimpered a second time as a dark stain spread downward from the crotch of his tactical pants. About half of the warm liquid ran into the kid's boots, while the other half trickled in a rivulet along the sidewalk. Ashe glanced down, then back up with a look of pure disdain. Without another word, he pulled the Claymore back and walked away.

Amber emerged from the convenience store, a large bag of road snacks in her arms. She watched as the terrified kid bolted past her and around the back of the gas station as fast as his legs could carry him.

Ashe was just pulling the straps tight on the ALICE pack when Amber arrived at the Bronco.

"What's up?" she asked, arching a brow.

"Nothing," Ashe replied, slamming the Bronco's back door shut. "Just helping that kid find the bathroom."

Chapter 22 : STRANGER SONG

1988

ASHE EMERGED FROM the bathroom, the steady thump of his cane against the wooden floor accompanying his measured steps. He was dressed better than she'd seen him in weeks. Well, better than she'd ever seen him, really: fitted dark jeans, a crisp button-down rolled at the sleeves, the color an understated green that matched some of the still-fading bruises on his skin. It wasn't formal, but it was intentional, which was what made it so surprising.

He looked at Dani across the dining room, which they had recently re-converted back to its original purpose, moving the remainder of the physical therapy down to the basement floor. Very little of the equipment there was still relevant, due to the rapid advance of her patient.

Ashe shifted slightly on his good leg. "Tell me again why Dr. Rosenbaum gave you concert tickets for us?"

Dani barely registered his question. Her head tilted, her gaze narrowing in on his face. Something was different. And then it hit her.

"You shaved," she breathed.

Ashe exhaled slowly through his nose, looking off toward the window as if scouting his optimal escape route. "I did," he admitted. "Since we're going out and all. I... I thought you might like it."

She stepped closer, peering at him under the glow of the wall sconces. Her fingers, clinical by habit, reached out to his jaw, tracing along the smooth skin where his grizzled beard had been. The outermost scars from the fringes of the shotgun blast—barely more than faint, pale tracks now—were all that remained of what had once been a brutal, gaping wound that removed a large portion of flesh. She'd seen men take injuries like that and not survive. But Ashe? Ashe had walked away from that and far worse injury, healed in ways that defied reason. She had been there for every painstaking step of that process, from fevered nights to the slow, agonizing struggle back to his feet. If she hadn't been there, she knew for a fact she would never believe it.

Now, her fingers lingered at the edge of his jaw. His skin was warm beneath her touch, unfamiliar in its softness.

She shook her head to clear it. Dropping her hand, she reached into her pocket and withdrew a small box.

"Hey! I got you something. A graduation gift." She held the box out to him.

Ashe reached out, almost timidly. Taking the small box, he braced himself on the cane and opened it. Thick, calloused fingers gingerly gripped the fine silver chain and lifted it in front of him.

"It's for your locket. The original chain could never be salvaged. Took me almost two hours to pick out all the tiny bits of it from your neck and back. But you were so concerned about the locket, I knew it was important to you. I wanted you to have another chain for it.

Dani smiled at him and continued, "When you value something, you keep it close to your heart."

Never a talkative man in the time she had known him, Ashe was speechless. But Dani could tell he was moved deeply by the gift. She suspected he was not a man accustomed to showing his feelings.

"Anyway, you clean up well," she murmured, still distracted, still turning the image of this kinder, gentler Ashe over in her mind.

"Thanks," was all the reply he made.

But something was still bothering her. Ashe never did anything without a reason. Her fingers dropped away, suspicion creeping into her voice. "You didn't just shave and clean up because we're going out," she stated in a firm voice, almost accusing.

His expression remained neutral.

She stepped back, crossing her arms. "You're trying not to be recognized."

Ashe exhaled. "What? No. No idea what you mean."

"You're hiding from the police."

"No. Don't be ridiculous." His shoulders tensed as he glanced at the clock they'd mounted on the wall. "We're going out. I just wanted to look nice. Why is that so hard to believe?"

Dani's sharp gaze drilled into his grey eyes.

"What?" he demanded.

"It's out of character."

"How do you know what's out of character? Have you ever seen me go to a concert before?"

"It's out of character," she repeated.

"Is it now?" said Ashe, appearing to warm to the argument. "And you know this due to your vast experience of watching me go on dates with beautiful women?"

"Stop trying to distract me." Dani's voice was level, unwavering. She walked her eyes up and down Ashe's clean-cut frame. "It's out of character."

"Really? I feel like trying to distract you fits my character just fine."

Dani just stared at him. She had let this nonsense go as far as she was willing to go. Ashe sensed the change in her demeanor. He exhaled again, his fingers flexing around the handle of his cane. "Yeah, okay, maybe a little of both," he admitted. "We don't need that kind of trouble tonight. Best if nobody recognizes me at all."

Dani took that in, pressing her lips together. Over the past couple of months, she'd pieced together more of his story than he'd probably wanted her to. Some of it had come from Ashe himself: fragments of truth he let slip when he thought she wasn't listening. Stray comments that seemed meaningless until cross-referenced, associated with, and related to other tidbits of conversation. Other background had come from the neighborhood kids. She'd gathered still more from people nearer the outskirts of the police investigation into the drug war that reunited her with Ashe—people who whispered in awe about what had gone down that night, many of them uniformed police officers.

She had tried not to pry. She had told herself that leaving the Bureau meant leaving that obsessive need to know behind. But several parts of the puzzle had forced themselves together for her, whether she wanted them to or not.

Ashe had been injured in the largest incident of drug-related violence in Chicago's history. Ashe had a history with that kind of violence; she had seen it firsthand in 1976. Ashe had a rage in him, an anger that had festered since Vietnam and had only grown sharper over the years. Ashe had money, but he deliberately made himself look like a vagrant—a disguise, she decided, that let him move through the city and go about his work unnoticed, overlooked, invisible. Ashe healed faster than was humanly possible. That fact, before she'd even come home to Chicago, had managed to draw Wolfe Linder's attention.

And Linder had been hunting for someone just like him. Linder had seen through the cloud of rumor, myth, and innuendo that was Ashe's best disguise. No rational person would ever find him. Unfortunately, Linder was probably the most irrational man Dani had ever met. Sure, Linder was a crackpot, but Dani wasn't a fool. She had to agree with Linder. She had pieced together who Ashe was, or at least who he had been. The Pusher's End Killer. Wolfe Linder's most recent object of attraction.

So now here she was. Less than three months ago, she had told Linder only an idiot could see someone like Ashe in that folder full of insanity. Now? She was dressing him up for a concert, watching the man. Watching the way he tried, however reluctantly, to fit into her world for just one night.

And none of the rest of it mattered. Over time all her justifications had crumbled, and she had admitted the truth to herself: she was falling for Ashe, despite his resistance, despite all the warning signs.

Despite every last shred of common sense she possessed.

And just like that, her thoughts were no longer those of an FBI Special Agent who had probable knowledge of a crime. They were the thoughts of a woman staring at a man she had come to love.

She reached out, adjusting the collar of his shirt before smoothing the fabric down over his chest. A small, private smile curled the edge of her lips. "Lena offered us the tickets because nights like this are good," she told him quietly. "They give us a chance to breathe."

Ashe studied her, apparently reading the layers beneath her words.

Dani straightened, shaking off the weight of her thoughts. "Who's going to recognize you anyway?" she asked, voice lighter now. "You're still worried about the drug ring, aren't you?"

"No," he said, shaking his head. "At this point, I'm more worried about looking domesticated."

❧ • ❧

THE EVENING AIR outside the Park West was clear, a welcome change after several days of damp cold and overcast skies. The crisp, dry breeze carried the scents of fallen leaves and the occasional waft of roasted nuts from a street vendor. The city hummed around them, but here, in this moment, Dani felt wrapped in the quiet anticipation of the night ahead. The Park West's marquee lights cast a glow onto the pavement, flickering against the restless energy of the gathering crowd.

"Are you sure this is a good idea?" Ashe asked, his voice low, steady. He looked around at the encroaching mass of humanity with a wariness Dani could only describe as comical.

"I am sure this is a *great* idea," she corrected, flashing him a smile.

She turned to get a proper look at him. Standing there on his cane, clad in the olive Henley sweater Lena had sent—against what she called the "November chill factor"—he looked absolutely handsome. The color was almost military, of course, a possibly unconscious nod to Lena's obsession with Ashe as a soldier. He still wore his blue jeans and navy Oxford button-down beneath the sweater. That color balance helped tether him to the present as a civilian, at least in appearance.

His hair had grown in enough to warrant an actual haircut, and to her surprise, he'd agreed to sit for one. Earlier that afternoon, they'd stopped at a small barbershop just off State Street, where the old-timers still read newspapers while waiting their turn. The barber had raised an eyebrow at the post-surgical mess Ashe's hair had become, but a few expertly placed snips later, his unruly locks had been tamed into something almost respectable.

"In for a penny, in for a pound," Ashe had muttered as the barber draped the smock around him.

Dani had watched with hidden amusement. Ashe sat with all the wariness of a man unaccustomed to the experience, almost like a child brought in for his first haircut and eagerly anticipating the candy he'd been promised if he sat still. His fingers flexed around the chair's wooden armrests as if readying for a fight. The old barber had worked with quiet efficiency, sparing his surly client the usual small talk. When it was over, Ashe had paid, given himself a cursory glance in the mirror, and grunted something that might have been approval. Like many such ambiguous experiences with Ashe, Dani had decided to count that as a win.

Now, as they stepped forward in the line outside the Park West, Dani passed their tickets to the box office clerk. Around them, fellow concertgoers exhibited a collective sense of relief, buoyed by the uncharacteristic clear skies and the rare break from Chicago's typical November gloom. Conversations were lighter, punctuated by laughter. Concertgoers chatted in the chilly air, rubbing their hands together for warmth or cupping cigarettes between their fingers. A couple behind them debated Cohen's best album, the argument punctuated by sharp laughter and nostalgic reminiscences.

Inside, the venue was filling up. The Park West was general admission, which meant arriving early had been a necessity. Dani had insisted they allow Ashe plenty of time. His recovery had been nothing short of miraculous, but he still moved slowly, the cane taking on much of the burden his legs used to bear without effort. They found good seats near the front, with an unobstructed view of the stage.

Ashe settled into his seat, his movements measured and slow. He exhaled slowly, casting a glance around the venue.

"Lena knew this guy, you said?" he asked.

"Yes!" Dani turned toward him, warming to the subject. "They grew up a couple years apart in the same area of Montreal. Lena and her mother migrated to Quebec after World War II. Her mother had been severely traumatized by the camps, and the Jewish community in Montreal was welcoming. That's why Lena ended up in Chicago too, when you knew her in the seventies. Anyway, she and Cohen overlapped for a couple of years at McGill University. He had just started writing then. But once she left for medical school in New York, she lost contact. Still, she goes to his concerts every chance she gets. She's been waiting three years for him to come to Chicago."

Dani let the atmosphere settle in around them. The Park West had a charm that some of the newer venues lacked: a space that felt intimate without being cramped, alive with the quiet hum of conversation. The energy of the night was subtly different from what she had expected: lighter, more open, as if the collective mood of the crowd reflected their relief at the break in the weather.

She looked at Ashe. "Lena was really glad when you agreed to come. She wanted to do something to say 'thank you' for helping people at her clinic, I guess."

Ashe's expression didn't shift much, but his answer was immediate. "Getting me out of the hospital and burning my records was thanks enough."

Dani didn't press the point. Around them, the lights began to dim. The noise in the venue ebbed as conversations tapered off, replaced by the soft rustle of shifting seats and the anticipatory silence that always settled just before a performance. The musicians took their places.

Then, the singer stepped forth.

Dani felt the reaction beside her before she saw it. Ashe stiffened, a subtle but undeniable shift to his posture. His body tensed; the cane he had been resting his hand against was now firmly gripped.

His eyes locked onto the man standing alone in front of his musicians, pale and gaunt, appearing to stand in darkness even under the bright stage lights.

"So that's Leonard Cohen?" Ashe murmured, his voice nearly inaudible.

Dani frowned, momentarily thrown, as the first doleful chords began to dance around the room. "Yeah. Who else would it be?"

But Ashe didn't answer. He just kept watching. And for the first time since they had arrived, Dani sensed something different: a new focus, some level of tension she couldn't quite name yet.

Something other than just discomfort.

రొ • ళ

THE FIRST CHORDS of *Dance Me to the End of Love* drifted like wisps of smoke through the Park West. The voice of a wandering violin threaded through the air, mournful and rich, weaving a path that led to a hush of the audience.

The methodical pacing of the rhythm soon settled into something hypnotic, and then Leonard Cohen's voice, deep and weary, poured over the room. His baritone was like dark honey, thick with time and experience, edged with something both tender and raw. The female accompaniment singers provided a sultry counterpoint, their harmonies full of longing, curling around his words like hands grasping for something they were forbidden to reach.

Dani hadn't known what to expect. Judging by the way Ashe sat stiffly in his seat, neither had he. She turned slightly, watching him in the low smoky light of the venue. His face was unreadable, but she caught the way his fingers rested lightly against his cane, the same way a man might touch the hilt of a knife he wasn't sure he'd need to draw. Guarded, always. Yet, as the song stretched on, she noticed something else: he was listening. Really listening.

As the applause died down, Cohen leaned toward the microphone and let the silence linger for a moment before speaking in a rumbling voice. "When you surrender, you take a wound. And, uh... the wider the surrender, the deeper the wound. That's why there ain't no cure for love."

The drummer counted off time with four sharp clacks of sticks, and an electric guitar wove a pensive intro that seemed to hover in the air. The song rolled forward, the melody both mournful and exultant, carrying a strange but vibrant optimism through its sadness.

Dani smirked to herself, thinking about recent events: her unexpected entanglement with Ashe, the way he had folded, however tenuously, into her life. She glanced at him again, ready to tease, but something in his face stopped her cold. He wasn't relaxed. If anything, he was harder than before, his eyes locked onto Cohen as if searching for something only he could see.

What is going on in there, Ashe?

The third song brought something unexpected. A stocky man with dark, wavy hair sat near center stage, plucking out a tune on a peculiar instrument that Dani had never heard before. Its sound was unlike anything in the previous arrangements—a twangy but resonant voice, older than time, both haunting and strangely soothing. She was no musician, but she couldn't shake the feeling that the scales used by the instrument were not the ones she had learned in grade school music class.

Dani leaned toward Ashe, whispering, "I've never heard a mandolin played like that before."

Ashe didn't look away from the stage. His eyes were riveted on the hands of the featured musician. "Oud."

"What?"

He finally turned his head just enough to glance at her. "Oud. It's an Oud."

Dani raised an eyebrow. "What's an Oud?"

"That," Ashe said simply, pointing toward the musician. "Not a mandolin. Oud. Middle Eastern. Originally from Persia."

Dani huffed, waving him off as she turned back to listen. The song unfolded like a macabre roll call at the gates of eternity. Cohen's voice listing the fates of souls, categorized by the method of their demise, as the instrument twanged and hummed beneath it. Each note was something ancient and inevitable; the tune was both mesmerizing and chilling. When it ended, Cohen gestured toward the musician in what appeared to be a signature practice: introducing the musicians just after they had done a notable work. His voice was laced with that quiet, poetic elegance that made even the smallest words seem significant.

"Mr. John Bilezikjian on the Oud."

Dani refused to look at Ashe. She could feel his smirk without seeing it.

The rest of the first set played out in shifting tones: earnest longing, weary sophistication, the strange levity that came from Cohen's ability to balance cynicism and sincerity on the edge of a knife. Dani could see what Lena saw in this old acquaintance of hers as a performer; the man had a skill for giving even the most mundane conversation a poetic elegance that transcended language.

Dani found herself lost in the music, but more than that, she was fascinated by the way Ashe engaged with the performance. He wasn't just watching; he was studying, absorbing, unraveling something she couldn't quite grasp. Still, he had relaxed, and she could tell she wasn't the only one enjoying their evening.

Then came the last song of the set.

Cohen introduced it playfully, making some quip about world domination which failed to amuse Ashe. By the time the instruments played the first few bars of *First We Take Manhattan*, Ashe had stiffened. His posture remained unchanged, but Dani had been paying too much attention to him to miss the shift.

She leaned in. "What is it?"

"Nothing."

The song itself was an unexpected change, its driving rhythm different from the quiet reverence or poetic expressions of need in the previous songs. Ashe's fingers drummed against his knee, tapping out the beat with an unconscious precision. A quiet response to the song's undercurrent of menace and defiance?

Dani didn't believe in coincidence. She filed it away.

A break. Dani slipped out to the restroom and returned to her seat just as the musicians were coming back onstage.

The second song again elicited a response from Ashe. An acoustic guitar played a soft arpeggiated sequence to support Cohen's introduction. He briefly described his journey from Montreal to New York and his lodgings there. Dani found parts of the story amusing, especially a sarcastically droll part about going to the hotel desk at two in the morning with a pygmy and a polar bear and simply being handed a key to a room.

At the hotel, Cohen described having met Janis Joplin. Dani found the story a humorous but respectful homage to the dead singer, and it seemed to unfold like a surprise to some of the concert attendees around them, despite their every appearance of being regulars at Cohen's venues.

And yet, Ashe seemed anything but surprised by the story, and less than amused by the following song, despite its melancholy humor.

Before she could worry about Ashe spiraling out of control, however, Cohen started to introduce the next song. For some reason she didn't quite follow, he did so in French, and although Dani couldn't understand what the man was saying, a few others here and there in the audience must have. They evidently found it to be a grand joke, for they responded with scattered chuckles, and Dani was about to brush it off until she heard Ashe, of all people, chuckle quietly along with them.

She turned, eyes narrowing. "You speak French?"

Ashe looked at her with the appearance of having been caught in a lie. "Some," he responded.

Dani filed that away as well.

A few songs later, just as *The Partisan* was beginning, Dani felt someone squeeze in beside her. The familiar scent of lavender, coffee, and winter air preceded Lena's voice.

"Sorry I'm late," she murmured. "Traffic was horrendous."

Dani grinned. "I had no idea you were coming!"

"Wouldn't miss it! Been waiting years for this." Lena patted her knee before glancing at Ashe. "And how are we holding up?"

Ashe grunted. Which, in Dani's estimation, was about as much as anyone could expect from him at this point.

Lena leaned in conspiratorially. "I have one more surprise for you both. But you'll have to wait until after the show."

At the end of the song, Cohen reintroduced Bilezikjian and another musician whose name Dani couldn't make out. At the first few solemn notes of the next song, Lena pressed a finger to her lips, signaling Dani to listen. The opening strains of *Hallelujah* filled the space, wrapping itself around the audience like an old lover's embrace. The song built into a pensive self-immolation, testifying to the existence of salvation and vision, laced with sacramental overtones. Dani found herself drifting with the lyrics into a place removed from a world where love's supreme role was regularly denied, and where those who sought it above all else were mocked without mercy as a matter of rote.

The song ended too quickly, as did the remainder of the concert—and not just for her.

During one of the last songs, *If It Be Your Will*, Dani turned to look at Ashe and what she saw made her breath catch. The hard lines of his face had taken on an almost rapturous softness as something raw and unguarded settled into his features. This darker offering seemed to resonate with Ashe, as if the words, the melody, the lament, had all somehow belonged to Ashe long before Cohen ever put them to song.

For once, Ashe wasn't thinking. He was *feeling*.

And for a man like Ashe, that might be dangerous territory.

At the end of the concert, Lena suggested waiting for the crowd to thin, and they lingered as the venue emptied.

Then, from the shifting crowd, a man approached. His jacket was emblazoned with the word, "SECURITY" in fluorescent yellow letters, and Dani could see that Ashe was instantly on guard again, preparing for an altercation.

"Miss Rosenbaum? Mr. Cohen has asked me to escort you and your guests backstage."

Dani blinked. "Wait. What?"

Lena grinned at her. "That would be my surprise."

Dani turned to Ashe, expecting a smile, sarcasm, anything. Instead, he looked... uneasy.

"Ashe, what's wrong?" she asked.

He hesitated, then muttered, "Nothing. Let's get this over with."

ॐ • ॐ

THE BACKSTAGE AREA of the Park West was a tangle of cables, crates, and people moving everywhere in a barely controlled frenzy. The scent of sweat, old wood, and hot electronics mingled in the close air, a tangible reminder that this place had been here for decades, steeped in chaos just like this. Road cases hugging expensive equipment clattered as they were stacked and rolled, their wheels squeaking over the scuffed floors. Overhead, banks of stage lights still glowed faintly, casting long shadows over exhausted techs hunched over soundboards. Roadies wrapped cables with the weary precision of men who had done this a thousand times before and would do so a thousand times more.

The murmur of voices was constant, punctuated by occasional shouts: a request for another hand moving a speaker, someone laughing hoarsely over a joke barely heard in the din, a reminder from a stage manager about call times for the next city. A scrawny man in a worn denim jacket and fingerless gloves hauled a lighting rig toward the loading dock, cigarette clamped between his lips, smoke curling around his head like mist in the dim light. A woman with a bandana tied around her dark curls barked out instructions to a much younger crew member she just called, "kid," who fumbled with a coil of cable nearly half his size.

Lena led Dani and Ashe through this world with the practiced ease of a hospital administrator accustomed to similar chaos, nodding to a few familiar faces as she passed. "You know, Leonard wasn't even going to play here," she said over her shoulder. "This stop wasn't part of the original tour. He's been running himself ragged: sixty concerts, most of them one-nighters. Chicago wasn't a priority. Till he made it one."

"Rough schedule," said Dani. She stepped over a tangle of wires as they followed a crew member through a narrow passage behind the stage. "And yet he did three encores?"

Lena smiled, though there was a flicker of something else in her expression. "Good stuff, too. He doesn't have to do that. I like to think he was enjoying himself."

They emerged into a slightly quieter pocket of the backstage, where a folding table sagged under the weight of water bottles, half-eaten plates of food, and stray setlists scrawled in black marker. Ashe kept his head down and reached for a bottle of water, twisting off the cap with one sharp motion. Dani grabbed a beer from the table, but her attention was drawn to Lena, who was standing a few feet away and scanning the room.

Before Dani could ask, the shift in atmosphere told her something had changed. A quiet ripple, a gravity to the air. Then, she saw him.

Leonard Cohen approached, moving through the chaos with every bit of the slow, deliberate grace Dani would expect from him. His suit was still immaculate despite the heat of the lights, his dark eyes sharp beneath tired lids. He spotted them, and a wide smile cracked his face as he strode toward them.

"You," he said, pointing as he neared. "I know you."

Dani blinked, but Cohen wasn't looking at her. He was staring straight at Ashe.

"Ashe, right? The teetotaler Marine," Cohen said with amusement. "We shared a table in '69 at that place near the Chelsea. The Bitter End, right?"

Ashe's shoulders stiffened. He looked as though he wanted to fade away into the walls. Dani, who had spent weeks learning to read his slightest movements, caught the subtle way his fingers flexed around the neck of the water bottle.

Cohen, oblivious or perhaps just ignoring Ashe's discomfort, continued. "Janis wanted to buy the Marine a drink, but you were drinking water, so she drank a few for you. Found it hilarious to find a Marine who didn't drink. And even funnier that a Marine named Ashe only drank water. Like you were trying to put out a fire or something."

Cohen chuckled. "Maybe I should try shifting to only water myself. Looks like it's done you a world of good."

Then, more softly, Cohen tilted his head and studied Ashe. "How is it that you seemed so old back then, and you seem so young to me now? I don't think you've aged a day in twenty years, despite the cane."

Dani's eyes narrowed. She snapped her gaze to Ashe, waiting for his response, but none came. His face was set in that mask he wore when he wanted the world to forget he existed.

"You know," said the singer, "the cane is a good look. I think I'll get one."

Dani stared at Ashe. He hadn't moved, but his grip on the bottle had tightened. He tilted his head back and drained it in a single long pull, something almost defiant in the motion.

Cohen, sensing his tension, smiled again. "You know, I've seen a lot of people drink liquor like water, but I've never seen anyone but you drink water like liquor."

Dani watched Ashe swallow hard. He desperately wanted to be somewhere else, but Dani could not imagine why. If Cohen noticed, he had the grace not to say so.

"Well, friend," Cohen said, clapping Ashe lightly on the shoulder. "It's great to see you again. Thanks for coming." Then he turned to Dani, his eyes twinkling. "Don't let this one wander too far. He's special."

Dani felt herself flush under the weight of Cohen's gaze. She cleared her throat, managing only, "Yes... I know."

Cohen moved off then, stepping over to Lena, who greeted him with a warm hug and a few whispered words of gratitude. Dani stood still, her mind a tangle of questions, her heart still hammering from what she had just witnessed.

Beside her, Ashe exhaled sharply. "Can we go now?" he growled.

She wasn't sure what she was supposed to do with all of this. But she nodded.

"Yeah," she said softly. "Let's go."

Chapter 23 : BLUEPRINTS AND BEAVERS

PRESENT DAY

AMBER SHIFTED UNCOMFORTABLY in her seat, her right knee bouncing madly. The lights of another semi flared in the side mirror as it thundered past, the air displacement rocking the Bronco slightly. She barely noticed.

"Ashe."

He didn't look away from the road. "Hmm."

"Ashe..."

"Still listening."

"Can we stop now? I'm about to explode."

A rumbling sigh. "Yeah," he said, glancing at the fuel gauge. "Coming up on Crossville. We need to stop for gas again anyway. Last stop before Virginia."

Amber folded her arms, pursing her lips. *I think we both know better than that, Mr. Camel Bladder.* But she had the good sense not to say it out loud.

They were back on I-40, Ashe having chosen it as the most efficient route eastward to Virginia. Amber had nodded along when he'd explained it earlier: something about taking 30 out of Fort Worth to pick up I-40 again near Little Rock, after their top up in Weatherford, Texas... But tracking numbers like that had never been her strong suit. Besides, she'd napped through most of the last leg, dozing off between bouts of munching on snacks and pestering Ashe with trivia and inane conversation.

They'd covered nearly 900 miles since Weatherford. "Okay, but not great" time, Ashe had mumbled when she'd asked how they were doing. Just over 13 hours of driving, with two grudging stops for her biological needs along the way. But at least she had gotten him at one point to admit that, despite her presence, this hadn't been the worst trip he'd ever taken.

That much was obvious. From the story he'd been telling her—his time as Hitler's pet project—Amber could easily imagine he'd seen worse.

"I'm so sorry you had to go through that," Amber told the old man, once she had cajoled him into resuming his narrative. "If the Nazis were taking your blood all the time, how... how did you ever escape?"

Ashe's hands flexed on the wheel. He tapped his blinker and switched lanes to slip around a large diesel truck towing what looked to be half of someone's home. Once he'd passed it and the pickup in front of it with the flashing lights and banner reading, "OVERSIZE LOAD, " Ashe answered calmly, like he was talking about the weather. "Through no fault or strength of my own, I'm afraid."

She waited. He finally sighed, adjusting his grip.

"Sometime in June 1940, Churchill and the boys caught wind of my predicament. They'd figured me for dead before that. By late June, Allied spies learned Hitler was planning to move me—"

He cut himself off, eyes moving toward the rear-view mirror, and flicked the turn signal.

Amber frowned. "Why are we stopping the story?"

"Because we're stopping for gas."

The Bronco rumbled off the highway and into the sprawling, neon-lit expanse of a gas station parking lot. Amber blinked, momentarily stunned by the sheer scale of the place; it was like nothing she had ever seen. The building was enormous, a brightly lit temple of excess dedicated to gas, snacks, and questionable life choices. The service and parking area seemed to stretch on forever. Amber reflected that she'd seen sports stadiums with less parking, and amusement parks that looked like less fun.

Streams of customers of every shape and size and walk of life poured into the several entry doors of the station despite the lateness of the hour, and other streams handled the flood of contented shoppers headed back to their vehicles, treasures stuffed into large plastic or paper bags. Children ran in circles around their smiling parents and laughed joyously. In their approach to the endless row of shining gas pumps, Amber saw a purple pickup truck headed past them with a twelve-foot tall stuffed giraffe in the bed.

And above it all, the benign visage of a massive cartoony beaver wearing a red ball cap smiled down upon his subjects from his place atop the building's main entry. One hand pressed against her window, Amber smiled back at the beaver from the passenger seat, which was suddenly feeling like a prison.

Ashe rolled past several pumps before slowing near an empty one. He surveyed the scene with mild distaste. "This place is huge. I think we should find somewhere else to fill up."

Amber's door was already open before he'd come to a complete stop. "Are you kidding me? This place looks amazing."

She hopped out, stretching limbs stiff from hours on the road, and took in the wonder of it all: the towering aisles of snacks visible through those oversized glass doors, the staggering number of gas pumps stretching out in neat rows, the ridiculous mascot grinning exclusively at her, beckoning her to marvels untold.

Amber looked back over her shoulder, grinning. "That sign says they have fudge! Want anything, Ashe?"

She wasn't surprised at all when the grumpy old man just turned away from her and toward the gas pump.

☙ • ❧

AMBER TORE OPEN her prize, releasing its pungent aroma into the confined space of the Bronco. Ashe wrinkled his nose.

"That stuff smells like a dead raccoon," he muttered, side-eyeing the bright yellow bag in Amber's lap. "Looks like one, too."

Amber, who had just torn off a large chunk of jerky with her teeth, made sure to chew extra loudly for maximum irritation. "It's really good, though." She tilted the bag, inspecting the label. "It really is sweet and spicy!"

Ashe exhaled through his nose in a way that was neither a sigh nor a snort, but something in between—his signature brand of disapproval. Amber had come to thrive on the sound.

"You should've come in! They had an entire wall full of nothing but beef jerky," she said, waving a piece at him like a prize.

"And of course, you had to try all of them," Ashe said, resigned.

"Obviously. Duh." Amber grinned, her new best friend—the cartoon beaver on the packaging—grinning back at her in full agreement. "How else would I know which ones I like and which ones I don't?"

Ashe rolled his eyes, gripping the wheel with both hands. "I'm sure that logic is airtight."

They drove on in companionable silence for a few minutes, the highway stretching ahead in a parallel set of long, dark ribbons. The glow from the dash cast warm light over Ashe's face, sharpening the hard edges of his expression. Amber studied him for a moment before speaking.

"You didn't finish your story," she reminded him.

He was quiet for a beat, his fingers flexing on the wheel. Then, with a shake of his head, he picked it back up. "In July, the SS was moving me to the Bavarian Alps. They had plans for me up there. Plans I didn't particularly care for. But we never made it. The convoy was ambushed along the way by a joint mission between MI6 and the French Resistance."

Amber blinked. "MI6? Like, British James Bond MI6?"

Ashe let out a small chuckle. "They wish they were that glamorous. But yeah."

Amber tried to picture the scene but found it difficult, a far-away look creeping into her eye as she imagined any number of spy books that she'd never read. "I have a hard time visualizing what kind of guys it must have taken to rescue you; they must have been really something."

"They were," Ashe agreed, his tone grudgingly respectful. "And none of them was more 'something' than Conan Everling."

She narrowed her eyes. "Conan Everling," she repeated, testing the name. Rolling it around and off her tongue. It sounded like it belonged to someone important. "Who was he?"

Ashe's expression shifted slightly, the kind of look he got when recalling someone he respected. Perhaps even admired.

"Everling was a former Royal Navy Intelligence officer. One of MI6's best infiltrators. He'd spent nearly a year working undercover as Hitler's wine steward in the Berghof."

Amber nearly choked on her jerky. "Wait, what?"

"That was his cover. He was deep inside Hitler's inner circle, working on ways to destabilize him from the inside."

She shook her head in disbelief. "That's insane. What was he doing?"

Ashe's lip curled slightly. "One of Everling's favorite personal projects was an attempt to slowly pump Hitler full of estrogen."

Amber's eyes went huge. "Hold on! That was a thing?"

Ashe nodded. "You bet it was. Everling figured that if they could suppress his testosterone levels, it might dull his aggression, cloud his thinking, make him more passive."

Amber snorted. "Turn him into history's most homicidal Karen?"

"Something like that," Ashe smirked. Amber wasn't sure Ashe knew what a 'Karen' was, but she was glad he played along. He continued. "The idea was to make him easier to manipulate, maybe even weaken his control over the inner circle. Everling managed to get a few doses into the Führer's meals before the plan had to be scrapped."

"Why'd they scrap it? That sounds amazing!"

"Because they had to lay in a rescue op for me," Ashe said. "Everling got pulled from his assignment and reassigned to leading the mission that got me out. He wasn't thrilled about it—he loved that estrogen plan—but he followed orders for once. MI6 had reason to believe Hitler wasn't planning to keep me alive much longer, so they figured they'd better grab me while they could."

Amber shook her head. "So, this Everling guy. He's just out here spiking Hitler's food, pretending to be a butler, then suddenly leads a full-scale rescue mission in occupied territory?"

Ashe nodded. "He had style, to say the least. After the war, he gave me a bottle of wine he'd stolen from Hitler's cabinet at the Berghof. He said it was his way of thanking me for letting him rescue me."

Amber barked a laugh. "That's… ridiculous."

"That's Everling." Ashe's tone held a rare note of warmth. "You're right; the man was something else. I've served with a lot of brave men in my time, but he was one of a kind."

She let out a slow breath and paused to wipe her brow. Sparing a glance at the most recent flavor of jerky she was trying, she was confronted by the words, "ghost" and "pepper," in that order. She wondered if that should be a point of concern and looked at her smiling beaver friend. That smile was starting to look a little shifty.

"Were you like that back then, too?" she asked, for distraction's sake if nothing else. "All swashbuckling, running secret missions and rescuing people?"

Ashe huffed. "Nah. The guys like Everling, they were the stylish ones. They got into all that flashy spy stuff. I just wanted to go in and blow stuff up." He paused, then added, "But I was instrumental in one of Everling's ops right after we got out of Germany. Just because I had a friend in New York."

Amber perked up, curious for the new angle. "Oh? What happened?"

"The Brits were running a misinformation operation to get the U.S. into the war. Everling was reassigned to America, tasked with manipulating various U.S. news agencies to drum up support for intervention."

Amber frowned. "Wait—are you saying MI6 was out here planting fake news?"

Ashe nodded. "Exactly. Americans weren't keen on joining another European war. Support for intervention was very low and MI6 needed to change that. So they started running stories—entirely fabricated—about British military victories behind enemy lines. A particularly good one was about a British commando raid on an airfield in Nazi-occupied France. Thirty German planes destroyed, forty prisoners taken, the British commandos escaping unscathed. Every newspaper from the Baltimore Sun to the New York Post ran it."

Amber's jaw dropped. "And it was fake?"

"Completely made up."

"When was this?"

"June 1941," Ashe said. "A few months before the U.S. entered the war. The British had been working hard for almost two years to get public opinion on their side."

Amber shook her head. "That's insane."

"That wasn't even the best one," Ashe continued. "In October, they got Roosevelt himself to deliver a speech about a top-secret Nazi map showing Hitler's plan to redraw South America."

"And it was fake, too?"

"Every line on the map."

Amber exhaled, still sweating profusely. "So... were you doing stuff like that, too?"

Ashe smirked. "My contribution was... smaller."

Amber raised an eyebrow. "How small?"

He glanced at her. "Comics."

She frowned, not sure what to make of this. She felt this was another one of those tests that Ashe liked to give her just to see if she could figure stuff out. Try as she might, she wasn't getting it, though. She looked again at the beaver. She was convinced he was laughing at her. She wadded up the rest of the insanely spicy beef sticks and threw them in the back.

"...Comics?" she repeated at last.

Ashe nodded. "While I was in New York, I spent a couple weeks visiting an old friend of mine from England. Harry Simon. He'd emigrated from Leeds in 1905. Harry was one of the few people ever, until you, that knew how long I'd been around. But he always kept it to himself; not even his family knew anything about me. It was our little 'in joke' of sorts. One night at dinner, I shared some crazy, obviously made-up story of my experiences as Hitler's captive with Harry's son, Joe, who'd mentioned he was looking for a superhero idea. Snippets of my experience, not all the rough stuff. But I made sure to include Hitler's desire to create a super soldier with blood infusions..."

Amber's breath caught. "...Ashe."

Ashe's gaze stayed on the road. He didn't elaborate; just raised one eyebrow and let the silence rest in the cabin of the vehicle. Amber's mind was no longer on his story, however. She was suddenly acutely aware of every rumbly vibration of the Bronco's big engine.

Whatever it was that Ashe wanted her to figure out, it was just going to have to wait. Something in her gut lurched and her face scrunched up.

"Uh... Ashe? I hate to say this, but I really need another quick stop."

Ashe glanced over, unimpressed. "That beaver finally turned on you, huh?"

"...Maybe..."

He shook his head, merging into the right lane. "Rest area in five miles. Try not to explode before then."

Amber groaned, clutching her gut. "I make no promises."

☙ • ❧

AMBER GRIMACED AS she pulled the heavy metal door open and stepped out of the rest area's dimly lit women's room. Buzzing fluorescent tubes cast way more light against the stained tile than Amber wanted. The air smelled of damp paper towels and industrial cleaner failing to mask something worse. She didn't want to think what it tried to mask, especially knowing how much she'd just contributed to the problem.

"That stupid beaver may have tried to kill me," she muttered under her breath, her stomach still making its displeasure known, "but he did have nicer bathrooms than this dump."

She tightened the drawstring on her hoodie as she stepped out into the cool night air. The summer heat had given way to the crispness of the high-altitude night, the humidity thinning out as they climbed deeper into the Great Smoky Mountains. The air was thick with the scent of pine and damp earth, a refreshing change from the indoor aroma. A soft breeze carried the distant, whispering sound of a creek somewhere beyond the parking lot. The moon was high, a silver-blue coin casting its glow over the hulking silhouette of the Bronco sitting alone on the rest stop's too-new pavement.

"Guess they spent all the tax money on new blacktop," she mused, thrusting her hands into her sweatshirt pockets.

Amber took a deep breath as she walked down the pathway past the pet relief area, soaking in the contrast between the sterile artificial air of the bathroom and the raw, wild openness of the mountains. Even in the dark, the looming ridgelines swallowed the horizon. The mountains had a way of making you feel small, like an afterthought. She might be a California girl, but there was something here that she could get used to.

She trudged toward the Bronco, adjusting the sleeves of her hoodie. As she approached, she caught the sharp edge of raised voices cutting through the stillness. Ashe's voice, low and steady but laced with irritation, filtered out from the open driver's side window.

"You realize that by conducting an exhaustive search, you're actually making it easier for the FBI to find what they're looking for?" Ashe snapped. "You are conveniently providing them with a long list of places the server *isn't*."

Amber stopped a few paces away, hesitating before climbing into the passenger seat. She decided to prolong her view of the mountains a while and just eavesdrop on the conversation. Owen Spirit's voice crackled over the speakerphone, dripping with exasperation.

"Okay, what do you want me to do, old man? Sit on my hands while the Feds crawl all over us? We've looked everywhere. There's no secret server room. It's a wild goose chase."

Spirit was using short sentences. It must be bad, indeed.

Amber opened the door and slid into her seat, carefully shutting the door. Ashe barely acknowledged her, his silvered eyes fixed on the tree in front of them by a park bench. He wasn't driving, of course, but his hands were clenched on the wheel as if he were trying to keep himself from reaching into the phone and strangling Spirit from a few hundred miles away.

"It exists," Ashe said, his voice firm. "I've dealt with more monsters like this than you ever got to read about in your history books. Dragons always have a lair where they hide their treasures."

"Well, not this one, I guess." Spirit's voice dripped with sarcasm. "If Task had a place, it's not here."

Amber looked from the mountains to Ashe, whose jaw flexed in irritation.

"You're throwing caution to the wind with this search," Ashe pressed. "Every door you kick open, every wall you scan—it's a roadmap, I'm telling you. You're laying it all out for them. The only thing you haven't done is draw them a stinking treasure map."

Spirit scoffed. "Well, if you're so knowledgeable about where monsters like Task hide their secrets, you need to get here."

"Working on it," Ashe replied.

Amber leaned back in her seat, listening to the exchange unfold. She could picture Spirit, pacing back and forth in some server room, ruffling a hand to muss his perfectly coiffed hair, grinding that ever-present practiced smirk of his into dust between his perfect clenched teeth.

"Well, work on it faster," snapped the lawyer. "What happened to that review of the plans? I sent you the schematics of the building. If you think this is so easy, why don't you just point me in the right direction?"

"That file you sent—what did you call it? A PDF?—it's garbage," Ashe railed. "Image clarity's too poor, and the file itself is just a stripped-down variant of the real plans.

Absolutely nothing in there I can use. Probably meant for tax assessments or some other bureaucratic nonsense."

"You think I don't know that?" Spirit shot back. "It's all we have. Fry and I have torn through every document in the building, and there's nothing. Nothing. No hidden server room, no blueprints, no schematics, no mysterious notes scribbled on a whiteboard somewhere. Just a big empty hole where all of Task's dirty secrets should be. We can't even find the architecture firm that built the place."

Ashe exhaled through his nose, rubbing his fingers against the bridge of his nose like he was trying to press down a headache. "Well, you're gonna have to. You're going to have to get me some real schematics," he said, his voice like steel. "I need everything. Every vent, every structural beam, every rivet. If it's in that building, I want to see it."

Spirit let out a sharp, humorless laugh. "Oh, sure. It'll just happen. Because that's what I do. That's my skillset. I wake up every day trying to figure out the best way to stage a heist."

Ashe's eyes darkened. "Tomorrow, you do."

Spirit's voice raised half an octave. "How am I supposed to do that? Where do I find these magical plans, Ashe? Tell me that, O wise one!"

"What did the Fire Department say?"

Silence settled over the line.

Ashe stared at the tree.

The silence continued.

Ashe stared at the tree as if willing it to wither and die.

Ashe spoke slowly, enunciating every word. "Please tell me you've already tried asking the Fire Department for their plans on file."

Spirit finally broke the silence, his tone all business. "Fine. I'll get you the best actual printed copies of the facility's plans I can find. We'll reconvene when you get here."

Ashe's teeth were locked together. "We can be there in six to eight hours," he growled.

"Lovely. I'll have the champagne on ice," Spirit deadpanned.

The call disconnected with a quiet click. It was the closest thing to humility Amber figured she'd ever see from Owen Spirit.

Chapter 24 : I WANTED A UNICORN

1988

DANI CLIMBED THE worn steps to Ashe's house, pausing at the top when she found the door locked. She frowned. All the time she had spent here, it had never been locked. Ashe only locked the door when he was gone.

That wasn't a good sign.

She exhaled slowly, tamping down her unease. Maybe he had just gone for a walk. Maybe he had needed some air after last night's disaster of a conversation. She rubbed her arms against the cool morning breeze, replaying the argument in her mind. After the concert, everything she had said had only made him angrier. She had been flippant, and he had shut down. He had barely said goodnight before she had left to find a hotel to check into, and the silence between them had felt heavier than anything either of them had said aloud.

Dani had told herself she would give him some space. Let the dust settle. But she had already decided she would be here every day for at least another week. That was her excuse, anyway: he still needed to heal, to rebuild his strength with a sense of independence. That was her professional justification. The truth, the one she would never admit to herself without criticism, was far more selfish. She simply wanted to be near him.

Ashe would be back to his old life soon, whatever that entailed. Helping out around the neighborhood, going back to his so-called job. And her? She would finalize her withdrawal from the Bureau, resume her position under Lena at the hospital. She had already made that decision. It would put her right where she needed to be. Here in Chicago, working at Sacred Cross, just over in Ashburn.

In case Ashe got hurt again. Yes, that was the reason.

She sighed, running a hand through her hair as she stepped back from the door. Last night, despite everything, had still revealed something important. Something Ashe could never take back, no matter how he tried to retreat. He had felt something. The concert had shown that. And no amount of irritation, evasion, or denial could erase the look she'd seen on his face.

Dani swallowed hard. Feelings.

She had them. Deep ones. And she was almost certain Ashe did too, even if he refused to name them. The problem was, she had spent weeks pushing aside a truth that now sat heavy in her chest, demanding attention.

She was still married.

Her hands curled into fists at her sides. Linder had done this to her before. She had given him divorce papers—twice—and both times, he had refused to sign. He had ignored them, convinced her to stay, told her things would change. That he could change.

He had never changed. He had only wanted *her* to change.

That was why she had left. That was why she had quit the Bureau and walked away from her marriage in the same breath. But walking away wasn't enough. The legal ties were still there, still binding her to Wolfe Linder, a man who wouldn't let go unless she forced him to.

She had to tell Ashe.

Then she had to go to D.C. and make Linder finalize the divorce. He could keep the apartment. He could have everything. She didn't care. She just wanted her freedom.

Her freedom and Ashe.

The thought sent a pulse of panic through her. And suddenly, the weight of it all—the fear, the uncertainty, the failures—pulled taut in her chest. She had been so consumed by her denial, her infatuation, that she had missed something crucial. Something she should have told Ashe about weeks ago.

Linder had come to their apartment in Alexandria. He had brought a file; one of his mystery cases. A case he had still been working when she left.

Linder had been tracking the Pusher's End Killer. And if he kept following that trail, it was only a matter of time before he realized the recent incident here in Chicago was related.

Linder was coming to Chicago.

Linder was coming for Ashe.

Dani's pulse spiked. Spurred on by this new urgency, she grabbed her key and wrenched open the door, stepping inside before she had even finished processing the thought.

"Ashe!"

The house was silent. She moved quickly through the main floor, calling his name again. No response.

Her stomach clenched. He shouldn't be climbing stairs yet, but he had done so before to put her to bed after their celebration dinner. She hurried up to the second and third floors, then down all the way to the basement. Empty.

She returned to the main floor, forcing herself to think. Ashe had to use one of the entry doors to come back inside. If she positioned herself just right, she could see both, and could catch him immediately, warn him of the danger. She took a breath, moving to the perfect vantage point.

She sat down to watch and wait.

DANI HAD DOZED off.

A noise downstairs jolted her awake, adrenaline chasing away the sluggish remnants of sleep. She sat up abruptly, heart hammering against her ribs. The house was quiet now, but she knew what she had heard— someone moving below. Not the groan of the building settling, not the wind rattling against the old windowpanes. Footsteps.

She swung her legs over the side of the couch, moving swiftly and silently to the basement door. The scent of dust and oil met her as she descended, the air thick with the unique scent of the old house. The basement was the same maze of oil drums, stacked crates, and furniture draped in dusty sheets it had been for weeks, but the light coming from the bathroom ahead was new.

Her breath caught when she finally spotted him.

Ashe stood hunched over the small bathroom sink, his bare back marred with fresh cuts. Blood slicked his skin, dripping sluggishly from a deep gash along his ribs. His left shoulder hung low, the unnatural angle clear even in the dim light. He was struggling to keep his breathing steady as he pressed a towel to the worst of the wounds.

Dani stepped into the bathroom doorway, her voice low and sharp. "What happened to you?"

Ashe flinched at her voice but didn't turn. "Working down here. Got careless."

"Liar."

She stormed forward, yanking the towel from his grasp and replacing it with a fresh one from the cabinet.

Her hands worked automatically, cleaning the wound with an efficiency that gave her something to think on besides the anger boiling within her.

"How did you even get past me? I was in the living room, Ashe. There's only one way downstairs."

He did his usual trick she hated—pretending he hadn't heard.

"Ashe."

No response.

Her eyes narrowed. "What were you really doing?"

He exhaled sharply. She wasn't being gentle. "I told you. Just some work."

Dani clenched her jaw. Fine. If he wanted to play it that way, she'd make him regret it.

"Sit."

He hesitated.

"Now."

With a sigh, he eased onto the closed toilet lid. Dani placed one foot on Ashe's thigh. She braced her knee against his ribs, just below his armpit. Taking his arm firmly in her hands by the wrist, she paused.

"This is going to hurt."

"It usually does," he muttered.

She yanked, hard, driving his shoulder back into place with a sickening pop. Ashe let out a sharp grunt, his whole body tensing before he slumped forward, breathing hard through his nose.

Dani's anger surged. She released the arm. "What were you really doing? What happened?"

"I already told you—"

"Stop lying to me!" she snapped, stepping back, hands clenched at her sides. "I've been forcing myself to turn a blind eye to your activities because you've been healing. But if you're starting again—"

"Activities?" Ashe interrupted, his voice low. "What activities?"

Dani threw her hands up. "Don't deny it! And don't lie to me. Even if I ignore what you're doing—and that's getting harder by the day—you're not ready. You could be seriously injured."

He let out a short, humorless laugh. "More seriously than I've already been?"

Dani stared at him, mouth agape with disbelief. "How can you take your healing for granted? You should be thankful for the miracle you've experienced."

Ashe's expression darkened. "Miracle?" he snarled. "That's what you think this is? Yes, it is a miracle! Every day. So why is it also such a curse?"

Dani's chest tightened. "A curse? What is a curse about any of this? You've recovered from injuries in just a few months that should have had you in a wheelchair for life!"

He shrugged. "Yeah, I do that. And you know what it means? It means I have to get back to work."

Dani's breath caught. "Work? You mean killing people."

"If necessary, yes. Bad people. People who prey on the helpless."

Her voice dropped, barely more than a whisper. "Dangerous people, Ashe. What if something happens to you? What if you die?"

His gaze softened, but his voice remained firm. "I won't. Trust me."

Dani's throat tightened. "You're awful glib about it when it's not your feelings at stake, aren't you? What happened to you? Have you been alone so long you can't see how I feel? You don't care how I feel, do you?"

Ashe's jaw tightened. "We should stop this conversation, Dani. Right now."

"No!" Her voice cracked. "I'm done being told how I should feel. Who I should love. What I should do. You're not the only one who's been alone."

Ashe exhaled sharply, running a hand through his hair, wincing at the pain it caused his abused shoulder. "Dani—"

She didn't let him finish. She grabbed him, her hands fisting in his shirt as she kissed him.

For a moment, he was rigid, frozen in shock. Then his body melted into hers, his hands sliding gently up her arms before gripping her waist, pulling her closer. She felt his resolve crack, just for an instant—

Then he stiffened. He turned his head away, breaking the kiss as though it had burned him.

Dani's breath was shaky. "Ashe..."

His voice was hoarse. "You should go."

"Ashe, you know how I feel about you," pleaded Dani.

"Yeah. And I'm sorry you do."

She stared at him, waiting for him to take it back. To say something—anything—that would help her make sense of this. But he wouldn't even look at her.

Her chest ached as she turned and left.

By the time she reached the street, she could barely see through her tears.

ॐ • ॐ

THE SUN HUNG low in the sky as Dani climbed Ashe's front steps for the second time that day. Her earlier departure had been a storm, a whirlwind of emotions she had still yet to process. Now, her pulse beat steadily, driven less by the heat of their earlier argument and more by determination. She had failed to warn him. That realization gnawed at her, pulling her back here.

In the heat of everything that had happened, Dani had lost sight of her purpose. All her resolve had been swept away by the chaos of their confrontation. But she hadn't come to confront Ashe about his injuries or his dangerous habits. No, she had come to tell him something far more pressing: Wolfe Linder was bound to be coming for him.

She unlocked the door, the key turning with a soft click. For the second time that day, she stepped inside, tension coursing through her muscles. Her footsteps echoed softly on the hardwood floors as she moved further into the house.

"Ashe?" she called, her voice steady, but the silence that followed was unnerving.

She walked through the rooms one by one, her eyes scanning for any sign of him. The house felt hollow, like it was holding its breath. The scent of antiseptic from his wounds earlier in the day lingered in the air, mixing with the usual scent of aged wood and old books.

Empty.

Dani swallowed the knot rising in her throat and leaned against the doorframe.

Her plan had seemed so clear just an hour ago. She had convinced herself that this news—Linder's impending arrival—would finally wake Ashe up. Make him realize how dangerous his vigilantism had become.

She would appeal to his fear of being captured, she'd reasoned. He had told her how much he feared becoming a lab rat, how his special blood would turn him into nothing more than a research project if the wrong people got their hands on him. Dani suspected that strange blood was a key factor in his ability to heal, and she could easily imagine how misinformation and half-truths would spread like wildfire, turning him into the centerpiece of one of Linder's infamous "supernatural" cases.

Surely that fear alone would be enough to make Ashe stop.

Or so she hoped.

She also hoped that the bombshell that Wolfe Linder wasn't just coming for him but was also her husband might somehow be something they could work through. How exactly that was supposed to happen, she had no idea. But hope was a stubborn thing.

Maybe she'd get lucky. Maybe they could find a way to push through it.

Or maybe she'd look into getting a unicorn.

At least then, she'd have a unicorn.

The silence in the house was almost a physical thing. Her fingers tightened around the strap of her bag, the weight of everything sinking deeper into her chest. She had come here determined to help him, to warn him, even if it meant throwing away the fragile relationship they had started to build. If keeping him safe meant losing him, then so be it.

She could live with sadness. What she couldn't live with was standing by and watching him destroy himself.

With a sigh, Dani pulled the door shut behind her as she stepped in again to wait.

She walked through the old house, possibly for the last time, turning on the occasional light as a talisman against the encroaching dusk. She slipped her hands into her pockets and forced her feet to carry her around as she searched for her heart. It wasn't here. There was nothing here.

For now, there was nothing more she could do but hope.

Hope for Ashe.

For herself.

And maybe, if the universe was feeling generous, for a unicorn.

❧   •   ❦

THE SUN HAD long since set by the time Dani found herself back in the basement. The dim overhead light threw long shadows over the cluttered space, highlighting the maze of oil drums, boxes, and forgotten furniture that filled the long, narrow room. Her steps slowed as she moved further into the basement, her eyes scanning the disarray with growing curiosity. Something wasn't sitting right with her.

She stopped near the far wall, her gaze drawn downward. A small, dark stain caught her attention—a spot of blood on the concrete floor, doubtless from Ashe's misadventures earlier in the day. But why was it back here, among the ancient heating oil drums? Had Ashe been telling her the truth? Had he actually just been working down here and hurt himself? Her heart quickened, grieved at how badly she might have hurt their fledgling bond because of a misunderstanding and her lack of trust.

Or had she been right?

No. It wasn't just one spot. There were more, a sporadic trail of droplets winding through the boxes and drums, leading her deeper into the basement.

Her investigative instincts flared, sharp and familiar, like slipping into a well-worn jacket. She crouched, following the blood trail as it snaked through the clutter. It wove an odd, deliberate path, like Ashe had been moving cautiously—or deliberately avoiding something. The trail ended at the rear wall, just below a set of exposed conduit pipes and an electric meter.

That made no sense.

Dani straightened, her hand resting on the cold brick. It looked solid enough, but something about it felt off. She looked over the entire wall but couldn't identify what was setting off the alarms. Something just... wasn't right. Her fingers brushed over the surface, searching for irregularities. The brick beneath her hand gave slightly— a nearly imperceptible shift, accompanied by faint clicks at the floor and ceiling level. She pressed harder, and with a low, grinding noise, the wall began to pivot inward.

Her breath caught as the hidden door swung open, revealing a dark passageway beyond. The doorway was clever—ingeniously disguised behind the piles of junk and electrical equipment. When closed, it blended seamlessly with the rest of the wall. When opened, it pivoted around the metal conduit and meter, which she now saw were free-standing and contributed to the illusion. Dani hesitated for only a moment before stepping inside.

The passage was narrow, dimly lit by a series of small bulbs strung along the ceiling. The air was cool and carried a faint scent of dust and damp stone. Her footsteps resounded softly as she moved deeper into the corridor, each step taking her further into Ashe's secret world. The tunnel opened into what seemed to be another basement, this one beneath the neighboring row house.

A heavy metal door blocked her way, modern and reinforced with a high-quality lock. Dani frowned, studying the mechanism. It was sleek, state-of-the-art—

not the kind of thing you'd expect to find in an old row house. Her fingers danced over the lock, assessing it with skill before grabbing a slim lock pick from her wallet. It took longer than she liked, but after a few tense moments, she heard the soft click of success.

The door swung open, and Dani stepped inside.

Her breath caught.

Weapons lined the walls: rifles, shotguns, and handguns meticulously organized on racks and shelves. Ammo crates were stacked neatly throughout the large room. On the far wall, a massive corkboard dominated the space, covered with newspaper clippings, photographs, maps, and handwritten notes. Red string connected various elements in a chaotic jumble of connections. Dani's eyes flicked over the names and locations scrawled in bold ink: street corners, gang leaders, unsolved murders... All tied together by one common thread: vengeance.

Her stomach twisted. This wasn't just a collection of notes. It was an intricate web, forming what could only be described as a literal murder board.

She walked along the long board almost in a trance, her fingers brushing over the framed edge of the corkboard. Familiar names leapt out at her: names from recent news reports, places she recognized from case files. This was meticulous, calculated. Dani's head spun as she realized how much planning had gone into this.

It was a blueprint for war. And Ashe was the architect.

Dani felt her pulse quicken as she realized just how far down the rabbit hole she had gone. She was an FBI agent, for God's sake. This wasn't just a man she cared for, this was a vigilante on a national scale, and by keeping his secrets, she had become an accomplice.

"How long have you been doing this?" she whispered to herself.

Her gaze wandered to a nearby table cluttered with personal items. A stack of old photographs sat next to a battered comic book. Captain America #1, signed by Joe Simon with an inscription that read, "To Ashe—thanks." Dani barely registered the comic, her attention drawn instead to the photos.

One showed Ashe standing with a woman in what appeared to be the mid-1800s. Another captured him with a group of soldiers during World War I. There were more: images spanning decades, each one with Ashe in it. His face never changed. He stood in different uniforms, among different people, in different wars and times. But it was always him, always the same, ageless face.

Above a small table bearing a few melted candles was a rich wooden shadowbox, fronted with glass and affixed to the brick wall. Inside the box was an ancient manuscript of some sort. Written in Latin on stretched calfskin—dry and brittle and cracked by long centuries— it was an illuminated page from an ancient Bible, penned long before the printing press had been imagined. The page, displaying the first eight verses of 1 Chronicles 22, was unfinished, the hand of the scribe so long ago having been interrupted before he could finish his holy work. Though the Latin of the text was far different than what she'd learned in medical school, she recognized enough of it to sense not only the weight of the page's history, but of its words.

A nearby box sat half-open, filled with an odd assortment of items: an old MI6 badge bearing the name Ashe Bridger, a well-preserved Roman gladius in a worn scabbard, and several battered Roman legion markers. Each a valuable relic in its own right, these items were unceremoniously dumped in the box together as if they were mismatched plates or papers, too precious to throw away but not important enough to feature.

But it was the paintings that truly caught her attention.

Two full-length portraits, lovingly framed and carefully displayed, stood on a shelf by the far wall. The first depicted a woman in Roman garb, holding a sprig of herbs, her eyes bright with a gentle smile. The second showed the same woman bending over a crib, a red-haired child cradled within. The brushstrokes were intimate, the details meticulous, the sense of light almost ethereal. Dani felt an inexplicable pang of sadness as she stared at the woman's face.

The door behind her creaked, and Dani spun around.

Ashe stood framed in the doorway, a bag of groceries in his hand. His eyes flicked to the open cabinets, the scattered photos, and the unlocked door. His jaw tightened.

"You weren't supposed to see this."

Dani's voice shook with barely restrained fury. "Really? Because it sure feels like I was meant to see it. I feel like the universe just came riding up to me on a frigging multicolor unicorn and said, 'hey, Dani, come follow me; you have *got* to see this. Wouldn't want you to miss out on a chance to tour the Ashecave!' You've been lying, Ashe. For how long?"

He set the bag down on a nearby table, his eyes never leaving hers. "I guess the whole time... But I wasn't lying. I just... didn't tell you everything."

"Not 'how long have you been lying to me?' I think we *all* know the answer to that one. No, I mean, how long have you been doing this? How many years have you been chasing around, waging your own little war? Ever since we met back at the clinic, I'm sure. Before that? How long, Ashe? How long?"

Ashe was unable to form an answer before Dani continued her tirade.

"Didn't tell me everything? Didn't tell me everything? Well, there's a shocker!" Dani threw a handful of photos onto the table. "Did you tell me anything? Anything at all? How on earth could you tell me all this? How could you *not?!* This is another world! Another life! What the... What is all of this?" Her voice rose with each word, cracking under the weight of her anger and confusion.

Ashe set the bag of groceries down and ran a hand through his hair. "It's... complicated."

"Oh, don't even give me the 'it's complicated' bit." Dani gesticulated wildly, windmilling her arms as she spoke. "'Dani, I don't like your meat loaf.' That's pretty simple. 'Dani, I have a girlfriend. She's an alpaca.' That's complicated." Dani's voice echoed in the room, harsh and raw. "Complicated doesn't even *begin* to cover this! I've been dragged into another zealot's crusade! Do you have any idea how far off track I've gotten? I'm supposed to be an FBI Agent!" She grabbed a stack of photos and waved them in his face. "Who are these people? Where did these guns come from? Who are you?!"

Her voice broke, but she didn't stop. She couldn't. "How many wars have you fought in, Ashe? How many lives have you taken? How many outside of wars? Do you even keep track anymore? Were you planning on telling me any of this, or was I supposed to just keep stitching you up while pretending none of it mattered? That's got to be the greatest thing in the world to a murderous vigilante, right? Your own personal doctor?" Her breath hitched, her words spilling out faster, barely coherent. "I thought I knew who you were. I thought I could trust you! I—"

She slammed her fists into his chest, once, twice, her voice climbing into a near-hysterical pitch. "Why didn't you tell me?! Why did you let me fall into this madness with you?! I thought you were off on another mission! I thought you were going to get yourself killed!"

Her strength gave out, and she crumpled against him, her sobs raw and unrelenting. Ashe caught her wrists gently, holding her hands against his chest, not flinching, not pulling away. His breath remained steady as he waited for her storm to break.

"I wasn't," he said softly. "I was picking up groceries. I decided... Last night, after the concert. I'm done. No more missions. No more war. I was going to make you an apology dinner."

Dani blinked, caught off guard, her breath coming in gasps. "You... what? You—"

"I went by Sacred Cross," he said. "You weren't there. Lena hadn't seen you."

"I was here," Dani whispered, her voice hoarse and broken.

Her eyes drifted back to the photos, her mind reeling. For now, she just leaned in Ashe's arms, too weak to stand without him. "The woman in the paintings, Ashe," she asked, "...who is she?"

Ashe followed her gaze. "Magdaia. Maggie, my first wife, when I lived in England the first time. Hadrian's Wall," he said, as if any of it made sense.

He pointed to the second painting. "Her with our daughter, Aurelia. I had those commissioned from a young guy I met later in Italy, named Zocchi. The photos? Those are Lorena, my second wife. Just before the war came to Winchester and wouldn't leave."

Dani's eyes moved again to the yellowing black and white photos, the woman in antebellum dress, Ashe in an officer's uniform from history books. "Winchester... you fought in the Civil War. For the South."

"I wasn't a slaver, if that's what you're thinking. Never owned another man. Not in Rome, and not then. Man can't own another man; goes against all that's right. But like most wars, that one didn't ask what a man believed, only where he stood when it arrived. It arrived in Winchester.

It took everything; and I fought back. The other pictures are from various other wars I've fought in. My friends, my men, and the honored dead."

Dani's breath hitched again, her voice trembling. "Ashe... Why did you never tell me any of this?"

"I never tell anybody. Would you have believed me?" Ashe's voice was calm, almost sad.

"No," Dani admitted, shaking her head. "I guess not... I mean, I don't know. I'm not sure I believe it now."

Ashe glanced at the faded Civil War photo of him and Lorena. "Yeah, me either. I haven't cared for anyone in a long time. Not since Lorena. I think I've forgotten how."

A silence fell in the room, the weight of his words hanging heavy between them. Dani's pulse slowed, her anger giving way at last.

"Maybe it's time you remembered," she said quietly, her voice barely above a whisper.

ঌ • ঌ

DANI STOOD SILENTLY, her fingertips brushing the edge of a photograph of Ashe. The sepia-toned image felt heavier than it should, loaded with a strange sense of permanence. Ashe and the woman beside him—Lorena—stood in front of a grand house, her arm linked with his. She looked serene, her eyes bright with a confidence that made Dani's chest tighten.

"How old are you?" Dani's voice was quiet but firm.

Ashe glanced at her. "I already told you. Too old for you."

"I mean it," she said, turning to face him fully. "I want a number. I'll know if you're lying."

He studied her for a long moment, his eyes dark with something ancient and unreadable. Finally, he exhaled. "Two thousand years. A little over that."

Dani's breath caught. Her eyes widened. "My God."

"Yeah," Ashe said dryly. "Mine too."

The room seemed to grow colder as Dani tried to process his words. It didn't make sense, but at the same time, it did. Every scar, every story, every inexplicable fragment of Ashe's past suddenly slotted into place, forming a picture that was simultaneously awe-inspiring and terrifying.

"People hunt me," Ashe continued, his voice low and steady. "When they find out about my blood, they want to harness it. Use it. They think it'll make them immortal. Give them power. But it doesn't work like that. My blood has never done anything for anyone else. Never healed them. Just me. Never made them stronger. It just... is."

Dani's eyes searched his face, looking for the tell she knew so well. That slight shift in his expression when he was hiding something. But it wasn't there. His gaze was steady, unwavering. For the first time since she had known him, Ashe was an open book.

She shook her head, trying to clear the fog of disbelief. It went against everything she knew as fact, every rational instinct she had. But she believed him. She didn't know how or why, but she did.

"I... I knew you'd seen war," Dani said, her voice soft.

"I'm pretty sure I've seen 'em all," Ashe replied.

Dani's mind raced back to the 1970s, recalling the network of scars across his body. Vietnam. That's what had been nagging at her all this time.

"Vietnam," she said, her eyes narrowing at the web of red string across Ashe's murder board. "That man you told me about, Ming. The leader of that gang that hit the clinic. He's the one behind all this recently, isn't he?"

"He is," was the simple reply.

"What's your connection to him?"

Ashe's face darkened, his expression turning grim. He looked away, acting as if he hadn't heard her. Dani figured that was a question he wasn't going to answer for her. Instead, after a long pause, he began speaking in a heavier tone.

"That mess on the South Side... it wasn't just a turf battle. Ming was consolidating his power, trying to take over all the distribution coming in. He wanted leverage on the rival gang, so he abducted their kids. Gave them his 'belts of compliance.'"

Dani frowned. "What's a belt of compliance?"

Ashe's voice was flat, technical. "It's a belt or a harness made from det cord. Detonation cord. Ming invented it back in Vietnam. He would strap it onto village kids to ensure their families did anything he wanted. It's a bomb, Dani. A human leash."

Dani's stomach churned. "And he's using that here?"

"Yeah. That's who Ming is." Ashe's eyes grew distant, his voice quieter. "In everything he does, Ming's driven to prey on the weak, use the helpless, flaunt his power. It was never enough for him that he was big and powerful. He has to have others acknowledge it... I've dealt with more than one man's share of monsters in my life. Ming was the first time I ever played a part in the making of one."

Dani looked at him, confused. Her breath caught in her throat. Ashe's story was coming in fits and starts, little of it making much sense without combining it with all the other parts that hadn't even been shared yet. She wanted to ask more, but she could see in his eyes that he'd already said as much as he would right now about that past. He switched back to the recent events, his voice steady but grim.

"When I showed up on the South Side, I didn't know the kids were there. I was making progress, wiping out Ming's men and the rival gang at the same time. But as I closed in, Ming detonated the kids' belts. He didn't care who died. His own men, the rival gang, those kids, it didn't matter to him. He just wanted to cover his escape."

Dani felt her blood run cold. "That's... horrible."

"That's war," Ashe said, his voice tinged with something bitter and resigned. "My war. And I'm not making enough progress in it. That's the problem with war. In every war, we start out fighting the last war and suffer because of it. The side with the most rigid doctrine, the most closed mind, usually loses."

He paused, his eyes locked on hers. "I'm cursed, but I'm just not evil enough to stop him."

After a pause, he went on, "Those kids? Their blood is on my hands." Ashe's hand brushed along the wooden frame holding the parchment page from the Latin Bible. "And of all the responsibility I bear for death, this is just the smallest portion."

Dani's breath caught at the weight of his words.

Ashe began pacing, his voice gaining a strange cadence as he returned to his time in Vietnam.

"My unit wasn't just recon," he said. "We were an autonomous special forces group. We studied enemy tactics, adjusted constantly, tried to stay one step ahead. It's tough for young men to do that and not become monsters themselves. Turns out, all they needed was an ageless man who had already been a monster for centuries. I could walk into a village and know immediately which villagers would shoot us in the backs, where the weapons were hidden. I knew where the booby traps were, and which traps were meant to funnel us into worse ones. And I taught them."

Ashe's voice faltered slightly. "But my ability to read men failed with Ming. I didn't see the darkness in him early enough. My method of keeping boys from becoming monsters was based on the assumption that they weren't monsters to begin with. Ming... he got through the gate."

Dani stayed silent as she absorbed his words.

"Ming isn't building a drug empire because he wants wealth," Ashe explained. "He thrives on power. On enslaving others. Drugs are just the fastest way to put a city under his control. That's why I've been fighting him for so long. Fighting for justice."

Dani blinked. "Justice? Or justification?"

"What do you mean?"

"Justice and justification are two very different things," Dani said softly. "Justice is about fairness, about the rule of law. Justification... it's an excuse. A way to rationalize something. You're seeking justice, but you can't justify what you've done."

Ashe paused, considering her words. "Maybe, maybe not. But either way, Ming's consolidating power. He's not just taking over Chicago. He's aiming for the entire Midwest and half the Southwest."

"You need to let the authorities handle him," Dani said.

"Yeah, that's always worked out so well," Ashe said dryly. "He owns half the Chicago police force. He's untouchable."

"But... but—"

Ashe shrugged. "But nothin'. I'm done. It's over."

A nearly interminable pause hung between them, the weight of everything said and unsaid pressing down on Dani, slowly robbing her of the ability to breathe.

Finally, Ashe smiled faintly. "Come on. Let's just go out and get some dinner."

Chapter 25 : THE GHOSTS WE CHASE

PRESENT DAY

A LONE FIGURE stood at the darkened window, hands clasped. Midnight had come and gone, and the building had fallen into the quiet of its usual late-night routine. The sprawling complex visible out the window was bathed in a soft glow, manicured lawns and polished walkways were faintly illuminated by security lights. Beyond the perimeter, the treetops of Northern Virginia stretched away in rolling waves, cloaked in darkness and gently swaying in the late-summer breeze. A rare flicker of headlights cut through the wooded horizon as late-staying workers wound through the complex headed for public roads. To the east, the dull red glow of Washington, D.C. was evident, a stark reminder that this corner of Virginia, nerve center that it was, never truly slept.

It had taken years—decades, even—to reach this office. Hard-fought battles and endless compromises paved the path here, step by step. And at every step, the figure had wondered if the objective was worth the effort. The sacrifice. The engraved plaque on the door read: Assistant Director Linder. It was a door many in the Bureau viewed with reverence, or at least caution. It was a door most would rather avoid. But it was a door to an office where things got done, where problems got addressed.

One of those problems should be arriving any time now.

The phone on the left side of the desk rang. The black line. Non-secure. The figure leaned down, pressing the speakerphone button.

"Linder."

"Director Linder, this is Mitchell at the main gate," came the response. "Wanted to let you know that badge you had us watching for just pulled through."

"Thank you, Mitchell."

The assistant director turned back to the window, listening to the faint hum of cable news in the background. The soft knock at the door was expected, and the figure didn't turn.

The door cracked open.

Reggie, the assistant director's administrative assistant, poked his head through the crack. "AD Linder? I have Special Agent Standish for you."

"Thank you, Reggie. Send him in. And go home. Just because I'm here this late doesn't mean you have to be."

Reggie smiled faintly. "Understood." He disappeared, leaving the door open just a crack. The assistant director knew full well Reggie wouldn't leave until the office was empty. Still, it was worth a try.

Moments later, the door swung open, and Special Agent Lamentation Standish entered. His severe black overcoat seemed to suck up all the light in the room, but aside from that, the man seemed almost intimidated, in awe. The assistant director was accustomed to nervous people in the office, but this agent's rigid posture suggested someone always a little bit on edge.

AD Linder tapped the remote to mute the television and turned to face the new arrival.

"Special Agent Standish. I was wondering when you would darken my doorstep."

As the AD had been told to expect, Standish got right to the point.

"Ma'am, I have a plan to have a subject in custody shortly. I was hoping you would like to identify him yourself."

Dani crossed her arms. "Identify who myself? Some corpse I shot thirty-five years ago?"

Standish paused, taken slightly off balance.

Dani's eyes narrowed. "Yes, Standish. I know why you're here. Who, exactly, do you think this man is?"

"Ma'am, I believe this man is the Pusher's End Killer, and he is still very much alive."

Dani shut her eyes, trying to show patience. "Based on what evidence?"

"I hope to get the evidence once we execute the warrant in the morning."

"You hope." Dani's eyes snapped open again, locked on the man's face. "Have you built a career at the FBI based on hope, Special Agent Standish?"

"No, ma'am."

"So... you hope that you're on the tail of a mysteriously elusive serial killer that the bureau closed the case on decades ago. Is that it?"

"No, ma'am. I firmly believe that this man is Pusher's End."

"Belief. I'd heard that you were just like my late husband. Maybe you are after all. He always wanted me to believe. So, you want me to believe that you've tracked an elusive killer who I myself shot through the heart and has not been heard of or seen for decades."

"Yes, ma'am. I have every confidence that this man—"

"Confidence? Do you know what rhymes with confidence, Special Agent Standish?"

"No, ma'am."

"Evidence. Evidence rhymes with confidence. Almost. Are you seriously basing your case on rhymes? On almost rhymes? Where is your evidence?"

Standish's face turned beet red.

"Ma'am, you and I are both aware of Cameron Task's history for riding the line between cooperating with authorities and obstructing justice. Once I have that warrant activated in the morning, I will—"

"You'll what? You'll arrest a ninety-year-old man who's been officially dead for thirty? You realize that Pusher's End was at least ten years older than I was, right? And I'm ten years past the age any sensible person would retire."

"And you are still very active, ma'am."

Flattery will get you nowhere, twerp.

Standish continued, "I met this man, face-to-face. I would estimate his age at around seventy, maybe eighty—"

Dani waved a hand. "Either way, I'm sure you'll get your geriatric suspect. Based on what you *hope* and *believe* you will find in some files that *may* exist and were *possibly* sequestered by an eccentric billionaire who's every bit as dead as your *potential* octogenarian suspect who was—wait... *definitively* declared dead by the bureau thirty plus years ago?"

"Ma'am, how can you be sure it was a fatal shot? By your own account, he fell back into the river and the body was never recovered."

"Excuse me?"

"How can you be sure he was dead?"

The already-chilly temperature in the room dropped by several degrees. Dani turned her head slowly to her right. Standish followed her gaze to an entire wall full of medals, badges, and certificates won in various bureau and inter-agency shooting competitions.

"I haven't missed what I was shooting at since I was seven years old. Not once." Dani knew this was a slight exaggeration, of course. But it carried the weight of her conviction and got her point across to the younger agent.

"And just so you know this for later," she continued, "the only way a woman survives in this boys' club is by being *better* than the boys. You do know that I was in the Tactical Section of the CIRG in the late nineties, right? And since that time, I spent six years training snipers for HRT at Quantico? As I recall, I was on the instruction rotation when you went through the Academy, wasn't I?"

Standish sheepishly acknowledged that fact with a curt nod.

Dani knew there had been one time she'd missed, however, and it had haunted her for decades. Every day since that one, despite Ashe being officially dead, she had questioned her motive and whether she chose subconsciously to miss. Her self-doubt was only made worse when forensics revealed that Ashe had not killed her husband after all.

The findings had shown that Ashe had instead been trying to defend Wolfe Linder, a fact the reporting forensic analyst had conveniently omitted from his official report, rather than cast a positive light on a serial murderer. He'd probably thought he was doing Dani a favor.

Returning to the present, Dani continued. "You are on very thin ice here, Special Agent Standish. I read your file, as you might imagine. You've been passed over for several promotions, haven't you? Your obsession with chasing 'abnormal phenomenon' cases hasn't done you a lot of good."

Standish looked confused. "You have a problem with my work? I... I thought you, of all people in the bureau, you might understand what I am trying to achieve."

"What? Because of my late husband? My husband had an obsession with the impossible. If you care anything about your career, I would advise emulating anyone's career but his. What you're doing is chasing ghosts. Impossible ghosts. That case has been closed for three decades."

"But... your husband," Standish stammered. "He was a legend for his pursuit of cases that touched on the supernatural. And this case—"

Dani cut him off, raising her voice. "Legend? He was a laughingstock. My husband was a marginally unhinged individual who managed to get a superstitious AD sucked into his flurry of craziness. And he wasn't all that good at police work."

Standish stared at Dani, stunned.

Dani continued, "What he was good at was imagining impossible situations and somehow convincing others that his ridiculous ideas had merit. That the kinds of windmills he loved tilting at were plausible. That there was such a thing as real dragons."

"Ma'am, please. I am convinced that—"

"So convince me," Dani snapped.

Standish took a step forward. "The trip to Sacred Cross in Ashburn in Chicago was only marginally successful, but—"

"Do tell."

"I was able to subpoena all the hospital's records from the drug war in 1988."

"And?"

"And the records and blood samples I was looking for had all been destroyed, long since."

Dani glared at the man.

"But there was a record from an ambulance crew that brought in victims from the event," Standish continued, sounding like a man grasping at straws.

"A record, but no definitive sample."

"Well, no. But, the warrants I served there and at the suspect's location in Auburn Gresham—"

"Right, the house. What did you find at the house?" Despite herself, Dani's pulse quickened a bit.

Standish held up the file he had carried into the room. "Nothing directly incriminating. Personal effects, some art, evidence of an array of weapons that had been removed—"

"But no weapons."

"No, no weapons. But many of the personal effects were very similar to a lot of the items I found in the cave in the L.A. Exclusion Zone—"

Dani's eyes snapped to Standish, her neck reddening with anger. "The what?!"

"The Exclusion Zone," he explained. "The area west of Los Angeles that—"

"I know what the Exclusion Zone is. All too well. Of all people, I am fully aware. What were you doing there?"

"There was a cave that was raided by Task. I went and looked at it, and—"

"My office never approved you to do that."

Standish tried to stand his ground. "Ma'am, all due respect, but your area is counter-terror, not domestic crime. I thought—"

"You didn't do your homework, Standish. My office has all oversight over that area. My office." Dani's tone lowered with an air of menace. "Me."

Standish paled before Dani's wrath. "Yes, ma'am. The... the items from the cave were all destroyed, ma'am," he said, trying to repair any damage done to the discussion. "There is no risk of radiological exposure, or of the items falling into the hands of—"

"I want a catalog of all the items from the cave," Dani snapped. "Every. Single. Item. Destroyed or not."

"Of course, ma'am. Everything is already in this folder, with photos and description of each item."

Dani reached out to take the folder from Standish.

Nervous in the silence, Standish tries to return to the previous discussion. "But the warrants in Ashburn there were just lures, anyway, and—"

Dani looked up from the folder. "Yes, I see your proposal. And how did that lure work out for you?"

Standish informed Dani that he believed the trap he'd laid out was working, even if the suspects hadn't come to Chicago. Dani noted that the term now being used was "suspects" rather than "suspect." Standish suggested that the killer and his accomplices mistook his intent regarding Ashburn—the Chicago neighborhood with which the killer would be very familiar—and interpreted that he was instead headed to Ashburn, Virginia. A welcome, if surprising, coincidence, because it had spurred them into action.

"Whatever is there—here—in Task's data center must clearly be incriminating for them to rush here. The Lawyer and the biologist have been here for several days, and we have sightings of the waitress and the Pusher's End Killer—"

"Alleged."

"Alleged. Yes." Standish paused, his momentum faltering. "They are moving in an arc across the lower States. Headed here, I am certain."

"Are they maintaining a low profile?"

"As low a profile as someone like Pusher's End would be capable of."

"You'd be surprised. If this man were Pusher's End, he'd be able to disappear pretty effectively if he wanted to. What's the butcher's bill?"

Standish scratched his chin. "The what?"

"How many dead?" Dani asked bluntly.

Understanding, Standish answered, "Several rumored or possible encounters, but—"

"Rumored? Possible?"

"Two confirmed altercations. In one, two would-be robbers were hospitalized, one is still in an ICU in New Mexico. The second incident ended with nothing more than an embarrassed teenager."

"An embarrassed teenager," Dani said flatly. "No deaths? No collateral damage? Have you even read the file on the Pusher's End Killer? For him, that is an *impossibly* low profile. He wasn't the kind to stop at embarrassing teenagers. What else?"

Pointing, Standish indicated the folder he had handed Dani. "The witness in the second encounter reports weapons visible in the suspect's vehicle. Possible explosives as well."

Dani paged through the file.

"The teenager. The teenager who..." Dani looked up and continued, "...wet himself?"

Standish shuffled on his feet.

"Yes, ma'am."

Dani slapped the folder down hard on her desk, rattling the chipped purple mug Dani had received three years ago as the only physical inheritance from her mentor. The intellectual and spiritual inheritances from Lena she carried inside her, and both were in use tonight.

"Inadmissible. Let me remind you one last time, just in case you've missed it. You are out on a limb here, Standish. Way out. I want this man and his associates alive for questioning. Alive. You have zero latitude here. Zero. If any single one of them, or one officer or agent comes to harm, you are finished. Do you copy?"

Standish was silent.

"Are we clear?" Dani demanded.

"Crystal clear, ma'am," he muttered at last.

∽ • ∝

DANI SAT IN silence. The air in the office seemed even colder now, heavier. She let out a slow breath and leaned back in her chair, staring at the folder Standish had left behind. She folded the cover back with careful precision and regarded the first photo.

Ashe.

He and his men stood framed against the jungle of Vietnam in black and white like resurrected ghosts. His eyes held the same intensity she remembered, the same guarded strength that had always drawn her closer, when it tried to drive her away.

She turned the page and stared into his world. The next set of images showed the cave where he'd hidden out, where he'd lived like some wounded animal. Her fingers tightened on the photos as she took in the stark, miserable details.

A rough cot, made from bent and weathered wood. A small cistern for water. Marks of a fire pit, black ash scuffed and strewn around by some struggle. Empty food tins and burst water bottles. A life stripped to its barest bones.

He survived like this... for how long? The whole twenty-five years?

Dani continued, flipping through more photos: images of personal effects pulled from the cave. A battered footlocker and its contents, too irradiated to salvage, and then...

Lorena.

The photograph struck her like a physical blow. The woman stood in front of a modest antebellum house, her face lit with a shy, quiet smile. Dani remembered this picture well. She had questioned Ashe about it once, a lifetime ago. He hadn't said much about the image, but the way he held it had told her everything.

Dani's throat tightened, but she pushed the emotion back where it belonged, into that locked box deep inside her. She'd spent years fortifying herself against these moments. She was tougher now. Harder. She had to be.

The file explained in sterile words that the original photos had been destroyed, the chemicals in the prints having absorbed radiation from the cave. Even the smallest piece of Ashe's past was dangerous, corrupted beyond repair.

Like everything he touched, he had once told her.

She turned another page—and froze.

There, lying in a shallow evidence tray next to a ruler for reference, was Ashe's silver locket.

Or what was left of it.

A bullet hole pierced the center, ripping through the silver in a brutal tear. The edges were jagged and brutally torn, the locket bent and twisted from the impact. The note beneath the photo simply read: *Recovered from Site Alpha. Contents destroyed.*

Her finger traced the path of the silver locket's destruction, following the line where the bullet had struck at an angle, punching through the locket before being deflected away.

The realization hit her with the force of that long-ago shot.

It had saved him.

The locket. That locket with his long-gone wife's picture. It had taken the shot that should have killed him, absorbing the impact, altering its course just enough.

Dani's breath stopped, and for a brief second, she felt herself back there, on that dock in 1988. She felt the gun in her hands, heard the sound of the shot she had taken out of reflex. Ashe falling, the dark river swallowing him. Standing there, her hands trembling, her heart frozen in her chest. Ashe had stumbled and eventually fallen, and she had stood there, numb and cold on the Chicago dock, not believing it was over.

But it hadn't been. He had lived. He had survived their next encounter ten years later as well, as the cave photos attested in silence.

Her fingers brushed lightly over the photograph. The locket was ruined, just like everything else in that cave, reduced to an artifact of loss and survival. The picture it had held was gone. Just another piece of Ashe's history lost to time.

Dani closed her eyes, swallowing hard. She had spent years trying to forget that night, and the day ten years later. Years convincing herself that shooting Ashe had been the right decision. Both times. She had been so sure. So convinced that she'd done what had to be done. That it was about justice, not vengeance. That she had done what needed to be done.

She didn't know what was worse: that she had missed that shot... or that something he loved had saved him.

The room felt suffocating. Dani leaned back, her gaze drifting to the wall of medals across from her desk. She had built a fortress around herself since then: a career, a reputation, an armor of discipline and precision that no one could penetrate.

But ghosts weren't troubled by fortresses. They thrived in their frigid halls.

Dani closed the folder with a sharp snap. Her fingers lingered on the cover for a moment longer before she pushed it aside.

Some wounds never really healed.

Chapter 26 : THE BLOOD TRAIL

1988

THE MORNING SUN reflected off the glass facade of Sacred Cross Hospital, washing the entrance in antiseptic light. Dani made her way up the steps, her breath steady but her thoughts in a tangle. She needed to talk to Lena. With Wolfe on his way, every record of Ashe had to be dealt with. No loose ends, no connections. Not to the recent chaos, not to the clinic in 1976.

She barely made it past the sidewalk when Ashe appeared, stepping out from the shadow of a nearby tree.

His posture was relaxed, but there was a sharpness in his eyes that immediately set her on edge.

"Dani," he called, catching her before she reached the door. His voice was calm but insistent. "Forget about the records. Whatever you were planning to do, just leave it."

Dani stopped. "Ashe, I—"

"Look," Ashe cut her off, glancing around as if ensuring no one was listening. "You've already meddled enough in this. The last thing you need is to draw attention to yourself by messing with hospital records. We can just disappear."

"Disappear?" Dani frowned.

"I've done it before," Ashe said, his tone light but his words laden with meaning. "More times than I care to admit. I've got a couple of other places. Not as nice, maybe, but isolated. You're right. The cops will eventually get Ming. It's time I moved on."

Dani folded her arms, considering his words. She had been so preoccupied a moment ago that she only now realized something odd about how he was speaking.

"We?" she asked, raising an eyebrow.

Ashe smiled faintly. "Of course. I'm sorry. Yes. *We* can move on."

A voice behind her made Dani's blood run cold.

"Move on where?" the voice asked.

Dani turned sharply to find Wolfe Linder standing just a few feet away, that ever-present crooked grin plastered on his face. He had slipped up behind her without her even noticing. Maybe she was too preoccupied with what

Ashe was telling her. Dani hadn't even noticed him approach.

"Linder," Dani said, trying to steady her voice. "What are you doing here?"

Wolfe held up a grainy photo, his eyes sparkling with excitement. "There's been another sighting of the Pusher's End Killer. Right here in Chicago. I came to chase down the lead. Look at this."

Dani leaned in, taking the photo from him. It was barely more than a shadowy figure, indistinct, grainy and blurred. "I can't make this out. You'll never get a height or weight from this, let alone a full ID." She cast a glance at Ashe, whose expression refused to show what he had to be thinking. "Is this all you have to go on?"

"Yes and no," Wolfe said with a shrug. "The photo's worthless, I admit. But I have this." He handed her a paper, his grin widening.

Dani's stomach sank as she scanned it. "Another untypable blood sample?"

"Exactly!" Wolfe practically bounced on his heels. "Same as before. Someone sent it for a test from this hospital." He pointed at the entry to Sacred Cross. "I'm pretty sure it's related to that big cartel blowout a couple of months back. Giant drug war event, exactly the kind that draws the Pusher Killer out into the open. Half the victims were brought here. Surprised you didn't hear about it."

"Linder..." Dani started, but he was already continuing.

"And get this. There's going to be another big meeting between the cartel and local gangs tomorrow night at the South Branch Docks. A local guy's trying to consolidate power against some new common threat. I'm pretty sure it's my perp they're after. I've contacted the local DEA boys, and they're letting us ride along for the bust. In case the Pusher Killer shows."

Dani's chest tightened on her heart like a vise. "How did you get this?" she asked, forcing her voice to remain calm.

Wolfe grinned. "After you headed this way, I got to thinking about Chicago. Since most of the Pusher Killer's activity has been here for over ten years, I set up alerts for anomalous blood test results. This one popped up. And there's more! How's your German?"

He handed her another sheaf of papers, so excited he barely cared that they were standing exposed on the street.

Dani's eyes widened as she glanced at the papers. Nazi insignia and unintelligible scribbles filled the margins.

"You're trying to tell me you think this is the same blood?" she asked, her voice steady but edged with disbelief.

"Of course it is! And look at the date—1936! How cool is that?"

Dani cast a glance at Ashe. He remained perfectly still, his face a mask of calm indifference. It amazed her how he could stand there, right in plain sight, and somehow remain unseen. Linder had completely overlooked the fact that she'd been talking to someone when he arrived, so singular was his focus.

Wolfe leaned in conspiratorially, his voice dropping. "Come on, you know you want in on this."

"No, Linder!" Dani snapped. "I told you. I'm out! I resigned from the FBI!"

Wolfe chuckled. "Not really, Mrs. Linder. I knew you didn't mean it, so I had the director just put a hold on your letter of resignation."

Dani's temper flared white-hot. "You what?! I don't even know why I'm surprised. You want so badly to ignore reality that you've created your own alternate universe! And stop calling me Mrs. Linder! Have you even signed the divorce papers yet?" she shouted.

Her outburst had drawn attention; passers-by turned their heads to look at her.

Wolfe's grin widened. "No. I knew you didn't mean that either, Mrs. Linder." He winked.

Dani's heart stopped. She suddenly realized what she had done.

She spun back around, but Ashe was gone.

Her breath caught in her throat, and a cold wave of panic rolled over her.

"Dani?" Wolfe asked, his tone only slightly more serious now. "You okay?"

"Yeah," Dani lied, her eyes scanning the street for any sign of Ashe. "I'm fine."

But she wasn't fine. Not even close.

Chapter 27 : PRICE OF ADMISSION

PRESENT DAY

THE SUN WAS just beginning to rise over Ashburn, Virginia, the first pale light breaking across the horizon and illuminating the glass-and-steel façade of the Task Industries data center. Mist clung to the ground, swirling in soft eddies around the tires of parked cars.

Ashe and Amber climbed out of the Bronco, the air cool and damp around them. The parking lot was nearly empty of employee vehicles, but an abundance of black SUVs and marked police cars along the outer edges of the lot more than made up the difference. The tension was palpable; the whole scene resembled the world's biggest Ikea waiting to open on annual Law Enforcement Sale Day. Walking around to the front of the building, they saw Frymet and Owen Spirit already waiting near the entrance, their faces drawn and tired.

"We've got a couple hours, right?" Amber asked as they approached the building, yawning and stretching her arms. "In and out. Easy peasy."

Ashe's eyes narrowed. Every uniformed and plain-clothes eye in the parking lot was on the new arrivals. "Yeah. We'll see."

Amber glanced at the growing number of vehicles gathering at the perimeter. Agents in dark windbreakers hovered near their SUVs, exchanging clipped conversations. A small army was forming, and Task Industries' security personnel were massing to hold them at bay on Owen Spirit's instructions.

Complicating the picture was a quartet of FBI agents in windbreakers at the main entry doors. While they were being disallowed entry by Spirit's men, Spirit himself and his group were barred entry by the agents. No one was entering the building until the warrant arrived, they said, and when it did, the FBI had first dibs.

Spirit handed a large blueprint tube to Ashe. "Got these from the fire department. Full blueprints. I hope you know what you're looking for, because we couldn't find a thing. We're out of time."

Ashe slid the blueprints a few inches out of the tube, and then recapped it. "I thought you said we'd have a few hours."

Spirit's jaw tightened. "That was before Standish moved up the timetable. Go time is at 0800. He's waiting on an updated warrant, but he's already called in half the FBI and every cop in the county. My security team is blocking them from entering, but once that warrant is active, it's over."

"Back to the parking lot," Ashe said, already turning on his heel. "Come on."

In the parking lot, Ashe spread the blueprints across the hood of the nearest non-official vehicle. Frymet peered over his shoulder while Spirit paced.

"They can see us," Spirit muttered.

"Let 'em," said Ashe.

Owen Spirit's eyes flicked around the parking area and a scowl spread across his face. "Where's the Corvette?"

"Back in Texas," Ashe replied, not looking up. His focus was on the blueprints. "You can go get it when we're done here."

"How'd you get here?"

Ashe jerked a thumb at the Bronco.

Spirit stared at him in disbelief. "You left the Vette to drive this monstrosity?"

"I don't see what was so special about that Corvette," Ashe said calmly. "Can we please focus?"

"That car is a piece of history!" Spirit's voice rose a notch.

Amber mumbled, "It's definitely a piece of history now."

Spirit spun toward her. "What do you mean by that?"

Amber smirked. "I mean it might need a little detailing before you send it to the Smithsonian."

"Detailing?"

"Well... a lot of detailing."

Spirit's eyes narrowed at Ashe. "You promised it would be driven carefully."

"It was driven very carefully," Ashe said, still studying the plans.

"So the car's fine?"

"I wouldn't say fine, no. Can we focus?"

Spirit looked as if he might burst a blood vessel. "Omigod! Why did I ever get involved in this? You're like a bull in a China shop! I should've known this would go badly. It's like you've got 'willful destruction of property' tattooed on your forehead!"

Ashe looked up at last, his voice steady. "If we all get caught, the Smithsonian won't care about the car anyway. Can we please just move on?"

The group studied the plans in silence. Frymet traced her finger along the diagram. "There's nothing strange here. No secret rooms, no weird power drains. It looks... normal."

Spirit sighed. "It is normal. That's what's driving us crazy. We've torn the place apart. There's nothing to find."

Ashe's eyes narrowed. He asked Spirit, "What was it you said about your IT guys? 'If those guys can't find something, it's because it isn't there,' right?"

Spirit shrugged, unclear what Ashe was saying.

"Okay..." Ashe murmured, scanning the plans again. He traced a finger over the building's central support column, eyes narrowing as the dimensions shifted from floor to floor.

On the second floor, above the warehouse area, something was off. The dimensions didn't match up.

"The core structural column," Ashe muttered. "It's huge, to handle the span of the floor joists. Like a giant tent pole. But it's larger on the second floor than it is anywhere else. By eight feet. Thing is, the plans don't acknowledge it; they list the wrong dimensions."

Spirit leaned in, his brow furrowing. "What does that mean?"

"You'd never see it unless you look at the dimensions of everything else, and then do the math. Only the math doesn't add up." Ashe tapped the blueprints. "Here. This second floor doesn't officially exist. Not as a floor, anyway. It's all ductwork and utilities, and the plans show it as being four feet tall. But look at the building as a whole. The second floor isn't four feet; it's eight feet. And right at the center is a dead space."

Amber raised an eyebrow. "An eight-foot cube in the middle of nowhere?"

"Exactly. And it's hidden in the fact that everybody expects it to be a massive steel girder. That, and all the false measurements from sheet to sheet." Ashe's voice grew sharper. "Enough room for a server rack."

Ashe stopped for a moment; a strange look clouded his expression for just a moment.

"When you value something, you keep it close to your heart," he said. He stabbed his finger at the paper. "And there—right there—is Task's heart."

Spirit's eyes widened. "Great! Now what do we do about it?"

Ashe turned to Fry. "You've been inside, right?"

Fry nodded. "Yeah. Plenty of times."

Ashe pointed at another section of the plans. "What's this space here?"

"That's a common area outside the cafeteria," Fry said. "The mezzanine has a coffee shop, and there are vending machines over there."

"And this space here?"

"That's just a big open area with some seats. But the secure server area is—"

"Yeah, I know. It's up here," Ashe cut in. "What about this stairwell heading downstairs?"

"What about it?"

"Is it secured?" Ashe asked her.

Fry frowned. "No, I don't think so. The whole basement level is just a big supply area. Kind of like a warehouse."

Ashe straightened up. "Okay," he said. "I think I see the way in. Just me, though."

"What do we do?" asked Fry.

Ashe glanced over at her. "You're gonna figure out what comes next, what we do after the server is taken care of. We'll want alternate transportation."

Fry herself looked down. "Because your truck is a two-seater, and the walking cast is a problem."

"No, Fry," said Amber, trying to help. "The FBI has seen the Bronco now. It's not exactly an inconspicuous getaway vehicle."

"Sure," Ashe replied, rolling up the schematics. "Something like that."

"We'll need a way to communicate, probably. I figure my hands are going to be full, so the phone's out."

"What do you mean 'the phone's out?'" demanded Spirit.

"Not going to try something like this holding a phone to my ear."

"Use the AirPods," said Spirit.

Seeing the quizzical look on Ashe's face, Amber went to the Bronco and returned with the small box of headphones. Handing them to Ashe, she quickly demonstrated their use.

When they were connected to Ashe's phone, he looked around strangely, frowning at Spirit and the others when they asked him if everything was working correctly. Finally pulling out one of the earbuds, Ashe realized that he was unable to hear ambient sounds with the devices in his ears.

Once this realization dawned on him, he turned slowly to Amber. "You mean to tell me," he said in a rumbling voice, "that all the way here, I've had a set of earphones that cancel out noise...?"

Amber shrugged, an angelic smile spread across her face.

Spirit raised an eyebrow at Ashe. "So... you have a plan?"

Still frowning at Amber, Ashe turned, closing the blueprint tube and tossing it into the back of the Bronco. He grabbed his ALICE pack and dropped it onto the passenger seat.

"Sure," Ashe said, getting into the driver's seat. "Time to go willfully destroy some property."

ക്ക • ൳

KNOWING WHERE SOMETHING was—or in this case, where it officially wasn't—was different from actually reaching it. Plans could tell you a lot, but they didn't whisper the real secrets. Task's hidden server room wasn't just concealed; it was forgotten on purpose. Getting to it would require something besides blueprints.

It would take a little brute force, and a little chaos. Maybe a lot of both.

Ashe eased the Bronco into gear, the engine rumbling. The old warhorse was ready for one last charge.

The lights of the parking area whipped by in a blur as he drove toward the back of the facility, his foot planted on the floorboard. One eye on the broad expanse of wall, he slowed just enough to make sure no police or FBI were patrolling this side. They weren't; there was nothing official to guard. No entrances here, just a solid brick wall with windows set high above the ground.

He found the spot he was looking for and veered sharply toward the building. His foot slammed down on the accelerator. The Bronco surged forward, its tires squealing in excitement. Fifty miles per hour. Sixty. Seventy.

At eighty miles per hour, Ashe's grip tightened on the wheel. His eyes locked onto the brick wall rushing toward him. His mind was silent except for one thought: *I hope that cowcatcher's still as tough as it was when I welded it together forty years ago.*

The Bronco plowed into the wall, the cowcatcher tearing through brick and steel. The wall exploded inward in a hailstorm of shattered bricks and twisted metal. The vehicle ground to a violent halt three-quarters of the way into a vast open common area, glass raining down from the now-obliterated windows above.

The wall, miraculously, held together, for now. Ashe had identified that spot as a weak area, and was gratified that it wasn't too weak.

Alarms blared instantly, their shrill cries filling the cavernous space. Due to the hour and all of the commotion at the front of the building, there were thankfully just a few people in the vast lunch area. They froze at the sight of the Bronco bursting through the wall, their wide-eyed shock quickly turning to self-preservation.

They bolted.

Ashe shoved the crumpled door open and swung himself out of the wrecked vehicle. Pain stabbed through his ribs, sharp and insistent. Broken, probably. He pressed a hand to his side, gritting his teeth as he snatched the ALICE pack from the back seat.

He had no time for injuries. Move, he told himself.

Ignoring the pain, Ashe set off, limping across the common area toward the door leading to the basement supply room. The building's internal alarms echoed around him as he descended the concrete stairwell two steps at a time.

The basement was just as he remembered from the blueprints: massive, open, filled with towering metal shelves and crates stacked on pallets throughout. His eyes swept the room, locking onto the massive central column in the middle of the space. And from there, to the ceiling.

There it was. The air intake vent, just as the plans had shown. Four feet square. Easily big enough to climb through.

The only problem was that it was thirty-five feet above him.

Ashe scanned the room, his eyes landing on a forklift parked near the corner.

Perfect.

He jogged toward it, ignoring the fire in his ribs, and started the machine. It roared to life with a shudder, its headlights cutting through the dim space. He maneuvered it toward one of the tall shelving racks and rammed the metal frame until it teetered and toppled against the central column. The top shelf reached twenty feet, still a good ten feet short of the vent.

Not enough.

He raised the forklift's tines and used them to shove the shelving rack even higher, jamming it precariously against the ceiling. The whole thing groaned and bent under the strain, but it held.

The structure swayed like a house of cards as Ashe climbed. His boots clanged against the metal frame, each step a dance between urgency and disaster.

At the top, he reached for the vent. It swung open, revealing a secondary mesh of metal bars. Locked tight.

There was no time for subtlety.

He pulled a grenade from his ALICE pack, popped the pin, and shoved it through the bars.

A second passed.

A second second passed.

BOOM!

The blast blew a ragged hole in the vent and ceiling above it, sending a shockwave through the room. The shelving rack trembled violently beneath him, the metal frame groaning in protest.

Then it gave way.

The entire structure collapsed in a cacophony of twisted steel and splintered pallets. Ashe fell with it, plummeting thirty-five feet and crashing into the concrete floor with a bone-jarring thud.

Pain lanced through his shoulder: a hot, blinding agony that left him breathless. He lay on his back for a moment, staring at the ceiling, his mind swimming through the pain.

Dislocated. He knew the feeling well.

Gritting his teeth, Ashe rolled onto his knees and reached into his ALICE pack, pulling out a claw hammer. He slipped the pack onto his back again and looked up at the central column.

The grenade blast had weakened the double-thick sheetrock around the column, leaving it a web of cracks and exposed steel.

But at least it hadn't collapsed..

Gripping the hammer like a climber's pick, Ashe drove it into the fractured surface and hauled himself upward, one brutal swing at a time. Each movement sent fresh waves of pain through his body, but he didn't stop.

Climb. Focus. One step at a time.

The column stretched above him, its surface rough and unyielding. He ignored the sweat dripping into his eyes, the fire in his shoulder, the blood staining his shirt.

The only thing that mattered was the server room above.

The heart of Task's secrets.

The heart he meant to tear out.

And nothing was going to stop him from reaching it.

æ • ﻉ

ASHE DRAGGED HIMSELF through the jagged hole in the ceiling, every muscle in his body screaming in protest. His dislocated shoulder throbbed with each move, and his ribs felt like someone had driven nails into them. The hammer, still clutched in his good hand, slipped against the crumbling edge, but he forced himself upward, biting down on the pain.

Almost there.

He pulled himself up into the hidden floor, collapsing onto the cool metal grate beneath him, sucking in a breath. After a moment, he rolled to his knees, the weight of his ALICE pack pressing against his back like a familiar burden.

The space around him was cramped and dark, the low ceiling brushing against his head as he crawled forward.

Ahead, the wall looked weaker—a seam in the panels where they hadn't been properly reinforced. Ashe raised the hammer, and began smashing his way through.

The sheet metal crumpled under his relentless strikes. Dust and shards of plaster burst free as the wall gave way. One last swing and the barrier caved, leaving a jagged hole large enough for him to crawl through.

Ashe climbed through and emerged into a brightly lit corridor, his boots echoing on the polished floor. The overhead fluorescent lights buzzed faintly, casting a sterile glow.

He glanced to his left: an empty hallway leading into parts unknown. To his right, just a few feet away, was a solid steel security door. No markings, no windows. Just a keypad and a biometric scanner set into the wall.

Task's hidden server room.

The phone rang, and Ashe tapped the AirPod that had miraculously stayed in his right ear.

"Ashe, are you there?" Spirit's voice crackled in his ear through the AirPod.

"Yeah," Ashe muttered. His voice was rough, his breath ragged. "I found the room. Steel door with... looks like some glass panel instead of a lock."

"Biometric?" Fry's voice chimed in, sharp and concerned. "It could be fingerprint, retinal, voice recognition—"

"Not exactly in a position to figure it out." Ashe leaned against the wall, studying the panel. "What are the odds Task left a cheat code for this thing?"

"About zero," Spirit said.

Ashe grunted. "Then it's time for the tactical application of brute force."

"Ashe, no!" Spirit's tone went from annoyed to panicked. "Don't do anything until we figure something out—"

Ashe hung up.

His phone immediately began to vibrate again. He ignored it. A second call followed.

"Enough!" Ashe growled, yanking out the AirPod and throwing it and the phone back through the hole in the wall. He heard them clatter to the floor far below, the sound strangely satisfying.

Ashe opened his ALICE pack and pulled out a Claymore mine, turning it over in his hands. He hadn't been entirely honest with the kid at the gas station. The backblast from a Claymore wasn't always lethal within 10 or 20 feet, but it sure wasn't something you wanted to be holding when it went off.

He placed the mine carefully against the keypad and secured it with a length of duct tape. His eyes flicked toward the air vent nearby: a perfect makeshift shelter. Not ideal, but better than nothing.

Sliding into the vent, Ashe braced himself. He pulled out the clacker and took a deep breath.

Click.

The explosion was deafening, the concussive force shaking the entire corridor. The Claymore's blast tore through the door panel, sending fragments of steel and plaster skittering across the floor. The vent rattled violently around him, the metal groaning at the abuse.

Ashe coughed, wiping dust from his face as the smoke cleared.

He clambered out of the vent, boots hitting the floor with a thud. The steel door hung ajar, its locking mechanism reduced to twisted shreds of metal. Ashe pushed it open with his good shoulder, the door groaning in defeat.

Inside, the server room was bathed in an eerie red glow. A single rack of servers was shielded by the central column, embedded within its steel girders like a heart within an iron ribcage. Lights blinked in rhythmic patterns, an electronic heartbeat pulsing in the dark.

"Gotta hand it to you, Task," mused Ashe. "You knew how to protect your stuff."

Ashe stepped closer. This was it: the sum of everything Task had hidden, including everything the world knew about Ashe. The countless secrets too dangerous to leave behind.

The beating heart of the dragon.

And he had just cracked it open.

ꜱ • ꜱ

WHAT NOW, THOUGH?

The server room hummed around Ashe, the red lights blinking like the pulse of a slumbering beast. His eyes scanned the hardware as he caught his breath, sweat dripping from his brow. Then, from the distance, barely audible through the low hum, he heard it.

The sound of a phone ringing.

Ashe frowned, genuinely surprised. He stepped back through the hole he'd blown into the corridor and looked down 35 feet to the floor below. His phone was still lying there where it had landed.

No answering it now, he grinned. Or, was there...?

Reaching into his pocket, Ashe grabbed his second AirPod and stuck it in his ear. His ears were still ringing from the explosion, so he tapped the AirPod and spoke louder than necessary.

"Hey, Spirit, speak up. I'm a little deaf at the moment."

"Ashe! Did you get in? You found the server?" Spirit's voice crackled through the tenuous connection.

"Yeah, I found it. What's the situation down there?"

"You've got a bigger problem than the server. The FBI's in the building and headed your way. You need to wipe that thing now and get out!"

Ashe glanced back at the server. "Wipe it, huh? Sure. Tell me how to do that."

A pause.

"Fry, help him out!" Spirit barked.

Fry's voice cut in, calm but urgent. "Ashe, look for a degausser. It's a machine that—"

"No degausser," Ashe interrupted, looking into the empty room from the hallway. "And I wouldn't know what to do with it if I found one. This thing looks like a sci-fi movie set. There is nothing but lights."

He stepped back into the server room to search for alternatives, but the call cut off almost immediately.

"Great," he muttered, stepping back toward the hole. The connection returned.

"Spirit? Fry?"

"We're here," Fry said. "You lose the signal when you're inside the room. It's the material in the walls combined with the distance. Bluetooth won't reach that far."

"Fantastic. So, I'm on my own in there."

Spirit's voice turned grim. "Yeah, you are. Whatever you do, make it fast. Those agents are going to be coming your way once they find out how."

Ashe slipped the AirPod back into a pocket and turned toward the server rack. His mind raced. No time for finesse. No time to learn what parts held the data or how to delete it.

He opened his ALICE pack and pulled out the remaining Claymore mines.

Three left. No shaped charges. Claymores would have to do.

Setting the Claymores around the server rack, he angled them inward toward the center of the hardware, careful to position them so the backblast would go away from him as much as possible. He didn't have a fourth mine to complete the square, but three would have to do.

He stood beside the last Claymore, securing it with a strip of tape. He double-checked the placement, giving a small nod of satisfaction.

This'll do.

Time for the hard part.

He crawled back to the hole he'd blown in the ceiling, knowing he was going to need better shelter than just the air vent. He slipped through the hole and pushed over to the central column. Again using the claw hammer like a climbing pick, Ashe hung through the hole by the hammer with his good arm. With his injured arm, despite the blinding pain, he raised the clacker, fingers trembling as they curled around the grip.

"Here we go," he whispered.

He clicked the clacker.

Nothing.

He frowned and tried again.

Still nothing.

"Why do I have to be right all the time?" Ashe shouted at no one through gritted teeth, his frustration boiling over. He cursed himself for not checking the clacker's shelf life. It must have been dead or defective—a fatal flaw in his plan.

No time to fix it.

His grip on the hammer tightened as his mind churned for alternatives. Below him, the distant sound of footsteps echoed through the building.

The agents were coming.

                                ❧ • ☙

THE CLACKER DANGLED uselessly in Ashe's hand, its stubborn silence mocking him. His grip on the hammer tightened as he clung to the central column, his breath coming in shallow bursts.

He didn't have time to troubleshoot. If he was going to blow those Claymores, it would have to be done the old-fashioned way—by hand.

Just like old times.

He climbed back up through the hole, each movement a fresh jolt of pain through his dislocated shoulder. His ribs protested with every breath, but he pushed the pain aside. The bones would still be broken later. Deal with it then.

Back in the server room, he stood beside the Claymores, eyeing the tripwire pins. The mines were relics from a half-century ago, their fates as unpredictable as the man who'd brought them.

"Brilliant plan, Ashe," he muttered under his breath. "Using explosives from the Nixon era as Plan A. What could possibly go wrong?"

The question hung in the air.

What if they don't go off?

He paused, fingers hovering over the tripwire pins. These mines had been sitting in storage for over 30 years, untouched, untested, exposed to who knew what kind of conditions. Them not working was a real possibility.

He really should have thought this through better. What he needed was a couple pounds of fresh C4 and a reliable detonator.

Not having that, his fingers tightened on the tripwire cord, threading it through the pins with practiced precision. The last time he'd rigged a setup like this had been decades ago, in a war half the world had forgotten.

And here he was again. Same game, different battlefield.

The cord was set. He straightened up, glancing around the room for better shelter. Hanging halfway out of the hole with a busted shoulder wasn't exactly going to be ideal.

Ashe glanced at the server rack, encircled by the Claymores. The blinking red lights seemed to pulse faster, mocking him with their rhythm.

What if the mines didn't even go off? Ashe shook his head. It wasn't like him to have doubts like this, but this time, other people's fates lay in the balance also, not just his. He was beginning to seriously doubt that the mines were still good. But he was out of time to find some kind of backup plan for when this contraption fell through.

Ashe started to step backward down the hallway slowly. Something caused the hair at the back of his neck to tingle and he suddenly realized that he had not even considered the other possibility: that instead of being duds, the ancient explosives might actually detonate before he…

ೊ • ೕ

THE CONCUSSIVE WAVE preceded his perception of the white-hot flash almost imperceptibly. It caught Ashe full in the chest, lifting him off his feet like a rag doll.

He was airborne for a fraction of a second before slamming into the wall of the hallway. The impact bounced him cleanly through the hole in the floor, like a deflated basketball, his body tumbling into open space.

A wave of orange flame roared behind him, crackling hungrily as it chased him down through the opening.

Ashe's body reacted before his mind could catch up. His arm shot out, fingers scrabbling for purchase against the shredded edges of the floor.

His good hand found the lip of the hole, gripping a warped floor joist. The force of his fall was enough to snap three of his metacarpals with a sickening crack. Pain shot up his arm, his fingers clenching instinctively, clawlike and desperate.

Ashe's hand tore free with the jolt and most of the meat of his palm sheared away from his hand. Blood splattered across the air as his grip failed, and he plummeted the full thirty-five feet to the floor below. He twisted midair, his instincts trying to guide his body toward a safer landing, but there was no safety to be found.

Agony flashed in his vision as his wrecked shoulder slammed into the extended rail of the forklift, filling his vision with the second blinding white flash in as many seconds.

As bright as the flash of pain was, everything went instantly black as his skull slammed into the cement floor.

Unconscious, Ashe failed to notice the sprinklers activating and starting to flood the warehouse with water.

Chapter 28 : LYING BENEATH

1988

DANI SAT CROSS-LEGGED on the bed in her hotel room, her fingers wrapped around a cup of cold lobby coffee in a styrofoam cup. The television flickered in the background, but she wasn't paying attention. Wolfe's sudden arrival replayed in her mind on an endless loop, each detail sharper and more unbearable than the last.

"That man's timing is supernatural, I'll give him that," she muttered, setting the cup down harder than she intended.

She had gone to Sacred Cross with a purpose, determined to stay one step ahead of Wolfe, to protect Ashe and make sure there was nothing left to find. Instead, Wolfe had appeared like some ghost from the shadows, derailing everything. Worse, Ashe had heard it all—every word—and now he was gone.

Her jaw tightened. She couldn't just sit here stewing. She had to talk to him.

Dani grabbed her coat and headed for Ashe's house.

The lilies along the front stairs swayed gently in the breeze as Dani climbed the steps. The house was quiet, as it had been before. The key was where Ashe always left it, tucked beneath a loose board on the lilies' soil box. But as she slipped it into the lock, a strange weight settled in her chest.

Inside, the air was cool and still. Ashe had covered the furniture again with white sheets, the way people do when they're leaving for a long time. Dani's pulse quickened as she moved through the house. It felt like a mausoleum, empty and waiting to be forgotten.

The door to the secret passage swung open on oiled hinges without a sound. Dani hesitated on the threshold before stepping inside. At the end of the hallway, the entry door to Ashe's lair stood slightly ajar, as if beckoning her inside one last time.

"Ashe?" she called, her voice echoing in the silence.

No response.

The lair was dimly lit, not that it had been bright before. Some of the items had been boxed up, the paintings and a few personal treasures carefully crated. Dani ran her fingers along one of the still-open crates, recognizing the portraits of Magdaia padded in straw.

The murder board was gone, dismantled and dumped unceremoniously into a trash bin. The photos, the clippings, the red string that had once formed an intricate web were now nothing more than a tangled mess of loose threads lying on the floor to the side of the bin. Dani swallowed hard.

He was leaving.

"No," she whispered. Her fingers tightened around the edge of the crate. "You're not doing this," although she knew he was.

Her eyes swept over the room again, taking in the packed boxes, the covered furniture, the hollow emptiness of a life abandoned. Ashe was gone, or was about to be. He had overheard Wolfe's plans, and now he was going to the docks.

He was going to finish things.

He was going to finalize his war before he disappeared.

Before he moved on without her.

The thought hit her like a blow to the chest. What must he think of her? She had led him on all this time, giving him reasons to stay, reasons to trust her. And what had she given him in return?

Betrayal.

She had been foolish enough to let herself fall for him.

And fool enough to never mention Wolfe.

Wolfe. Her husband.

The husband Ashe had only learned about when Wolfe had appeared out of nowhere, smiling that stupid smile, ready to ruin her life all over again.

Dani's breath caught. She paused, her heart racing.

Wolfe.

Wolfe, who was setting up at the docks alongside the DEA force he mentioned.

Wolfe, who was going to catch Ashe up in his net.

Her stomach twisted. She bolted for the exit, her footsteps echoing through the empty house.

"No," she muttered, breathless. "No, no, no."

She had to stop Ashe. She had to warn him.

ϑ • ϖ

THE SOUTH BRANCH docks were a war zone.

Dani arrived to the sound of gunfire, the acrid stench of burning rubber hanging thick in the air. Sirens blared everywhere, their flashing red and blue lights bouncing off the cold multicolored steel of shipping containers. The port district was now a battlefield, littered with overturned crates and burning cars and shattered glass.

She sprinted toward the chaos, her heart pounding with urgency. Weaving as she ran, she ducked instinctively as an explosion ripped through several drums near the pier she was passing, adding another plume of smoke into the sky.

Dani dropped to her knees behind a white van riddled with bullet holes. A small group of police officers and DEA agents huddled there, exchanging frantic radio calls and loading fresh magazines into their weapons.

She flashed her badge, glad it had come in handy after all. "Special Agent McKendree, FBI," she said, not catching her Freudian slip. "What happened here?"

A DEA agent—a wiry man with blood trickling down his temple—looked at her, his eyes wide with adrenaline. "It's been a nightmare! This was supposed to be a routine bust. That other FBI guy—Hinder or something, he said— You with him?"

"Yes and no. Mostly no. Is he here?"

"He was. But he took off, chasing after those military guys that showed up. I told him to lay low; he seemed pretty outclassed. But he wouldn't listen."

"Never does," Dani confirmed. Her heart was in her throat. The gunfire was abating quickly, but a stray bullet hit the van, causing them all to squat down.

"What military guys?" Dani asked.

"Rival gangs started shooting it out at each other, and then us, while we were still getting set up. Then this other crew showed up—moved like military, way too organized for the street. Explosions, ambushes. Way outside our lane, but they met their match before too long. It's been nuts. No sooner does one group attack, somebody else shows up and attacks them. I don't know what's going on. I am not looking forward to the paperwork on this fiasco. Getting things wrapped up now, at least."

Dani pressed her back against the van, scanning the chaos. "A crew with military skill? Was their leader a shorter guy with dark hair?"

The agent shook his head. "No, big guy. Blond. Built like a tank. Led his men like he'd been doing it a while."

Dani's stomach dropped. That description was familiar. She had seen that face before—in one of Ashe's old photos from Vietnam. It sounded like Ming was continuing his takeover bid.

"What about the other group? The one that attacked the military crew?" she asked.

The agent risked standing up tentatively. Emboldened when no gunfire came his way, he cast a glance around the surrounding carnage. "Wasn't really a group. One guy. Fought like a holy terror. Never seen anything like it. Drove the military group back that way. Saved our bacon, five times over."

Other agents and CPD were slowly emerging from their scattered shelter as the main battle concluded. Numerous gang members were slowly coming out as well, laying down arms, choosing jail cells over the cold ground where their fallen comrades now lay.

Dani's voice tightened. "One guy? Smaller guy? Dark hair, maybe plainclothes?"

The DEA agent nodded. "Yeah. We thought he was CPD plainclothes, but honestly, no idea who he was. Didn't stick around long enough to ask questions, but... we're glad he was here."

Dani's pulse quickened. Ashe. It had to be.

"Where did they go?" she demanded, gripping the agent's arm.

The agent pointed toward a cluster of stacked shipping containers in the distance. "They all went that way. The big guy and his group, the guy in the suit, and the plainclothes cop. Sounds like it's not wrapped up yet over there."

Dani followed his gesture, her eyes narrowing at the labyrinth of shipping containers and shadows beyond. Gunfire echoed faintly from that direction, the sound sharp and relentless.

She released the agent's arm and took off at a run, weaving through the wreckage and chaos. Her instincts screamed at her to hurry.

As she drew closer to the gunfire, a single thought was alone in her mind.

Please don't let me be too late.

THE WAREHOUSE REEKED of blood and gunpowder, the metallic tang sharp in the cold, stagnant air. Broken glass crunched beneath Dani's boots as she stepped over the twisted remains of a metal shelving unit and the equally twisted remains of a black man in military-style clothing. The man was dead, but Dani kicked his weapon far to one side out of habit. Her own Sig Sauer was gripped tight in her hand, finger poised just outside the trigger guard. Shadows stretched out ahead of her under the flickering glow of a failing fluorescent, painting the chaos in stark, fragmented lines. Other bodies lay scattered: dealers, gang members most of them, slumped in grotesque angles, blood seeping into cracked concrete.

But none of it registered.

All she saw was Ashe.

Ashe and Linder.

Standing over Wolfe's crumpled body, Ashe's silhouette was framed by the flickering light, a pistol hanging loose in his hand. His posture wasn't triumphant, wasn't defensive. He was just... still. The barrel of his gun dipped toward the ground, smoke wafting up from its barrel. The pistol's barrel shone brightly, its characteristic chrome slide catching the warehouse's overheads.

She knew that gun.

Dani's breath caught in her throat as her eyes locked onto the gun in Ashe's hand. That gun. Satin black with a chrome slide that gleamed in the flickering warehouse lights, its open breech mocking her tardiness. She knew it well—too well. Wolfe's trophy gun. The one given to him by President Reagan himself.

Linder had not cared much for the sitting president, but he had loved that gun. A custom Smith & Wesson Model 459, hand-fitted with polished ivory grips and etched with a small presidential seal on the left side of the frame. A gift from the highest office in the land for solving a high-profile case—a case Dani had practically solved for him. She had done all the shooting. Linder had done all the talking. And in the end, it was Wolfe who got the handshake, the ceremony, and the gun.

She swallowed hard. Now that gun was empty, its magazine spent, and the man who had once carried it proudly lay crumpled and bleeding at Ashe's feet.

Smoke curled from the open breech, curling lazily upward, dissipating into the stale warehouse air. Ashe hadn't just fired it; he had emptied it. He'd emptied it into Wolfe.

His face was obscured by shadow, but the rigid line of his shoulders spoke volumes.

No. No, God, no.

Her breath hitched. In a heartbeat, her world was reduced to the dark shape of her husband sprawled on the floor, crimson spreading like a grotesque halo beneath his head. Wolfe. The man she'd married, the man she'd planned to leave—but never like this. Not sprawled on cold concrete with his life bled out.

And Ashe, the man who had unraveled her, standing over him.

She didn't think. Muscle memory took over, cold and precise. She raised her Sig, sights aligning with Ashe's chest in less than a heartbeat. Her finger squeezed the trigger before she even realized it was happening.

The gunshot shattered the fragile silence, a single, violent punctuation to the scene of carnage.

Ashe staggered. His head snapped up toward her, surprise registering on his face. Not pain, not guilt. Just confusion.

Dani was surprised herself. Not that she had shot him; that was reflex, and justified by his murder of her husband. No, she was mystified how Ashe was still standing. She'd made that exact shot so many times in so many competitions and many more in the field. She'd never missed once, not at this range. How was Ashe still upright?

He stumbled backward, toward the open warehouse door facing the loading dock, a look of utter betrayal on his face. He teetered for a breathless moment, then fell, disappearing into the dark, frigid waters of the Chicago River below with a muted splash.

Dani rushed forward, her pulse a deafening roar in her ears. The Sig slipped from her hand, forgotten as she reached the dock's edge, peering into the black water. Ripples spread where Ashe had vanished.

Was it a mistake?

Only now her mind raced through it all, replaying the scene with brutal clarity. The position of Wolfe's body, the discarded shell casings rolling at Ashe's feet.

She didn't want to believe.

She didn't want to believe Ashe had killed Wolfe. But the gun in his hand, the blood, the stillness...

Dani stood trembling, staring into the dark water, her heart as fractured as the shattered glass crunching beneath her feet. She hardly noticed as the paramedics arrived and gently guided her back from the edge of the dock.

Dani wept. She was unsure whether she wept for her husband, whom she had just watched die, or for the man she'd come to love, whom she'd just had to kill. In the end, as the paramedics walked her out of the warehouse, she decided to just weep for herself.

Chapter 29 : DRUNK RHINO

PRESENT DAY

LIGHT. FLASHES OF light. Heat. Water. Screams. Wailing screams. Something cold was soaking into his back, and everything spun in strange, lurching waves.

He wasn't walking. He was floating. On a boat? His funeral skip? No. Not floating. He was lying down, moving. Rolling. The world jolted roughly beneath him, sending spikes of pain through his body with every bump and rattle.

His shoulder throbbed, a brutal, relentless pulse that blurred the edges of his vision.

Then a voice, loud and panicked, crashed through the noise like a hammer:

"Move! Move! Out of the way! This man is dying!"

Spirit?

"Critical case of combustion trauma! He needs immediate care!"

Hands slapped his chest violently. "Stay with us, buddy! Hang in there," the lawyer shouted theatrically. He looked like he was wearing... scrubs?

Spirit started feigning CPR on him. Ashe's broken ribs screamed in protest, but his head was spinning too badly to even react. *The idiot is doing it wrong,* was all Ashe had the energy to think.

And then he passed out.

Ashe cracked one eye open, his gaze swimming. Overhead, red and white lights spun in dizzying circles. Smoke curled around the high ceiling, mingling with the spray of sprinklers, drenching everything in cold mist.

"Who's in charge here? We've got a live one!" Spirit's voice climbed another octave. "This guy's been hit with a... thermokinetic vapor scorch! From the explosions. I've only seen this once, during my second tour in Shrapnelistan, and it was bad! Really bad!"

Definitely Spirit. *What a moron,* Ashe thought, and passed out.

Another flash of light. The gurney slammed into a wall, jolting Ashe's ribs and sending a fresh wave of pain crashing through his body. His breath caught and his throat heaved with nausea. He gritted his teeth, trying to ride it out, but it was like trying to swim through broken glass.

He blinked again, harder this time, and his surroundings snapped into fractured focus.

Amber's face hovered above him, soaked and blurry, her red hair plastered to her forehead and cascading downward past her face in his direction. Her eyes locked onto his, calm but intense.

"Almost there, sir. Don't you dare quit on me now," she said, her voice loud enough to be heard over the chaos.

And then she winked at him.

The gurney bounced again, and Ashe felt the world tilt sideways. Water poured from the ceiling, cold and endless, drenching his clothes and pooling beneath him.

He closed his eyes, trying to hold onto something solid. Anything.

A bright light seared through his eyelids, and for a second, everything was peaceful again.

"Coming through! Outta the way!" Spirit bellowed. "You there, Agent. Yes, you! Step aside unless you want a front-row seat to this guy's funeral and your forced retirement!"

They hit another bump, and Ashe's head lolled to the side, his cheek pressing against the soaked sheet beneath him. The coppery taste of blood was rich in his mouth.

A cluster of uniformed agents parted before them, caught off guard by the chaotic energy radiating from Spirit. One of them raised a hand, trying to stop them.

"Whoa—what's going on here? Who is that?"

Spirit flung a hand in the air theatrically. "Who is that? What difference does that make? He's a victim of some psycho back there with explosives! And he's going to be the end of your career if he dies, mister 'tax dollars at work!' Now get out of our way!"

Ashe tried to follow what Spirit was saying, but that wasn't an easy task when he was lucid. It all slipped through his fingers like sand. His thoughts swirled and twisted, fragmented and fleeting.

Spirit leaned in conspiratorially towards the agents, his voice dropping just enough for dramatic effect. "It's pure bedlam in there. Seriously, you're all lucky to—"

Blackness.

Another jolt.

Fresh air.

Cool, brisk air that bit at his skin. Outside.

Ashe breathed in deeply, relishing the cool dryness of the air. He felt Amber's hand on his arm, her grip firm and steady.

"You're out, Ashe. We've got you," she said with a wide smile. She looked like a drowned rat. An orange one. Water overflowed her carrot-colored eyebrows and ran into her eyes, flashing green in the sunlight.

Ashe's eyelids fluttered, the darkness pressing in from the edges of his vision. Spirit's voice floated above him, fading in and out.

"Old man, you're gonna owe me so much after this," Spirit said, dead-center between smug and breathless.

Ashe tried to laugh, but it came out as a shallow cough. The wispy clouds overhead blurred, melting into a curtain of darkness.

Then nothing.

☙ • ❧

THE WORLD WAS a blur of noise and light. And chaos—still chaos.

Ashe's eyes fluttered open, his vision swimming in and out of focus. An oxygen mask pressed tightly over his face fed him sharp bursts of cool air. Everything felt wrong: tilted, unstable, and moving.

He squinted, trying to make sense of the spinning ceiling lights above him.

A muffled siren wailed, blending with the clang of metal objects bouncing around the cramped space. A plastic IV bag smacked into the side of the gurney, followed by a box of bandages that skittered across the floor and disappeared into the corner.

Another jolt sent Ashe rolling halfway off the gurney, stopped only by the frayed waist strap barely holding him in place. His head lolled to the side. Two figures hovered nearby, both struggling to stay on their feet.

Spirit and Fry.

In paramedic uniforms.

Spirit caught his eye and gave him a half smile. Fry reached down and adjusted the oxygen mask with practiced calm, her other hand braced against a cabinet.

The ambulance took another violent turn, throwing them both off their feet.

"Amber!" Spirit barked, one hand gripping the edge of the gurney for balance. "What are you doing up there? We're not fleeing Fallujah! Slow down!"

"I'm driving!" Amber shouted back without looking. "Do you want me to focus on that, or do you want me to make polite conversation? You said to get us away from the FBI back there as fast as possible!"

"You know, between arrested and dead in a smoking car wreck—!"

The ambulance swerved again, hitting something metallic with a crunch. Spirit stumbled, crashing into the cabinet behind him. A small rolling cart shot across the floor, slamming into the opposite wall with a metallic clatter.

"Oh, come on," Spirit grumbled, pulling himself upright. "You hit a trash can? Kind of easy to track us if you hit everything we pass, Amber!"

Ashe craned his neck to see her through the open partition. Amber was hunched over the wheel, her eyes locked on the road, red hair plastered to her forehead from sweat and the damp mist of the sprinklers still clinging to her.

"I'm sorry!" Amber called back. "This thing handles like a drunk rhino!"

"Then stop driving it like a getaway car!" Spirit shot back.

"That's what it is!" Amber jerked the wheel again, narrowly missing a parked car. "If you think you can do better, why don't you come up here and take over?"

"I'm wearing a stolen EMT uniform! Do you know what the FBI would do if they found me driving an ambulance? I'd be in prison by lunch!"

"You'd talk your way out of it."

"Not if they find you've turned it into a bumper car!"

"Wait a minute!" Amber yelled over her shoulder. "*I'm* wearing a stolen EMT uniform!"

Ashe coughed into the mask, his voice weak but audible. "We're stealing an ambulance?"

Spirit looked down at him, surprisingly unruffled given the chaos. "Technically, no. We're commandeering it under the doctrine of necessity."

Ashe raised a brow, the dull throb of pain in his ribs subsiding a bit. "Uh-huh."

Spirit straightened up, adopting the tone of a professor addressing a first-year law student.

"The necessity defense," he began, "allows for the violation of certain laws in situations where following the law would result in a greater harm. The courts have consistently upheld it in cases involving life-threatening emergencies. The principle applies to the unauthorized use of a vehicle during a medical emergency. Given the circumstances, our actions are not only reasonable but entirely defensible under both statutory and case law. R v. Dudley and Stephens is a foundational case on necessity, though admittedly more about cannibalism than ambulance theft, but the logic—"

The ambulance hit another bump, jarring Ashe's shoulder and sending a fresh wave of pain shooting through his body. He clenched his teeth, deciding to focus on the searing heat in his muscles rather than Spirit's droning voice.

"Spirit," he croaked, his voice muffled by the mask. "You made the mistake of assuming I cared."

Spirit smiled. "Suit yourself. But when this goes to trial, you'll be glad someone thought this through."

Chapter 30 : ASHBURNS

PRESENT DAY

AMBER SLAMMED BOTH feet hard on the brakes, and for a brief, ridiculous moment, she imagined the ambulance nose-diving like in a cartoon, its back wheels lifting clear off the ground.

The vehicle skidded with a deafening screech, metal groaning in protest as it ground to an abrupt stop. Behind her, the compartment exploded into chaos: a storm of crashing equipment, bodies colliding, and Spirit's accusing shout rising above it all.

"What the—*Amber*!"

Amber winced and glanced over her shoulder. The gurney, which had been barely secured at the best of times, now lay in a heap at the front of the compartment. Ashe had fallen from it, sprawled on top of Fry, who was awkwardly pinned beneath one of the ambulance's rolling carts. Spirit was wedged sideways against the wall, glaring daggers at her.

"Sorry!" Amber offered weakly.

She turned back to the windshield and squinted. The morning sun glowed faintly in the sky, but the flashing red and blue lights ahead of her overpowered it.

There sure are a lot of them, she mused.

The street in front of the ambulance was filled with emergency vehicles: black FBI SUVs, police cruisers, tactical vans—all arranged in a two-deep semicircle, forming an impenetrable wall. The flashing lights lit up the surrounding buildings, no mean feat in broad daylight. There were a lot of tax dollars standing in the road ahead of them.

More concerning, however, was the staggering collection of firearms pointed directly at her.

Amber's stomach sank.

"Uh... guys?" she said, slowly raising her hands. "I'll see you outside."

She eased out of the ambulance, hands in the air. The warm morning air hit her skin, and her sneakers crunched on the pavement as she walked forward cautiously.

An array of stern faces greeted her. FBI agents and uniformed police officers focused exclusively on her and her passengers. Assault rifles and handguns were trained on her, their polished barrels gleaming in the sunlight.

A moment later, the back doors of the ambulance swung open. Spirit, Fry, and Ashe climbed out. Slowly, carefully. Ashe's right arm hung limply at his side, his movements stiff and awkward. His face was pale, and every step brought a fresh wince of pain.

The four of them stood together, surrounded by flashing lights and armed officers.

Front and center, just beyond the line of weapons, was Special Agent Lamentation Standish.

His sharp eyes settled on Ashe, curiosity flashing in their depths. He took a step forward, his gaze lingering.

"Curious," Standish murmured. "You look… younger than I remember."

Several officers moved in closer, guns still raised. The unmistakable click of handcuffs echoed across the tense silence.

Standish gestured to his men. "Arrest them."

The officers closed in.

Amber held her hands higher as an agent grabbed her arm. Pulling the arm around and back, the agent secured one wrist, and then the other. "Remember what I said about this not ending without a lot of guns?" she said wryly.

Ashe, already in cuffs, tried to shrug. Only one shoulder responded. He winced sharply, his face contorting in pain.

Amber, being shoved toward a waiting FBI vehicle, grumbled under her breath.

"'Amber, you're just being superstitious,' he says," she muttered, shooting a glance at Ashe. "'Chekhov's gun is just a myth,' he says."

Ashe gave her a lopsided smirk, despite the pain. "Technically, it's a dramatic principle, not a myth."

"Shut up."

$$\approx \quad \bullet \quad \lessgtr$$

THE RIDE WAS uncomfortable in every possible way.

Amber sat crammed between Spirit and Ashe in the back seat of the unmarked SUV, her shoulders pressed tightly against theirs. The seat wasn't designed for three adults, much less three who had just fled a war zone soaked to the bone. The air inside the vehicle was damp and thick with the smell of sweat, smoke, and spent explosives.

Spirit kept shifting beside her, trying to find a more comfortable position, while Ashe sat rigid on her right, clearly in pain. His right arm hung limp at his side, his shoulder misshapen beneath the sleeve of his soaked jacket. Every bump in the road sent a fresh jolt of discomfort through him, and Amber caught him wincing out of the corner of her eye.

She felt bad for him. Really, she did. But there wasn't much she could do while handcuffed and jammed into an FBI SUV. Sitting on the crack.

A glance at the road signs told Amber the SUV was rolling along Route 267, heading east toward McLean. Amber stared out the window, trying to distract herself from the ache in her shoulders and the uncomfortable closeness of the three-person pileup in the back seat.

The countryside blurred past, a mix of rolling hills and office parks, dotted with clumps of trees that looked like they had been transplanted to give the illusion of nature. They passed Dulles Airport, its control tower standing like a lone sentinel against the pale sky. Planes sat motionless on the tarmac, their windows glinting in the early light.

A green highway sign loomed ahead. Exit for Wolf Trap National Park.

Amber smirked to herself. Wolf Trap. It sounded like the kind of place where Ashe might've vacationed a thousand years ago, assuming wolves were actually involved and the trap wasn't metaphorical.

The SUV hit a pothole, jarring her out of her thoughts and into Ashe's ruined shoulder. Ashe grunted beside her, his teeth clenched as the collision sent fresh pain through his shoulder.

"Sorry," Amber said quietly, though she wasn't the one driving.

The front passenger seat creaked as Standish turned to face them. His pale, angular face looked even more severe in the shadows, his thin lips curling into a small, smug smile.

"Well," Standish said, his voice calm and measured. "I do have to thank you all for making this far easier than it could have been."

Amber's attention snapped to him, her body tensing instinctively. Spirit shifted beside her, but said nothing, his eyes flicking toward the agent.

Ashe, still pale and visibly exhausted, gave Standish a tired glare. "Glad we could help," he muttered.

Standish ignored the sarcasm, his gaze moving slowly across their faces. "You gambled on something being somewhere on Task's servers. An understandable move. But Task was far too meticulous to leave anything useful behind. I would never have tried looking there," he gloated. "The likelihood of the FBI ever really learning anything substantial from those drives is... well, we can assume it would be minimal."

Amber blinked. "And you're telling us this because...?"

Standish's smile widened slightly, without involving his eyes. "Because, Ms. Olsen, this was never about the data. The warrants for Chicago? That was bait: a lure for a trap I knew Mr. O'Reilly would not be able to resist."

Ashe's eyes narrowed. "And yet, somehow I resisted."

"Indeed," Standish replied, nodding thoughtfully. "But it all worked out, it would seem. Having two Ashburns to choose from came in rather handy, even if I could never have planned it that way. Thank you for incriminating yourselves in this Ashburn. The one where the judges are far more... friendly to me."

Amber's wrists flexed against the tight metal hoops restraining her. She glanced sideways at Ashe, who sat motionless, his breathing slow and controlled despite the obvious pain he was in.

"At long last," Standish said, his voice softening with satisfaction, "after decades in hiding, you will die for your crimes, Mr. O'Reilly."

Amber laughed, a sharp, humorless bark. "Sounds to me like you've got nothing but a bunch of legends and campfire stories. You're insane if you think any jury's gonna convict over that."

Standish raised an eyebrow, clearly unimpressed. "I have legends, yes. Thanks to another agent who paved the road for me. But it matters not if those legends are true. I do not need legends to convict. Not when I have eyewitness testimony linking Mr. O'Reilly to the Pusher's End killings."

"Eyewitness testimony?" Amber blurted. "From the eighties?"

"That's right, Ms. Olsen. An eyewitness from the eighties. *The* eyewitness. And now that I can also connect him to the recent events at Task Industries... well, that is more than enough reasonable doubt for a jury. He will at least be convicted for the murder of Cameron Task, having established Task's discovery of his actions in the eighties as the motive. By extension, all the other murders will land at his feet as well."

Amber opened her mouth to respond again, but Ashe shot her a warning glance, his eyes narrowing just enough to make her pause.

Spirit, ever the lawyer, remained silent. His expression was blank, but Amber could practically hear the wheels turning in his head.

Standish turned back to face the road, his voice growing quieter, almost conversational. "You must know how this ends, Ashe O'Reilly. You have been running for a very long time. But no one can run forever. Not even you."

Amber clenched her jaw, resisting the urge to say something cutting. A city skyline was just visible in the distance now, rising beyond the endless sprawl of suburbs and highways.

She hated how calm Standish was, how sure of himself.

The trap had been sprung, and Standish was already celebrating his victory.

Chapter 31 : GILLIGAN'S SPLEEN

PRESENT DAY

THE INTERROGATION ROOM was a windowless box of cold efficiency: too clean, too quiet, and too bright, Owen thought. The stainless steel walls reflected the harsh fluorescent light overhead, making the space feel smaller and more sterile than it already was. The only furniture in the room was a heavy, bolted-down steel table and two metal chairs, one of which waited for him by the table. The room reeked of disinfectant, the kind that burned your nose if you inhaled too deeply.

The aluminum chair waited for him, positioned at the table in the center of the room beneath the harsh glow of an overhead light. The off-the-shelf FBI agent escorting Spirit led him to the table, his grip firm but not rough. He said nothing as he gestured toward the chair.

"Such a warm welcome," Spirit quipped as he took his seat.

The agent ignored him, pulling a set of keys from his belt. Spirit raised an eyebrow but said nothing as his wrists were shackled to the table's steel loop, the cuffs still cold and snug around his wrists.

Once he was secured, the agent nodded once and left the room, the heavy door clanging shut behind him.

Spirit leaned back in the chair as far as the restraints would allow, flexing his fingers experimentally. "Well, this is cozy," he muttered to no one in particular.

He glanced at the ceiling, catching sight of the small black camera mounted in the corner. Its red recording light blinked steadily at him, unblinking and indifferent.

Seconds stretched into minutes. Spirit kept his gaze on the door, waiting, his lawyer's brain already working through a dozen scenarios and counter-strategies.

A light on the high-tech panel next to the door flashed green and the door finally swung open.

Special Agent Lamentation Standish entered with slow, deliberate steps. His black suit was perfectly pressed, his tie knotted with surgical precision. His face was as severe as the room around him: sharp, angular, and utterly humorless. He was really feeling this inquisitor role, mused Spirit.

He said nothing as he took the seat across from Spirit, his cold eyes remaining locked onto Spirit's with unnerving intensity.

Spirit smiled. "So, Agent Standish. We meet again. What brings you to Virginia?"

Standish didn't blink. "Special."

Spirit tilted his head. "Excuse me?"

"Special Agent," Standish clarified, his voice clipped and cold with menace.

"Oh! Right. Sorry," Spirit said, his smile widening.

A long pause followed. Standish remained silent, his eyes boring into Spirit like twin drills.

Spirit cleared his throat. "Special Agent," he said, nodding once.

Nothing. The silence thickened.

Spirit leaned forward slightly, his voice dropping an octave. "Special Agent Standish."

Standish's jaw tightened. His eyes narrowed, but he said nothing.

Spirit raised an eyebrow. "Special Agent *Lamentation* Standish," he added, drawing out the syllables as if savoring them.

The air seemed to hum with tension. Standish's glare darkened, his lips pressing into a thin line.

Spirit tilted his head thoughtfully. "Are you, though?"

Standish's brow furrowed. "What?"

"Special," Spirit said lightly. "Are you really all that special? Because it seems to me that if you were, we'd all be in cuffs in the same room, not split up in different cells while you try to break one of us."

Standish's eyes flashed with irritation.

"You don't have anything on us," Spirit continued, his tone growing softer, more confident. "At least not on me."

"You are all under investigation as accessories to murder," Standish said, his voice icy and precise.

Spirit leaned back as far as his shackles would allow, arching an eyebrow. "Murder? Whose murder would that be?"

"Your former employer," Standish said, his words deliberate. "Cameron Task."

Spirit's face lit up in mock surprise. "Oh, you must mean Cameron Task, the one who shot me in the back and then took a nosedive out a skyscraper window? That Cameron Task?"

Standish's eyes flickered with something—frustration, perhaps—but he quickly masked it. "You are continuing to maintain that he committed suicide?"

"Of course he did," Spirit said smoothly. "He'd just lost the best lawyer he'd ever had. He was... distraught."

Another tense silence followed. The only sound in the room was the faint hum of the overhead lights.

Spirit glanced around theatrically, as though searching for something. "Speaking of lawyers, I'm not even sure why I'm talking to you without mine here."

Standish leaned forward slightly, a sneer curling at the corner of his mouth. "Without your lawyer? Are you not planning to represent yourself, mister Spirit?"

Spirit gave him a slow, confident smile. "Oh, you'd better hope I don't represent myself, pal. I'd mop the floor with you."

❧ • ❧

"AND WHO IS your lawyer, then?" asked Standish, his voice low and deliberate.

"Owen Spirit," Fry replied without hesitation.

Standish's lips curled into something resembling a smile—though not the friendly kind. "Well, you have a problem, then."

Fry tilted her head. "Oh?"

The room was too bright. Not warm, inviting bright—more like laboratory under observation bright. Every surface seemed to gleam, from the stainless steel walls to table in front of her. The table had been bolted down, as if it wanted to get up and walk away. The overhead light buzzed faintly, adding to the sterile hum that filled the space.

Fry shifted in her chair, her leg cast propped awkwardly on the floor in front of her. They hadn't bothered to offer her a more comfortable setup, leaving her to wrestle her position into something only vaguely tolerable.

The cuffs around her wrists clinked softly against the metal loop affixed to the center of the table. The presence of the cuffs was ludicrous. They had decided it was probably the safest approach just to charge her as well, to be thorough. So, they had read Fry her rights and slapped on her own fresh set of cuffs once they arrived at this facility. Whatever "this facility" was.

She tested the shackles, just to see how tight they were. Tight enough to annoy, but not enough to stop her from tapping a rhythm on the tabletop with her fingers. Good to know, she thought.

Special Agent Lamentation Standish sat in the chair across from her, folding his hands neatly on the table. His eyes, cold and predatory, locked onto hers. His severe black suit absorbed what little warmth the room had left.

Standish leaned in slightly, his tone dripping with false sincerity. "Mr. Spirit is just next door, providing some very interesting information about your little conspiracy."

Fry blinked once, expression calm. "So, you're telling me my lawyer is here, but I can't talk to him?"

Standish straightened. "Yes," he said smugly.

"And Miranda says I needn't talk without my lawyer?"

"Yes..."

Fry folded her arms, leaning back in her chair as far as her cuffs would let her. Her eyes narrowed just slightly behind her glasses, her lips curling into a faint, satisfied smirk.

"Sounds like a 'you' problem," she said.

The silence that followed stretched uncomfortably long. Fry held his gaze, daring him to say something else.

Standish's nostrils flared. His jaw tightened. His fingers tapped the table once, twice. He opened his mouth, thought better of it, then closed it again.

Fry let the silence hang for another beat before adding, "I'll be here if you need me. Oh wait—no, I won't. Because I don't need to be here. Miranda told me so."

Standish's eyes darkened. "This is not a game, young lady."

"No, I think you're mistaken," Fry replied, her voice light and steady. "For me it is a game. As I said. For you, it's a problem."

∾ • ∽

"SO, YOU SEE my problem, then," Standish said, his voice low and deliberate.

Amber tilted her head and studied him for a long moment, considering.

"Yes," she said slowly. "Yes, I think I do."

The room felt like a dentist's office, except without the chair, the Highlights magazines, or any of the warm charm. The walls were stainless steel, the table bolted to the floor, and the light overhead buzzed incessantly like an angry bee.

Standish's black suit looked just as severe as it had been in the diner. So did his face: sharp lines, pale skin, eyes that were far too interested in everything she was about to say in front of a brain that knew how to use it against her.

Amber squirmed in her chair, the cuffs around her wrists clinking softly against the table. The air was sterile, cold, and smelled faintly of cleaning solution. She glanced at the camera in the corner and raised an eyebrow.

Standish leaned in slightly, sensing blood in the water. His thin smile widened just enough to show teeth.

"And you're going to help me, aren't you?" he said.

Amber looked down at her hands, then back up at him, wide-eyed. "I... I don't know."

Standish thought he had identified the weak link. He slid a legal pad across the table toward her, placing a freshly sharpened pencil neatly in the center.

"Here, Ms. Olsen," he said, his voice dripping with false warmth. "We can help each other. You are a writer. Now is your chance to pen your magnum opus."

Amber blinked. "I don't know what that is."

"It is your defining masterpiece," Standish explained with a touch of exasperation. "It is the truth you wish to cry from the rooftops."

"Oh!" Amber said brightly. "Why didn't you just say that?"

She took the pad gingerly, turning it over in her hands, and set it down on the table with a resigned look. She hung her head slightly and paused for a moment. With a sigh, she began to write. Her handwriting was slow at first—careful, deliberate. But soon, the words came faster. Her pencil scratched furiously across the page, her brow furrowing in concentration.

Several minutes passed in silence, broken only by the hum of the light and the rhythmic scratch of graphite on paper.

Standish watched her with barely contained satisfaction, his eyes gleaming as he leaned back in his chair.

Amber paused for a moment, chewing on the end of the pencil. She stared off into space, lost in thought, then resumed writing with renewed intensity.

The pencil wore down to a nub. Amber held it up like a queen summoning a servant.

Standish jumped to his feet, grinning like the Cheshire Cat, only too happy to help. He disappeared into the hallway for a moment and returned with a small box of pencils. His fingers trembled slightly as he handed her a fresh one.

"Thank you," Amber said sweetly, and returned to her work.

Two pencils later, she stopped writing. She read over the pages carefully, pausing now and then to erase and make corrections. Satisfied, she set the pencil down beside the others with exaggerated care and leaned back in her chair.

Standish reached for the notepad with trembling hands, his eyes filled with anticipation. He scanned the first page, his lips moving silently as he read. His expression shifted from curious to confused.

He looked up at her, narrowing his eyes, then returned to the pad, flipping through the pages faster and faster. His face turned beet red as he reached the end.

"What is this?" Standish demanded, slamming the notepad onto the table.

Amber placed her palms on the table and half rose from her seat, an excited look in her eye. "Pretty good, isn't it?" She smiled widely.

Standish's eyes darted back to the title scrawled across the top of the first page and he read it aloud. "'I Was Captured and Tortured in an FBI Black Site Without Due Process: An Exposé by Amber Olsen'?!"

"Catchy, right?" Amber beamed. "I think it'll resonate with readers. Very timely."

Standish's nostrils flared. He slapped the notepad down, his fingers curling into a fist on the table.

Amber leaned forward, a look of angelic sincerity on her face. "Want me to sign it for you?"

❭ • ❬

THE LIGHT IN the room seemed brighter than before, or maybe it was just Standish's presence making everything feel sharper, more cutting. His eyes never left Fry's, watching, calculating.

Standish had left for some time and had returned with a digital recorder in hand—a small black device with a blinking red light. He placed it on the table between them with exaggerated care and pressed the "play" button.

A burst of static crackled from the recorder, followed by a woman's voice.

"911, what's your emergency?"

Fry's voice answered, high-pitched and jittery, each word laced with panic. "There's been a murder! And I've been shot!"

ASHBURN

The 911 operator's calm response followed, asking for details. Fry's recorded voice gave a frantic account of the incident in Task's office—rushed, vague, and peppered with ambiguity. She winced slightly hearing herself again, the panic in her tone almost foreign now.

Standish let the recording play out before pressing stop. His eyes gleamed with satisfaction as he leaned forward, folding his hands neatly in front of him.

"That was the call where you reported Task's murder," Standish said, his voice smooth, predatory.

Fry blinked. "No, it wasn't."

Standish's expression darkened slightly. "You're telling me that wasn't your voice? You have a very distinctive accent, Ms. Cieślak."

"Well, sure it was me," Fry admitted. "But I wasn't reporting Task's murder. Is that what this is all about?"

Standish's lips thinned. "You know very well what this is about, Ms. Cieślak. Are you changing your story about the call?"

"I'm doing nothing of the sort," Fry said, sitting up straighter. "Didn't you read the initial LAPD reports? I was reporting Owen Spirit's murder. By Task. I thought Task had killed him."

Standish's eyes narrowed. His tone dropped, becoming colder. "Owen Spirit is alive, as you well know."

"Yeah?" Fry shot back, crossing her arms. "Tell that to his spleen."

THE STORYTELLER TRILOGY BOOK 2

"MY SPLEEN!" SPIRIT exclaimed. "The man shot me in my spleen!"

Standish blinked, taken aback. The light in the room hadn't gotten any brighter, but it felt like it had. Owen shifted in his chair, resting his wrists against the cold steel of the cuffs. His leg bounced rhythmically beneath the table as he watched Standish with a bemused expression.

"You know people can live without a spleen, right?" Standish said after a moment, his tone flat.

"Yes, but at much higher risk of infection," Spirit replied solemnly.

Standish raised an eyebrow, clearly debating how much energy he wanted to spend on this conversation.

"I liked my spleen," Spirit added, his voice dropping into a pout.

An angry silence filled the room. Standish said nothing, his lips pressing into a thin, tense line.

"Do you know," Spirit continued, "I have to wash my hands after using the bathroom now?"

Standish's lips curled in barely concealed disgust.

"What I do know," Standish began, his voice tight, "is that you find yourself in control of Task Industries—"

"Temporary control," Spirit interjected, raising a finger.

Standish exhaled slowly through his nose. "Temporary control of Task—"

"Just until the board meeting," Spirit said helpfully.

"Temporarily in control until the board meeting," Standish corrected, his voice dangerously calm.

"I'm not really in control," Spirit mused. "It's more of a successorship."

The sound of Standish's palms slamming against the steel table echoed sharply through the room.

"Enough!" Standish snapped, his face turning several shades redder. "You've gotten your hands into the works, and that's more than enough to establish motive!"

Spirit blinked innocently. "Motive? For what?"

"Murder," Standish spat. "Colluding in the murder of Cameron Task."

Spirit gasped theatrically. "The man shot me in my spleen! Is it a better motive than him shooting me in my spleen?"

Standish's eye twitched. His jaw tightened as he leaned in, speaking through gritted teeth. "We both know I am not here to argue about your spleen."

"No?" Spirit leaned back in his chair, tilting his head in a look of genuine confusion. "Then what are we here to argue about?"

"We are not here to argue," Standish growled.

Spirit frowned. "Then why are we arguing?"

Standish's nostrils flared. "We are not arguing, Mr. Spirit."

Spirit shrugged. "Too bad. I came here to have an argument."

Chapter 32 : LASTING WITNESS

PRESENT DAY

THE ROOM WAS cold, clinical in both temperature and design.

It looked more like a control center from some futuristic thriller than a basement room in some government facility. Rows of sleek black consoles lined the walls, each one humming softly with power. High-resolution monitors displayed live feeds from the interrogation cells, the sharp clarity of the images leaving little to the imagination. The camera angles were fixed: positioned high in each room, capturing everything from the suspect's shackled hands to the complexity of their expressions.

A glowing array of buttons and touchscreens pulsed in the dim light, manned by two technicians who monitored the event. Another armed agent stood near the door. A big, burly man in a tailored suit that fit a little too tightly around his large biceps, his eyes regarded the tableau, his body language relaxed and ready.

This was the nerve center of Standish's operation: the heart of his investigation, where every word, every twitch of a suspect's face, was recorded and could be analyzed in real time.

Assistant Director Dani Linder stood with her arms crossed, her sharp eyes flicking from monitor to monitor. She'd come straight from her office, and the day-length morning was starting to show in the set of her jaw and the tension in her shoulders.

Standish stood beside her, his pale face lit by the glow of the monitors. He looked pleased with himself, smug even, as he gestured toward the live feeds.

"AD Linder," Standish said, his tone clipped and professional, seeking to redeem himself in his superior's eyes. "Thank you for coming down. If I can brief you on the progress—"

Dani raised an eyebrow. "Progress, huh? Let's hear it," she interrupted.

Standish cleared his throat and pointed to the first monitor, where Frymet Cieślak sat in her interrogation room. Her arms were folded across her chest, her expression calm and unreadable.

"Ms. Cieślak," Standish began, "has been… difficult. Deflecting at every turn. She's clever, but it's clear she knows more than she's letting on."

On the next monitor, Amber Olsen appeared. She was seated at the bolted-down table, her chin propped on her hand, an unmistakable smirk on her face.

"Ms. Olsen," Standish continued, his voice tightening, "is… creative. Let's just say she hasn't been particularly forthcoming with the truth. And yet, despite her predilection for falsity, she can come across as fully convinced of her own fictions."

Standish next drew her attention to Owen Spirit, who lounged in his chair, looking far too comfortable for someone in custody. He was bound, but his body language demonstrated anything but.

"Mr. Spirit, of course," Standish said, rubbing his temple, "is determined to turn this into a courtroom drama. He's deliberately evasive and thoroughly enjoying himself."

Dani's eyes narrowed. "And what have we learned from these interviews so far?"

Standish hesitated. "Not as much as I'd hoped. But their stories are inconsistent. Plenty of gaps for us to exploit."

Dani crossed her arms tighter. "So, what you're saying is, this operation of yours hasn't yielded any fruit."

Standish bristled. "I have made progress, but—"

"You have made a mess," Dani snapped. "You showed up at the Task data center with an army of agents and officers, causing a spectacle that escalated far beyond reason. Do you realize how many calls my office has gotten in the last twelve hours alone? Half the officials in this state and more than a few elsewhere want to know why the FBI invaded a corporate facility like it was a hostage situation."

Standish opened his mouth to respond, but Dani cut him off.

"The president called me. The President. Did you know he was a close personal friend of Cameron Task?"

"I—"

"You overreached," she said bluntly, not giving the younger agent a chance to defend himself. "You didn't have the authority to deploy that many agents. If you think I came down here to hand you a commendation, think again. Not while I have to deal with your media nightmare and justify a hare-brained operation that was laid in too quickly and is barely holding together."

Standish's lips thinned, but he said nothing. His gaze shifted to the largest monitor, where Ashe O'Reilly looked up at the camera.

Dani's breath caught for just a second. Ashe sat in his chair, his wrists shackled to the table. His shoulder hung at an unnatural angle, and despite the tension in his face, his expression was calm, watchful.

Her eyes lingered on him.

"Doesn't look much like an eighty-year-old man, does he?" she said quietly.

Standish stiffened. This was not a topic he was keen to discuss. "It must be the monitors. Distortion from the camera."

Dani gave a short laugh, gesturing at the screen. "It's a 4K camera on a matching-resolution monitor, and the room's lit up brighter than an operating theater. The distortion is in your head."

Standish shifted uncomfortably.

Dani leaned in to the monitor, her gaze sharpening. Ashe looked... familiar, as ageless as he had been when they first met, as rugged and attractive as when she had seen him last. She paused a moment to compose herself as her emotions whispered of buried memories and long-forgotten truths.

Standish's jaw had tightened as he misinterpreted her interest. "Perhaps he ages well," he said quietly.

Dani's gaze lingered on the monitor for a moment longer before she straightened and turned back to Standish.

"You've been at this for three hours with them," she said, her voice cold and measured, "and you've gotten absolutely nothing."

Standish cleared his throat, straightening his posture. "What I have gotten is—"

"What you've gotten," Dani reiterated, her eyes narrowing, "is nothing. The fact that Owen Spirit is with them and sanctions their actions makes this whole thing a nothing sandwich. You do know that he essentially runs Task Industries now, don't you?"

"Yes, ma'am," Standish said, his tone tightening, "but with all due respect—"

"Oh, now I'm due some respect?" Dani's voice sharpened, her eyes drilling into him. "Where was that earlier when I told you to drop this?"

"Ma'am, what I have done—"

"What have you done, Standish?" Dani snapped, taking a step closer. The room felt smaller, the air charged with tension. One of the technicians glanced nervously over to the armed agent by the door.

"What you've done," Dani continued, her voice low and deliberate, "is apprehended a group of miscreants who broke into what amounts to their own facility and blew up what amounts to an empty room. And nobody cares. They'll just say it was planned demolition or something."

"Ma'am, they drove a car through the back wall of the facility—"

"Their facility. Theirs. Their insurance will have that handled by five o'clock. And it was on private property, so we can't so much as issue a reckless driving citation."

Standish opened his mouth to respond, but Dani didn't give him the chance.

"No, seriously," she said, her words quick and deliberate. "What else do you have? Where's that super-secret server you assured me was going to turn up? Where's the weapons cache? Where's the proof that this man murdered dozens of drug pushers and distributors in a blood-filled vendetta starting fifty years ago?

"Where's your evidence that this man is the long-lost perpetrator of those crimes that I myself shot directly through the heart over thirty-five years ago?"

Standish's lips parted, but no words came out. His eyes flicked toward the monitors, then back to Dani.

"Where's the blood samples that tie all this together?" Dani pressed on, her wrath unrelenting. "The ones that connect my late, deluded husband's work with this insane crusade of yours?"

Standish tried to speak again, but his words faltered. "I—"

"You do realize," Dani said, her tone softening dangerously, "that the sprinkler activation in the data center washed that all away, right? No blood samples. Gone. Literally down the drain."

Standish's face tightened, his jaw clenching visibly. "I—"

"You what? Have you just asked the man for a blood sample? On what cause? None. No judge in this country would justify an invasive action like that without proper cause or the suspect's permission."

Dani leaned in, her eyes flashing. "What do you have them on? Nothing that holds up, that's what. At worst, maybe possession of explosives. Maybe transporting them across state lines. If we can even prove that was the case."

Standish paused, closing his eyes for a brief second. He inhaled deeply, visibly trying to regain control of the situation. When he spoke again, his voice was low and deliberate, carefully controlled.

"Ma'am," he said, "I will get that proof. I can break them down. It will just take some time. Each one of them is completely infuriating, but in their own unique way."

Dani's eyes narrowed further. "As are you, Standish," she said icily.

She turned her head back to the monitor, her gaze settling again on Ashe's image. His shackled form remained eerily calm despite the unnatural angle of his shoulder. His eyes, even through the remote feed, seemed to meet hers.

"You're out of time," Dani said softly, her words laced with quiet menace. "And none of the others are really the issue here, though, are they?"

Standish shifted uncomfortably, his silence more telling than any denial.

Dani kept her eyes on Ashe's face.

"*He* is."

                                     ◈ • ◈

THE ROOM WAS small enough to feel like a cage. The overhead light buzzed faintly; the cold steel of the table reflected its harsh glare. Ashe sat shackled to the table, his wrists bound tightly by cuffs bolted to the surface. His shoulder hung at a painful, unnatural angle, a dull throb radiating from the joint with every beat of his heart.

He ignored it.

The door swung open, and Special Agent Lamentation Standish strode in with slow, deliberate steps. His black suit was starting to lose its crispness, but his eyes remained sharp and watchful as they locked onto Ashe.

"Ashe... O'Reilly," Standish said, his mobile lips caressing each word, savoring its flavor. His voice was smooth but probing, like a scalpel searching for weakness.

Ashe remained silent.

"That is the only name I could find for you," Standish continued, pacing slowly around the table. "O'Reilly."

Ashe glanced up, his eyes flat and dull. "Oh, really?"

Standish's eyes narrowed. "Your dog tags. From your cave."

Ashe tilted his head slightly, his expression blank.

"Well?" Standish pressed.

"Well, what?"

"Nothing to say?"

Ashe said nothing.

"Nothing?" Standish repeated, leaning in slightly.

"I'm waiting for a verb," Ashe replied. "You're speaking in sentence fragments."

Standish's lips curled into a thin smile. His eyes gleamed with satisfaction as he circled the table, a predator searching for an opening.

"You want a verb?" Standish said, his voice hardening. "Kill. That is what you did to Cameron Task. Found. I found your cave. Destroy. That is what I did to the few belongings you still had. They could not even be kept as evidence due to the radiation. I destroyed it all. Every last photo of your ancestors, all of it. Gone."

A flicker of something passed across Ashe's face: anger, perhaps, or something colder.

"But you understand destruction, do you not?" Standish continued. "You pulled quite a number on Task's data center. It takes skill for one man to do that much damage. It takes skill to orchestrate the murder of a man like Cameron Task. And yet, you live in a cave in a radioactive wasteland. With nothing but some ancient handguns and older family photos. And your own filth."

Ashe's glare darkened.

"Lived, rather," Standish added, his voice dropping to a near whisper as he lowered himself into the chair across the table from Ashe. "You will not be going back there. You will soon be in another cave. For the rest of your life."

"Yeah, I kinda doubt that," Ashe said quietly.

"Whereas I do not," Standish said. "A small square cave, with no old family pictures."

Standish paused, his eyes gleaming with malicious delight. "She was not all that much to look at, you know. I saw the photos. Daguerreotypes, were they not? I examined them before they were incinerated. I suppose it was your great-grandmother or something? The old man was every bit as ugly as you. But his wife? Nothing more than average. Much more than he deserved, of course."

Ashe stood up suddenly, his manacled hands clanging against the table. Standish instinctively flinched back, his chair scraping across the floor as he jumped upright.

Ashe stepped around the immovable steel table, his eyes locked on Standish. He rotated his torso, aligning his dislocated shoulder precisely with the table's edge.

With one swift motion, he dropped to the floor, slamming his armpit into the edge.

A sickening crunch echoed through the room as his shoulder popped back into place.

Ashe's face went ghost-white, beads of sweat breaking out across his forehead. His feet slipped on the slick floor as he scrambled to stand, breathing through clenched teeth. The pain was excruciating, but he forced himself upright, his grin somehow growing through the agony.

He eased himself back into the chair, his face pale but triumphant.

"Be a good little boy," Ashe rasped, his voice low and rough, "and go get me some water."

Standish ignored the request.

"I have a witness, Ashe O'Reilly," Standish said, his voice trying to recover its lost momentum.

Ashe raised an eyebrow. "Oh? Who broke?"

Standish smiled thinly. "Which of your friends? None of them. You should be very proud of their loyalty. But I did not need them to break. I have an eyewitness who can place you as the Pusher's End Killer in all those murders in the eighties. A doctor—a physician—who can place you there and tie you to dozens of deaths."

Ashe's expression remained neutral.

"Do you remember that?" Standish asked, back on the offensive, savoring each word. "Just before you disappeared for months? I suppose you skulked off to your den to heal before you started killing again."

Standish leaned closer, his smile widening. "A doctor who also happened to be an FBI special agent."

Ashe's eyes narrowed.

"You were not aware of that, perhaps?" Standish's smile threatened to swallow his face.

"Mostly drug dealers, of course. Your victims," Standish said, his tone almost conversational. "But murders nonetheless. Then, another FBI agent came onto the scene, looking for you. And he died. The report says you killed him as well."

Standish paused for effect.

"Even without any new evidence from Task's servers, this doctor's eyewitness testimony will link you to all those other deaths. Did you know the dead agent was her husband? Your actions resulted in the death of the doctor's husband, Ashe O'Reilly. And I found her."

Standish's smile grew sharper. "It is over for you, Ashe O'Reilly. It is finally over for you."

The door opened with a soft click, and Dani Linder stepped inside, holding a liter bottle of water and a thick manila envelope.

Behind her stood the muscular watch officer from the observation room. His eyes flicked toward Dani's sidearm.

"Ma'am," the agent said, his voice cautious, "can I take your service weapon before you go in there?"

Dani tilted her head, her eyes narrowing. "I don't know. Do you *think* you can take my service weapon from me, Special Agent Wilkins?"

The man blanched, his face paling as he reconsidered. "Uh... no, ma'am."

"Then I don't think we need to fear a handcuffed, injured suspect taking it," Dani said coolly. "I'll retain my weapon."

Standish turned, his smile widening again. "Assistant Director Linder. Perfect timing! I was just—"

"You were just leaving," Dani said sharply, cutting him off.

Standish blinked, uncomprehending. "Ma'am? I don't think that's a good—"

"When I want you to think, Standish," Dani said coldly, "you'll be the second to know. I said get out. Now."

Standish hesitated, his eyes darting between Dani and Ashe, then nodded stiffly. Without another word, he turned and left.

The heavy steel door locked behind him.

༄   •   ༄

ONCE STANDISH WAS on what Dani considered to be the correct side of the door, she stepped over to the access panel and swiped her badge. She punched in the admin override code. A small light on the panel flashed orange, signaling that the door could no longer be opened from the outside.

They were alone.

Her fingers danced over the control panel. With a few more quick taps, the recording light on the camera in the corner blinked off. Transmission and recording stopped.

No one outside the room could see them.

Dani was sure she imagined it, but the room felt quieter, more peaceful, without the hum of the live feed. It was certainly more peaceful without that twerp, Standish.

Dani crossed the room and stood over Ashe. He sat slumped in the metal chair, his wrists shackled to the steel table, his right shoulder still visibly swollen from the brutal realignment. His face remained calm, though a faint sheen of sweat clung to his forehead.

Without a word, Dani unlocked his shackles and set them aside on the table with a soft clatter. Ashe rubbed his shoulder, wincing slightly.

A smile flickered across her face. "Still fighting with that same shoulder, I see."

Ashe glanced up at her. Dani saw the light of recognition in his eyes. Of course, he remembered her. How could he not? Twenty-five years was a long time, but some things didn't fade.

"Yeah," Ashe said, his voice gravelly but steady. "Some things take longer to heal if they're not fixed right."

Dani knew there was a deeper meaning in his words. It was not only a callback to a different time, a different injury. There was also the unspoken wound of old regrets, old betrayals.

She sat across from him, pulling a clear plastic evidence bag from her jacket and dropping it onto the table. Inside was a silver-splashed, copper-jacketed bullet.

"If I recall correctly," Dani said, tapping the bag, "you had a lot of these in you at one point. What's so special about this one?"

Ashe picked up the bag and turned it in his hand, studying the bullet. "I think you probably know."

Dani looked chagrined. "I do. I had forensics run it. Rifling was a match for my old service weapon. The docks."

A pause hung between them, heavy with the weight of memory and silent accusation.

"I'm sorry about that night, Ashe," Dani said, her voice quieter. "I'm truly sorry I shot you."

Ashe's eyes never left hers. "I been shot a lot of times. None of 'em hurt like that one."

Dani looked away, exhaling slowly. "You fell in the river. We searched for your body. Dredged it. You were gone. At first, I wanted you to be. I thought you'd killed Wolfe."

"At first?" Ashe asked.

"Yes," Dani said, nodding. "Forensics eventually proved you hadn't done it. The ballistics alone cleared you; Wolfe was full of holes from other combatants. Combatants you killed. With Wolfe's own gun."

A quiet beep sounded at the door, followed by a soft, rhythmic pounding. The sound was dull and distant but persistent: a background hum to accompany their conversation.

Dani folded her hands in front of her, her tone thoughtful. "Forensics showed you killed the last three gang members after they shot Wolfe."

Ashe's eyes narrowed. "How do you know he hadn't shot them and I just picked up the gun afterward? That's what you shot me for, wasn't it?" he snarled at her.

Dani gave him a rueful smile. "Because Wolfe couldn't hit the broadside of a barn."

Ashe shrugged, relenting. "I noticed that. He wasn't a very good shot."

"He was not," Dani agreed. "That would've been enough, but the security footage verified it. You did your best to save him."

"Security footage?" Ashe asked, a trace of concern slipping into his voice.

"Too grainy and dark for identification," Dani assured him. "Don't worry about that. But more than sufficient to see what happened. Not good enough for them to write a report that cleared you, of course."

She paused, her voice softening. "You made some impressive shots that night. I'm not sure I could've made a couple of those, especially under return fire."

Ashe shrugged. "Had an advantage. Easier to concentrate when you don't need to worry about cover. Just point and shoot."

Dani leaned back, folding her arms. "Los Angeles, Ashe. I wanted to be the one to tell you that you were cleared. But you never gave me the chance. Your vendetta wasn't over, was it?"

"No," Ashe admitted quietly. "But you got him, finally, didn't you? Ming. That was you?"

"That's... complicated," Dani said, her expression guarded.

"Oh, now you're doing the 'it's complicated' thing?" Ashe shot back.

"It's complicated and classified," Dani said firmly. "I'm not discussing it, even with you. But then you disappeared. I always hoped you'd just gone to ground, but I feared..."

"Feared what?" Ashe asked, his eyes searching hers.

Dani looked away for a moment before meeting his gaze again. "I feared something had finally happened to the unkillable man."

"Something did. You did. When you came to the city for me."

"We found your cave," Dani said, wanting to discuss anything else. Her voice dropped to a whisper. "You spent over twenty years there? Why did you run there in the first place?"

"I figured you were there for me," Ashe said simply. "I'd never have fought you, and I couldn't let you take me in to become a lab animal."

"And you think I'd have done that to you?" Dani's voice cracked slightly as she fiddled with his shackles on the table. "A decade later?"

"You came after me because I was still after Ming," Ashe said.

"No, Ashe," Dani corrected. "No one ever connected what happened in Chicago. Not at the time, anyway. I came to Los Angeles for other reasons, ones I can't discuss, but I'm sure you're smart enough to figure out. You and Ming just got caught in the middle of it. And then your Ming problem went away."

Ashe leaned back in his chair, processing everything she'd said.

"You found my cave...?" he asked softly, finally accepting the new line of conversation.

"We did," Dani confirmed, her voice steady but tinged with something almost like regret. "What were you thinking? The amount of radiation you subjected yourself to... Did it...?"

"Just slowed me down," Ashe replied. "I didn't understand it. I thought I was finally dying, and I just didn't care at the time. Hoped for it, really. Still not quite over it, but I'll be fine. Been through worse."

Dani smiled at the memory of the stubborn man she'd known decades ago. "You have, haven't you?" she said quietly. "I guess I have to thank you again."

The rhythmic pounding at the door intensified, more insistent now, but Dani barely acknowledged it.

"Thank me?" Ashe said, raising an eyebrow.

"You opened me up to some... interesting possibilities," Dani said, her voice light. "Despite all of Wolfe's best efforts, I could never believe in things outside the boundaries of science."

Ashe's lips curled into a wry smile. "You've found there are more things in heaven and earth than were dreamt of in your philosophy?"

A faint smile touched Dani's lips before fading. "Speaking of 'not quite over it'... I'm sorry, Ashe. Most everything in the cave was too radioactive and had to be destroyed. Even your medals."

Ashe shrugged. "Don't matter. That stuff stopped meaning anything to me a while back."

"I know," Dani said softly. "But these didn't."

She placed the thick envelope on the table.

Ashe opened it slowly, carefully, pulling out a stack of photographs. His eyes flickered with recognition as he sifted through them, each one a window into his past.

"Those are all replicas. Reprints," Dani explained, watching his reaction closely. "I had them made by our graphics team. They're printed on archival stock, so they should last about forever... as long as you don't do something stupid like irradiate them."

Ashe's fingers brushed lightly over the photos, his expression softening. Then, something small and silver slid from the envelope onto the table: a locket, its surface gleaming in the harsh light.

Dani nodded toward it. "The locket had to be destroyed. What was left of the original, that is. That's the closest facsimile I could find at Tiffany's."

Ashe picked up the locket, turning it over in his hand before carefully opening it. Inside was a photograph: a perfect recreation of Lorena's face, smiling softly back at him.

"I'm sorry it's not the original," Dani said quietly. "It's the best I could do."

For a long moment, Ashe said nothing. His thumb lingered on the edge of the locket as a tear rolled down his craggy cheek.

Dani swallowed, her voice steady but warm. "There's something else in there I had made for you."

Reluctantly closing the locket, Ashe tilted the envelope and a smaller envelope slid out onto the table. It was sealed, so Ashe opened it carefully and pulled out a set of documents—a passport, immunization records, and other identification papers. His eyes widened as he looked them over.

"Is this real?" he asked, his voice tinged with disbelief.

"As far as legends go, yes," Dani said with a faint smile, "it's not backstopped, but it's as real as you're gonna get. I called in some favors from the other side of the river. Used some old photos of you. I see you haven't changed much." She winked.

"Golding," said Ashe, regarding his new passport.

"Yes," smiled Dani. "You just never seemed right to me as 'Ashe O'Reilly.'"

Her smile grew just a bit wider. "I'm not giving you a driver's license, though. Not after that stunt at the data center. I have a responsibility to the American public."

DANI WATCHED ASHE for a long moment. His fingers rested on the photos, the replica locket open again in his hand. His eyes—those same eyes she'd known for decades—held a strange mixture of gratitude and sorrow.

Without a word, Dani stepped closer.

Her hand rested lightly on his shoulder, careful not to press too hard on the still-healing joint. Then, with a tenderness that surprised even her, she leaned down and kissed his forehead.

"Stay out of trouble, Ashe Golding," she whispered, her voice barely audible.

Ashe closed the locket and slipped it around his neck. "No promises."

Dani turned and walked to the door. She entered her admin override code, the panel beeping softly in response as the camera blinked back to watchful life. The heavy lock disengaged with a loud clack, and she pulled the door open.

The hallway outside was filled with movement. Standish rushed forward, flanked by two uniformed officers. His face was flushed, his eyes gleaming with self-righteous determination.

"Assistant Director Linder," Standish said breathlessly. "I must insist... I need verification. This man is the Pusher's End Killer. I'm asking you for confirmation of that fact, as the only living eyewitness to that man's crimes."

The man seemed emboldened by the presence of the two guards behind him, ready to cart off the infamous mass murderer of evil men. Evil men who were all doubtless trying their best to kill him at the time.

Dani held her ground, her gaze cold and unwavering.

"Don't be ridiculous," she said calmly. "Of course it's not him. If it were, he'd have to be well over eighty years old."

She gestured toward Ashe, who remained seated, watching the scene unfold.

"Does that man look anywhere near eighty years old?" she demanded.

"But, Assistant Director, I am sure—"

"Sure of what, Agent?" Dani's tone was venomous, and she was sure that Standish caught the early indicator of his impending demotion.

"I am sure this man is the Pusher's End Killer," he stated. In desperation, he added, "This is the man who killed Special Agent Wolfe Linder."

Dani's eyes narrowed to fine slits. "So, are you telling me that I do not recognize the killer of my own husband? Perhaps I'm too old to recognize a murderer that I put down with my own gun? Is that what you're telling me here?" she hissed.

Standish remained speechless, furious at being spotlighted in front of the other agents.

"I thought not. Let this young man and his associates go," Dani said. Her voice left no room for argument.

Standish's mouth opened, then closed, his face darkening. "But—"

"Now, Agent Standish." Dani's tone dropped, her words cutting through the air like a blade.

The officers exchanged uneasy glances. For a moment, the hallway was filled with tense silence.

Then, with a glare, Standish turned and stalked off without a word, leaving the outer door to the observation room open. The two other agents, confused, looked to Dani for direction. She dismissed them, and big, burly Special Agent Wilkins turned away and set about freeing Ashe's compatriots.

Ashe rose from the chair slowly, flexing his fingers on the thick envelope, his gaze meeting Dani's once more.

"Thank you," he said quietly.

"Don't make me regret this," she murmured.

Chapter 33 : HELLO, GOODBYE, AND EVERYTHING BETWEEN

PRESENT DAY

THE LATE SUMMER air hung soft and cool, the day's warmth fading into the deep blue of early evening. The parking lot of the facility was nearly empty now, save for a handful of vehicles and the small group gathered near the entrance.

Dani stood with Ashe a few steps away from the others. Spirit, Fry, and Amber lingered a short distance off, speaking quietly among themselves. Amber's animated hand gestures stood out in the fading light, while Fry nodded calmly, leaning on her crutches. Spirit remained unusually quiet, his hands tucked into his pockets, his eyes flicking between Dani and Ashe with that lawyer's calculating gaze.

Dani's attention was nowhere but on Ashe. His silhouette was sharp against the darkening sky, his broad frame slightly hunched from lingering pain.

"You just can't stop destroying things and getting hurt for other people, can you?" Dani said, her voice betraying the fringes of her smile.

Ashe shook his head. "This one was all for me."

"I doubt that very much," Dani said, slipping her hands in her pockets. "We both know that if what Standish suspected about the Task affair and your part in it were true, they'd all be going to jail. Maybe not the redhead and her friend, but the lawyer? Definitely. And you couldn't allow that, could you?"

Ashe paused, considering her words. Finally, he spoke, his voice low and reluctant. "He's not a bad guy." It clearly galled him to admit it.

Dani chuckled. "And if Task Industries were to fail in such a spectacular way, thousands and thousands would suffer. This wasn't just for you. If there's one thing you're terrible at, it's self-preservation."

Ashe shrugged, carefully, due to the lingering pain in his shoulder.

Dani laughed again, reaching out to place a hand tenderly on his cheek. "You look so young, old man."

"What? Come on, I've aged a bit," Ashe replied, his eyes glinting. "The radiation in the cave slowed me down pretty good."

"But you've gotten over that for the most part, haven't you?" Dani asked.

"Yeah," Ashe said, his voice steady.

A pause stretched between them, not uncomfortable, but filled with the weight of too many shared memories, and too many missed opportunities.

"What will you do now, Ashe?" Dani asked at last.

Ashe looked out toward the horizon, the fading light catching the edges of his face. "I dunno. Stuff. What will you do?"

Dani followed his gaze, her eyes sweeping across the buildings and the quiet landscape surrounding them.

"I'm not sure," she admitted. "For years, I stayed in this job because I had something to prove. Then I stayed because I wanted to find you. Then... I just stayed."

Her voice softened. "I think maybe it's time I stopped staying."

⤝ • ⤞

A SOFT BREEZE brought the scent of nearby pine trees. Dani stood quietly beside Ashe now, watching the last traces of sunlight melt into the horizon. The others lingered a short distance away as Spirit talked animatedly on his cell phone. Amber, of course, had edged closer bit by bit, still giving Ashe and Dani space but was quite transparent in her efforts to hear what she could.

Ashe broke the silence.

"I've never had the chance to say I was sorry for the death of your husband," he said, his voice low and deliberate.

Dani looked at him, her gaze steady. Finally, she shrugged and looked back at the trees.

"And you never gave me the chance to thank you for trying to save him," she replied.

Her words hung in the air for a moment before she continued.

"It's ironic," Dani said, her tone reflective, "how Wolfe hunted incessantly for something supernatural. For years, I was trapped in the chaos brought on by his nonsensical hunt. Only when he found something—someone—outside the realm of rational science was I finally set free."

Ashe remained silent, his eyes on the horizon.

"And now," Dani said, her voice sharpening just a little, "a little runt like Standish is going to come along, pick up Wolfe's scraps, and take you down? The man who set me free?"

Her lips thinned into a tight line. "I don't think so."

Ashe chuckled softly. He knew she wasn't speaking literally about Standish's height, but the thought of the tall, lanky agent being labeled a runt was still amusing.

Their moment was interrupted by Spirit's approach. His confident stride didn't quite mask the tightness in his expression.

"I've got some loose ends to tie up," Spirit said. "Namely, retrieving my Corvette from Texas for the Smithsonian." He cast Ashe a theatrical glare.

Dani raised an eyebrow. "Oh, don't worry about that. Standish had it taken care of. It's sitting in the impound yard in Abilene." She reached into her pocket and handed him a card. "Here's the number of the wrecking service that towed it."

Spirit froze, staring at the card. "Towed it?"

His head swiveled toward Ashe, his eyes narrowing dangerously. "I do not like the sound of the words, 'wrecking service,' Ashe. That car better be alright!"

"It's intact, from what I understand," Dani stated, trying to be helpful. "It should be mostly dried out by now, I imagine. We dredged the river and I'm pretty sure we recovered all of it."

Spirit's face turned a shade of red usually reserved for emergency lights. His mouth opened, closed, then opened again. "Dredged...?!"

He shot a glare at Ashe, who remained utterly unfazed.

Spirit turned on his heel, looking like a man on the verge of a coronary. Muttering under his breath, he stomped away, already punching the number into his phone as he stormed toward the parking lot.

Dani chuckled softly as she watched him go, then turned back to Ashe. A quiet pause settled between them.

She took a step closer, her voice dropping to something almost like a whisper. "You know how I still feel about you."

Ashe met her gaze, his expression softening just enough to reveal the weight behind his words. "Yeah. And I'm still sorry you do."

Dani smiled at the familiar response, a memory flashing through her mind: that one moment, years ago, when she'd kissed him for the first and only time.

The evening air felt cooler now, carrying the scent of the pines and the quiet hum of crickets in the distance. Her smile lingered as Dani tucked her hands deep into her pockets and risked leaning into Ashe's broad shoulder.

* * *

About the Author

THE CREATIVE JOURNEY of pHil Rittenhouse has meandered from art to science to technology. Roughly in that order, and sometimes all at once. Once upon a time, pHil was a cartoonist. Of course, he also spent over a decade as a research chemist, so that probably cancels out any credibility he may have gained from cartooning.

As a chemist, he learned to approach the world through experiment and observation—habits that shaped his attention to detail as a storyteller. He also learned that explosions, while educational, are frowned upon in most laboratory settings.

These days, pHil (he insists on capitalizing his name that way for obscure reasons no one fully understands) works in software development at Microsoft, where logic and architecture meet imagination, and where he's spent nearly two decades wrangling SharePoint and Dynamics 365 into submission. The precision of coding and the chaos of creativity somehow coexist comfortably there, which might explain both his career longevity and his fiction.

A lifelong reader with a fondness for history, philosophy, and frequent esoteric rabbit holes, Rittenhouse draws from ancient texts, scientific theory, and forgotten myths to craft stories that blur the boundary between the known and the unknowable. His writing explores how obligation, guilt, and grace echo across time. Sometimes with explosions, but fewer than he'd probably like.

He lives in rural Illinois with his wife, four amazing kids, and a cast of household pets large enough to qualify as a small ecosystem. When not writing or debugging, he can often be found reading late into the night or volunteering at his church—still experimenting, still observing, and still sketching his next idea in the margins.

* * *